PRAISE FOR ROBERT BAILEY

The Boomerang

"Breathtaking! A brilliant concept, brilliantly told. *The Boomerang* sets the standard for big, palm-sweating thrillers, with the added extra that it positively brims with that element often missing in such books: heart. Word of warning: before you start, clear your calendar—I guarantee you won't want to stop until the very last page. Bravo!"

—Jeffery Deaver, *New York Times* bestselling author and creator of Colter Shaw, from CBS's *Tracker*

"The stakes couldn't be higher in this compelling and character-rich political thriller. As much about the shocking secret truths buried deep in the annals of power as it is about fatherhood, friendship, and the things we'll do for the people we love most, *The Boomerang* is thought provoking, riveting, and action packed. Don't miss it."

—Lisa Unger, *New York Times* bestselling author of *Close Your Eyes and Count to 10*

"*The Boomerang* is much more than a fast-moving thriller with a unique premise. It is a powerful story of family and friendship that will touch the heart of anyone who has had a loved one with cancer."

—Phillip Margolin, *New York Times* bestselling author of *An Insignificant Case*

"A master storyteller at the top of his game, Robert Bailey has woven an ingenious thriller with the perfect blend of political intrigue, high-octane action, and heartfelt emotion. *The Boomerang* had me on the edge of my seat with twists and surprises all the way to the very last sentence."

—Isabella Maldonado, *Wall Street Journal* bestselling author of
The Cipher

"A relentless, nail-biting thriller that pits a corrupt multi-billion-dollar industry against Washington, DC, newcomers. The stakes are unthinkable. The price demanded unconscionable. Bailey's novel will keep you turning the pages until the shocking conclusion."

—Steven Konkoly, *USA Today* bestselling author

"With razor-sharp pacing and high-stakes drama, Robert Bailey brilliantly merges the taut legal thrills of John Grisham with the rugged, wild intensity of *Yellowstone* in his latest must-read thriller, *The Boomerang*. Brace yourself for an epic roller coaster of twists, complex characters, and moral dilemmas that will keep you turning pages long into the night!"

—Ryan Steck, The Real Book Spy and author of *Gone Dark*

"Loyalty, secrets, and survival collide in this gripping thriller."
—Sara DiVello, author of *Broadway Butterfly* and founder, on-air host
of *Mystery and Thriller Mavens*

Rich Justice

"Sturdy legal thrills for readers willing to go the distance with a flawed hero in an even more flawed world."

—*Kirkus Reviews*

Rich Waters
An Amazon Best Book of the Month: Mystery, Thriller & Suspense

"A compelling dive into the life of a lawyer out way past his depth."
—*Kirkus Reviews*

"Small town, big story—*Rich Waters* works like magic as a mystery and a legal thriller, but what I loved best was Robert Bailey's attention to the details of character and place. I'd ride with Jason Rich to a courthouse anywhere!"
—Michael Connelly, #1 *New York Times* bestselling author

Rich Blood
An Amazon Best Book of the Month: Mystery, Thriller & Suspense

"Well-drawn characters match the surprise-filled plot. Phillip Margolin fans will be enthralled."
—*Publishers Weekly* (starred review)

"*Rich Blood* is a deliciously clever legal thriller that keeps you turning pages fast and furious. Robert Bailey's latest is wildly entertaining."
—Patricia Cornwell, #1 *New York Times* bestselling author

The Wrong Side

"Bailey expertly ratchets up the suspense as the plot builds to a surprise punch ending. Readers will impatiently await the next in the series."
—*Publishers Weekly* (starred review)

"Social tensions redoubled by race intensify a workmanlike mystery."
—*Kirkus Reviews*

Previous Praise for Robert Bailey

"*The Professor* is that rare combination of thrills, chills, and heart. Gripping from the first page to the last."
—Winston Groom, author of *Forrest Gump*

"Robert Bailey is a thriller writer to reckon with. His debut novel has a tight and twisty plot, vivid characters, and a pleasantly down-home sensibility that will remind some readers of adventures in Grisham-land. Luckily, Robert Bailey is an original, and his skill as a writer makes the Alabama setting all his own. *The Professor* marks the beginning of a very promising career."
—Mark Childress, author of *Georgia Bottoms* and *Crazy in Alabama*

"Taut, page turning, and smart, *The Professor* is a legal thriller that will keep readers up late as the twists and turns keep coming. Set in Alabama, it also includes that state's greatest icon, one Coach Bear Bryant. In fact, the Bear gets things going with the energy of an Alabama kickoff to Auburn. Robert Bailey knows his state, and he knows his law. He also knows how to write characters that are real, sympathetic, and surprising. If he keeps writing novels this good, he's got quite a literary career before him."
—Homer Hickam, author of *Rocket Boys/October Sky*, a *New York Times* #1 bestseller

"Bailey's solid second McMurtrie and Drake legal thriller (after 2014's *The Professor*) . . . provides enough twists and surprises to keep readers turning the pages."
—*Publishers Weekly*

"A gripping legal suspense thriller of the first order, *Between Black and White* clearly displays author Robert Bailey's impressive talents as a novelist. An absorbing and riveting read from beginning to end."

—*Midwest Book Review*

"Take a murder, a damaged woman, and a desperate daughter, and you have the recipe for *The Last Trial*, a complex and fast-paced legal thriller. Highly recommended."

—D. P. Lyle, award-winning author

"*The Final Reckoning* is explosive and displays every element of a classic thriller: fast pacing, strong narrative, fear, misery, and transcendence. Bailey proves once more that he is a fine writer with an instinct for powerful white-knuckle narrative."

—*Southern Literary Review*

"A stunning discovery, a triple twist, and dramatic courtroom scenes all make for a riveting, satisfying read in what might well be Bailey's best book to date . . . *Legacy of Lies* is a grand story with a morality-tale vibe, gripping and thrilling throughout. It showcases Bailey once more as a writer who knows how to keep the suspense high, the pacing fast, the narrative strong, the characters compellingly complex, and his plot full of white-knuckle tension and twists."

—*Southern Literary Review*

"Inspiring . . . Sharp in its dialogue, real with its relationships, and fascinating in details of the game, *The Golfer's Carol* is that rarest of books—one you will read and keep for yourself while purchasing multiple copies for friends."

—Andy Andrews, *New York Times* bestselling author of *The Noticer* and *The Traveler's Gift*

THE BOOMERANG

OTHER TITLES BY ROBERT BAILEY

JASON RICH SERIES

Rich Justice

Rich Waters

Rich Blood

BOCEPHUS HAYNES SERIES

The Wrong Side

Legacy of Lies

MCMURTRIE AND DRAKE LEGAL THRILLERS

The Final Reckoning

The Last Trial

Between Black and White

The Professor

OTHER BOOKS

The Golfer's Carol

THE BOOMERANG

A THRILLER

ROBERT BAILEY

THOMAS & MERCER

Published by Thomas & Mercer, Seattle

www.apub.com

Amazon, the Amazon logo, and Thomas & Mercer are trademarks of Amazon.com, Inc., or its affiliates.

EU product safety contact:
Amazon Media EU S. à r.l.
38, avenue John F. Kennedy, L-1855 Luxembourg
amazonpublishing-gpsr@amazon.com

ISBN-13: 9781662516658 (hardcover)
ISBN-13: 9781662516665 (paperback)
ISBN-13: 9781662516672 (digital)

Cover design by Jarrod Taylor
Cover image: © CHBD, © lcurtoicurto / Getty;
© EB Adventure Photography / Shutterstock

Printed in the United States of America
First edition

For the Baca family of Los Lunas, New Mexico

PROLOGUE

Lick Skillet, Alabama. July 4, 1994

The night was perfect. Or to paraphrase Randy Owen and the boys from Fort Payne . . . close enough.

The humid, sticky air smelled of hot dogs, Budweiser, and the ungodly awesome trifecta of hair spray, sunscreen, and cheap perfume. In the dugout, the opening chord of "Paradise City," by Guns N' Roses, blared out of a jam box. And on the infield dirt of the New Sharon baseball field, two boys played catch, the game long since over. Both still wore their green-and-gold jerseys, white pants stained with dirt and grass, caps cocked high on their heads. The kings of their tiny universe. Neither wanting to leave.

Or to say goodbye.

"My Gawd, that's Eli James's music!" Lionel Cantrell hollered and hurled the baseball submarine-style to Eli.

Eli caught the ball and took a deep breath of the intoxicating mixture of scents. In the outfield grass, kids and families milled about. Some were already lying on their backs and looking up at the dark, cloudless sky. Waiting with anticipation for the fireworks extravaganza. In the distance, even above the high-pitched wail of Axl Rose, roared the V-8 engine of Brent Lassiter's cherry red Camaro IROC-Z.

Up against the right field fence, under the old wooden scoreboard, two middle-aged men, clearly drunk, were engaged in a full-out fistfight.

Lick Skillet, baby, Eli thought, battling the sadness that grew with every passing second. He looked behind the backstop to the parking lot, where car headlights provided just enough illumination to see the baseball. Past Lionel in left field, a group of teenage girls sat in a circle passing around a bottle of Boone's Farm. Ruthanne Quick, Eli's crush since third grade, was with them.

Earlier that day, on this very field, Eli and Lionel had led the New Sharon team to a thorough beating of Walnut Grove in the annual Fourth of July game. Lionel pitched a shutout, and Eli slapped a home run and a double and threw out two base runners before being ejected in the final inning.

"Still can't believe you kneed Tommy Ledbetter in the nuts," Lionel said above the music. "Damn, son. I thought his momma was going to whup your ass."

"Mine would have swallowed his whole and shit her out for breakfast tomorrow."

Lionel whistled. "Foncie James is bad to the bone. And a genuine fox with that wild hair."

"Fuck you," Eli said, throwing the ball as hard as he could at Lionel.

Lionel caught it, and the pop of the glove sounded like a firecracker. "Easy, dude. Now tell me: Why'd you lose your mind out there?"

Eli put his hands on his hips. "Just throw the damn ball."

Lionel tossed it up in the air and caught it with his glove. "Not until you answer the question."

Eli felt a surge of anger. "Because he pointed his bat at you after an inside pitch and said he was going to break your face if you got that close again. I told him to shut the hell up, and he poked me in the rib cage with the handle of his bat right up under my chest protector. The umpire had his back turned and didn't see it. Then he whispered something at me. After that, I just reacted."

"What did he say?" Lionel again flipped the ball up in the air and caught it with his glove.

Eli cussed under his breath. "He called me a pussy."

2

"Well . . . I mean, to be fair, you are a *pussy!*" Lionel howled and hurled the ball even harder back at Eli.

For the next few minutes, the two friends played a vicious game of burnout on the dimly lit diamond, with Lionel finally holding his hands up. "Mercy."

Eli faked a throw and laughed, seeing that several kids had come in from the outfield to watch them. He strolled to the mound.

"Seriously, dude," Lionel said, coming over to Eli. "What were you thinking? Tommy Ledbetter's a monster, but you acted so fast. He never had a chance."

Eli gazed past Lionel and the gathering throng of mostly boys. The outfield had grown quieter. The fight had finally been broken up, and the two participants were leaning against the fence and drinking beer together. *Classic . . .*

He moved his focus to left field, and his stomach clenched when he noticed that Ruthanne Quick was staring at him. Her palms were flat on the grass. Legs extended with her bare feet crossed. Tight blue jean shorts cut high on her tanned legs and a crimson tank top that exposed her cream-colored bra strap.

"Elijah Longstreet James." Lionel mocked Eli's mom's voice. "I'm talking to you, brother."

Eli turned to him, still thinking about Ruthanne. "I don't know. I guess I got a mean streak when it comes to protecting my friends."

"But a heart of gold," Lionel said, punching Eli's shoulder and putting his arm around him. "Gonna miss you, man." Then he sighed, and for a few seconds, neither said anything.

"We still rooming together in Tuscaloosa in a couple of years?" Lionel asked after a moment.

"You know it."

"Then law school," Lionel said with a nod.

"Boom." Eli made a mock explosion with his hands.

"And after that, politics, baby. We'll start small, but someday . . ." Lionel tapped out a drumroll while Eli hummed the presidential jingle.

"Lionel Jefferson Cantrell is the first president of the United States from the great state of Alabama!" Eli proclaimed, cocking his head to the sky. "Can I get an RMFT?"

"Roll *motherfucking* Tide," Lionel yelled. "And you'll be right there with me, brother. Kneeing everyone in the nuts that tries to bring me down. And to think . . . we can say it all started in the 4-H club of Madison County."

Eli laughed. "Don't forget being sophomore class president of Hazel Green High," Eli said, chuckling as the first Roman candle lit up the sky with shades of purple, red, and orange.

Eli quickly glanced left and saw Ruthanne Quick still staring at him.

"Wouldn't hurt to talk to her," Lionel teased, elbowing Eli in the side.

Someone had changed the tape on the boom box to Skynyrd.

"No, it wouldn't," Eli said, as his feet started forward. But when he reached the spot where the dirt turned to grass, he turned and gazed back at Lionel Cantrell.

"Ball," Lionel said, holding up his glove.

Eli tossed the baseball to his best friend as another Roman candle sparked neon green above them and Ronnie Van Zant sang about Tuesday being gone.

"Lick Skillet forever," Lionel said.

Eli nodded. "Lick Skillet forever."

PART ONE

SILENT KILLER

The mood in the room is tense. The only sound, the television.

"As the clock strikes midnight and we turn to November 6, 2024, with all precincts now reporting, Lionel Cantrell carries New Mexico, Colorado, Utah, and Arizona. The senator from Alabama will be the next president of the United States."

A man snatches the remote and mutes the volume. General Kyle Randolph is tall and thin with salt-and-pepper hair cut high and tight, and blue-gray eyes. "Well . . . there you have it."

FBI Director Beth McGee sighs. "Not what I was expecting . . . but probably best for the country." She is a petite woman with short red hair and green eyes. Her tone is firm and no-nonsense.

"I beg to differ," the third person in the room growls. Robert Bellamy, the secretary of Homeland Security, is a short, squat man with a bald head. "Cantrell carries too much risk."

For several seconds, silence. As they stare at the map on the TV screen, McGee whispers the name they're all thinking: "Nester Alejandro Sanchez."

Randolph rubs the back of his neck. "We have a more pressing concern."

"Than the next president's connection to the most dangerous man in America?" Bellamy scoffs. "What could that possibly be?"

"Lionel Cantrell's colon cancer has recurred."

The air seeps out of the room as the other two look to Randolph. No words spoken, but McGee finally whistles through her teeth and crosses her arms. "Jesus H. Christ."

"Cancer? You've got to be kidding," Bellamy says. "He looks fine. Great, even." He points at the screen, where Lionel Cantrell is waving to his supporters at his campaign headquarters. He has his arm around his wife and is flanked by his son and daughter. At six-three and a little over two hundred pounds, the senator and soon-to-be president still projects the smooth athleticism that made him a starting pitcher on the University of Alabama's baseball team some two and a half decades earlier. "I don't believe it. When was he diagnosed?"

"Last week," Randolph says, fatigue creeping into his voice. "His annual follow-up. He had no symptoms, but the scope revealed a six-centimeter tumor." He pauses. "And that's not the worst of it."

"Metastasis?" McGee guesses.

Randolph nods. "To his pancreas."

"Another silent killer." She looks away and massages her temples.

"Good grief. He should've said something," Bellamy says. "The American people have a right to know."

Randolph raises his eyebrows. "That's a bit hypocritical, don't you think?"

The Homeland Security director grits his teeth and stares at the television screen.

"How long does he have?" McGee asks.

Randolph shrugs. "Six months . . . maybe ten. Possibly two years."

"But not the full term," Bellamy concludes.

"Not a chance."

Again, the room grows quiet. Finally, McGee breaks it. "Governor Yancey would be a disaster as president. He's . . . much too volatile."

Bellamy grunts. "As a figurehead VP, he can be tolerated, but that's it."

Finally, Randolph sits and slaps the table. "We don't have a choice."

"The boomerang." McGee's voice falters as she speaks the inevitable.

The three regard each other in the shadowy room.

"When?" Bellamy finally asks.

General Randolph hesitates, but only for a moment. "Soon."

1

On the morning of his inauguration, President-Elect Lionel Cantrell was escorted into the bowels of the Pentagon. While the public transfer of power would happen a few hours later, during his first address to the nation as president, the true changing of the guard took place now.

While being briefed by Strategic Command and the White House military staff on the arsenal of nuclear weapons that would be in his care during the next four years, Lionel had to concentrate to keep his shoulders from sagging. The weight of the burden he now carried felt staggering.

He was, quite literally, the most powerful person in the world.

He'd been expecting this briefing for some time, but no amount of preparation would have been enough to ease the heaviness of the moment.

Many people referred to the container holding the codes for the nuclear weapons that could destroy the civilized world as "the black box," but the actual nickname for this forty-five-pound briefcase was "the football." Lionel listened intently as personnel from Strategic Command went over the United States' vast nuclear arsenal.

Submarines in the Arctic.

Missile silos across the Great Plains.

And bombers on runways from sea to shining sea.

Then he was shown how the football served as the trigger for it all. And, finally, how he would use the device if, God forbid, the safety of the country required it.

"I understand," Lionel said over and over again. When the meeting finally concluded and the military personnel began to disperse, Lionel collapsed into a leather chair at the head of a long table. The seats, which moments earlier had been filled with uniformed men and women explaining the most apocalyptic nuclear arsenal in the world, were now empty except for Lionel and one other man.

"Is there something else?" Lionel asked, hearing the fatigue in his voice and knowing he had to shake it off. After all, in a few short hours, he would give his inaugural address. He needed to be *on*. The world would be watching. But here and now, God-knew-how-many floors below the Department of Defense headquarters, Lionel Cantrell felt overwhelmed by the magnitude of his responsibility.

"Yes, Mr. President. There is."

Lionel glanced up at the man. Kyle Randolph was a four-star general and had served as both secretary of defense and chairman of the Joint Chiefs of Staff under prior administrations. General Randolph was the most respected figure in the Pentagon—a literal living legend— but until a second ago, he'd yet to utter a word. "How are you feeling?" he asked.

The newly elected president snorted. "Honestly? Overwhelmed."

The general nodded. "That's to be expected." He squinted. "But you misinterpreted my question."

Now, it was Lionel who narrowed his eyes. "I don't understand."

"You suffered a recurrence of your metastatic colon cancer." Randolph spoke the words as if he were delivering the weather forecast. Firm. Almost monotone. No empathy or inflection in his voice. He spoke the words as absolute fact, which, of course, they were.

Lionel felt an icy chill run up his arms. Only one other person knew of his recent diagnosis, and it sure as hell wasn't Kyle Randolph. In fact, it was *impossible* for this man to know. "How?" was the only response he could manage.

"Mr. President, the national security of this country is a serious matter. Wouldn't you agree?"

Lionel nodded.

"A health condition that might cause your death before the end of your term affects the national security of the United States." He folded his hands into a tent. "And I make it my business to know anything that might harm our country."

"How could my cancer—?"

"It makes us vulnerable. The country can't voluntarily be in a transition state. Ever. And you can't effectively govern the executive branch with a debilitating illness."

"But the vice president—"

"Is the weakest person in your cabinet. It's a title, only. To be frank, sir, Governor Yancey is a complete joke."

Lionel managed a soft chuckle. On these points, he had to agree with the general. Sanford Yancey was the governor of Texas. He carried much political weight and was popular with the masses. But that didn't make him any less of a buffoon.

"Sometimes, it's necessary for the vice president to assume the role of president," Randolph continued. "But we never want to invite such a drastic change of power, especially if we know that the successor will be a disaster. And, based on our understanding of your diagnosis, it is very possible that Governor Yancey might become the president in a couple of years." He hesitated and rubbed his hands together before placing them palms down on the table. "We can't have that."

Lionel crossed his arms tight against his chest. "Setting aside how you somehow violated my patient privacy to learn the current state of my health, why exactly are we having this conversation? I have cancer. I may die in less than four years because of it. So what?"

At this, General Randolph actually smiled. "Lionel, how many presidents of the United States have died of cancer?"

Lionel raised his eyebrows. He couldn't think of one off the top of his head.

"Come on. Take a wild guess."

"Harrison?" But he knew that was wrong. William Henry Harrison had died forty days after taking office, from pneumonia. "Harding?"

"Wrong and wrong. Harrison died of pneumonia and enteric fever. Harding had a heart attack. The correct answer is one president. Ulysses S. Grant died of throat cancer in 1877."

"Okay, what—"

"Honestly, up until very recently, it was dumb luck that only Grant had fallen to cancer. But then Project Boomerang happened."

The tiny hairs on the back of Lionel's neck started to tingle. "What are you talking about?"

"What if I told you that you could take a drug that would make your metastatic colon cancer not only stop spreading but go away completely?"

Lionel forced a laugh. "I'd tell you that you'd lost your ever-loving mind. If such a thing existed, it would be out in the world. I would have already been offered it."

"You think?" Randolph gazed at Lionel with flat eyes.

The temperature in the room seemed to drop several degrees as the two men peered at each other. If Lionel's arms hadn't been tightly crossing his chest, they would have been shaking. "Yes, I do."

"Mr. President, do you know how many billions upon billions of dollars are wrapped up in the oncology market? What would a miracle pill do to that industry? How many jobs do you think would be lost? How much money?" The general leaned forward, and his massive hands were now on Lionel's side of the table. "Not to mention, how would you roll out such a drug? Who would be chosen to manufacture it? And who would receive the benefit of this miracle? *Everyone?*" He licked his lips. "It would be a logistical nightmare and would destroy this country, if not the world, as we know it."

Lionel held his mouth agape. He couldn't believe what he was hearing.

"The bottom line is that such a discovery, like your illness, represents a potential threat to national security."

Lionel Cantrell stood from his seat on trembling legs. "Are you telling me that there's a cure for cancer?"

General Randolph reached into his suit jacket and pulled out a gold key. "No, I'm not saying that. The FDA has never approved any such drug."

"But?"

"But let's just say the trials of one particular medication have been tampered with a bit. If a person were to research this *one particular medication*, according to tests conducted by the FDA, they would find that this immunotherapy drug had a forty-eight percent chance of killing cancer cells and a thirty percent chance of preventing the development of cancer cells." He paused. "Along with a laundry list of debilitating and devastating potential side effects."

Lionel leaned against the table to steady himself. "Most people with stage-four cancer would take those odds. What did the tests really show?"

"That this drug is ninety-eight percent effective across the board with few, if any, side effects."

"Good God Almighty." Lionel felt dizzy as he stared at the key in the general's hand. "What is that?"

"This . . ." Randolph glanced at the key and then back at the president. ". . . will open a small container hidden in the presidential suite of the White House. Inside it, you will find the medication, which we refer to as the boomerang. The dosage instructions are on the bottle." He placed the key on the table.

Lionel took a deep breath and slowly exhaled. A few moments ago, he had been overwhelmed by the responsibility bestowed upon him with the nuclear football. Now, how did he feel? As he looked into the steel-blue eyes of Kyle Randolph, one emotion overpowered all others: fear. Before he could ask his next question, the general answered it.

"You and the first lady each have your own walk-in closet. In yours, there is a framed photograph of President Ulysses S. Grant. Remove the frame . . . and you will see the medicine box."

"The *medicine box*?"

General Randolph ignored the question. He stood and extended his hand. Without conscious thought, Lionel shook it. The general's grip was firm, and he held on when Lionel tried to pull away. "Mr. President, the contents of the medicine box are a matter of the utmost national security. But we believe your health is a more pressing matter. As president, you are entrusted with this gift, and only you will receive its benefits. Take the drug, and in a couple of weeks, your new oncologist will perform some scans. I think you will be pleased with the results." He finally let go of the president's hand. "Please do not abuse this power."

Lionel knew a threat when he heard one, but he had gathered himself. Keeping his hand steady, he retrieved the key from the table. "I would think something so important would be guarded with secret codes. Why use something as antiquated as a key?"

"Because that particular key cannot be copied. And, even if it could, we know who comes and goes in the presidential suite. The only way this secret gets exposed to the world is if you violate the trust we are granting you." He patted Lionel's shoulder. "You want to get better, don't you? To be free of cancer and able to live a longer and fuller life?"

"Yes, but this seems wrong," Lionel said. "To keep something so important from the people and give it only to the president."

"We do not agree."

"And who's *we*?" Lionel gritted his teeth. "And who the hell are you to wield such power? And why wasn't any of this discussed when the Strategic Command was in here? Good Lord, man, if this is all true—"

Randolph held out his palms. "It's natural to have questions, Mr. President, and I'll do my best to answer them. Project Boomerang is a top secret defense initiative founded some years ago when I was secretary of defense. There are only a handful of people who are aware of its existence, and that small group now includes you." He licked his lips. "Offering the medication to you is something that we do with great trepidation, but . . . we feel it is necessary under these circumstances." He took a step back from Lionel. "Do you comprehend?"

"No. I don't."

Randolph glared at him. "You will." He walked to the door, then looked over his shoulder at the newly elected president. "We understand that your wife and family are not aware of your recurrence."

Lionel swallowed. "That's correct."

"Have you told anyone?"

"Yes. One person." Lionel figured it was pointless to lie. If they knew about his diagnosis *and* that his wife and kids were clueless, then they must know to whom he'd disclosed his secret.

"Your chief of staff? Mr. James."

Lionel nodded. "Eli James is my most trusted adviser. He's also my best friend. He understands better than anyone why my diagnosis must be kept under wraps." Lionel squinted at the general. "And he'll be thrilled if my health improves."

Silence engulfed the room for several seconds. Randolph walked toward Lionel and stopped when he was a foot away. "Mr. President, the contents of the medicine box are a matter of national security and must be kept confidential. You cannot share what I've told you with any other person . . . including Mr. James." He paused. "Are we clear?"

Lionel swallowed, his mouth dry. "Crystal," he managed.

Randolph's glare softened. He patted Lionel on the back. "I look forward to working with you, Mr. President." He turned and headed toward the exit.

Lionel Cantrell stood alone in the large conference room.

Sweet, merciful Jesus, he thought, collapsing into his chair and gazing at the gold key he still held in his hand. *There's a cure for cancer?* He took a deep breath. As he exhaled, he still couldn't believe what he'd been told.

"The boomerang," he whispered, closing his eyes and putting the key in his pocket.

2

Eli James walked into the coffee shop at 4:45 p.m. He was fifteen minutes late, and his tardiness was intentional. The person who had called the meeting was waiting at a corner table, and Eli sat down without ordering anything.

"Well?" Eli asked.

Hoyt Barnes, the chairman of the Federal Election Commission, took a sip of coffee. "Just show up whenever you can."

"It's been a busy day, Mr. Chairman. My best friend was inaugurated as president of the United States this morning, and, as you might imagine, the first day at work as his chief of staff has been a tad hectic. *This* bullshit didn't make the top five on the priority list." He paused. "What's the verdict?"

Barnes leaned back in his chair and tapped his fingers on the table. Then he cocked his head and sighed. "The FEC will issue a press release next week that there was no evidence of any illegal campaign contributions."

"It's about damn time," Eli said, forcing his tone to be defiant but feeling a jolt of relief laced with adrenaline in his veins. He glanced around the café, gathering himself. At this time of day, there were only a couple other patrons, which was likely the reason this site and time were chosen. "I trust the witch hunt is over."

The chairman gritted his teeth. "I take offense to that characterization. We were doing our job and investigating serious allegations."

Eli shrugged. "Whatever. Is it over?"

He shrugged. "Yes and no."

"What does that mean?"

"It means that we think you're dirty. We don't trust you or your wife, and we think there was an awful lot of smoke to the claims that your wealthy friend in New Mexico made contributions in excess of campaign-finance laws. Unfortunately, no one we interviewed would talk. They were apparently scared of someone else more than they were of us."

He waited for Eli to chime in, but Eli was no fool. He would not be supplying this man any information.

"So . . . ," Barnes continued, placing his hands on the small table, ". . . while our official inquiry is over, we will be keeping an eye on you."

Eli grinned and held out his hand. Reluctantly, Barnes shook it. "I'm certainly glad that the FEC will be looking out for me," he said, releasing his hand and standing from the table as Barnes did the same. "I trust you'll send me a draft of your release before it goes out."

"We're going to take Nester Sanchez down, Mr. James," Barnes said. "And it's not just the commission. The FBI, Homeland Security, and the DOD agree that his power and influence have become a danger to New Mexico and the country as a whole." He leaned forward, and Eli could smell the coffee on his breath. "A man like Nester Sanchez can turn on his friends in a heartbeat. I'd be careful if I were you."

"Oh, I will, Mr. Barnes." Eli smiled again, enjoying the contempt in the bureaucrat's eyes. As an attorney and political animal for the past twenty years, Eli had grown accustomed to getting under people's skin, and he rather enjoyed it. "I always am. But I'd watch myself if I were you, as well."

"Are you threatening me?" Barnes crossed his arms.

"Oh, no. Just making a promise. If there are any quotes that come out to the press from you or anyone else in the FEC, including any *anonymous sources*, that in any way impugn the integrity of the president of the United States, me, my wife, or Nester Alejandro Sanchez, then the FEC—including you, the vice-chair, all of the commissioners, and anyone else directly involved in this investigation—will be sued for slander, libel, obstruction of justice, willfully violating your own regulations . . . and any damn thing else we can think of."

Barnes raised his eyebrows. "You prick."

Eli mirrored the other man's gesture. "You have no idea."

The chairman's face reddened. "If the president grants the expected pardon request of Mr. Sanchez, there will be considerable pressure on us to launch another investigation."

Eli held his arms out wide. "Bring it."

———

Out on the sidewalk, Eli dialed the number.

"Well?" a woman's firm voice answered.

"It's over," Eli said. "The FEC will release a statement next week."

Silence on the other end of the line.

Eli broke it. "Tell him thank you," he told his wife.

"He will expect the favor we discussed," she warned. "Soon."

"Yes, I know. So, Dale . . . when are you coming—"

"Congratulations, Eli. Please give Lionel my regards."

The line clicked dead before Eli could respond.

Eli James, the chief of staff to the newly elected president of the United States, took a deep breath of the cold January air. He walked to his car, a black Range Rover, and slid into the front seat. After he turned on the ignition, he gripped the wheel with both hands and squeezed it. He wanted to be happy. Wanted to yell "Woo-hoo!" But he found it impossible. Jealousy, anxiety, and relief were having a tug-of-war with his emotions. Instead of being here to celebrate his triumph, his wife was on the other side of the country . . .

. . . *preserving our victory.*

Finally, he closed his eyes and forced the negative thoughts out of his mind. "We did it. By God, we *did* it."

3

Eli winked at the head of the president's Secret Service detail and closed the door to the Oval Office. He took in the iconic rug with the enormous seal of the United States, then his friend seated in the most powerful chair in the world.

"We did it," he said.

Lionel grinned, his face showing the exhaustion of the day. "Yes, we did."

The two men embraced, and Eli slapped him hard on the back. Then he placed the bottle of bourbon on the president's historic desk.

"Pappy Van Winkle," Lionel said, snorting. "We've come a long way from Jackie's Lounge in Tuscaloosa."

Eli laughed and opened the bottle. "Longer than that, brother." He breathed in the heavenly scents of oak, vanilla, and caramel. "As I recall, the dream started in the old red building of Hazel Green Junior High and was cemented on a dirt infield in downtown Lick Skillet."

Lionel stared wistfully at the ceiling. "From Charity Lane to Pennsylvania Avenue. Who would ever believe it?"

Eli poured two glasses of bourbon and handed one to the president. "You remember homecoming our first year of law school? Getting up at six in the morning and cooking steaks on the grill and drinking Bloodies. Then putting on those ridiculous tuxedos and riding on the float."

Lionel smiled at that. "The parade finished up at Jackie's, where we proceeded to drink beer and shoot pool until kickoff and then stumbled off to Bryant–Denny Stadium."

"As I recall, we fleshed out our crazy plan for the presidency that afternoon."

Lionel grinned. "Yes, and today we crossed the goal line."

Eli held his glass up high and peered out the window to Pennsylvania Avenue. "To big dreams and the fools that dream them."

"Amen, brother," Lionel said.

Eli turned to his friend. "To the president of the United States."

Lionel again touched Eli's drink with his own. "To my best friend. Who believed in me when I didn't believe in myself."

The president plopped down in his chair, and Eli walked around the table, reveling in the joy and ecstasy of the moment. Outside, they had to play their roles and be professional at all times. But in here, at least right now, they could take measure of the great journey.

"Three years of law school for both of us," Eli said, his voice wistful. "Two years of private practice for me, and a couple years in the Tuscaloosa DA's office for you. Making contacts. Pressing flesh. And then—"

"State senate," Lionel chimed in, closing his eyes and taking a sip of Pappy. "Then lieutenant governor of the great state of Alabama." He'd dialed up his southern accent a notch, but his voice came out hoarse and weak.

"Then the by-God US Senate," Eli added.

"And now . . ." Lionel moved his drink in a circle around the room. "I can't believe it."

Eli frowned. "I can. We worked hard, man. We pushed it. You're forty-six years old. Older than Kennedy but younger than Obama and Clinton. I'm forty-five. What we've accomplished in just over twenty years is—"

"Freakin' amazing," Lionel interrupted, holding up his now-empty glass, and Eli poured him another.

For a few minutes, the two friends drank in silence. Eli was buzzed on both the bourbon and the energy and excitement of the day. Finally, he dropped the good news. "I met with Hoyt Barnes this afternoon. The FEC is closing their investigation. I suspect there will be an under-the-radar announcement next Tuesday or Wednesday." He raised his glass. "Nothing to see here. Move along."

Lionel sipped from his glass. "And our friend in Los Lunas?"

"Happy for us, Dale says."

"But?"

"Wanting his favor."

"And what happens if we can't deliver?"

The smile that had been affixed to Eli's face drifted away. "Nester Sanchez is a lot of things, but he's not stupid. We promised we'd do all we could do, and regardless of whether he gets impatient, he knows he backed the right horse. At the end of the day, his money was well spent. The last thing he wanted was Isaiah sitting in that chair." Eli pointed at Lionel, who took a long pull from the glass and nodded.

"I guess not," he agreed.

Isaiah Blankenship, the two-term governor of the state of Illinois, had been Lionel's opponent for the presidency. Two days after the election, Isaiah's campaign manager had filed a complaint with the FEC alleging that Lionel had taken illegal contributions from Nester Sanchez, the largest landowner in New Mexico and one of the wealthiest individuals in the world, and asked for a full investigation. The claims were serious but hardly new in US elections.

They were also difficult to prove. Could they show smoke? Yes. Absolutely. Many individuals, PAC groups, nonprofits, and other foundations with a connection to the rich land baron had donated to Lionel's campaign. But was there fire? To prove a violation, the commission needed a whistleblower. Someone on the inside who could connect the dots.

But, as Hoyt Barnes had indicated a few hours earlier, not a single person had talked. Not under condition of anonymity. Not for immunity. Not for any damn reason.

Such was the power of Nester Sanchez.

"Do you think Isaiah will back off now?" Lionel asked.

"Who cares?" Eli said. "He's old news, and you're the president. He can't override the FEC."

Lionel gazed into his glass but didn't say anything.

"Something wrong?" Eli asked.

The president blinked but remained silent.

"Lionel?"

"What?"

"You went away there for a minute, bud. You okay?"

Lionel rubbed his eyes. "I was thinking . . . about my meetings at the Pentagon this morning."

Eli frowned. "The football?"

Lionel nodded his agreement. "Yeah." He sighed, but it sounded forced to Eli. "Lot of responsibility. It was . . . a bit overwhelming."

"I saw the briefcase when I walked in." Eli downed the rest of his glass and studied his friend. "You sure there's nothing else?" He spoke in a lower tone. "How are you feeling? I mean, you know, with the cancer—"

"Fine," Lionel snapped.

Eli held out his hands as if to block a punch. "Hey, I'm sorry. I just . . . I know you've been through a lot these past couple of months, what with the treatment and the stress of the election and inauguration." He hesitated. "And I know it's been tough hiding the truth from Vanessa."

"I'm fine, Eli. Just exhausted."

"Then I take it you won't be making an appearance at the Four Seasons tonight to revel in the glory of our victory?"

"Not tonight, old buddy. I'm afraid it's past my bedtime." Lionel stood and extended his hand.

Eli swiped the hand away and hugged his friend. "We did it," he said again. Then he walked to the door, leaving the bottle of bourbon and glasses on the desk.

"Hey, Eli," the president called after him.

Eli turned and looked over his shoulder as he grabbed the knob. "Yeah?"

"Everything okay with Dale? I noticed that she wasn't there today at the ceremony." He paused. "I suspect I wasn't the only one who took notice of her absence."

For a moment, Eli's buzz faltered. He pursed his lips. "She hated to miss, but Nester needed her in court. There was a motion hearing today in Albuquerque on the charges against him."

"Well, that's a relief. I think our understanding with Nester depends a lot more on Dale than it does on either of us. Don't you agree?"

Eli forced a smile. "All is good, my powerful friend. Get some rest."

He opened the door, but again the president's voice stopped him. "Elijah Longstreet James?" The southern accent was dialed back up.

The chief of staff bowed, the two bourbons having fully kicked in. "At your service."

"Thank you, Eli," Lionel said. "I mean it, brother. Thank you. None of this would have happened without you."

Eli nodded and winked. "Lick Skillet forever."

"Lick Skillet forever."

———

Once his chief of staff was gone, Lionel Cantrell gazed out at Pennsylvania Avenue. He sipped from his glass and tried to recount the day. There had hardly been a second to spare until now. But though the nuclear football briefing had been overwhelming, the reaction to his inaugural speech exhilarating, and the walk to the White House with his wife, Vanessa, joyful, the entire day had been clouded by what General Randolph had told him after the briefing on the football.

"The boomerang," he whispered. He was standing so close to the window his breath formed a circle of fog on the glass. Lionel turned and gazed down at his desk. He was too tired to work, and even the thought of another party like the one Eli had mentioned made him cringe. Vanessa was upstairs, already in bed. The stress and anxiety of the day had knocked her out minutes after the inaugural dinner.

"But we have to break in the presidential mattress," Lionel had teased while she put her pajamas on. "I mean, John and Jackie Kennedy did the nasty in this room. George and Martha Washington. Barack and Michelle."

"You'll have to take a rain check," she said but giggled from under the covers as Lionel continued calling out president and first lady names.

"Bill and Hillary. Ronald and Nancy. George and Barbara. George W. and Laura."

"Don't you have work to do, Mr. President?"

He kissed her cheek and hugged her tightly. Then he'd descended the stairs and headed to the West Wing to await his celebration with Eli.

He'd enjoyed reminiscing with his old friend, but he couldn't take his mind off what was hidden in his bedroom closet. Finally, knowing he had stalled long enough, Lionel drank the rest of the bourbon in his glass in one swallow and walked up the stairs and down the long hallway. When he entered the suite, he could hear Vanessa's snores, and he couldn't help but smile. His beautiful, petite wife snored like a sailor, and he loved giving her grief about it.

He stepped into his closet, closed the door, and turned on the light. He saw the framed photograph of President Ulysses S. Grant and removed it from its place on the wall. His breath caught in his throat when he saw the safe.

He took the key out of his pocket and held it with both hands. Lionel thought back to three months ago. "You've had a recurrence," his oncologist, Dr. Paul Englert, had said. "And it has metastasized to the pancreas. I'm sorry, Lionel, but we need to start chemo and radiation immediately."

Lionel had done four weeks of chemotherapy and radiation starting the day after the election. He'd stayed hidden from the public eye for almost two months, and he'd told Dr. Englert that he did not want to do any treatment at all during the three weeks before the inauguration. He'd also managed to hide his treatment from Vanessa, but he knew if he had to undergo anything else, he'd have to tell her. He'd dropped fifteen pounds, but on his six-foot, three-inch, 220-pound frame, the lost weight wasn't that noticeable and, if anything, was an improvement. He could write that off as wanting to thin down for the inauguration. But how long could he keep the truth from the American people?

Lionel took a deep breath and inserted the key. He turned it and heard the unclicking of the lock.

He opened the medicine box and exhaled. Inside was an orange pill bottle. He grabbed the container and, on the label, saw his name: *Lionel Cantrell.* Then he read the simple instructions out loud.

Take one capsule by mouth every day.

Lionel felt his heart pounding in his chest. He was scared to death, but he had to admit that he was also curious.

Could there really be a cure for cancer?

The president opened the bottle and removed a pill. *Dear God, please help this work. And . . . forgive me if it does.*

Then he put the capsule in his mouth and swallowed.

4

At 7:30 a.m., Eli pulled in to the driveway of his two-story townhome in Arlington. His head pounded with a hangover despite the four Aleve caplets he'd popped last night before passing out in his hotel room. And the shower he'd taken that morning had done nothing to thwart the sluggish exhaustion that consumed him.

Now, as he parked in the three-car garage next to his wife's Lexus sedan, he winced at the reception that would await him. He cut the ignition and lumbered toward the door leading into the house. When he entered, the smell of bacon and coffee hit his nostrils, and his gag reflex kicked in. He ducked into the hall bathroom, put his hands on his knees, and then puked into the toilet. After straightening, he ran cold water over his face and gritted his teeth. He knew his daughter was here—Bella's Jeep was in the garage, and she was likely eating breakfast before going to school.

You gotta tighten up, he told himself, echoing something his alcoholic father used to say both to Eli and to himself after a night spent partying. He looked in the mirror and wanted to spit at the reflection. Then, grinding his teeth together, he sucked in his chest and forced a smile onto his face.

"I smell bacon!" he yelled as he entered the kitchen.

Bella was eating at one of the stools at the huge island. She had just put a forkful of eggs in her mouth. She didn't look at Eli as he walked toward her and planted a kiss on her cheek. "How's my favorite daughter?"

She rolled her eyes. A few years ago, she might have giggled and said, "I'm your only daughter," but the joke, like Eli himself, had worn thin, and Bella James wasn't having it.

Eli stepped back and looked at her. She had her mother's blond hair but Eli's brown eyes. There were a few freckles on her nose that Eli had adored since she was a toddler. But she was no child anymore. She was a seventeen-year-old high school senior with a full scholarship to Belmont University School of Music in Nashville, Tennessee.

"I'm late, Dad," she said, picking up her plate and taking it to the sink.

"No, you're not," Eli said, glancing at his watch. "It's seven thirty-five, and the drive to school is only five minutes."

"I have a meeting this morning with my calc teacher. I got a B on my last test, and I need to bring that up."

"A *B*? Heaven forbid."

She stuck her tongue out at him, and he returned the gesture. Then, as she moved around him, she grabbed her back and grimaced. She leaned against the island.

"Still hurting?" Eli said, his head beginning to clear. Bella had been complaining of back pain for a couple of weeks and had already been seen once by her pediatrician. Since she was a soccer player and the club season had just started, the physician had equated the pain to a strain. Physical therapy had been ordered, which Bella had religiously been attending three days a week.

"It's not that bad," she said.

"Probably need to see Dr. Upchurch again," Eli said. "It should be getting better—"

"I'm fine, Dad," Bella snapped. "I don't have time to go to the doctor again. I've got tests every day this week, two soccer games, and dance and voice every night. Plus, my recital is in twelve days, and I'm not ready. This will be my last one . . ." She trailed off and bit her nails.

Eli put a hand on her shoulder. "Hey, easy. You're gonna nail that solo."

Bella had been practicing her final dance-recital solo for weeks. It was to Sarah McLachlan's "I Will Remember You," and it was something she had choreographed herself, with a little assistance from her mom, who had been a hell of a dancer in her day.

She hugged him but then pulled back. "Dad, did you throw up?"

"Yeah . . . I had a little food poisoning at the party last night."

She tilted her head. "Right. Bourbon poisoning, you mean."

Eli sighed. "Aren't you late for school?"

She giggled and pushed past him, then snatched her backpack from a hook on the wall by the garage door. "I'm sorry I wasn't at the inauguration yesterday. I really wanted to go, but Mom . . ." She stopped and looked down at the floor.

"It's okay," he said. "I understand."

"I'm really proud of you . . . and of LC."

He grinned. Bella had always called Lionel "LC." She'd had a hard time pronouncing his name when she was a baby, and he'd told her to just use his initials. The nickname had stuck. "Thank you, sweetie." She turned to go, but he called after her. "Keep me posted on your back, okay? I want you to see Upchurch again if it's not better in a few days."

She again rolled her eyes. "Okay," she agreed.

He started to head for the coffeepot, but now it was her voice that stopped him. "Dad, I'm worried about Mom." There was a pause. "I'm worried about you and Mom."

Eli looked down at the floor. "Me too," he managed, not able to meet her gaze.

Seconds later, he heard the door to the garage swing open and close shut.

After pouring himself a steaming cup of coffee and having several sips to make sure his stomach could handle it, he ambled out of the kitchen to find his wife.

As he expected, Dale was in her home office. He rapped on the open door a couple of times, announcing his presence. His wife held her phone and was pacing back and forth across the floor, speaking into it. Because she had dictation software on the device, he wasn't sure if she was on a phone call or dictating a memo. He took a seat in one of the chairs across from the desk, knowing full well that she would not halt what she was doing until she reached a stopping point.

"Overall, the deposition of the plaintiff went about as well as expected. She makes a good impression, and a jury will probably like her. But she didn't say anything that will hurt Dr. Porter's chances for a defense verdict. The case still hinges on whether his differential diagnosis for the stomach pain was appropriate and whether it was reasonable to treat the symptoms as a potential kidney stone and not an ulcer." She glanced up at Eli and blinked. "All right, that's it." She flung the phone down on the desk and crossed her arms. Her nostrils were flaring, and her blue eyes blazed with anger. "Well? Enjoy your night?"

He took a sip of coffee. "When did you get back?"

"Don't ignore me. Did you have *fun* last night?"

"As a matter of fact, I did. My best friend was inaugurated president of the United States yesterday." He glared back at her. "It was kind of a big thing."

"So was the hearing in Albuquerque."

"I know that," Eli said, choosing his words carefully. "I'm not the one fussing, here."

"Why are you just dragging your sorry ass home now? Did all of Lionel's cabinet spend the night at the Four Seasons? Are they all having flings with lobbyists for special interest groups that supported Lionel?" She gritted her teeth. "Or just *you?*"

"Dale—"

"Oh, spare me the bullshit. You've been carrying on with Sarah Kate Moss for over a year. 'SK,' right? Isn't that what you and everyone in Washington calls her?" She blew a stray hair out of her eyes, and Eli studied her.

Dale Davis James had blond hair that she usually kept tied in a ponytail. She had Carolina blue eyes that could be as warm and inviting as the waters of the Caribbean or as cold as Antarctic ice.

"What are you staring at?" Dale snapped. He wasn't getting warmth or ice from her gaze today. Only red-hot anger.

"The most beautiful woman alive," Eli said, winking at her.

"I'm going to throw this phone at you," she growled, snatching up her iPhone.

"Please do. I have a massive hangover, and getting nailed with a hard object might put me out of my misery."

"Don't tempt me," she said, but she placed the device back on her desk.

"Bella's having back pain again," Eli said, desperately wanting to shift gears.

Dale continued to glare at Eli. Then, finally, she placed her hands on her hips. "I know, and I'm not sure what to do about it. I mean, she's a teenager. With all her activities . . . there's no telling."

"I know. I'm just worried about her."

"No, you're not," Dale snapped. "You're trying to change the subject."

Eli gave a weak smile. "Right and wrong. I am trying to change the subject, but I am worried about Bella."

Dale plopped down in her chair and leaned her elbows on the table, running her hands over her face, before peering back at Eli. "I'm sorry. I know you care about Bella, and you are a good father. But—"

"Thank you," Eli chimed in.

"I'm not finished."

Eli waited.

"But you have become a bankrupt husband, and your playboy lifestyle is finally starting to embarrass me. I've looked away for a while, but I will not have you parade that slut around as if she's your kept girlfriend."

"She's not a slut."

"I'll call her any damn thing I want, and I dare you to sit here and defend her."

"Dale, when was the last time we had sex? Can you remember? I can't."

She blinked but recovered fast. "Don't you *dare* make this about me. While you've been out playing Johnny Playboy, I've been busting my ass around the clock making this family work. Practicing law and making sure that Bella is on top of everything, and I think I've done a pretty damn fine job, thank you very much."

Eli walked around the desk and dropped to a knee in front of his wife. It was a desperate move that he'd used many times before. Dale rolled her eyes as he grabbed her hand, but she didn't pull away.

"You have done an amazing job, honey. You're an incredible mother. You're a fabulous trial lawyer. And what you've done for us . . . for Lionel . . . with Nester has been—"

She ripped her hand free of his. "That's what this is all about, right?" She stood from her chair and walked around the desk, arms crossed, again scowling at him.

Now it was Eli who collapsed in her chair. "Dale—"

"Oh, fuck off. I don't want to hear it. Don't worry, sweet prince, I'm not going to do anything to mess up your arrangement with Nester." She laughed ruefully. "You know, it's funny: he is one of the most ruthless people I have ever known, and I trust his character more than I do yours."

"You don't really believe that," Eli said, feeling a surge of anger.

"Oh, yes, I do. Nester Sanchez isn't a two-faced, kiss-ass pimp who uses charm and lies to get what he wants. He tells it like it is, and he is who he says he is. That's a far cry from what you've become."

Eli bristled and stood to his full height, done cowering. "I'm the chief of staff to the president of the United States. I'm one of the most powerful people in the civilized world. Just because you don't think it is a big deal and, worse, directed our own child to miss the inauguration doesn't diminish my success or power."

"And none of that happens without *me*. Without me and, more importantly, my friendship with Nester, you're still an aide to a scrub in the Senate."

"Fuck you."

"No, thanks."

For several seconds, they stared at each other. Finally, Eli dropped his hands to his sides. "Dale, I'm really sor—"

"Don't," she interrupted, her voice cracking. "Please don't. I can take anything but your empty apologies."

Eli gritted his teeth. "The inauguration was a big deal. You should've been there. Bella should've been there. She'll regret that one day." He paused. "And so will you."

Dale approached the desk and leaned forward, hands on her hips. "Don't talk to me about regret."

"Dale—"

"I want a divorce."

"Dale, honey, no. We can work this—"

"No."

She said it with such force that Eli recoiled as if struck.

"I can't do this anymore, Eli." She wiped her eyes. "I can't do us. We don't work."

"Dale, please. Not now."

She narrowed her eyes and shook her head. "All you care about is the timing. You're worried that a divorce might look bad for the newly appointed chief of staff. You don't care anything at all about our marriage ending."

"That's not true."

"It is true. The only thing you give a shit about is your precious role in the White House and making damn sure no one knows how you got there." She lowered her voice to a whisper. "That no one ever finds out that Lionel's campaign was financed heavily and quite illegally by Nester Alejandro Sanchez."

He looked down at the desk, feeling defeated. All he could muster was, "You're wrong."

"No," she said. "I've never been more right." She walked toward the door. "I've already seen a divorce lawyer, and the petition has been drafted."

Eli continued to peer at the mahogany desk. "When are you planning to file?"

"By the end of the week."

Eli felt like he'd shrunk a full foot since he'd entered the office. What he said next made him feel even smaller. "Dale, regardless of what happens with us, we may need you to run interference with Nester. He is an impatient man, and he'll be very concerned when he hears about this."

When she didn't immediately respond, Eli glanced up at her.

The look on her face was pure disgust. "You are such a narcissist. I'm literally sitting here telling you that our nineteen-year marriage is over, and all you can think about is the pirate you climbed into bed with to pave your friend's way to the presidency and whether I'm going to throw you and your precious dream under the bus."

Eli bit his lip, feeling weak and stupid. "I need to know that you won't pull the rug out from under us. Please."

"Oh, worry not. I'm every bit as guilty as you for what happened with Nester. Hell, I set up most of the foundations and PAC groups that funneled the money. I'm not going to sell us out. That would be suicide for everyone." She paused, and then a faint smile played on her lips. "Besides . . . Nester's my friend."

The words stung as badly as any she'd said up to that point. "Dale, please think about this."

She crossed her arms again. "I have. A lot." Her tone grew colder. "Now, I'd like you to finish your coffee, get dressed . . . and get the hell out of here."

Then she slammed the door behind her.

5

Nine hours later, at just past 5:00 p.m., Eli was pacing the floor of his new office at the White House and drinking a Diet Coke to stay alert. After his confrontation with Dale, he'd done what she'd asked. He'd finished his coffee, gotten cleaned up, and hightailed it out of there. Not so much because she had asked but because the day had demanded it. His first hours as chief of staff were important, as he had to set the tone for the cabinet. He'd conducted meetings with each member until 1:30 p.m., going over the first-ninety-days agenda. Then, the lobbyists had started knocking on the door, and he'd handled each in thirty-minute increments. Now, as darkness began to descend on the nation's capital, he finally had a few minutes to himself, and he had no choice but to think about the ramifications of Dale's words.

In truth, he had known divorce was on the horizon and perhaps, in the nether regions of his soul, had hoped for it. He and Dale hadn't been right for almost a decade—not since her last miscarriage—and he had grown tired of the daily stress of trying to make it work. If he were honest with himself, he knew she was absolutely right. The only problem with ending their marriage at this pivotal moment was the impact such a development might have on Nester Sanchez. In particular, the tycoon's patience.

As three swift knocks on his door mercifully interrupted his thoughts, he glanced out the window to the Washington skyline. *By the end of the week,* he thought. He'd have to tell Lionel. And then he'd need to call Nester. Maybe a meeting.

Three more knocks, and Eli sighed. "Come in."

SK Moss cracked open the door. "Room for one more meeting?" she asked, sliding through the tight space. Eli felt a tingle of excitement as he admired Big Pharma's most powerful lobbyist.

SK was in her midthirties. She had brown hair that was typically put up in some sort of no-frills do, though Eli had seen her let it down on several occasions, including last night. She had brown eyes and a slim, athletic figure. She wasn't as striking as Dale, but she was beautiful, funny, and smart as hell.

"You look like shit, chief," she said, sitting down in the chair across from him.

"Thanks," he said.

"Trace Pharmaceuticals wants some assurances from the president that he won't be supporting any legislation promoting cost-cutting measures on oncology products. A little birdie told me that Senator Wiggins is working on a bill that, if passed, could radically affect Trace's bottom line and also, more importantly of course, the production of medication that could prolong the lives of people battling cancer."

"Of course," Eli said.

"We want to make sure that the president is not going to get behind Wiggins's bill or do anything that would affect what Trace charges for the latest and greatest immunotherapy medications or what the insurance companies are willing to pay for these wonder drugs."

Eli placed a pen in his mouth and began to chew on the end of it, a habit he'd had since middle school. "Does Chad have the support of the Senate?"

Chad Wiggins was a junior senator from Minnesota who'd only been on the Hill for one term.

"He does. He's got a lot of energy, and a personal stake. He lost his son to leukemia, and he wants to make sure that families can afford medication that could make a difference."

"That seems like something we should all be promoting."

SK frowned. "Any type of drug that lowers the risk of cancer or reduces cancer cells is expensive, Eli. Trace can't just give it away, nor can any pharmaceutical company that comes up with something new. It took forever to negotiate the contracts with Blue Cross, TRICARE, and Medicare. If the government steps in and puts ceilings on what Trace can charge that are lower than the contracted amounts—which is my understanding of Chad's bill—then we are back to the drawing board, and the people who need these medications are going to suffer. Can we count on the president to have our back?"

Eli set the gnawed pen down and made a tent with his hands. "I don't think the president will do anything that harms the interests of Trace Pharmaceuticals or any of the companies under pharma's umbrella."

SK squinted at him. "I would hope not. We supported him in the election."

"And the president remembers that and truthfully believes in your lobby. We need to promote the manufacture and distribution of better medications to treat cancer. While Chad's bill has good intentions, the end result will be catastrophic to those he seeks to protect."

Now SK smiled. "Exactly." She cocked her head. "You've already read his bill, haven't you?"

He winked at her. "I might've had a sneak preview."

SK crossed her legs. "My folks are going to be so pleased that the president is already on top of this. Is there any way I can show my appreciation?"

Eli raised his eyebrows. "I think . . . maybe there is."

———

An hour later, they ate room service cheeseburgers and drank longneck beers while sprawled across the king-size bed of the Four Seasons suite. Eli had booked the place for the night, not wanting to go home after his fight with Dale. The room smelled like sex, onions, and beer, and Eli breathed in the scent that brought back memories of college and law school.

"Did you enjoy the appetizer?" SK asked.

"Very much."

"Mind telling me what's going on?"

"What do you mean?"

"I mean why are you staying in DC tonight? Shouldn't you be home? Eating dinner with your wife and daughter? It is a school night, right? And you spent last night here. Won't Dale be getting her dander up?"

"Dale's filing for divorce," Eli said, taking a long sip of beer.

SK sat up straight and put her bottle on the nightstand. "Since when?"

"She told me when I got home this morning."

"I'm . . . sorry. I guess," SK said, fumbling her words.

Eli took a breath and exhaled. He started to say thanks, but his cell phone began to ring on the table next to him. He looked at the screen and cringed when he saw the name.

"Speak of the devil," he said, not answering the call. He turned his attention back to SK, but she only stared at him. "What's wrong?" he asked.

"Nothing. I'm surprised."

Eli snorted. "Really? Why? I'm not. We've been having an affair for over a year. Dale didn't even come to the inauguration, for God's sake."

"I know," SK said. "It's just—"

The phone had stopped ringing, but now the device dinged to announce a new text message.

Eli looked and saw that it was from Dale. Call me. It's an emergency.

He snatched the cell, feeling his heart begin to speed up. He clicked on the message and then called his wife back.

She picked up before the first ring finished. "I'm at the Virginia Hospital Center. Bella passed out at soccer practice. When she woke up, she was feeling dizzy, and her back was really hurting. I've taken her to the ER."

"Has she been seen yet?" Eli asked, putting her on speakerphone, beginning to put his pants on. He tried to keep his voice calm.

"She's having a bunch of tests run. MRI of the brain. Carotid ultrasound. Chest x-ray."

"Good grief. What do they think—"

"They're trying to rule out a stroke."

"A *stroke*? She's seventeen years old. It can't be—"

"Eli." Dale stopped talking, and for a moment, the line went silent. Then came the sound of soft crying.

Eli glanced up and saw SK staring at the phone. Her face had turned pale.

"Eli, please come down here," Dale said. "I'm scared."

He couldn't remember the last time he'd heard any fear or even the slightest hint of vulnerability in his wife's voice.

"On my way," he said.

6

The emergency room of the Virginia Hospital Center was slammed when Eli passed through security and into the lobby. Every seat was taken, and many people were standing. He checked in at the front desk, and seconds later, the double doors to the back opened, and he walked through them. "Room four," the clerk called after him. "Straight ahead and then to the right of the nurse's desk."

Eli took a deep breath and braced himself as he saw the room with the numeral 4 above it. He walked inside, and his daughter was lying on her side on the cot. The lights had been dimmed, and she appeared to be asleep. Below her and up against the wall in one of two guest chairs sat Dale. She had her arms folded tight across her chest, and she was looking at Bella.

He knocked softly, and Dale jerked toward him. Her eyes were red, and when she saw him, she wiped them to stop the tears.

Eli took a seat next to her and placed his hand on top of her knee. She let her hand fall on top of his, and he grabbed hold. "Any news?"

"Still waiting to talk with the doctor."

"How many tests?"

She sighed. "I've lost count."

Eli nodded toward Bella. "How is she?"

"Exhausted," Dale said. "And so am I."

He squeezed her hand. "What can I do? Want me to go get you some coffee? Something to eat? Anything?"

She shook her head. "Not until we see the doctor."

"Okay," he said.

"Where were you?" she asked.

Eli bit his lip. "In meetings. First day on the job . . ." He trailed off.

"She has to be okay," Dale said, and a tear began to slide down her cheek. "She has to."

"She will." Eli managed to sound firm.

"I should have taken her back to the doctor last week. This is my fault."

"No, honey," Eli said. "No, it is most certainly not. This is no one's fault."

She shook her head. "I've been too wrapped up in my job," she said, peering at him. "And so have you. We've taken our eye off the ball, and now look what's happened."

Eli felt a familiar ache in his heart. Dale had made statements like these after each of her three miscarriages. The nagging sense that it was somehow their fault that the baby's heart had stopped beating. That they should have been more cognizant of the baby. Stayed home more. Been less active. And on and on. Dale never accepted that something bad could simply happen without anyone doing anything wrong.

He tried to think of something reassuring to say, but he didn't have the energy. Besides, it wouldn't work.

He squeezed her hand again and kissed her cheek.

And they waited.

———

When the doctor came at just past 11:00 p.m., Eli and Dale were both asleep.

"Mr. and Mrs. James?"

Eli's eyes shot open, and he sat up straight. Meanwhile, Dale was already on her feet. "Yes," Dale said. "What is wrong with our daughter?"

"I'm Dr. John McCormick," he said, shaking Dale's hand and then Eli's.

All three were now standing in the cramped quarters of the room. Behind them, Bella continued to sleep.

"I have good news and bad news," Dr. McCormick said. "I'll start with the positive. We've worked Bella up for the full stroke protocol, and there is absolutely no indication of a transient ischemic attack."

"Transient what?" Eli asked.

"A TIA," McCormick said.

"So, she didn't have a stroke," Dale chimed in.

"No," McCormick agreed. "Her brain MRI and CT scan were completely clear, and the carotid ultrasound did not show any evidence of a blood clot."

Eli let out a breath he'd been holding. "That is good news."

"What's the bad news?" Dale asked.

For a moment, the physician looked to Dale and then Eli. "It would probably be easier to show you." He walked past them to the computer next to Bella's bed. He clicked several buttons, and Eli stole a glance at his wife. Dale had spent a lot of her career in hospitals and doctor's offices. She could speak the lingo. Some of her colleagues liked to joke that Dale might as well have had an MD at the end of her name, because she could size up a medical chart almost as well as a doctor. But this time, her gaze showed no comprehension. She was as clueless as Eli.

"This is the x-ray we did of Bella's chest," McCormick said, touching the screen with his index finger.

"A chest x-ray?" Eli asked. "Why would that even be indicated for dizziness and passing out?"

"She also complained of back pain," McCormick replied. "And a chest x-ray is part of the workup to rule out a TIA." He pointed at the image. "So, this is the chest wall, and here is the right and left lung." He moved his finger in a circle around the area. "Now, do you see—"

"Oh, my God," Dale said, stepping back from them and putting her hands over her mouth.

"What?" Eli asked, looking from Dale back to McCormick.

"Do you see this area here in her right lung?" the physician asked.

Eli squinted as McCormick took a red pointer out of his jacket and highlighted a round object.

"Kind of looks like a grapefruit," McCormick added. "And then this one here?" He shone the light on a smaller but similarly shaped spot in her left lung.

Dale stifled a sob and collapsed into the chair.

"Honey, what's wrong?" Eli asked. Feeling stupid, he turned back to Dr. McCormick. "What are you telling us, Doctor?"

"Bella has a large mass in the lower lobe of her right lung and a smaller one in the upper lobe of her left." He paused. "We'll need to do a biopsy to determine what they are."

Eli blinked and gazed from McCormick back to the screen. "A . . . *mass*? You mean a tumor?"

"Yes."

Eli ran his hands over his face and through his hair. His legs felt weak, and he reached out for the table that the computer sat on to steady himself. "Dr. McCormick, are you telling us that our daughter has . . . cancer?" Eli could barely get the word out.

He glanced at Dale, who had her head up and back straight, as if waiting for a jury verdict. Then Eli saw that Bella's eyes were open. She was awake and listening. Eli reached forward and put his hand on her foot.

"I don't know," McCormick said. "There won't be a definitive diagnosis until after the biopsy, but . . . I'd prepare for the worst."

PART TWO

WAITING ROOM

Eli squeezes his wife's shoulder. They sit in hard chairs, staring at the wall across from them. Between them sits Bella, who plays a game on her phone.

The nurse opens the door to call another name, and Eli's stomach clenches.

He exhales as an elderly woman stands. A younger man is with her. Her son, maybe? They walk toward the nurse, and the door closes behind them.

Eli looks around the space. There are about twelve chairs, all filled. In one is a boy who appears to be around fourteen, but it is hard to tell. The boy is bald. He can't weigh over eighty pounds. He could be nine or sixteen. His eyes look older, but that doesn't matter. The minute you walk into this room, you age faster.

Eli thinks about Bella. She has barely uttered a word since the masses were found in her lungs.

The nurse opens the door again, and Eli feels Dale's hand clamp down over his own.

Again, he lets out a ragged breath of relief as the boy with no hair stands along with a woman wearing sweatpants who must be his mother.

Eli wants to know—he must know—but he also dreads with every fiber of his being what lies beyond that door. Does his seventeen-year-old daughter have cancer?

He looks at Bella, who is wearing a gray hoodie over jeans. She grips tight to her phone. Her eyes flutter up to meet his but only for a moment. It is too hard for them to look at each other. When they do, the hurt and fear seem overwhelming.

They have a life . . . a big, full, messy life . . . but the world has pressed pause. The pictures won't start moving again until they know.

The nurse opens the door . . .

7

"Mucinous adenocarcinoma in both lungs." Eli whispered the words as he typed them into his search engine. He sucked in a quick breath and then clicked Enter.

In seconds, he was staring at one article after another. He scrolled down and saw that there were at least ten pages of results. *Good grief.* He took a sip of bourbon over ice and winced as the alcohol made its way down his throat. He was sitting at the kitchen island with his laptop in front of him. The lights were off except for the sheen of his screen. Upstairs, his daughter's sobs had finally stopped.

They had gotten the news at 3:47 p.m.

"I'm sorry," Dr. Peter Jansen had started, pausing to lick his lips. Eli could literally hear his heart thudding in his chest as he waited. "The biopsy reveals that Bella has mucinous adenocarcinoma in both lungs. It is an incredibly rare diagnosis."

"*Both* lungs?" Dale had asked, and the heartbreak in her tone sent a shiver of pain through Eli's chest.

The doctor nodded. "Like I said. It is very rare."

"Is it curable?" Dale asked.

Dr. Jansen glanced at Bella and then back at Dale. "There are a number of treatment options, Mrs. James. My thought would be to start with radiation and—"

"Answer the *goddamn* question," Dale said. "I mean it, Pete. I've known you for fifteen years. I've represented several of your partners. I've given the continuing education seminar on how to avoid malpractice suits at least three times in this building." She hesitated and bit her lip, putting her arm around Bella. "Is my daughter's cancer . . ." She gained control of her voice. ". . . curable?"

Jansen blinked. "No," he said.

Eli remembered only bits and pieces of the rest of the consult. He and Dale had both sat as Jansen outlined his plan to radiate both masses in an attempt to shrink them, followed by several rounds of chemotherapy to try to prevent metastasis.

Eli felt numb throughout, realizing that he was holding Dale's hand only when she began squeezing it so hard that he winced. His wife had looked straight ahead, not making eye contact with the doctor while Bella fired off questions.

"Can I still graduate?"

"Will I be able to do my solo?"

"Can I finish the soccer season?"

"Am I going to lose my hair?"

Jansen was mostly noncommittal, saying her activity level depended on how she reacted to treatment. Radiation could be painful, and chemotherapy could cause nausea and other side effects. However, he was unambiguous regarding her last question: "Yes, you will lose your hair." Then he smiled and said, "Many patients go ahead and shave their head. I had a family last week take pictures of the event and try to make it fun."

"Make it *fun*?" Bella snapped.

"Well," Jansen said, easing off his stool. "The institute has a family counselor that is going to come in and talk with you now. A cancer diagnosis can be overwhelming, and I urge you to participate in the counseling. After that, please go down to scheduling so that your appointment with the radiation oncologist can be set up, as well as your first chemo session." He paused. "You'll also need to have a chemotherapy port inserted, which is done by a general surgeon. Do you have any preference, Dale?"

"Lawley," she said, glancing up at him. "Matt Lawley is the best in the area. He's been an expert for me in several cases."

Jansen nodded. "That is who I was going to refer, but I'm glad you confirmed my thought."

For a moment, the small room was silent. Then, Dr. Jansen looked at Bella. "I'm sorry to be the bearer of bad news, but you are young and strong, and there is a very good chance that you will do well with treatment."

"What does that even mean?" Bella asked. "*Do well?* Does that mean I'll live two more years?"

"Oh, no. The prognosis for this type of cancer is anywhere from three to ten years, and I think you have every chance to be on the latter end of it."

At this revelation, Bella finally lost it. Her eyes filled with tears, and she covered her face with her hands. Dale went to her, cradling her and stroking her hair. Eli stood and followed Jansen out of the room. Once out, he gently grabbed the doctor's arm. "Ten years?" he asked. "That's the best we can do?" He let go and waited.

"Under current guidelines . . . yes."

———

Now, Eli blinked at his computer screen and took another sip of bourbon. Based on the articles he'd read, Dr. Jansen was spot on. If Bella was lucky, she'd live ten more years. *Twenty-seven,* he thought. *That's not much of a life.*

He shut his laptop and took his empty glass to the bar in the den. He snatched the fifth of Jack Daniel's and poured the whiskey over the remaining ice. Then, before screwing the top back on, he took a slug straight from the bottle. And then another. He looked at himself in the mirror above the bar and felt a deep hatred in his heart. *I'm Eli fucking James. Chief of staff to the president of the United States. I'm one of the most powerful people in the world.*

He took another hit from the bottle and finally screwed the top back on. He leaned against the counter and felt the weight of the news bearing down on him. His daughter had cancer. *Terminal cancer.* She was going to die, and there wasn't a damn thing Eli could do about it.

This is punishment, he thought. *God is punishing me for my sins. For adultery. For making a deal with the devil himself, Nester Sanchez. For . . . everything.*

Eli glanced around the den and focused on the portrait of Bella that Dale had given him for Christmas last year. She was nine in the picture. Blond hair in pigtails. Big smile and a pink-and-white dress.

Eli's cheeks were damp, and his chest convulsed. *Our only child . . .*

All the miscarriages. The dreams they'd had of a big family shattered. The lost intimacy. The lost life.

But at least, above all, they had Bella.

And now she would be taken away too. Just like all their babies that had never made it out of the womb. Eli felt his face contort with grief, and he gripped the glass of whiskey with both hands. He was shaking . . . he took a long sip to steady himself. Whiskey dribbled down his chin and neck, but he took no notice.

He ground his teeth and trudged toward the stairs, grabbed the railing, and blinked upward. The staircase wall was covered with photographs of Bella. Her one-year-old photo shoot. As a toddler at the beach. And then, as he reached the top, her soccer picture from last year. Number 32.

Eli reached the landing and took another sip of Jack Daniel's. He felt dizzy. He glanced down the hallway and saw that Bella's door was cracked. He wiped his eyes and steeled himself. He wanted to hug her. He wanted to make this day go away. He wanted control. The one thing he'd sought all his life. *Control . . .*

But he had none. He was powerless. Weak.

He forced his legs forward and peeked inside the door. Bella was lying on her bed with her hands clasped behind her head. The lamp on her nightstand was on. She was staring up at the ceiling with a scowl on her face.

Eli cleared his throat, but Bella didn't look at him. "Honey," he started. "We . . . we're gonna—"

"I'm still going to Belmont," she interrupted. "I will graduate high school and start in the fall, and nothing is going to stop me. Not Dr. Jansen. Not you and Mom. Not cancer. Not any damn thing." She glared at him. "You hear me?"

Eli met her fierce gaze and gritted his teeth. He nodded. "I hear you."

She leaned over and flicked the switch on her lamp, and the room went dark. "Good night, Dad."

"Good night, sweetie," he said.

"I love you," she said.

He bit his trembling lip. "I love you too."

———

Eli walked down the stairs and poured out his glass. He looked toward the bedroom; the door was shut. He blinked and then walked out the door to the backyard.

It was snowing. Eli still had on the suit he'd worn to work that morning. He hadn't bothered to change when he got home, but he must have thrown his tie off somewhere in the house because it wasn't hanging around his neck anymore. For an odd moment, he wondered what time it was. It was dark, so it must be past 5:30 p.m., but he hadn't checked his phone in what seemed like hours. Not since Dr. Jansen had handed down his terminal verdict.

Eli folded his arms across his chest and breathed in the cold air. He stuck out his tongue and felt a snowflake land on the tip of it. He swallowed. Then he opened his eyes. He took another deep breath and then another. Eli James had many failings in his life, but he also had his talents, and one of them began to take hold of him now.

To guide a political career from the state senate to the White House, you had to be able to think while everyone else was panicking. To focus on the challenge and find the solution. To take the emotion out of it and solve the problem.

Eli again breathed in the frigid air. He felt his heart rate slow down, and his mind began to clear. They would get a second opinion. Peter Jansen wasn't the only game in town. Dale knew every oncologist in the region, and she could get Bella seen tomorrow. They'd run more tests. Perhaps Jansen was wrong.

Eli looked down at the snow-covered grass. Though he was a world-class bullshitter when it came to other people, he couldn't pull the wool over his own eyes. He knew Jansen wasn't wrong. *But we will check, regardless. We'll do our due diligence.*

Eli glanced up at the quarter moon and opened his mouth, catching a few more snowflakes. The storm was picking up. Then he looked back at his house. Bella's upstairs light was back on. He remembered the scowl on her face and her proclamation that she was still going to Belmont. No one would stop her.

He nodded at the window and felt a deep resolve come over him. The fog of shock, sadness, and alcohol had lifted, giving way to one all-consuming thought.

This will not be, he told himself. *I sit at the right hand of the most powerful person in the world . . .*

. . . and this will not be.

8

At 4:30 p.m. the following afternoon, Eli sipped from a Styrofoam cup of coffee and sat on the edge of his desk. Seated in the guest chairs in front of him were the chairman of the Appropriations Committee, Ted Jackson, and the committee's senior member, Nancy Holgan. Eli nodded and rubbed his chin as Ted went through a series of bills related to discretionary spending that his committee would be presenting to the president. For each bill, Ted would lay out the big picture, and then Nancy would fill in the details. Eli crossed his arms tight across his chest, asking questions where appropriate, but mostly listening. When he felt his cell phone vibrate in his pocket, he abruptly stood.

"Ted. Nancy. Thank you both for the introduction and summary of these bills. I'll report to the president and get back to you with his position very soon."

"Eli, we fully expect the president to support—"

"I'm sorry, Ted," Eli interrupted. "I have to take this call." He clicked to answer the phone. "One second," he spoke into the device and then nodded to both of the senators. "Soon. I promise."

Ted bowed, and Nancy gave a frustrated nod as Eli opened his door and gestured them out. He took a deep breath and walked behind his desk to the window overlooking Pennsylvania Avenue. "Well?" he asked.

"Dr. Falkenburg's opinions are the same as Jansen's," Dale said, her voice firm, but the fatigue was evident. "Mucinous adenocarcinoma in both lungs. Terminal. Radiation followed by chemo is the accepted treatment."

Eli leaned his forehead against the cold glass. "You trust her?"

"Yes. She's not as experienced as Pete Jansen, but her credentials are impeccable. Johns Hopkins med school. Fellowship at Vanderbilt followed by residency back at Hopkins. Board certified in oncology and has practiced for over twenty years." Dale paused. "She's also a friend, and that's why I was able to get in to see her so soon."

Eli took a deep breath as his heartbeat picked up speed. He had arrived at the office at 6:00 a.m. and had barely eaten anything all day, fueling himself on coffee. He'd gone through the motions of his job but had been unable to think about anything but his daughter's diagnosis.

"Did she have any advice? Anything . . . outside the box?"

"Yes," Dale said. "She said she was going to look into the current trials going on at MD Anderson in Houston. Bella might qualify for one of them. We are going for genetic testing tomorrow and will have a follow-up appointment with Amy after that. Probably early next week."

"Good," Eli said, pacing his office. "Did she say anything else?"

"Yes," Dale said. "She . . ." Her voice began to crack, and Eli could hear a tremor in her breathing.

"What did she say?"

"That we should probably get Bella into counseling . . . and also ourselves. That, if Bella didn't qualify for a trial, the first round of radiation and chemo would be a painful process."

Eli sat on the desk. "Do you want to stick with Amy or Jansen?"

Silence for several seconds. Then a suppressed sob. "I don't know, Eli. I mean, they're both good, but it doesn't sound like it's going to matter." She let out a sigh. "Let's see how the genetic testing goes and whether she is a candidate for a trial."

For a moment, the only sounds were their breathing, and Eli realized that his heart was now thudding. He felt dizzy and sat down in one of the guest chairs. "How is Bella?"

Another sob. "She's been pretty good . . . most of the day. Talking about the soccer season and her solo. But after the meeting with Amy, she's been just . . . numb. On the way to the car, she said she didn't want to go to dance practice tonight. And her back pain is getting worse. She took a Norco when we got home."

"Where are you?" Eli asked, feeling nauseated.

"Out walking. Trying to decompress, but it's not working."

"Okay, I'll see you at home. Dale . . . we have to stay positive."

"I know. I'm just . . . I know." Then the phone clicked dead.

———

Eli paced a couple more laps around his desk, running his hands through his hair and concentrating on his breathing. He glanced at his to-do list, seeing that he still owed Chad Wiggins a call. Wiggins was the senator from Minnesota whose young son had died of leukemia. He wanted a bill passed to lower the price of cancer medications. Eli had told SK that he'd advise the president to veto the bill if the legislation made it to Lionel's desk, but now he had a personal interest in this bill . . . and Chad Wiggins. He snatched his landline, asked the White House dispatcher to call Senator Wiggins, and, seconds later, was on the phone with Wiggins's administrative assistant. They scheduled a late lunch meeting for tomorrow, then Eli clicked his speed dial for SK.

"Hey, stranger," she greeted him.

They had not spoken since Eli had bolted for the emergency room to meet Dale the week before. She had sent texts, inquiring about him and Bella, but Eli had yet to confide the truth. Only that more tests were being done and that Bella was feeling okay.

"Can you do dinner or a drink tonight?" Eli asked.

"I'm sorry, but there's a banquet I have to attend at seven. It'll be over at ten. A drink then?"

Eli bit his lip. That would have to be good enough. "Four Seasons bar?"

"I'll be there," she said. "Is everything okay?"

"Yes," Eli lied. "But something's come up, and I . . ." He closed his eyes. ". . . need your counsel."

"Need anything else?" There was a tease in her voice.

"Not tonight," Eli said. "See you at ten." He ended the call.

For the next thirty minutes, Eli jotted thoughts and ideas down on a legal pad. It was one of the ways he coped with stress. Dale had contacts throughout the country in the health care field. If he knew Dale, Eli would bet that his wife was making calls at this very moment to find other treatment avenues. Specialists in lung cancer. New treatment modalities. Anything. There was also Eli's father, a retired physician in Destin, Florida. Frank James wasn't an oncologist, and Eli hadn't spoken to the man in years, but shouldn't Eli at least get his thoughts?

He's a drunk . . . What possible good could come from involving him?

Eli slammed his fist on the pad. *Hell, what good am I?*

He was great at raising money, smearing political opponents, and pressing the flesh. He honestly could think of nothing else constructive to do now other than talking with SK Moss, having lunch with Chad Wiggins, and . . .

. . . one other thing, which he'd been avoiding all day. He glanced at his watch, knowing that the president would be free for the next hour, followed by an evening dinner engagement with the prime minister of England.

Eli took a deep breath and left his office. Seconds later, he was knocking on the outer door to the Oval Office.

"Come in," Lionel said, his voice full of energy.

Eli entered and faked a smile. "Mr. President, may I have a word?"

"You may indeed, my friend."

Eli took a seat across from the president.

"How did things go with the Appropriations folks?" Lionel asked.

"Fine. What we expected. A lot of bills relating to boosting the military, most of which I'll recommend that you support. I'll have a summary to you on it soon."

"Good man," Lionel said. "How about your meetings with the lobbyists? Anything pressing there?"

"Chad Wiggins's bill to lower prescription costs for oncology medications probably has the most heat. I met with Sarah Kate Moss last week. Pharma fully expects you to veto the bill if it gets past the House and Senate."

"Will it?"

"It might. Chad has a lot of support in Congress and a personal stake due to his son's death from cancer." Eli paused. "I'm having a late lunch with him tomorrow to hear his side."

"Smart," Lionel said. "Hear both sides. But it sounds like I may be taxed with vetoing a bill the public will likely be in favor of. I'm sure there will be negative press."

Eli walked around the desk and looked out the window. "There always is." He sighed. "But you know the drill."

"Dance with the one that brought us."

Eli nodded. Aside from Nester Sanchez's creative financing, pharma had been the campaign's largest contributor.

Lionel stood, leaning his arm against the window. "Well, I'm sure my chief of staff will figure out a way for us to save face."

When Eli didn't respond, Lionel lightly punched his shoulder. "Hey, you okay?"

Eli kept his gaze focused on the cars trudging along Pennsylvania Avenue. He wasn't sure he could meet his friend's eye. "Bella has lung cancer. Mucinous adenocarcinoma in both lungs." He cleared his throat. "It's, uh . . ." Eli bit his lower lip to keep it from trembling. ". . . terminal."

When Lionel didn't respond, Eli turned to face him. The president's mouth hung open.

"*No*," Lionel finally said, his voice shaky. "That can't be. Did you get a second—"

"Yes," Eli interrupted. "This afternoon." He paused. "Same diagnosis and prognosis. She goes in for genetic testing tomorrow. See if she can qualify for a trial at MD Anderson."

Lionel turned and walked away from Eli and around the desk. He massaged his neck and hung his head.

Eli wasn't surprised by his reaction. Lionel was Bella's godfather. Lionel and Vanessa's children functioned as cousins to Bella—and always had. They were as close to family as you could be without sharing blood.

The president sighed deeply. "Eli . . . damn, man. I am so sorry."

"I know."

"What can I do?"

Eli turned back to the window. A few seconds later, he felt his friend's hand on his shoulder.

"Whatever you need, brother. Just let me know."

Eli took a ragged breath, trying hard to control his emotions. "Time," he finally said. "I may need some time to go over treatment options . . . and possibly travel to Houston with Dale and Bella if a trial is recommended." He hesitated. "Lionel, you know this world. You've been through it . . ." He lowered his voice. ". . . and you're going through it again now. Do you have any advice? You went to Houston once, didn't you?" He looked at his friend, who was nodding.

"Yeah. I did a trial during my first go-round. It was a medication that was supposed to reduce the size of the tumor. It worked, which allowed me to only have to do radiation afterward."

"But the cancer came back," Eli said.

Lionel blinked and looked down at his shoes. "Yeah."

"But this time, your doctor didn't send you to MD Anderson."

"No," Lionel said, stepping away from his friend.

"Have you had any treatment since the round of radiation before the inauguration?"

Lionel again began to rub his neck as he paced to the door. "Not yet," he finally said. Then he sighed. "Listen, man. I'm sorry to have to do this, but . . ."

"You have a dinner to attend with the British prime minister," Eli said, walking toward him with two long strides. "I understand. I just wanted you to know my deal."

"And I'm glad you told me," Lionel said. "I . . . wish there was something I could do." He moved away from the door, making way for Eli.

Eli grabbed the knob and then pulled back from it. "There's one more favor I'd ask," he said, staring at the floor and then finally raising his eyes to meet his friend's gaze. "Could you ask the head of the FDA if there are any new treatments . . . medications . . . anything that might help my daughter?"

Eli could make those same inquiries, but the president of the United States obviously had more stroke than he did. Lionel also had his own stake in the answer to that question, given his current battle with colon cancer. For all Eli knew, the president might have already started that process. *I hope he has . . .*

Lionel again squeezed Eli's shoulder. "Of course."

———

Lionel Cantrell sat in his chair and closed his eyes. He thought of his own children, Leon and Kisha. Both now in college at Alabama. What would he do if he learned they had cancer? How would he react? His eyes grew misty, and he wiped them hard. Eli James and he were best friends. He loved Bella like his own.

Lionel opened his eyes and grabbed his coat. He slipped it on and stepped out into the hallway. Most of his office staff had gone for the night, and Lionel was alone with his thoughts. He could do as Eli asked. He could call the FDA. He was sure he'd get a nice summary of the most up-to-date oncology drugs, none of which would save Bella James's life. He could and would give Eli all the time he needed.

As Lionel entered the presidential suite, Vanessa came out of the bathroom. "We need to get going or we'll be late," she told him.

"Give me a second," Lionel said, brushing past her and closing the bathroom door behind him. He walked into his closet and took out the key. He glanced at the portrait of Ulysses S. Grant. Then he removed it and opened the medicine box. He grabbed the bottle and took out one of the white pills, then held it close to his eyes. He'd been on the medication for only a couple of weeks, but he felt better. Stronger. He'd had an appointment yesterday with the oncologist assigned to him by General Randolph, and the tumor in his colon had shrunk by half, and the PET scan showed considerably less activity in the pancreas.

"In another two weeks . . . maybe a month, it should all be gone," the doctor had said, patting his shoulder. The appointment hadn't been in a physician's office or a hospital, but in the basement of the Pentagon.

Again he closed his eyes.

Over the next weeks, months, and years, Bella James would go through radiation, chemotherapy, and perhaps a few trials at MD Anderson. Then, her body wasted and ravaged, and her mind, heart, and soul broken, she would die. His best friend would be devastated. Not only by the death of his daughter but from the awful torture Bella would have to endure before mercifully dying. Lionel knew the terrain of the cancer patient intimately. He had been lucky during his first go-round to reach remission. But after his recurrence, his own oncologist, with Eli present, had delivered a death sentence: *"We can treat it and buy you some time, but the chances of a cure are slim."*

The president opened his eyes and gazed at the pill.

"Are you coming?"

"Yeah, hon," he answered, then put the medicine in his mouth and swallowed.

God forgive me, he thought, turning and looking at himself in the mirror.

"The country comes first," he whispered as he straightened his tie.

9

Eli nursed a bourbon and branch at the bar of the Four Seasons. He'd taken a few sips but wasn't interested in the drink or getting a buzz. Since his meeting with the president, he'd gone for a long walk in the cold. He'd bought some hot chocolate at a stand and sat on the steps of the Lincoln Memorial, looking out at the Washington Monument. Normally, when he did that, he thought of Forrest Gump's speech in the movie and his epic kiss in the water with Jenny, but today his thoughts were consumed by Bella. His daughter was the only pure thing in his life. The only part of his world that was true and good. He remembered her birth at Druid City Hospital in Tuscaloosa, holding her close to his chest and feeling her heartbeat. Eli knew he wasn't a great man, but he had done his best to be a good father. Despite his hectic travel schedule pushing Lionel to the top of the political ranks, he had made every birthday party and spoken to Bella each day, even if only by telephone. They had a healthy relationship, and he was proud of her good grades, athleticism, and talent as a musician.

It isn't fair.

Though Eli knew that nothing about life was fair, he couldn't help but think how ridiculous it was for a young girl with her whole future in front of her to have lung cancer. A lifelong smoker, sure. An old person who didn't take care of his or her health? Of course. An asshole who's cheating on his wife? Absolutely.

It should be me, he thought. And not for the first time.

But it wasn't.

Finally, Eli had trudged off the steps of the memorial and started walking toward his car. But instead of stopping at the vehicle, he'd walked on to the hotel, thinking the whole way that Bella's diagnosis was punishment for his sins. For his affair with SK Moss. For failing to comfort Dale enough after the last miscarriage. For working with a criminal like Nester Sanchez to fill Lionel's war chest. He knew blaming himself for Bella was counterproductive and amounted to the same type of torture that Dale had inflicted on herself, but he couldn't seem to stop the train of self-loathing from running through him.

A mile and a half later, he'd walked into the Four Seasons and ambled to the bar. He'd ordered his whiskey and water and watched the people mingle. So many smiles. Laughs. Muffled whispers. People going about their lives. How many of them were dealing with cancer? Did they have children with a debilitating disease? He knew he wasn't the only person in the world facing dire circumstances, but it seemed that way now.

Eli closed his eyes and brought the glass to his nose, inhaling the smoky scent of bourbon. He felt SK slide into the stool next to him, and as he set the glass down on the mahogany surface, the scent of bourbon was replaced by her citrusy perfume. He opened his eyes.

"You look like you've been run over by a car," SK said, squinting back at him. She ordered a cosmopolitan and then leaned close to him. "What's wrong?"

"Bella has cancer," he said, hearing the fatigue in his tone. Normally, he was playful and flirty during his meetups with Sarah Kate Moss, but he would be neither tonight. He needed her help.

SK leaned back as the bartender placed her drink on a napkin in front of her. She kept her eyes locked on Eli. "There's a table over by the window," she said, scooting off her stool and walking that way. Eli told the bartender to put SK's drink on his tab and then followed behind her. He plopped down in the seat and placed his barely touched bourbon on the table.

"When did you find out?" SK asked. Her voice was calm, her demeanor cool.

"A couple of days ago. Confirmed with a second opinion today. Mucinous adenocarcinoma in both lungs."

"*Lung* cancer?" SK asked in an intense whisper.

"Yes. Very rare. Because there are masses in both lungs, it's . . ." His voice started to shake, and he stopped.

"Oh, Eli. I'm so sorry." She took a sip of her drink and glanced out the window. "I . . . can't imagine." Then she looked back at him. "How is Dale handling it?"

"She's a wreck. Trying to be strong, but she's dying inside." Eli brought his drink to his lips and then set it back down. "So am I. And Bella . . . ?" He shook his head, already fighting tears.

"Have you told the president?"

Eli nodded. "A few hours ago. He was devastated. He's Bella's godfather."

For a few moments, neither of them spoke. Then SK touched his hand. "What are you going to do?"

"What do you mean?"

"Are you taking some time off? Will Bella start radiation or chemo? Or both?"

"We're still . . . evaluating our options."

She set her drink down and crossed her arms. "Why did you want to see me tonight?"

Eli had thought through how to bring this up with her and had come up with nothing other than a fastball down the middle. "Are you aware of any oncology medications that are not available to the general public that might help Bella?"

She stared back at him. "No."

"Oh, come on, SK. You're the head lobbyist for pharma, and you have been for over a decade. Oncology medications are easily their most expensive and lucrative product. Surely there's something you can tell me. My daughter is seventeen years old. She's got terminal cancer.

There's no amount of radiation and chemo that is going to save her life. Surgery isn't an option." He paused and narrowed his gaze. "You work for people whose sole objective is coming up with cancer-fighting medications. Tell me there's *something* you can do to help."

She glanced out the window and let her arms fall to her sides. "Eli, I wish I could help you, but I'm a salesperson. That's all. I sell people on the positions that Big Pharma assigns me. You more than anyone else should know that. We're the same, Eli. You sell people on Lionel Cantrell, and I sell them on pharma."

"There's a difference," Eli said, growing angry. "I believe in Lionel."

"Oh, bullshit. You believe in the same things that I do. Money and power. Lionel means both for you. Just like pharma does for me." She stood from her chair. "I'm sorry about Bella, Eli. I really am. But I can't help you." She touched his shoulder and walked away.

Eli glared at her pink drink and his own. He took the glass of bourbon and brought it to his lips, forcing it down in three sips. Then he strode to the bar. *She's holding back,* he thought. He paid his tab and trotted through the bar to the lobby and then out the door. SK never drove anywhere downtown, so perhaps she was waiting for a cab or an Uber.

As he stepped out of the revolving door and onto the sidewalk, he caught no sight of her. He hung his head, feeling flushed from the bourbon he'd just consumed. He hadn't wanted it before, but now he thought he might go back inside and have another. *No,* he told himself. He took out his phone and called an Uber. He didn't feel like walking back to his car, and, at this time of night, it probably wasn't safe. He saw a dark-blue sedan pull to a stop at the curb and then felt his elbow being squeezed and hot, citrusy breath in his ear.

"This is completely off the record," she whispered, "and if you tell anyone about it, I will deny it and do everything in my power to bring you and Lionel down. Understand?"

Eli froze and nodded, his heart racing.

"About seven or eight years ago, there was a brouhaha in pharma about a man from Mobile, Alabama, who'd come up with a product." SK paused. "I can't remember his name, but there were rumors that he'd found a cure. Honestly, I wouldn't have put any stock in them. But a *very* close colleague of mine told me of a hush-hush meeting between the FDA and the DOD that took place right after the rumors started. And then . . ." She paused. "The man and the rumors . . . went away."

"What do you mean they went away?"

SK stepped in front of him and grabbed the lapels of his overcoat. As she pressed them together and fastened the top button, she spoke in a calm, clinical voice. "Eli, do you know how powerful the Department of Defense is?"

He felt a chill envelop his body that had nothing to do with the January cold.

SK took a couple of steps backward and turned away. As she grabbed the door handle of the waiting blue car, she looked over her shoulder at him. "Think about it," she said.

10

Chad Wiggins had curly brown hair that fell almost to his shoulders. The junior senator from Minnesota was waiting on Eli when he entered the restaurant. Chad stood, and the two men shook hands. At six feet, five inches tall with a wiry frame, the congressman still looked like the shooting guard he'd been for the Timberwolves for six years before arthritic ankles ended his NBA career. Chad had made a seamless transition into politics, moving up the state ladder before obtaining a US Senate seat five years ago. There had been rumors of a bid for the presidency when Lionel was making his decision to run.

But then Chad's twelve-year-old son Patrick was diagnosed with leukemia. Less than a year later, the boy was dead. Chad grew his hair out long as a tribute to his son, and his political stances changed. His primary target was Big Pharma, which Chad argued was killing the American people with its outrageous prices on oncology products. It was a personal mission that had galvanized many of his constituents, but it had also made him a list of powerful enemies.

"Thank you for meeting with me," Chad began, as a waiter took Eli's drink order. For a few minutes, the two engaged in small talk. Once the beverages had been returned to the table and the two men ordered lunch, Chad got down to brass tacks.

"Is there any help the president can give me regarding the prescription drug bill?"

"The president has an open mind," Eli said. "As I'm sure you know, Big Pharma was one of his biggest supporters."

Chad's mouth curved into a sheepish grin. "Of course. I'm actually surprised . . . pleasantly, I mean . . . that you'd meet with me."

"There are two sides to every story. I've read your bill, and I've spoken to a lobbyist for Big Pharma."

"Sarah Kate Moss," Chad said.

Eli nodded.

"She's tough," Chad said. "Knows the issues. Smart as hell. I admire her . . . I just don't think she or Big Pharma understand the gravity of these ridiculously high prices."

"I think they understand that if prices are cut, then contracts with insurance companies, Medicare, and Medicaid will have to be adjusted or completely reworked. Their worry is that if your bill is successful, it will hurt cancer patients because the medication that might make a difference in their treatment won't be produced anymore."

Chad looked down at his hands. "I get that, Mr. James."

"Eli, please."

He smiled and looked up. "I get that, Eli, but even with health insurance, many of these medications are going to cripple the middle- to lower-income American family. Do you want that? Does the president?"

Eli started to say something, but Chad held up a hand.

"This isn't fairyland for me. I've *lived* this, man. My son's medication was outrageously expensive. If I hadn't been lucky enough to play basketball in the NBA and saved some of my money, I never could have afforded it." He looked away, and his eyes misted over. "And it still wasn't enough. My boy died."

"I'm sorry," Eli said, thinking of Bella. "My . . ." Eli stopped himself, not wanting to share too much. "Did you ever go to MD Anderson? Do any of the trials there?"

"Patrick didn't qualify for a trial. He was genetically tested, and he didn't have the right genomes or whatever they call them to match up with the trial. He got several rounds of chemo and there was discussion of a stem cell transplant, but he never got that far. His form was too aggressive. Ten months, man. That's all we had with him after we found out."

Eli allowed for a few seconds of silence. He'd already said he was sorry, and sometimes there were no words. As he waited, looking at his glass of iced tea, he thought again of Bella.

"Since he died," said Chad, "I've spoken with so many parents of patients who are struggling to make ends meet. Having to take out second mortgages, home equity lines, second and third jobs, et cetera, just to get another round of chemo. And it's not just leukemia, Eli. Every single cancer has the same issue with costs being astronomical for the best and newest meds. It's not fair."

Eli remembered his trek from the Lincoln Memorial to the Four Seasons, thinking the exact same thing: *It's not fair.*

"And that's not even the worst of it," Chad said. "The bill I'm proposing only scratches the surface. It's a shot across the bow, but it won't make a dent, win, lose, or draw."

Eli narrowed his gaze. "What are you talking about?"

Chad took a sip of tea. "Off the record?"

"Sure."

"I think there needs to be a full-scale investigation into Big Pharma, the FDA, and the oncology business. Some serious questions need to be asked. What's out there? What's been approved? What's the process? Who makes the decisions? I think the American people deserve that." He let out a weary sigh. "I think *I* deserve that. So does any other person who's lost a loved one to cancer or is dealing with a diagnosis."

Eli forced a shrug, but his hands had begun to sweat. He thought of what SK had said to him last night. About the man from Mobile, Alabama, who'd *disappeared.* Still, he knew it would be foolish to do anything but toe the line now and say what the pharma folks . . . and Lionel . . . would expect him to say. "Come on, Chad. The FDA has regulations on—"

Chad interrupted him with a sigh. "The FDA is just a group of people, Eli. Subject to the same weaknesses in morality the rest of DC falls to every day. Cancer has been around long enough for there to be better options than the current chemo, radiation, and surgery modalities. Why no miracle drugs?" He paused. "Why won't they ever let us have something with a greater than fifty percent cure rate?"

"That's crazy talk, Chad."

"The oncology market is a multi-billion-dollar industry. I doubt it will be long before it reaches into the trillions. If the FDA approves a medication that cures cancer, it could cripple them, and then the entire economy." He shook his head. "I think the government might . . . put the brakes on such a drug."

"Are you serious?" Eli asked. His armpits were wet with perspiration. In his mind, SK whispered, *Do you know how powerful the Department of Defense is?*

Chad leaned back in his chair. "Still off the record?"

Eli nodded.

"As a heart attack."

11

Eli booked his flight to Mobile that evening. He packed his suitcase for a three-night stay, but he wasn't sure how long he was going to be gone.

As he zipped up his bag, he heard voices entering the kitchen. And then the sound of his daughter's laughter, which made him smile despite himself. He slipped on his jacket and overcoat and trotted down the hall, where he found Dale and Bella standing and eating pizza at the island. There was a six-pack of Coors Light between them, and they both were taking a sip from fresh longnecks.

Eli didn't know what to make of this scene. "Bella, aren't you a bit young to be drinking alcohol?" He glanced at Dale. "Honey?"

"Don't 'honey' me. We both know Bella has already had a beer in her life. She's a high school senior, for God's sake. I just thought, after the day and week we've had, that I wanted to share a pizza and beer with my best girl. Do you have a problem with that?"

Eli shook his head and took a step toward them. He leaned down and kissed Bella on the cheek. He thought about doing the same to Dale, but her glare made him think better of it.

"Where are you going, Dad?" Bella asked, gesturing at the case in Eli's hand.

He blinked his eyes and swallowed. He could almost taste the guilt in his mouth. "To see Nana and Papa." It wasn't a lie. Eli did plan to see his parents, but it wasn't the whole truth either. *Not even close . . .*

"Oh," Bella said, her voice cracking. "Okay."

When she looked away, Eli gave her neck a gentle squeeze and spoke in a soft voice. "I haven't told them about your diagnosis yet, and I want to do it in person. Your grandpa is a physician, so he may have some thoughts on your treatment, and your grandmother is . . ." He felt emotion swelling in his chest. "Well . . . the toughest and smartest human being I've ever known."

For a moment, the kitchen was silent. Finally, Bella reached back and patted his hand. "Give them my love."

Eli gritted his teeth to keep from losing it and glanced at Dale, whose eyes had reddened.

"I assume Lionel is good with you being off?"

"He said take as much time as I need. How about the firm?"

Dale took a sip of beer. "Supportive . . . for now." She gave her head a jerk, and her expression was tense. "The genetic testing got rescheduled for tomorrow, and the results should come back in a day or two. Then we'll have to make some decisions."

"I know," Eli said. "Keep me posted, and I'll do the same."

Dale crossed her arms and finally nodded.

"All right, enough with the serious talk, people," Bella declared. "I'm not going to die tomorrow. I've still got seven to ten good years." She winked at him and turned up her bottle.

Eli winked back. Then he grabbed a beer and popped the top. "Room for three?" he asked, then took a swig.

Dale studied Bella, who shrugged and clinked Eli's bottle with her own. They smiled at each other, and then Eli looked at Dale.

Her scowl softened, but only a smidge. "Why not."

———

For the next forty-five minutes, they ate pizza, drank cold beer, and laughed at each other. The c-word wasn't mentioned. Bella talked about wanting to go to soccer practice the next day, and both parents agreed that was fine. She also said she was still doing her dance solo, which was early next week.

"You'll be back for that, won't you, Dad?"

"Oh yeah," he said.

Bella pushed back from her chair and downed the rest of her beer. Dale had only let her have one, while the two adults had drunk two each. "Thanks for the brewski, Momma. And the pizza." She looked from one parent to the other. "It was nice to have a meal together without you two at each other's throats." She walked around the island and leaned into Eli. "Love you, Dad. Be careful and give Nana and Papa a hug from me."

"Will do, hon."

She gave her mom a fist bump and walked to the stairs. "Good night, everyone." She got to the newel post and wheeled around, holding her arms out wide. "I have an announcement to make," she said, looking over their heads as if she were addressing a large crowd. "I have decided to beat cancer's ass." She nodded, bowed, and then ran up the stairs.

Eli grinned and glanced at Dale, who turned away, her shoulders heaving.

Reality had returned with a vengeance.

"Well, I guess I should go," Eli said. He walked over and touched his wife's back. "Let me know about the genetic testing, okay?"

She said nothing, nor did she nod.

He sighed and walked to the garage door. When he touched the knob, her voice, hoarse and weak, stopped him.

"Eli?"

"Yeah." He lowered his eyes to the floor.

"She's going to beat this, isn't she?"

It had been a long time since he could remember his wife talking to him like this. It reminded him of her questions before the last miscarriage. *He's going to make it, isn't he, Eli? Our son is going to live, right? God isn't going to take another child from us, is he?* Eli had answered all the questions the way he thought he should. He'd comforted his wife, and they'd lost the baby anyway.

"I don't know," Eli finally said, speaking through clenched teeth. "But I'm going to do everything in my power to make sure that she does, starting now." He raised his gaze and saw that Dale was looking at him. The sadness was still there, but also a hint of curiosity. His answer had surprised her.

"What are you up to?" she asked, cocking her head.

He wanted to tell her the truth. That he was going to Alabama not just to see his parents but to learn the name of the man SK Moss referred to, the medication he supposedly manufactured, and anything and everything else he could discover about this person who may, or may not, have found the cure to cancer. *Including what happened to him . . .* That his conversations with SK Moss and Chad Wiggins had lit a fire in him. SK, a pharmaceutical lobbyist, and Chad, a senator with opposing views, both of whom had implied the same horrific thing.

"I think the government might . . . put the brakes on such a drug." Chad. Intense. Passionate. Off the record. Serious . . . *"as a heart attack."*

"Do you know how powerful the Department of Defense is?" SK. Scared . . . whispering . . . also off the record. *There was a man from Mobile . . .*

Eli could hardly fathom the implications. Could the United States government . . . his own employer . . . be involved in covering up the medical miracle of the century? Of all centuries?

He didn't believe it, but he also couldn't let it go. If there was even a 1 percent chance that there was a cure . . . that Bella might possibly be saved . . . he ground his teeth and stared at the kitchen floor. He couldn't do this alone. He'd get his father's ideas and hope the old man was sober enough to help.

But it was his mother's expertise . . . and toughness . . . that he'd lean on the most.

But he couldn't tell Dale or Bella about the man from Mobile. Not yet, anyway. He wouldn't . . . couldn't . . . give false hope to Bella or Dale until he was certain. Besides . . . *They'd both think I'm crazy . . .*

. . . which I very well might be.

"Eli?" Dale again. Closer. He felt the heat of her gaze.

He looked up from the floor and forced a wink. "Got to go."

12

Eli met SK Moss at the District, the presecurity bar at Reagan National Airport. "Thank you for coming," he said, as she took a seat across from him.

"You said it was an emergency." Her voice was cold. Distant. It was as if her revelations had built a wall up between them. If that was the case, his next request would only fortify the barrier.

"I need to know more," he said, after a waiter had delivered their drinks.

She took a long sip of her cosmopolitan. "I've already told you more than I should."

"Do you have a name? An occupation? A description? You didn't give me enough to go on. It will be like trying to find a needle in a haystack."

She took another gulp from her drink and spilled a bit on her chin. She looked flustered, her face red. Nervous. These were not traits that Eli would typically associate with Sarah Kate Moss. "Eli, I can't. If my employer or my friends in the FDA knew I was meeting with you like this . . ."

"They'd think you are trying to make damn sure that I don't advise the president to approve of Chad Wiggins's bill. I met with Chad earlier, by the way, and he's very persuasive. I imagine they might also think that we're having an affair, as my wife certainly didn't have any problem connecting the dots. I wonder how many other folks in DC think the same . . ."

"You sonofabitch." She glared at him.

"This is my daughter, SK. She has terminal cancer, and if there's something out there that can help her, then I'm going to find it. I will not watch her . . ." He bit his lip and took a sip of Diet Coke, looking around the crowded airport and trying to keep his composure. "My daughter isn't going to suffer the same fate as Chad's son. I won't allow it." He kept his tone measured and finally felt her hand cover his own. He looked at her.

"Life happens, Eli. You aren't immune. There are some things even Eli James can't control. I'm sorry about Bella. I really am."

"Do you think there's a cure for cancer?" Eli asked. "Do you believe this 'man from Mobile' really came up with a cure and got killed because of it?"

She let go of his hand and stood from her chair. "I can't do this, Eli. I'm sorry."

He rose and clutched her arm. "Please, SK."

"Let me go," SK said. "Or I'm going to scream at the top of my lungs."

He released his grip, and she took a step back from him. "I'm sorry." For a long moment, she stared at him.

"What?"

She extended her hand, and he shook it. She pulled him toward her and leaned close to his ear. "The man sold his products at farmers' markets on the gulf coasts of Alabama, Florida, Mississippi, and Louisiana."

"Thank you," Eli breathed.

"I'll expect the president to veto any bill from Chad Wiggins that comes before him," she told him, letting go of his hand.

SK turned to go, but Eli stepped in front of her. He tried to think of something else to say but couldn't. "Thank you," he repeated.

"Our personal relationship is over, Eli. From now on, it's strictly professional."

He began to nod, but she continued:

"If my people or the FDA gets wind of you digging into this stuff, then they'll suspect that I told you. I'm risking my career."

"Hey," he said, raising his palms, "I could have heard this man-from-Mobile story from other sources. I'm Eli fucking James, and my home *state* is Alabama, remember?" He offered a reassuring smile. "You have *nothing* to worry about, okay?"

She frowned.

"Okay?" he pressed, but SK was already walking away. After a few strides, she stopped and turned to him, her expression dead serious.

"*Be careful,*" she mouthed silently, then disappeared.

13

Fairhope, Alabama, was a quaint hamlet that sat on Mobile Bay. Known for its charming boutique shops, fabulous restaurants, and one of the world's greatest bookstores, the iconic Page & Palette, the town had always been close to Eli's heart. When most people thought of Fairhope, they envisioned sunsets at the nearby Grand Hotel, the Mardi Gras parade in February, or perhaps the annual jubilee when all manner of shrimp, crab, and other fish would leave deep waters and swarm in the shallower parts of the bay. But for Eli James, the town of Fairhope and, in particular, the farmland north of the area, meant one thing.

Mom . . .

Eli pulled his rental up the long gravel drive of Indigo Farms. He parked between the barn and the one-story house with its wraparound porch. As he stepped out of the vehicle, he breathed in the mixed scents of hay and manure. It was a smell he remembered well. He shut the door and strode toward the barn. As he got closer, he could hear her raspy voice singing "Camptown Races."

Eli smiled and touched the wooden door, thinking back almost thirty years. Dad had been offered a huge pay raise to be the head of the emergency department physician's group in Mobile, but Mom didn't want to leave their spread in Lick Skillet. Ever the shrewd salesman, Dad found a compromise in "this little slice of heaven," as Mom had called it the first time she'd laid eyes on the pasture, the farmhouse, and the barn. And . . . at least for a few years, they'd been happy. Eli's eyes misted over, and he wiped them. Then he opened the door to the barn and stepped inside.

She was in the second stall. Her back was to him, and she was grooming the animal's side with a brush, using smooth strokes. Her once-brown hair was now solid white and put up in a no-frills ponytail. A red bandanna covered her forehead, and she was dressed in faded jeans and a dirty white T-shirt.

Eli didn't want to startle her, so he cleared his throat.

She turned and looked him up and down. "You're overdressed," she said, continuing to brush the horse, but a grin formed on her lips.

"I need your help," Eli said.

"Figures," she said, leaning down and examining the horse's front left hoof. Then she did the same thing with each of his other feet, nodding to herself. When she was done, she slapped her hands together and approached him.

"Money?" she asked.

He chuckled. "No, ma'am."

"That's good. 'Cause I don't have any."

"I need you to help me investigate something." He hesitated and walked back into the main area of the barn, looking down the aisle, where there were three other horses waiting to be groomed or to be fed or both.

"Oh, no. The campaign was my last hurrah. I've given up that life forever." She laughed. "Besides, how am I ever going to top my work digging up dirt on Lionel's opponent that won him the damn election?"

Eli rubbed his chin and nodded. She was right. After the financial contributions of Nester Sanchez, painting Isaiah Blankenship as a sexual deviant had been the biggest component to winning the presidency. Isaiah had been charged with assault in college at Illinois, but the case had been dismissed and swept under the rug. Mom had found the victim, who had signed a statement that Isaiah Blankenship had pulled her panties down in the bathroom of a fraternity house and would have raped her, but a drunken partygoer heard her screams and banged on the door until Isaiah gave it up. It was shocking. Awful. Criminal.

And it was also pure-grain bullshit. The woman was a meth head who had been in and out of jail since college. She wasn't credible. But Eli was able to clean her up, arrange for a job and some new clothes, and she looked perfectly presentable during her interview on *Good Morning America*.

"You were brilliant. As always."

"And I'm done. Like I told you in the fall, I can't do it anymore. I'm too old, and I don't have the juice anymore. I just want to take care of my horses."

"I know that. And I wouldn't ask if there were any other way."

She sighed and walked over to a sink. She scrubbed her hands and dried them on a towel that hung on the wall. "How long has Lionel been president? Not even a month? And you already need me?" She glared at him. "What kind of trouble are y'all in now? Has somebody finally figured out that Lionel isn't the saint he makes himself out to be? You know I'm an investigator and a damn good one, but I'm no magician."

"This isn't for the president. It's for me."

"Same difference," she said, shaking her head. "Working for you is working for him, and I'm done. I don't have any desire to be a gumshoe anymore, no matter how good I am at it."

Eli took a step closer to her, feeling his face begin to flush. How long had it been since he'd seen her? She hadn't come to the inauguration, so it had to be at least five months. He took another step and touched her shoulder. "This is personal."

She pulled away and strode back to the horse. "Oh, no. I'm not going to investigate my daughter-in-law, no matter how I feel about her. She's the mother of my grandchild, and that's sacred, and I'm not crossing that line. No way. No how. No will."

"Mom," Eli's voice finally cracked and his shoulders heaved. "It's not for me. It's for Bella." He peered down at the concrete floor and heard her footsteps approach him. Then her hand was on his chin and forcing it up.

Her green eyes burned with intensity. "What?"

"It's bad."

"Then spit it out. Ain't no problem too big for Foncie James."

He wiped his eyes and held his mother close. "This one might be."

14

Dale sat in a lawn chair with her laptop balanced on her knees. She wore a Patagonia jacket over a pullover and wool leggings, but she could still feel the January cold. On her computer screen was a string of emails from an insurance adjuster regarding a uterine-rupture case against an ob-gyn set for trial in just over a month. Should they make a final run at settlement? Was the causation defense strong enough to overcome the doctor's questionable decision to increase Pitocin after several late decelerations? Could they trust the trial judge to keep out the literature offered by the plaintiff's expert?

It was all typical pretrial banter, but Dale didn't have the energy for it. The irony of what she did for a living sometimes kept her up at night. She'd had three miscarriages, none of which she could claim were medical malpractice, but she wondered whether twenty years of defending the judgment of doctors had somehow made her a pariah to God. That he was punishing her for what she chose to do. Now Bella had cancer, and that old feeling of needing to do penance was as strong as ever. Almost overwhelming.

She slammed her laptop shut and gazed out at the field. Bella was a center midfielder, and she was cutting toward the goal. The ball was sent her way, and Bella stopped it with her right foot, hesitated, and then began to dribble toward the sideline. She was moving well. Not showing any ill effects from the cancer in both her lungs. She sent a thunderous kick across the field to a teammate breaking for the net. Seconds later, the ball was sailing into the goal, and Bella let out a fierce scream.

It was an assist, and Bella's team was up 1–0 in the scrimmage. Dale was thankful that she'd looked up from her work at the right time, but she wasn't completely free of the guilt either.

As a working mother, she felt guilt was her constant wingman. Always chiding her for every decision she made. *You should be at home taking care of your only daughter. You're wasting time at home when you should be billing hours and prepping for trial. You ought to make dinner for your family, but here you are, scarfing down pizza at your desk and prepping for a white-knuckle deposition that your client will screw up no matter how hard you prepare. If you were home more . . . and willing . . . then maybe Eli wouldn't stray.*

And on and on and on. Guilt was relentless, and she could never win. Dale felt a tear forming in her left eye, and she swiped at it. Then she smiled as her daughter looked at her. *I have to be strong. I can't let Bella see me cracking.*

Dale gave a fist pump, and Bella returned the gesture. It was so good to see her outside, doing what she loved, but the dread was never far away. *How much longer does she have?*

Dale had received a call just before practice. It was news from Dr. Amy Falkenburg: Bella qualified for a trial at MD Anderson. It started next Monday. *The day after the recital . . .*

They would go. Dale had already decided. They would go and see what was offered. She'd heard incredible things about the cancer facility in Houston, and she owed it to Bella to try every alternative. Chemo and radiation were the standard, but they would never cure her daughter. They would only prolong her life, making the days she had left a living hell. Dale had seen her own father go through cancer when she was in middle school. Ten months of chemotherapy, radiation, and torture for what? He lost eighty pounds and looked like a skeleton by the time hospice was brought in. Before he died, he made her promise that if anyone she loved ever got cancer, that she would encourage them to go without the poison that kept them alive longer but destroyed any quality of life.

I would have much preferred four months of golf, hiking, and spending time with you, your sister, and mother than ten months of this bullshit.

Bullshit. That's what he'd called cancer treatment then, and Dale wasn't sure there was a better name for it now. *It runs in my family . . .*

Guilt. Ever-present and heavy. Like one of those weighted blankets designed to help you sleep better. Never far from Dale James's consciousness.

Her father's death had been the defining moment of her childhood. He'd been a beloved history professor at the University of North Alabama in Florence. His office had been near the cage of the mascot, a real-life lion. Dale had loved visiting her dad at work after school. They would go for long walks between his afternoon and evening classes, sometimes stopping for ice cream at Trowbridge's or lunch at Ricatoni's and always checking out the lion.

Most of the time, the glorious animal slept far away from the fence that separated him from humans. But occasionally, he would walk toward Dale. His yellow eyes would bore into hers. It was a strong, fierce, and aggressive stare. A hunter sizing up prey. But also, somewhere in those lids, there was a calm, peaceful quality. A contentedness. The lion was the king of the jungle. He was a killer. He knew what he was and was okay with it.

Dale liked that. She figured that's what had drawn her to Nester.

"Mom!" The sound of her daughter's strong voice broke Dale's reverie, and she glanced up. Bella was sipping Gatorade from a bottle, her forehead streaked with sweat. "Did you see that pass?"

Dale smiled. "Amazing," she said. "You led her perfect."

Bella nodded, then peered down at her. "You hear from Dad?"

"No," Dale said, feeling another pang of guilt combined with irritation. "Not yet."

"You think he'll be back for the recital?"

Dale squinted at her daughter. "If he's not, I'll break his legs."

Bella laughed at that. "Oh . . . kay." Then she ran back onto the field.

Dale put her laptop in its case and stood from the lawn chair. She began to walk laps around the field, thinking as she moved. Eli was up to something, she knew that much. Her husband was a lot of things. An asshole. A charmer. A consummate bullshitter. A hard worker. An incredible lover . . . *when he wanted to be*. Dale bristled, thinking of SK Moss. Angry at Eli, but also herself. When had it all gone wrong? Then she watched Bella and remembered that none of that mattered anymore. They were in a crisis, the worst they'd ever faced.

After the recital, she would take Bella to MD Anderson. They would search every avenue. Every street corner. They would exhaust all alternatives. *I won't lose her.*

As the lights to the soccer field came on, she again thought of her estranged husband. Eli had a lot of faults, but if there were one quality she admired most about her husband, it was this: *Eli James is at his best in a crisis.*

She'd heard Lionel say it; ditto many of the congressman they'd worked with. When the bullets were flying, Eli was fast, swift, and strong.

Dale crossed her arms, watching her daughter dribble the soccer ball across midfield, her hair flowing behind her.

Then she prayed to a God she wasn't sure she believed in. *Help us, Lord. Help my daughter.*

She wiped tears from her eyes. If anything, the prayer made her feel weak, and she cursed herself. She pulled out her phone. When Dale James needed to talk with someone, it wasn't God she turned to.

After her father died, her mother had hauled Dale and her sister a thousand miles cross-country to Albuquerque, New Mexico, to start a new life, enrolling them in a small private school. Dale had been so scared. Angry. She'd even contemplated suicide.

But then she met a kindred soul, and ever since that moment, it had been him to whom she'd turned to in life's darkest moments. She scrolled through her contacts. There were three with only one name:

Bella.

Eli.

Although she loved them both, neither was her rock.

She'd last seen her closest friend a little over a week ago, when he'd flown her out to Albuquerque for the hearing on the motions to dismiss the various federal charges against him. Though criminal law wasn't her specialty, he'd still wanted her there. She didn't attend the hearing, but she took part in all the preparation beforehand and the discussions afterward.

Then, in the intense quiet of his construction trailer, she'd broken it all down for him, feeling the eyes of the lion on her.

Her finger stopped scrolling, and she stared at the name. Then she whispered it out loud.

"Nester."

15

Eli awoke at dawn to the smell of coffee and bacon. He swung his legs off the ancient bed and trudged to the bathroom. He gazed at his bloodshot eyes in the mirror. He'd had a fitful sleep, unable to turn his mind off.

He splashed water on his face, threw on some sweatpants, and plodded down the hall toward the kitchen. He could hear his mother's voice as he got closer.

"I don't give a rat's ass whether you're tired, busy, or booked on a vacation to the French Riveria, you owe me, Darren, and I want you to hit every damn farmers' market in Louisiana by five p.m. tomorrow afternoon, or the most intriguing decoration in my house is going to be your balls in a jar on my mantel. Got it?"

A pause and then she scoffed. "Don't yes-ma'am me, just get it done. You'll be compensated handsomely."

Eli smiled and poured himself a cup of coffee. Since his parents' divorce a decade earlier, Darren had been his mother's on-again, off-again love interest and also her investigative partner. He was a good detective when motivated, and Foncie had just provided the necessary kick in the ass.

She hung up and slammed her phone down. "He's going to do it."

Eli sat at a stool on the kitchen island. "Thank you," he said.

"I'm going to handle Alabama and Mississippi. Darren's got the boot, and you're going to take Florida, right?"

"Yes," Eli said, taking a sip of the strong coffee. They'd gone over the plan last night after he'd told her everything. She'd handled it better than he thought. No tears. No bullshit. She'd grabbed a broom and gone into an empty stall, hitting the walls over and over again until there was nothing but the handle left. Then, eyes blazing, she'd broken down the territories she knew best and where she would need help.

"And you'll see your father while you're there?"

Eli bristled and looked away.

"Elijah Longstreet James?" His mom was the only person besides Lionel that liked to belt out his full handle, but she was never joking when she did so.

"Yes, Mom. I'll see him."

"He's a drunk and a sonofabitch, but he's still your daddy. He's also a brilliant doctor. You'd be stupid not to run this by him."

"I know, and I had planned to get his thoughts."

"When it comes to his grandchild, Frank will give you all he's got."

Eli squinted at her. "I thought you hated him."

She turned to the sink. "I do. But I also still love the SOB." She peered at Eli over her shoulder. "It's complicated."

Eli took a sip of coffee and felt adrenaline and caffeine flowing through his veins. When was the last time he'd seen his father?

All hands on deck . . .

He stood and kissed her cheek. "Thank you."

As he strode toward the hallway, Foncie's voice stopped him. "I hope you and Dale are working together. She's a frosty one, but smart as almighty hell."

"We're on the same page," he managed.

"I hope so," Foncie said, approaching him. "You realize that if these rumors are true . . . if there is actually a cure for cancer . . ." She scratched her neck. ". . . and if we find this man or discover what happened to him—"

"How dangerous that could be," Eli completed the thought.

Foncie nodded, her green eyes burrowing into him. "If we learn the truth and it's that explosive? You might have to lean on Dale for something else."

Eli looked out the window, where the orangish-yellow sun rose over the crimson barn.

"Do you understand what I'm saying?" Foncie asked.

Eli sighed and rubbed his chin. *All hands on deck,* he thought again, feeling goose bumps prickle his arms. Then he peered back at his mother.

"Yes, I do."

16

Lionel was jogging on the treadmill when he saw General Kyle Randolph step inside. He slowed his pace to a walk and wrapped a towel around his neck.

"Mr. President," Randolph said.

"General. To what do I owe the pleasure?"

It was 10:00 a.m., and the day was relatively light in terms of activity for the president. After his workout, there were plans for a helicopter trip to Camp David. Lionel was looking forward to the excursion and his first trip to the presidential getaway.

"Nice to see you exercising, sir. How are you feeling?" Randolph met his eye in the wall mirror.

"Fantastic," Lionel said.

"I trust that your . . ." He paused. ". . . *training regimen* is paying dividends." Randolph's voice was just loud enough for Lionel to hear over the hum of the treadmill.

You already know, Lionel thought, but he smiled. "It's working well." He peered around the room that presidents had used for nearly two decades to keep their bodies toned. He knew there were cameras in here but was curious as to the quality of the audio. Had Randolph said anything incriminating? *No.* And even if he had, would the head of Project Boomerang think twice of destroying video or audio evidence if it threatened national security?

"I'm glad," Randolph said. "When you finish, I'd like a brief word with you in the Oval Office. I'll be waiting."

Before Lionel could respond, the general strode out of the gym. He guessed that answered the question about how willing Randolph was to speak openly in this room.

Lionel resumed his jog, looking at the screen on the running board. He still had twelve minutes left. He knew he didn't hold the cards with respect to the contents of the medicine box, but he was, after all, still the president of the United States.

The general could wait.

———

When Lionel stepped into the Oval Office a good thirty minutes later, after finishing his workout and taking a quick shower, General Randolph was not alone. With him was Chet Michaels, the attorney general.

"Mr. President," Randolph growled, clearly annoyed by the delay.

"Mr. President," Michaels added, his voice gruff and no-nonsense. Chet Michaels was a bald man with a barrel chest whose suit always looked a tad tight on him. He'd been one of Lionel's last cabinet decisions, and Lionel had been torn in appointing him. A senator from Arizona who'd spent forty years in Congress, Chet brought a lot of experience to the table, along with his popularity among his colleagues and in his home state. However, there was one significant drawback to picking Chet, and Lionel's instincts figured he was about to hear about it now.

"We need to discuss Nester Sanchez," Chet said, leaning forward and resting his elbows on his knees. "You can't possibly be considering granting him a pardon."

Lionel crossed his legs, remembering Eli's strong admonition to pick someone besides Chet. *We shouldn't have someone in the cabinet who's enemies with Nester,* Eli had pleaded.

But, in the end, that's exactly why Lionel had chosen Chet—as cover. Choosing Chet would make it seem impossible that Lionel was also in bed with Nester.

"I must consider all pardon requests that come across my desk," Lionel said, picking his words carefully. "Mr. Sanchez has made sizable donations to many good causes in the Corners, particularly in New Mexico, and he has a letter of support from Governor Florez."

"He's killed federal agents on the border." Michaels spat the words. "He's murdered at least two tribal chieftains of the Pueblo nation. He uses the Catholic Church to launder money made from the illegal sale of marijuana and opioids. He is a very *dangerous* criminal that deserves to rot in prison."

"And he has yet to be convicted of a single one of those offenses."

"There are at least fifteen charges pending," Michaels said, but Lionel heard the weakness in his voice.

"Will any of them stick?" Lionel asked. "Will even *one* result in an actual conviction?" He jerked his head. "All that taxpayer money being thrown down the drain trying to crucify a man who has donated millions to the state universities of New Mexico, Colorado, Arizona, and Utah. Who bailed out the Catholic Church last year when it almost went bankrupt. Who has donated land and resources to the reservations."

"He does all of that to own the people, Mr. President." Chet paused. "Just like his contributions to your campaign. Nester Sanchez craves power. He took over New Mexico by gaining influence with the Catholic Church, the Pueblos, and the border drug cartels. He did business with each, learned where the bodies were buried, and now he dictates all of it."

"Still waiting for the negative in all that, Chet. Seems to me that the good outweighs the bad when you really look hard at it."

"So, are you really going to pardon him?"

Lionel glanced at General Randolph, who had yet to utter a word. He didn't quite look amused, but he certainly wasn't angry like Michaels.

"I don't know yet," he said. "There is a lot to unpack there. I just don't see it as black and white as you do. General, what do you think?"

Randolph shrugged. "I agree with Mr. Michaels that Mr. Sanchez is a dangerous man. However, the Department of Defense doesn't view him as a national security threat . . . at least not yet. If he weren't the one in power, then it stands to reason that the Mexican border cartels would be causing as much, if not more, problems for state and federal government. I hate to use the term, but he might be considered a necessary evil."

"I don't believe this," said Chet. "I thought you were with me."

"I'm not with or against, Chet. I don't see this as political, per se. As the president suggests, there is a lot to unpack, good, bad, and ugly, when it comes to Nester Sanchez."

The attorney general rose from his chair, glaring at Lionel. "Are you prepared to deal with the fallout of negative public attention that a pardon of Nester Sanchez will bring?"

Lionel also stood. "Are you, Mr. Michaels, prepared to deal with the whispers, yells, and shouts from the Four Corners if you take down Nester Sanchez and leave the people he protects to the wolves?"

Chet flung up his arms. "You have *got* to be kidding me."

"I'm not. I like the term that General Randolph used. He's a 'necessary evil.' Dangerous, yes. But worse than a cartel off its leash? I'm not so sure."

Michaels walked toward the door. "Mr. President, you're going to regret this stance. So will you, General. If Nester Sanchez gains any more power . . ." He trailed off and then let himself out.

Lionel sat back down in his chair. "Thank you," he said, nodding at General Randolph.

"No need. I worry about a man of Nester Sanchez's power. Especially with his perceived ties to you by virtue of Mr. and Mrs. James."

Lionel waved a hand at him. "Perception is not reality."

"So you say," Randolph said. Then he folded his arms across his chest. "I'd like to discuss something I consider more pressing."

"Okay."

"Your health, Mr. President. As I understand it, the tumor in your colon has shrunk by more than half, and the metastasis has evaporated."

Lionel nodded. "It's . . . incredible. I feel like myself."

"I'm happy for you, but I just want to make sure that you are abiding by the terms of our agreement." He paused. "Have you told anyone?"

"Absolutely not. My wife still doesn't even know of my recurrence, nor do my children. I obviously haven't told them about the treatment."

"So Mr. James is the only one in your circle who knows that you have cancer."

"That's correct."

Randolph stood from his chair. "Has he asked any questions about your improvement?"

Lionel thought about his last visit with Eli. How broken he'd been when they discussed Bella's options. How guilty Lionel had felt to be holding the key to the cure and keeping it hidden from his best friend and goddaughter. "No," Lionel said.

"He will," Randolph said. "And when he does, what will you tell him?"

Lionel swallowed. "That the radiation and chemo are working their magic."

The general slapped his knee. "Good man."

He doesn't know, Lionel realized. *He knew everything about me, but he doesn't know about Bella's diagnosis.*

The daughter of the chief of staff was a bit far removed for the operatives of Project Boomerang to be monitoring, but still. Lionel had been dumbfounded at what they knew about him.

Should I tell him myself? Alert him so that he knows why Eli might be more curious than normal?

"Mr. President, as I've told you before and reiterate every time we talk, we hold the contents of the medicine box to be a matter of national security. Any breach . . . any disclosure about those contents could . . . and likely would be catastrophic." He paused. "Do you understand?"

"Yes," Lionel said.

General Randolph extended his hand, and Lionel shook it. "If Mr. James does . . . become curious, let me know at once. Do you agree?"

Lionel nodded. His mouth had become dry. "Of course."

17

Eli found his father exactly where he thought he would. Belly up to the bar at AJ's Lounge, the iconic seaside saloon in Destin, Florida, where Eli himself had spent many spring-break nights and early mornings. The old man was already several drinks in.

"Need to talk," Eli said, sliding into the stool next to him.

Frank James lifted the glass of vodka and tonic water and took a long pull, then smacked his lips. The old man had long silver hair and a deep tan. His face was bright red, both from the steady stream of alcohol he consumed and the sun, as he spent most of his days on the golf course at nearby Kelly Plantation practicing his two favorite vices.

"This can't be good," Frank said, grunting.

"Bella has cancer. Mucinous adenocarcinoma in both lungs." Eli decided to just spit it out. He was on a tight timeline and didn't have the time to chitchat or the energy to break the news gently. He'd spent most of the day scurrying the litany of farmers' markets on the Florida gulf coast. He'd come up dry and was fighting fatigue and a growing sense of depression. *This is a wild goose chase . . .*

The old man blinked and brought his glass up to his mouth again. He didn't drink from it, staring at Eli with wide eyes. "Is it . . . ?" he rasped, unable to say the last word, but Eli knew. It was the first question that had come to his mind upon learning the news.

Eli nodded.

Frank stood from the stool and flung two twenties on the bar. His face shone pale suddenly in the neon glow of the bar lights. Somewhere in the huge establishment, a band was playing "Baby Blue," a sad George Strait classic. He stared down at Eli.

"Let's get out of here."

———

An hour later, they were seated in a booth with two steaming mugs of coffee in front of them. Eli had barely touched his java, but Dr. Frank James had already demolished almost a pot. The old man had a napkin out on the table and was writing notes in his indecipherable scribble. The penmanship that scratched out thousands of prescriptions. Eli watched him, grateful to have him engaged. His father was a scoundrel. A womanizer. A man high on ambition and low on morals. Eli came by all these faults honestly. But Francis Henry James had also been one of the finest emergency room physicians in the state of Alabama. Whatever came through the double doors of the ER at Huntsville Hospital and later Mobile Infirmary Medical Center, Frank had seen it and dealt with it. Gruesome car-wreck injuries. Gunshot wounds. Trauma of every kind and description. Ruptured colons. Perforated ulcers. Even phantom pains that were the seedbed of cancer. Dr. James had treated it all. He'd spent over forty years in emergency medicine and doing the occasional shift in intensive care. Eli knew that the calmness he felt during adversity also came from his dad, and he hoped and prayed that the old man would be at his best now.

As he watched his father think and work, Eli gazed around a place he knew well. The Donut Hole was a café a couple of miles from AJ's on Highway 98. Eli had finished up a few nights here as well. Even panicked, tired, and on edge, it was hard not to wax nostalgic for simpler times when he and Lionel had come down to the gulf and drunk cold Miller Lites from cans and dreamed of their political futures as they chased tail on the beach by day and haunted AJ's by night. Eli had been such a stereotypical frat-boy asshole. Most of those days were a blur of alcohol, oysters, and late nights, but Lady Luck had smiled on him his third year of law school.

That's when he met Dale Davis at the weirdly shaped condo unit on Holiday Isle. *The Aegean.* He could still remember the name of the dark-orange building where he'd seen the striking blonde snorkeling for hermit crabs at dusk. Instead of going out with Lionel and the boys, Eli had stayed behind and offered to help her. Then, as the sun set over the jetties that divided the ocean from Destin Harbor, they took a walk.

Which lasted almost twenty years . . .

Eli stared at his mug. He hadn't thought much about Dale's threat of divorce since Bella's diagnosis, but he knew their marriage, if not over, was on life support.

"Smart getting Foncie involved," his father finally said, as he motioned for the waitress to refill his cup. He squinted at Eli. "Not sure why you came here."

"Mom said I should run it by you, and I reluctantly agreed." He gestured at the three napkins' worth of notes the old man had taken. "You must have something to say."

Frank sighed. "I haven't practiced medicine on a regular basis in five years. I'm nothing but a part-time has-been."

"But you were the best ER doc in south Alabama for four decades."

Frank grunted. "Emergency medicine is a far cry from oncology." He glanced down at his notes and sipped more coffee.

"Dad, please. You practiced in Mobile for a long time. Have you ever heard any rumblings about an actual cure for cancer?"

He folded one of the napkins and sighed. "Mary Frances Bruce," he whispered.

"Who?" Eli asked, squinting at him.

"She's the reason your mom sent you here. Not because I'm a doctor or might have any specific knowledge of cancer treatment."

"Okay . . ." Eli took a sip of his own coffee, which was now cold. He fought the urge to spit it out, not wanting to distract the old man.

"Why would Mom think Mary Frances Bruce was important?" Eli swallowed the cold coffee and waited.

Frank rubbed his hands together. "What I'm about to tell you violates the HIPAA privacy law."

"Dad, we're talking about Bella."

"I know that, but I want you to know the magnitude of the disclosure. If I was still practicing, this could cost me my license." He glared at Eli. "But I'm not practicing anymore . . . and even if I was . . . this is my granddaughter."

"Did you tell Mom about Ms. Bruce? Is that why she said I should come?"

Frank shrugged. "Your mom is an intuitive woman. Did you know she had a cancer scare a few years ago?"

Eli's eyes went wide. "No. What the—?"

"You know how private she is. She swore me to secrecy, so I'm not surprised she kept it from you. It was breast cancer. She found the lump a couple years after our divorce. Stage one. She had a lumpectomy and, as far as I know, has been in remission ever since. But . . ."

"But what?"

"Before we knew there was no metastasis, in those first few days after she told me, I confided to your mom that there might be alternative remedies. I never mentioned Ms. Bruce's name. Just that I'd seen and heard some things and to let me know her prognosis as soon as she knew it. Thankfully, she caught it early, but I'm sure she remembered how insistent I was about the possibility of other avenues." He sighed. "Smart woman. You know, even though your mother and I aren't married anymore, I still . . ." He trailed off, and Eli remembered his mother's description of their relationship.

"It's complicated," Eli quoted his mom.

"Fucked up is what it is," Frank said, chuckling. Then he cocked his head at Eli. "Did you know that, for about two years, I was a concierge doctor?"

Eli shook his head. "I don't even know what that is."

"It's basically a family physician for the rich. No lines. No waiting to get appointments. They call me and I come, sometimes at my office, but on many occasions to the patient's house. I did it right after the divorce with your mom. My drinking then was even worse than it is now, and I needed a change. I stayed on in the ER on the weekends and worked as a concierge doctor during the week."

"I had no idea."

"I did it for about a year and a half and made a fortune. Mostly bad colds and pain management. Typical PCP stuff, but occasionally I'd get a patient with back pain or a cough or blood in the urine, and tests would reveal cancer." He paused. "Ms. Bruce was a lung-cancer patient. A lifetime two-pack-a-day smoker who just happened to be the widow of a maritime lawyer who owned a lot of valuable real estate in Baldwin County. She was rich, impatient, and not afraid to try things. I remember she insisted on going to MD Anderson, even though she had a cancer variant that could have been treated just as effectively in Mobile."

Eli flinched at the mention of the oncology facility in Houston. Dale would find out any moment—or she possibly already knew by now—whether Bella qualified for a trial. He pushed his cup away so he wouldn't be tempted to drink more of the frigid brew. "What happened next?"

"Not much in terms of my care. I referred her to an oncologist and would see her for noncancer issues over the course of the next year." He paused. "But then a funny thing happened. She came to me for her annual physical and said her cancer was gone."

"Gone?" Eli raised his eyebrows.

Frank snapped his fingers. "That was my exact reaction. I said, What do you mean, *gone*? I saw the bone scans. I had a copy of the chest CT. She had a huge mass in her right lung that had spread throughout her body. It was stage-four lung cancer. There was no way. After her examination, I reached out to her oncologist, Dr. Walter Dana, who was a good friend and drinking buddy of mine." Frank stared at his coffee mug and grimaced. "Walt died of liver failure last year." He shook his head. "I'm probably next."

"I'm sorry," Eli said. "What did Walt say?"

"He affirmed everything Ms. Bruce had said. The patient was in remission. He was even more shocked about it than I was. He said he had seen cancer reverse itself on occasions where there was no metastasis, but never where the cancer had spread to the bone."

"What happened?" Eli asked.

"Walt said he didn't know. Ms. Bruce had not undergone any of the treatments he had recommended. No radiation. No chemo. And yet . . ."

"It was gone." Eli sat in the silence for a moment. "Did you see Ms. Bruce again?"

Frank nodded. "She came in to go over her blood work the following week. I remember everything was fine. There were no squirrelly results, and you would expect a high white count if she still had cancer, but the disease in her body was gone. I couldn't help myself. I said, Ms. Bruce, how can this be? How did you cure yourself without any treatment?"

Eli felt gooseflesh raise the hair on his arms. "What did she say?"

"She said a friend of hers had a niece who liked to smoke pot. The young woman ran in a circle of earthy types who believed in alternative and holistic medicine. Mushrooms. Herbs. Natural everything. All that bullshit. One of the gal's friend's fathers was a pharmacist who had come up with a pill that several cancer patients had taken and gone into remission soon afterward. Ms. Bruce tried it and . . ." Frank snapped his fingers. "Voilà. Magic. She felt better within a week or two, and after a month and a half, the cancer was gone."

"That's unbelievable," Eli said. "Where did this pharmacist sell his wonder drug?"

Frank met his son's eyes. "Guess."

"Farmers' markets?"

Eli's father nodded. "Ms. Bruce bought her batch at the one in Gulf Shores."

"Did she say anything about the man who sold it to her?"

Frank scratched his neck. "I can't remember. She didn't mention his name and was rather coy about it. Ms. Bruce was in her late sixties, and I think she enjoyed knowing a secret."

Eli leaned forward, feeling his heart racing in his chest. "Dad, this is incredible. How many years ago was this?"

"Eight," Frank said, staring down at the table.

"Do you know where Ms. Bruce is now? Jesus, surely she remembers the pharmacist's name. She could lead me right to him."

Frank continued to stare at the table, lost in thought.

"Dad?"

"Aren't you curious how I could remember her name? That was almost eight years ago . . ."

"I'm assuming because she mentioned that she'd taken a drug that cured her cancer," Eli scoffed. "I'm sure that piqued your interest."

Frank's lips formed a sad smile. "I thought it was pure horseshit. The whole damn story. I thought Ms. Bruce was a quack and that the original scans must have been faulty. There was no way. No *fucking way*." He gripped his mug but didn't drink from it. "No . . . her story isn't why I remembered her."

The goose bumps on Eli's arms crawled up his neck. "Why, then?"

"Because Ms. Bruce presented as a patient to the emergency room that weekend. Three days after she saw me. She'd been run over by a car. Her body was . . . mangled. Broken arms. Legs. Pelvis. Everything." He looked up from the mug. "She was dead on arrival." Frank shook his head. "There was a witness who was talking to the police. A neighbor who had seen the accident from his garage. He said a sedan just mowed her down. It was going too fast for him to get the plates." He hesitated. "As far as I know, there were no charges ever brought. Just a phantom hit-and-run."

"My God, Dad," Eli said. "Did you or Walt ever tell the authorities about Ms. Bruce's miracle remission?"

"That would have violated HIPAA. I couldn't have done that and, truthfully, I just thought the whole thing was ironic and sad. A rich widow run over in one of Mobile's ritziest neighborhoods—just after beating cancer? I figured Ms. Bruce had pissed off the wrong person. She had a mouth on her, and like I said, she seemed to enjoy having a secret. Her death may have also been penance for one of her husband's sins. I guess . . . I just didn't really think about the reason much then. Only that it was tragic . . . and very unusual."

Eli sat back in his seat and crossed his arms. "After hearing what I've told you . . . what the pharma lobbyist and Senator Wiggins said . . . what do you think now?"

Frank took a slow sip of coffee and spoke in a measured voice. "I think that you are swimming in shark-infested waters, Eli. And, if Ms. Bruce and this . . . 'man from Mobile,' as your lobbyist friend called him, were both killed over this wonder drug, then you and everyone you involve in the effort could become a target."

Eli felt perspiration pooling under his arms and on his back. A cold, uncomfortable sweat. "Do you think there could be a cure for cancer? Something that Bella could take that would heal her?"

Frank James leaned back and put both hands on the table. "I don't know, son. I'm a doctor. I deal in data and differential diagnoses. Medicine, like law, is a practice. There are few things that are black and white."

"Cut the crap and shoot me straight, would ya?"

Frank squinted at his son. "I believe that it is . . . *very possible* . . . that there may be medications that are much more effective at fighting certain cancers that the FDA has likely been encouraged not to approve."

"So it comes down to money."

Frank nodded. "And power." He reached across the table and grabbed Eli's hand, squeezing hard. "If I'm right, then anyone that sniffs close to the truth could end up in the same place as Ms. Bruce and your man from Mobile."

"Are you saying I should give up? I can't do that, Dad. This is *Bella*, for Christ's sake."

Frank shook his head and let go of his grasp. He pointed his index finger at Eli. "No, son. What I'm telling you is to watch your back."

———

Eli dropped his dad back off at AJ's.

"Remember what I said."

He nodded. "Thanks, Dad."

For a few seconds, the rental car was filled with a million unsaid things between father and son. Frank must have sensed it, because as he grabbed the latch, he grunted, "I'm sorry I wasn't a better father. You, uh, tell that little girl her Paw Paw is rooting for her. That she's a James and we might be stubborn as hell, but we fight to the bitter end." His voice cracked, and he wiped at his eyes. He climbed out of the car and then knocked on the window.

"Yeah," Eli said, looking up at him.

"Have you figured out what you're going to do if you confirm that these rumors and stories are true? That there is a cure for cancer and the government has been hiding it from us . . . and isn't afraid to kill to keep it hidden." He paused. "What then?"

Eli gazed out over the steering wheel. In the distance, he saw the lights of the boats still floating on Destin Harbor. Beyond them, the dark waters of the gulf. "I haven't thought that far ahead."

"You'd better. I know you pretty well, Eli. The apple didn't fall far from the tree. I know you aren't a martyr."

Eli shook his head. "No, I'm not. If there is a cure . . ." He gritted his teeth. ". . . then I'm going to get my hands on it and give it to Bella. I'm the chief of staff to the president. I have a good deal of power and influence. If it's out there, I'll get it."

"Good," Frank said, placing a toothpick in his mouth and beginning to chew. "Just remember. Your power that you're talking about comes from the federal government. The very institution that may be behind this cover-up."

"What would you do?" Eli looked up at his father, and Frank grinned. His sunburned face glowed in the lights coming from AJ's.

"I don't have a clue," Frank said. "I'm a doctor, and I've exhausted my expertise. But you've made it all the way to the White House by being craftier and meaner than the rest of the bastards."

Eli snorted. "What are you saying?"

Frank pointed at his son. "Don't forget who you are. And don't forget the two rules of fighting that I taught you in the fifth grade. Remember? Doug Bolden?"

Eli's face flushed red. "How on earth do you remember his name?"

"He was bullying my son. I was an absentee father most of the time, but that was my finest moment."

Eli nodded. "The two rules of fighting." He held up one finger. "Hit first and hit hard."

"Amen," Frank said. "And . . ."

"Never bring a knife to a gunfight."

"Yup. If your opponent has his fists, you bring a stick. If he has a stick, you bring a knife. If he has a knife, you bring a goddamn revolver."

"What if he has the power and might of the United States government?"

Frank James's bloodshot eyes blazed with intensity. "Well . . . you gotta ask yourself: What are *they* afraid of? What . . . or who . . . keeps them up at night?"

Eli rubbed his chin. *All hands on deck,* he thought again. "Thank you, Dad."

"I love you, son."

But before Eli could respond, the old man was gone. He trudged past the car toward the entrance to the bar and didn't look back.

In the coming days, Eli would wish he'd thought to hug his father. To tell him that, despite everything, he loved him too.

It would be a regret. One of many.

18

I'm going to kill him, Dale thought. She watched the stage with a fixed smile, but her fists were clenched. The opening song was a montage of rap and pop songs that introduced almost all the dancers that trained in the studio. Bella's part was small and not a big deal. But she would be in four other smaller performances, including her solo. *This could be the last time she ever takes that stage,* Dale thought, then realized she was sugarcoating it. *This* will *be the last time.* She glanced around the packed auditorium full of other parents, siblings, and friends. How many of these events had she attended over the past thirteen years?

Bella had always loved dancing. The costumes. The routines. The ambience of it all. Dale had never had to push her to go to practice. In fact, Bella rarely complained about any of her activities. She might fuss that she wasn't better at soccer, and she used to be frustrated that she was too slow in track. Or that she wasn't as tall as the other dancers or that her voice lacked the strength of some of the others in choir. She was hard on herself, which she no doubt got from Dale.

Her father was always ten feet tall and bulletproof, but Bella carried her mother's insecurities. Do these tights make me look fat? Is my makeup subtle enough or too much? Is my hair too curly?

Dale brushed a stray hair out of her eyes and realized that a couple of tears had fallen down her cheeks. She was so locked in that she hadn't noticed. She unclenched her fists and took the tissue in her right hand

and dabbed at her face, careful not to smear her own makeup. She glanced at the empty seat next to her.

Where are you? she thought, watching the stage as the last song of the ensemble ended and the curtain came up. Eli had called each night, giving a vague "just chasing a few leads on treatment options Dad had mentioned," but he'd been gone almost four days now, and Dale was losing patience. She knew he had to be doing something else, but what?

If Bella's diagnosis and her husband's strange behavior weren't enough, she was also dealing with her own issues. Yesterday, she'd requested a leave of absence from her firm. It was granted, but she could feel the angst. At least three trials would need to be continued. The law was a jealous mistress, and Dale knew all too well how quickly she could lose her power in the firm. She'd worked two decades to be a senior partner, but Bella's diagnosis had changed everything.

Sad that the destruction of her marriage hadn't budged her from wanting or even needing to work. But Bella falling ill had shaken her to her core. Dale James had never been one to be apathetic about almost anything, but she found that she didn't care about the sidelong glances her colleagues had given her when she left the office today. The uncomfortable exchange with her secretary and paralegal. Everyone lived the job in medical malpractice defense litigation. You couldn't afford to have much of a life outside of it, and Dale also had a rather important nonmedical client who occupied a good bit of her time. She clasped her hands, knowing she owed him a call.

She'd almost called Nester when she pulled up his contact while walking laps around the soccer field, but she'd stopped herself. She hated feeling weak and vulnerable. She didn't want him to see her that way. And yet, he was one of the only people who had.

Dale squeezed her arms across her chest as the curtain opened and the lights darkened. A spotlight on stage and then . . . there was Bella. Wearing white tights and a tank top, strutting around the stage to the song "Uptown Funk" and clapping her hands. She smiled, knowing she needed to embrace the moment, but her thoughts were consumed by the uncertain future. Their flight to Houston was later tonight. The dreaded red-eye. They could have gotten one in the morning, but Bella was due at MD Anderson at 10:00 a.m. Dale was never one to chance being late. That's why she always insisted on staying in hotel rooms for morning depositions or hearings that required more than two hours of travel. She would never be a victim of traffic or a flat tire or anything else. She controlled everything she could control.

She sighed. Perhaps, in that particular way, she and Eli were just too damn much alike. He also relished having things his way. Compromise and cooperation were two traits sorely lacking in their marriage. *That has to change,* she knew. For Bella's sake . . . *It has to.*

"Hey." Eli slipped into the seat she'd been saving for him, right out of central casting: Dark suit. White shirt. Maroon power tie. Overcoat draped over his lap. He leaned in and kissed her cheek, and Dale had to force herself not to recoil. "I watched the first dance from the back. She looks incredible, doesn't she?"

Dale bit her lip and focused on the stage. There were at least seven other dancers onstage now, but she watched only her daughter. Bella moved with grace and confidence. Sometimes, Dale wondered if she knew everything there was to know about her daughter. It almost seemed like Bella was too perfect sometimes. She thought the girl told her everything, but was that true? She glanced at Eli, knowing they had both been so busy these past few years. Bella had spent so much time on her own or with her friends.

Does she have a boyfriend? Or a girlfriend? Dale didn't think so, but would Bella share that kind of thing with her? Based on how she had taken down that beer the other night with pizza, Dale assumed that her daughter had drunk alcohol enough to enjoy a brew. What else did she drink? Vodka? Whiskey? Alcoholism ran in both their families.

Does she smoke pot? Take THC gummies?

Dale felt that huge cloak of guilt falling down on her, all set to strangle what should be a positive and emotional experience. Then she felt hot breath in her ear. "I hope it's okay, but I bought myself a ticket for the trip to Houston."

She didn't look at him. Could hardly believe her ears. "What about Lionel—?"

"I've already told him, and he understands."

Dale finally couldn't help herself. She moved her eyes from the stage to her husband. His jaw jutted out, and his eyes were focused, but she could tell he was thinking about something far away from the auditorium. "What are you up to?" she whispered.

For a moment, Eli said nothing, staring at the stage as the song died down. Finally, he turned to her, and the intensity in his gaze was almost palpable. She felt a tickle of gooseflesh rise on her arm.

"Leaving everything on the field," he said.

19

In the parking lot of the civic center, as Bella James prepared to perform her solo, a man and a woman sat in a Toyota Sienna minivan. Both sipped from Styrofoam cups of coffee. The man spoke into his cell phone. "The chief of staff just arrived. His wife and daughter drove separate."

"Did he come straight from the airport, or did he make any stops?"

"No stops. He arrived at Reagan National on a flight from Atlanta and drove his own car here. The itinerary we received from FAA says he flew into the Mobile International Airport last Wednesday."

"James has family on the coast," the voice on the other end of the line said. A statement, not a question. "Did you do what I asked at his home?"

"Yes, sir. There's a team there now. Hidden mics set up in every room, the garage, and the back porch."

"And his and Mrs. James's vehicles?"

"Bugged and so is the daughter's Jeep."

There was a pause. "Excellent." Then the phone clicked dead. The man behind the wheel let out a long sigh. "Seems a bit . . . over the top, don't you think? I mean, they're best friends, for Christ's sake. How could Mr. James be doing anything that might endanger the president?"

The woman in the passenger seat kept her eyes on the entrance to the civic center. "We aren't paid to ask those types of questions." Then she punched his shoulder, and he looked at her. She made a circular motion, pointing to all areas of the van. "*They're listening to us too,*" she mouthed slowly. Then she muttered under her breath: "Jackass."

The man raised his eyebrows and nodded. "Yes, ma'am."

———

Inside the conference room in the basement of the Pentagon, General Kyle Randolph paced the concrete floor. He, like all men and women in the military, hated surprises. Despised them. The success of missions depended on superb preparation and planning, but it was impossible to account for every contingency.

"Bella James has lung cancer." Saying it out loud sounded wrong. Like a guitar string struck off-key. It couldn't be. "*Lung cancer,* for God's sake."

"It happens," Beth McGee said. "It's very rare, but the research my people in the FBI have done confirms that mucinous adenocarcinoma of the lung without the presence of smoking is a growing trend among women. Bella is much younger than the average age of those affected, which is late thirties, early forties. But it's out there. Still . . . there was no way for any of us to predict it."

"And it wouldn't have mattered," Robert Bellamy, the former director of Homeland Security, offered. "Handing the president the key to the medicine box was the only way to avoid Yancey ascending to the office. Nothing has changed. We just need to remind the president what's at stake."

"I've been doing that on a regular basis," Randolph said. "I think the president is well aware of Bella James's diagnosis and chose not to tell me during our last discussion."

"Which isn't necessarily an act of defiance," McGee said. "He and Mr. James are friends, and I believe he is the girl's godfather. I'm sure he is probably feeling a degree of guilt to have access to the boomerang."

"The question is, Will he talk?" Bellamy said. "If he keeps his mouth shut, then we have nothing to worry about."

"I'm not worried so much about the president disclosing the secret," Randolph said. "Lionel Cantrell is a political animal and a survivor. He's not about to do anything, not even for his best friend, that could dismantle his presidency or future. My concern is Mr. James's knowledge of the president's illness . . . and his reaction to Lionel's impending remission. Mr. James is a resourceful man . . ."

"With some dubious connections," Bellamy added.

Silence for a few seconds. "What have your operatives uncovered about his trip to Mobile?" Randolph gazed at both department heads.

"Still working on it," McGee said. "We know he had dinner with his father and that he spent the night at his mother's."

"It would be natural to see his family after the news about Bella," Randolph noted.

"Alone? Without his wife or daughter?" Bellamy snorted.

"The Secret Service was in the dark," McGee said. "Just that the trip was 'personal.'"

"We've got to know," Randolph finally said. "Given Mr. James's connection to Sarah Kate Moss. I'm worried . . ."

"How would Moss know about what happened in Mobile eight years ago?" McGee asked.

"She wouldn't. Or shouldn't," Randolph said. "But she could have heard rumors."

"I'll reach out to our friends in pharma and the FDA tonight," Bellamy said, also standing.

The three now made a triangle, with Randolph at the high point. "Good," he said. "I'm certainly hoping that Mr. James is simply dealing with grief by taking a trip home to clear his head."

"He's going to MD Anderson with his wife and daughter tonight," McGee told them. "That's consistent with a grieving father trying to do everything he can do."

"It's also in line with someone trying to learn every bit of information about cancer treatment . . . after acquiring classified information under the covers with Big Pharma's favorite lobbyist." Bellamy spat the words, and his gruff tone irritated Randolph. As did his willingness . . . almost eagerness . . . to be boorish in a professional setting.

But he's right, Randolph had to admit.

"Let's not jump to conclusions," McGee said. "Not until we hear back from both of our teams."

"But we need to be ready to move," Bellamy fired back. "Right, General? And I believe we all know what that means."

"Right," Randolph said, glaring at Bellamy. "I know exactly what it means."

20

As the jet took off from Reagan National, Eli peered out at the lights of the nation's capital. Next to him, his daughter leaned her head against his shoulder, already asleep. Bella was exhausted after the recital. Her solo, in particular, had been . . .

. . . *incredible.* Her choreography and performance had won her a standing ovation. Eli had struggled to hold his emotions together. After, he'd shaken hands and accepted hugs. With Bella being a senior, this was her last hurrah with the dance troupe she'd been with since she was four years old. At the end of the show, the owner recognized all the girls who had been with the studio for longer than ten years, and Bella was the last to cross the stage. That had brought another standing ovation. And more tears.

Now all Dale and Eli had was fear and hope.

Eli knew that the treatment offered in the trial in Houston would not heal his daughter. Dr. Falkenburg had been clear on that. Because Bella had certain genes, she qualified for this trial, which might shrink the tumors faster than traditional methods. It also might not be effective at all. There was a less than 1 percent chance that the tumors would completely go away, and zero chance that if they did evaporate, they wouldn't come back.

"We're buying time," Dale had said, repeating what Falkenburg had told her.

Buying time, Eli thought, as the plane reached its traveling altitude. *Over a hundred years of treating cancer, and that's the best we can do.*

He rested his head against the cool window and thought through the events of the past few days since dropping his father off at AJ's Lounge. After three consecutive days of cruising the Florida gulf coast and asking questions at farmers' markets, he had no leads. None. He'd worn a cap and dressed casually in order to disguise himself, even though he knew it was unnecessary. He was the chief of staff, not the president. No one was going to recognize a behind-the-scenes operator like him. Still, he couldn't help a sense of paranoia growing while he followed the lead that SK Moss had disclosed. In fact, he had left his phone in the hotel room he'd rented for the weekend and bought a burner model from Target for use in the field.

He'd used it only twice, both times to check in with his mother. Foncie had hit all the markets on the Alabama and Mississippi coasts and was now chasing the Mary Frances Bruce angle.

Eli pulled the burner out of his pocket and looked at the last text he'd received from his mother. He glanced to his left and saw that, on the other side of the aisle, Dale had reclined her seat. She wasn't sleeping, and her eyes peered up at the ceiling of the plane. Lost in thought. Since his departure to Mobile, Dale had seemed even more distant than usual. Bella's diagnosis had obviously been like an F5 tornado, destroying and disrupting everything in their lives. On the way to the airport, she'd told him that she'd taken a leave of absence from the firm. What would that mean for her career? A litigator, even an experienced one like Dale, couldn't just walk away from an active caseload. She hadn't been bitter or even sad when she told him. Only resigned to their new normal, whatever it would be. Divorce hadn't come up since that night in the emergency room when Dr. McCormick showed them the tumors in both of Bella's lungs. Dale had acted cordially throughout the recital and afterward, but her mind, like now, had seemed a million miles away.

Is something else going on? Eli wondered.

With the rush of getting home after the recital, packing, and driving to the airport, there hadn't been time for him to inform Dale of his adventures on the coast, but he would soon. He was still piecing it all together, and they didn't have anything definitive. But that could change on a dime. He glanced at the text on the burner's screen:

> I think I may have something. Meeting with a woman tomorrow who knew Ms. Bruce well. We need to talk about the police investigation of her death. It stinks, Eli. This whole thing stinks to high heaven.

Eli stopped reading and smiled. He loved his mother's sayings, and "stinks to high heaven" was one of her favorites. He closed his eyes and felt his daughter's breath on his neck. His father's recounting of Ms. Bruce's situation had been similarly suspicious.

None of it added up.

Eli shivered and opened his eyes. He again peered at his phone, feeling a cold chill come over him as he read the last sentence of his mother's text.

> I'm scared, Eli.

21

The man rose at 4:00 a.m.

He'd woken early since he was ten years old. Always before dawn. The last time he'd slept past the first light of the sun, he'd arisen, and his mother was gone. She'd cooked him and his father a dinner of cheese tortillas laced with her own batch of green chiles. The former Olivia Rodriguez had grown up in Hatch, and had learned from her own mother, who had worked in the fields, specializing in the spicy peppers known the world over. For dessert, she'd made sopapillas, which the boy loved. She'd tucked him in and read him a story about the ghosts that inhabited the Luna mansion. Ghost stories scared most kids, but not him. Not when his mother told them. Not when she kissed his cheek after finishing and told him that she was proud of her big boy.

She died in her sleep on February 14, 1984. Valentine's Day morning. She might have died the night before, but his father had been adamant that the date of death be the fourteenth. She was his Valentine. She was their everything.

The boy never forgot that the coroner didn't care about the date. He rolled his eyes as the boy's father wept. His father hadn't noticed, but the boy had.

He'd been angry after that. And his anger never fully went away. He'd learned to harness it. To exploit it. To use it for good. But it was always there. Smoldering like a furnace. His mother and father had meant nothing to that coroner. His mother's corpse had been hauled out of their adobe shack like a sack of trash.

The boy's father had never recovered. He hadn't been angry like his son. He hadn't seen the way the coroner looked at them. His father had been blinded by grief. He died three years later. The boy was in the eighth grade when his father passed. He made good grades. Was smart and a good athlete. He had an uncle who didn't much care to raise him and, even if he had, didn't have the time. The uncle knew a coach at a private school in Albuquerque. The boy was given a scholarship because of his grades and ability to play basketball. He was a "boarder," as the rich kids called the students who lived on campus.

The boy had been alone in the world . . . until he met the girl. The girl who told him his eyes looked like a lion's.

They'd both been new kids at the school. Bound by circumstance and tragedy. She'd understood his anger. Around her, he'd been his best self. And she had motivated him to not just be the best.

But to be the only.

She'd been his sunshine. Warming his heart, mind, and eventually, his body. They should have been together forever, but the girl had her own dreams, and he did not stand in her way.

She returned to Alabama after high school. Gone, but never far from his thoughts. His motivation to be number one remained. As did the anger, never far from the surface.

He'd seen that coroner again. About ten years ago. He wasn't quite as powerful as he was now, but he was well on his way. This time, the man who had rolled his eyes averted his gaze. Staring at the ground instead of meeting the eyes of the lion. Afraid of the man that the boy had become.

The man sank to his knees and did fifty push-ups by the twin bed in which he slept. He had no cell phone here, only a landline with an answering machine. The red light on the archaic device was blinking, notifying him that he had one new message. He'd noticed it before bed last night but had decided to wait until morning to listen. If it was an emergency, they would have kept calling. His number was unlisted. Only his inner circle had it, and that included precious few people. He knew the message would be important, but he liked to be fresh to hear important news, good or bad.

He pressed the button to listen, and his heart raced when he heard her voice. "Hey, I just wanted you to know that I'm taking a leave of absence from my firm. Bella has cancer and we are exploring all options. My leave doesn't apply to you. If you need me, call. I haven't forgotten about the promises made to you, and I'll make sure that they are met. I just wanted you to know the situation. I . . . I'm scared. I . . ." A deep breath. ". . . I miss you."

The man stared at the answering machine for a long time. He did not have children. His parents were dead. After his father's death, his family . . . had been her.

My family is her.

He didn't make decisions based on emotion, and yet he'd supported a president that he didn't believe in because she asked him to. That wasn't so hard. He didn't believe in any politicians. He didn't believe in the Catholic Church, but he had donated millions to the New Mexico parishes last year. He didn't believe in the power or intelligence or even the entitlement claims of the Pueblos; yet, no one had given more money and resources to Native Americans than he. He didn't care for the Mexican drug cartels—in fact, he despised the sons of bitches— but he hadn't hesitated to grease the wheels of the local police and the immigration authorities to allow millions in contraband to enter New Mexico. The drugs would have come into the country anyway, so he took control and delivered the shipments while the three heads of the cartel ended up six feet under in an old landfill on the outskirts of Los Lunas.

The man didn't simply know where the bodies were buried. He did the burying.

He knew they were afraid of him. All of them. The cartel. The Church. The Pueblos.

And the government most of all.

The man did fifty more push-ups. Then he strode into the kitchen and put a pot of coffee on. It was piñon, which was his favorite. He didn't believe in much, but there were a few things he held sacred.

Family. His parents might be dead and the girl-turned-woman thousands of miles away, but they were never far from his heart.

Traditions. He relished that—in any Mexican restaurant, in Albuquerque, Rio Rancho, Sante Fe, Los Lunas, or anywhere else in his state—you were always asked whether you wanted green or red chiles. Sopapillas were offered as dessert after every meal. The delicacy he'd loved as a child was something you always got in a restaurant. He loved the annual balloon fiesta in October. And the way the aspen leaves changed colors every fall.

Love. It was what drove him most of all. The school he'd attended as a teenager, along with the girl, had saved his life. He continued to donate large sums of money to it every year. When alumni complained that he was too polarizing a figure to be recognized as a donor, he continued to give anonymously.

Love for his mother and father.

For his hometown of Los Lunas.

And for the girl. Always . . . the girl.

She's scared.

The man poured himself a cup of the coffee, smelling the roasted piñon pine nuts, and opened the back door of his adobe rancher. He could have lived in a castle in the richest neighborhood in Santa Fe or Albuquerque. Instead, he dwelled in Los Lunas on the first piece of property he'd purchased two years out of high school.

He gazed out over the twenty-acre spread. Modest by any description. A pen with cattle. Another with pigs. And a barn that could have held horses but instead hid something more . . . *explosive.* He knew that most men in his position would build a fortress, but he didn't believe in that kind of protection. He hid in plain sight. He watched over the people here. Supported their customs. Shielded them from poverty. From eminent domain. From the cartel and the government.

And, in return, the people kept their mouth shut.

He had so many nicknames in other parts of the state and even the country.

"The Scourge of New Mexico." Hadn't John Chisum called Billy the Kid that very same thing? Then there was "the Silent Killer," "the King of the Four Corners," "the Godfather of the Southwest," and, among the Pueblos, "the Beast," which was his favorite.

Here, though, in Los Lunas, they simply called him Nester.

———

An hour later, the man walked back inside his house covered in sweat. A brown pit bull followed him, and the man fed the animal before he poured himself some water.

He'd run three laps around his property with Dog, as he called his faithful companion, trotting next to him. Then he'd lifted weights in the bare-bones gym he'd put in the barn. Bench press, pull-ups, and dead lift today. Nothing crazy, but he felt the pump of blood pulsing in his veins.

He fixed himself a glass of chocolate milk and three over-medium eggs. Then he sat in the silence of the small, dark kitchen and ate.

He thought of the message from Dale. The fear and anxiety in her voice. *Her daughter* . . .

The man had backed Lionel Cantrell for two reasons. Because Dale asked him to and, even more importantly, because she promised him that he would be granted a federal pardon for the many offenses the government had brought against him.

He loved Dale. He always would, despite some of her ill-fated choices, the worst of which had been marrying a con artist like Eli James. But he held people to their promises.

After finishing his breakfast, he cleaned the dishes and strode to the bathroom. As he performed his morning routine, the man sensed a growing weariness in his chest.

Bella's sickness had made Dale weaker . . .

. . . and that weakens me.

He had countless lawyers, but it was Dale's counsel that he trusted above all. They shared a bond forged in tragedy, grief, and the pains of youth. Nothing, not her marriage to another man or his growing power and criminal reputation, could break it.

Nester Alejandro Sanchez glanced at the mirror, and the eyes of the lion stared back at him.

Nothing ever will.

PART THREE

THE TRIALS

The days pass in a blur. Are they there for a week? Two? The MD Anderson Cancer Center is . . .

". . . overwhelming," Dale whispers her thoughts out loud as they go to their fourth appointment in three hours.

What day is it? Eli wonders. Wednesday? Thursday?

As in the waiting room before Bella was first diagnosed, time seems to stop here. Then again, it also seems to be moving too fast. Decisions have to be made. Every meeting is another sales pitch. Bella qualifies for this six-week medication, but she could also take it in conjunction with this other drug that will likely never be approved by the FDA due to the potential side effects, but if you sign this waiver, we can give it to her too. And it might work.

Guinea pigs, Eli thinks. That's what we are. Grateful guinea pigs.

The place is huge. Enormous. The food is good. The people are friendly. Helpful. It's Disney World for cancer patients. Eli sees the desperation in so many people's eyes. The dads and moms and uncles and aunts and brothers and sisters waiting in the various lobbies as their precious guinea pigs are tested and treated.

Eli asks questions. He probes. He watches. He holds his daughter's hand and confers with his wife on all that's been offered. He tries to keep an open mind.

But he knows better. The Jameses have been to Disney as a family several times. The folks there have a way about making you feel so good about opening up your bank account. Money is no object. It's the happiest place on earth. You don't feel a speck of resentment as you swipe your card. Give me that fun. Give it to me now.

MD Anderson is not the happiest place on earth. But it is the last bastion of a resource that cancer patients and their families have precious little of:

Hope.

22

Eli propped his chin on his fist. His legs were crossed, his eyes focused on the attorney general. His head was throbbing, and no amount of Aleve, TYLENOL, or Advil had helped. He'd been at the White House since six in the morning, trying and failing to get caught up after almost two weeks in Houston. The cabinet meeting was his last of the day, but it had already dragged on for almost an hour.

"Mr. President, the world is watching," Attorney General Chet Michaels said without enthusiasm. "A pardon request by the Scourge of New Mexico is still waiting to be acted upon by you. There have been several articles asking serious questions. Allegations of campaign fundraising malfeasance. A possible bribe. *Newsweek* says that sources say you made a deal with the devil."

Lionel cleared his throat and shot Eli a casual glance. He appeared relaxed, but Eli could feel the intensity behind his friend's facade. The heat was rising.

"There is no urgency to act on Mr. Sanchez's request," Eli chimed in, forcing nonchalance into his voice. "There are over fifty requests for pardon on the president's desk, and I'm sure there will be more. These things take time."

Chet smirked at Eli. "The only request that the press or the country cares about is Nester Alejandro Sanchez's. The biggest criminal in New Mexico since Billy Bonney rode with his regulators."

"Ah yes, the Beast," Eli said, rolling his eyes. "The Godfather of the Southwest."

"The King of the Four Corners," the vice president joined in with a chuckle. "I agree with EJ. There's no urgency to this request."

Eli glared at the man, who sat with his hands in his lap and a shit-eating grin on his face. Sanford Hickock Yancey IV. The heir to the Yancey oil conglomerate. The ex–Texas governor had as much money as Bill Gates. *If only he had a tenth of his brains.*

Yancey had dominated Lone Star politics for a decade. His grandfather had dined with LBJ, and some said his father had been a living, breathing J. R. Ewing.

Unfortunately, the vice president's only similarity with his distinguished ancestors was his name. But he'd ridden that for all it was worth. Through the Texas state senate and all the way to the governor's chair. And due to good advisers and sheer luck, the economy in the Lone Star State was as strong as it had ever been. Yancey knew how to give a stump speech, and he looked the part of the strong, affable Texan. As a running mate for Lionel, he was a no-brainer, locking up critical electoral votes in one of the biggest states in the Union, clinching success where the Yancey name meant the most.

But, despite all that, among the power brokers of Washington, he was considered to be a first-rate moron. His support for Eli's position served only to weaken it.

"Well, thank you, Mr. Vice President," Chet Michaels said, the smirk never leaving his face. "Mr. President, there is no universe where you should consider Nester Sanchez's request for a pardon. Deny it now, and you'll seem strong and cut all these rumors at the root."

"Anybody else have a take?"

A woman cleared her throat and spoke with a throaty drawl. "All due respect to the attorney general, the chief, and the vice president, but I think there are more pressing concerns than a farmer's pardon request." Austill Baker, the secretary of state, had crossed her arms and glared at each of the men before studying Lionel. "Mr. President, we need to talk about our position with respect to the ongoing conflict in the Middle East, particularly in Iran. The Joint Chiefs are recommending that we increase our presence, but I think a diplomatic mission is the first step." Baker spoke with command, and Eli sensed the mood in the room shifting. She'd effectively changed the subject, and she was right. Nester Sanchez's request for a pardon, while a big deal to Chet Michaels, was penny-ante compared to the Middle East.

Eli saw that Michaels was staring at him, but he ignored him. Eli knew the attorney general would not quit with his agenda: Nester Sanchez must be stopped.

How will we ever be able to keep our pardon promise? Eli wondered, feeling a chilly wave of anxiety run through him. *And what will happen if we don't?*

———

Once the other cabinet members had filed out of the Oval Office, Lionel took the seat next to Eli. "How'd it go at MD Anderson?"

Eli shrugged. "She's in the middle of a trial now. Two and a half more weeks. They say it's worked in twelve percent of patients to reduce lung tumors." He rubbed the back of his neck. "But it won't cure her."

Lionel said nothing, but he patted Eli's knee. "Hang in there, buddy."

"How are you doing?" Eli asked, squinting at his friend. "You look . . . great. Weight seems to be coming back. Have you had any more treatment?"

Lionel shook his head. "Haven't needed it. The doctor says that the cancer is stable, and he's just going to watch it now. Scans every so often, but that's it. He says I've been very fortunate and that, based on the lack of growth or spread, my prognosis has improved."

Eli continued to peer at the president. Then he slapped his back. "That's great, man. If anyone deserves a break, it's you."

"Thank you, I . . ." Lionel trailed off before finally sighing. "I wish there was something I could do."

Eli started to ask if Lionel had ever inquired about new treatments from the FDA but decided against it. *He would tell me if there were something helpful.* Then, an odd, almost inconceivable doubt crept into his mind. *Would he?*

"You've already done plenty," Eli finally said, rising to his feet. "Thank you for keeping things quiet."

Lionel had granted him a personal leave of absence, but nothing else had been said or leaked to the cabinet or Congress. Eli figured they were all probably curious, and he suspected that many were hoping for the worst. Eli was a polarizing figure in politics. That's why he could never have been a candidate himself. A man like him could have any variety of ailments that could lead to "personal leave."

Divorce? Of course that was possible, given the rumors circulating about his relationship with SK Moss.

A stint in rehab? Almost probable, given Eli's family history and his past exploits.

Health problems for him or a family member? Also possible, but not nearly as sexy or interesting.

Eli trudged toward the door.

"Let me know if there is anything else I can do," Lionel called after him.

Eli turned, wondering when he would confront the president with what he'd learned.

Not until I know for sure, Eli thought. He was still waiting on Foncie. Her last text to the burner phone said she was close, but she still didn't have all the pieces.

As he peered across the most powerful office in the world at his old friend, Eli felt a tightness in his chest as more doubts flooded his mind. He had to wonder: *Does Lionel know the truth?*

Or is the truth that there are a bunch of unsubstantiated rumors?

Eli took a deep breath and forced a smile. "Will do."

23

Foncie James wanted a drink.

Whiskey. Gin. Vodka. Hell, a lukewarm PBR. It didn't matter. She felt a powerful urge and was having a hard time quelling it.

Frank had driven her to drink because he couldn't get through a meal without alcohol. Her ex-husband was still a practicing drunk, and, if she had to guess, he was probably lifting longnecks and chasing strange pussy at AJ's Lounge in Destin at this very moment.

Foncie had given up booze twenty years ago and divorced Frank some five years after that. She was seventy-one years old, now, and the phrase "too old for this shit" had never seemed more appropriate. But here she was. Eating DORITOS and drinking Dr Pepper with Alanis by-God Morissette blaring out of the car radio. Her eyes glued to a damn booth in a damn Whataburger.

She was in Niceville, Florida, about forty-five miles from the gulf coast. The town didn't seem to match the gentility of its name. Especially not at 10:00 p.m. on a Wednesday night in the parking lot of one of the few places still open for business.

Foncie did want a drink but wouldn't allow herself one. Her granddaughter had cancer, and the woman in the booth closest to the bathroom might have information about the cure.

It was crazy. But, hell, everything she had learned since her son's visit two weeks ago had been nutty, if not downright scary.

From the parking lot, Foncie squinted as the woman in the booth got up to go the bathroom. The man with her also exited, leaving out the side door nearest the drive-through. He walked . . . no, strolled . . . to a pickup truck parked in the back. A minute later, the woman navigated the same path. She carried a drink with her and stumbled twice on her way to the truck. She climbed into the passenger seat, and for several minutes, the two sat there talking. Then the woman leaned toward the man, and her head disappeared beneath the steering wheel.

"Oh, good grief," Foncie muttered. Apparently, the woman didn't have enough cash to close the deal and was resorting to other methods. "I don't have time for this shit."

Foncie glanced at the burner phone she'd been using to keep up with Eli. He'd sent her another text an hour ago.

Anything? The message had said. She could sense her son's desperation. She was so close to having something tangible, and she was convinced this woman could tell her. Alas, her efforts so far had been futile.

Foncie reached into the glove compartment of her Ford Mustang and pulled out a GLOCK 43x handgun. It had been a while since she'd been to the range, and the gun felt foreign in her hand.

I'm not going to shoot anyone. Just gonna scare them.

She glared at the truck, where the man had clasped his hands at the back of his head, clearly enjoying his payment for whatever brain-killing substance he was about to give the youngest and only surviving daughter of Mary Frances Bruce.

Foncie stuffed the gun into the front of her jeans and stepped out of the 'Stang. She spat on the concrete and breathed in the smell of ground beef and onions. "All right, then," she whispered. "Fuck it."

Candace Bruce had been called Candy since she was a little girl. It was a nickname her mother bestowed upon her, and she'd liked it, early on. Later, like everything in her miserable life, she'd started to resent it.

She wondered what her mother would think of her now. Candy Bruce, the honor student, most school spirit, Mu Alpha Theta, student government vice president who went to Alabama and pledged KD just like her mother, married a wealthy trust-fund kid, and bought a house two miles down the road from her parents. How did that person end up sucking the medium-hard dick of a drug dealer in the parking lot of a Whataburger in exchange for two grams of methamphetamine?

A lot of reasons went into it, and Candy used to think about them. Not being able to have children. The trust running dry. Her husband leaving her for a younger, more fertile woman.

My mother being murdered . . .

Candy had tortured herself for several years with these types of thoughts. Entertained some therapy. Even went to rehab after she got hooked on Xanax.

And those were "the good old days," compared to her life now. She'd been introduced to meth by an old high school friend. It was cheaper and more potent than anything she'd ever tried to kill the pain. The meth took everything away. It was a complete escape. Her failed marriage, inability to bear a child, and the questionable decisions she'd made after her mother's death all went away.

All replaced by the haze of meth. The inhibition. The bliss of being on a cloud of energy, far away from her mess of a life.

Sex in exchange for the product was nothing new to her. She'd done it so many times now, the fact that she was prostituting herself didn't even register anymore.

There was no shame. No anger at herself. No nothing.

There was only the buzz . . . and the restless desperation she felt every time the high ended.

The fact that this man's penis tasted and smelled like ass made no difference to her. She worked her mouth faster, anxiety fueling her pace. When his hand moved up her skirt and touched her, she barely felt it.

135

But she did feel the cold gust of wind when the passenger door swung open.

"What the—?"

"Shut the fuck up." The woman's voice was harsh and mean. It was also familiar. Candy lifted her head out of her dealer's lap and looked to the open door.

The woman had solid white, frizzy hair covered with a mesh camouflage cap. She pointed a pistol at the dealer.

"Kendall Jerome Schmidt," the woman said, spitting on the dash. "Niceville's foremost meth peddler. Also, judging by the sag in your britches, owner of a ridiculously unimpressive dick." The woman glanced at Candy. "Jesus, girl, you must be hard up as all hell." She reached into her jacket and pulled out a wad of cash, flinging it at Kendall. "I'm assuming that will buy all the poison you have on ya."

"Yes, ma'am," the dealer said, gathering up the bills and zipping his pants.

"Give the drugs to my friend here, and then she's coming with me." The woman pulled Candy out of the truck, and her feet landed awkwardly on the pavement, causing her to fall on her bottom.

"Hey!" Candy yelled, but then she looked down the barrel of the handgun.

"Don't test my patience, cum lips. I need you too bad to kill you, but I'm tempted. Just making me have to witness you sucking this turd's pecker is an emotional scar that all the shrinks at Bryce Hospital won't fix. *Go!*" She waved the gun toward the front of the restaurant.

Candy walked a few steps away and then watched. Her heart was pounding in her chest, and she was freezing. All she had on was a skirt and a tank top.

"Well, dickless," the old woman said. "You're having the best night of your miserable life. Now, hand over the goods and do it fast. I don't want to have to smell you any more than absolutely necessary." She shot a glance at Candy. "Seriously, dude, if his outer stinks this bad, I can't imagine the foulness of his inner."

Candy watched as the woman took the drugs from the place Kendall had dropped them on the seat. She put them in her jacket and then pointed the gun again at the dealer. Candy caught sight of Kendall now. His face was pale. Sweat edged around his neck. He was in shock.

"I'm kidnapping Candy, so don't hold this against her. In fact, based on the windfall I just gave you and the fact that you're not dead, you should be grateful to her." The old woman spat again into the cab of the truck and took two steps back, still pointing the pistol at the dealer. "Fuck off."

———

Foncie's heart was pounding as she escorted her hostage to the 'Stang.

"Get in," she said, digging the gun into Candy's neck and pushing her into the passenger seat.

She walked around the front of the car, keeping the GLOCK aimed at Candy's head, but she knew the girl wasn't going anywhere.

Not until she gets her fix, Foncie thought, feeling the baggies of meth in her jacket pocket with her elbow.

She opened her door and sat down. "There's a sweatshirt in the back seat if you're cold."

"Fuck you," Candy said.

Foncie chuckled, reaching into her pocket for one of the baggies. "I'm guessing you don't want any of this."

Candy said nothing and crossed her arms over her chest.

"We're going to take a little drive, Candace," Foncie said. "I trust you aren't going to make any trouble for me. After all, I just brokered you a much better meth deal than the one you were working on."

Candy didn't look at her, but finally she sighed. "What do you want?"

"You know damn well what I want. This is the third time that I've tried to talk to you in the past two days. You've blown me off the other two, but something tells me you're gonna cooperate this time."

"Why? Are you going to kill me?"

"No, Candy dear, I'm not. What I'm going to do is hold this meth until you can't take it anymore."

Silence filled the Mustang as Foncie set her pistol down in her lap and pulled a pack of cigarettes from the center console. She'd managed to quit drinking, but she still needed a smoke occasionally. Especially when she was knee-deep in an investigation.

Since she was in the process of holding a witness at gunpoint for the first time in her life and had just committed multiple felonies, she figured now was as good a time as any for an unfiltered Camel. "Want one?"

"Sure," Candy said.

Foncie lit her cancer stick and then Candy's. The irony of this situation floated into her head. Her granddaughter had lung cancer and had never smoked anything in her life. Foncie had been a three-pack-a-day inhaler for twenty years and now managed on a pack every two months. "Fuck it," she whispered, putting the car in drive and pulling out of the parking lot.

"What?" Candy said.

Foncie rolled down the windows, and frigid air blew into the car.

"Are you nuts?" Candy screamed, reaching for the sweatshirt she'd initially refused.

"What do you think?" Foncie growled, as they passed a green sign indicating that Destin was thirty-five miles away.

Fuck it all to hell.

24

Dale James covered her ears. She wanted to scream but knew it wouldn't do any good. In the bathroom of the on-campus apartment at MD Anderson, Bella continued to throw up.

For a while, Dale had stood behind her daughter, patting her back, making sure she drank water in between heaves. But Bella had finally yelled for her to leave.

So now Dale lay on the bed and stared up at the ceiling. The television was tuned to the news, but Dale wasn't listening. All she could hear were her daughter's wails. The vomiting and coughing were bad enough.

But it was the girl's crying that sank a dagger in Dale's heart.

She forced herself off the bed and snatched her phone from the desk. "Honey, do you—?"

The bathroom door opened, and Bella shuffled out. Her eyes were cast down at the floor, but Dale still saw the tears that streaked the girl's cheeks. In the glow of the fluorescent overhead light, Bella's face was pale. Sickly.

She's dying.

Dale shook her head, trying to force the ridiculous thought out of her mind. Bella was having an adverse reaction to the trial medication she was taking. Nausea was the primary side effect, and she'd been afflicted with it all afternoon and into the night.

"Do you need anything?" Dale finished her question. "Sprite? Water? Crackers?"

Bella didn't answer. She lay on the other double bed and curled her body up into the fetal position. Eventually, Dale heard sniffles, and the dagger dug into her heart again.

How many pounds had Bella lost in the two weeks since they'd been in Houston? Yesterday, it had been twelve, but after all the vomiting she'd done today, it was probably north of fifteen.

Is any of this worth it? Dale wondered, gazing around the small confines of the room. The accommodations were fine, but after fourteen days, the cramped nature of the quarters had become claustrophobic.

At least Eli is gone . . .

She glared at the worn carpet and crossed her arms tight across her chest. As her daughter continued to convulse, Dale let her mind drift to her husband's batshit conspiracy theory. There was no way. No *fucking* way. Eli was a smart man. A critical thinker. He hadn't guided Lionel Cantrell's career from the outhouse to the penthouse by following flights of fancy. He'd done it with brains and balls. By seeing things as they actually were. Not as he wished them to be.

He can't really *believe there's a cure for cancer . . .*

It's madness. Insanity. Beyond comprehension.

And yet . . . she wanted so badly to believe it too.

The morning after they arrived in Houston, while Bella was going through her first treatment, Eli took Dale to a nearby Waffle House. As bacon and eggs sizzled on a skillet behind the counter and the overpowering scent of coffee filled the air, he'd told her about SK Moss's "man from Mobile," Senator Chad Wiggins's postulations that the government might be hiding the cure for cancer, and, finally, about the woman his father had treated and who'd been cured after taking the miracle pill, only to be killed in a hit-and-run accident soon after.

A cold sweat had broken out on her neck as Eli had laid it all out, concluding that his mother was investigating the Mary Frances Bruce angle and that, if there were something to these rumors, Foncie would find it.

Dale had reluctantly accepted the burner phone he'd bought for her and told him that she'd keep an open mind . . . but she was worried. Eli's eyes, voice, and mannerisms reeked of intensity bordering on obsession. They also reflected something more primal. Something Dale herself felt more and more each day.

Desperation . . .

She glanced up from the carpet to the other bed, where Bella's chest continued to heave. She muted the television and closed her eyes. The girl's soft crying was the only sound in the tiny room.

Before leaving for DC, Eli offered to put them up at a nice hotel. They had the money. Why live like this?

"Because cancer doesn't give a shit," Dale had said then and thought again now. Rich or poor. Good or evil. Man or woman. Black, white, Asian. Hetero, homo, or trans. It didn't make a damn bit of difference.

Dale gritted her teeth and forced her voice to sound strong. "Honey, I'm going to go outside and get some air. Do you want to come?"

"No," Bella croaked.

"Okay. Be right back." Dale took a step forward, wanting to comfort her daughter, but stopped in her tracks. What comfort could she provide? Bella was sick. More from the medication now than the cancer.

Dale couldn't help but recall a deposition from a few years back. It was the husband of a woman who had died of breast cancer. The allegation in the lawsuit was that the disease should have been seen and reported to them over two years earlier than it was. The ultrasound and biopsy had shown cancer, but the chain of communication broke down, and the patient was never told.

The case was resolved before trial, but it was the man's deposition that haunted Dale now. She'd asked him to describe her treatment at UAB after learning the news. The husband had started out simply regurgitating the information. Radiation. Chemo. Loss of hair. Lost weight. Lost appetite. It was the same spiel he'd probably told a hundred friends and family members who had asked. But he'd finally lost his composure. The heat of a deposition could do that to a person. The nerves became frayed. Mouth dry. Eyes bloodshot from stress and lack of sleep. He hadn't even been looking at her, but instead the wall behind her. Dale remembered videoing the deposition and instantly regretting that decision when she saw and felt the man's hurt. *"The cancer didn't kill her. I mean, I guess it technically did. But she died long before her heart stopped beating. The treatment killed her. While poisoning the bad stuff in her, it killed all the good stuff."* He had paused then, and the sob that escaped him caused spittle to ooze out of the corner of his mouth. *"It killed her spirit. She was nothing but a shell at the end."* Then he'd lowered his eyes and glared at Dale. *"No one should have to go through that."*

The case had settled the next week for low seven figures, and Dale had moved on to the next.

Now, as she watched her daughter struggle to breathe, she thought of the husband from that deposition.

Had he moved on?

———

The complex had a courtyard, and Dale sat on a bench looking at dormant grass and dead flowers. The cold air was a refreshing change from the stuffy room. Dale took out a mini bottle of Kendall-Jackson pinot grigio. *Only the good stuff,* she thought but didn't chuckle or even smile at the poor attempt at humor. She took a long sip straight from the bottle and finally looked at her phone.

She scrolled through the mass of emails, texts, and missed calls, knowing that she would never be able to return them all. The office had put an auto-response on her email, but that hadn't stopped clients from trying to get to her. She owed the firm an update. Bella's treatment was set to last almost two and a half more weeks. By that point, Dale would have been gone from work for a *month*.

Lawyers were not known for patience. How long would they let her stay gone before giving an ultimatum? She'd asked for six weeks and been given a month.

I don't care, she thought. *All that matters now is Bella.*

Dale continued to scroll until she saw the missed call.

She knew she couldn't ignore him. She'd promised, in fact, in her answering machine message, that she would be available to him.

She hovered her thumb over his name but then clicked her phone off.

He might just want to console me. I'm sure that's what it is . . .

But as Dale crossed her arms to ward off the cold, she knew it was never that simple with Nester.

25

Eli waited until he saw Sarah Kate Moss exit the building to get out of his car. A light rain was falling, and SK was walking fast down the sidewalk with her jacket pulled up to cover her hair. Eli trotted toward her and opened his umbrella.

"Can we talk?" he asked, taking her elbow with his free hand.

"Eli . . ." Her voice was breathless, and he wasn't sure if it was because she was winded from walking fast or from fear at being accosted by him.

"Please, SK. I know I've put you in an awkward spot, but you were right. There *was* a man from Mobile, and he did come up with a miracle medication. And one of his customers ended up dead."

She stopped walking as they reached an intersection.

"Eli, please let me go. You're hurting me."

He relinquished his grasp and let out a deep breath. "I'm sorry. I just need something more from you."

"I've told you everything I know."

"A name, SK. I need the name of the man from Mobile."

She peered at him and leaned closer. So close that he could smell her fruity fragrance. Her brown eyes conveyed anxiety and concern. "I've told you everything I know."

"How far does the cover-up go? Beyond pharma and the FDA?"

She shook her head. "I *never* said there was a cover-up. I don't know *what* there was. I've shared too much, Eli, and I'm scared. For you . . .

and for me. If there is some kind of conspiracy or cover-up, and the powers that be get wind of this . . ." She trailed off.

Eli glanced behind him. The sidewalk was crowded with people rushing to their cars or to hail cabs or Ubers to get out of the rain, which had picked up since he'd joined her. As the pedestrian sign changed from **DON'T WALK** to **WALK**, Eli placed his hand on her arm again, this time much gentler. "Please, SK. I need his name."

"I don't know it," she said. She crossed the street with Eli still covering them with the umbrella.

"I'm desperate. Bella isn't handling the trial well at MD Anderson. Her options aren't good, and she's fading fast."

As they reached the sidewalk, SK came to an abrupt stop. They were in front of Martin's Tavern, a popular watering hole among the political elite. "I'm meeting someone for drinks, Eli."

"Who?" he asked.

She glared at him, and her face flushed red. "None of your business."

Eli knew it was ridiculous for him to feel jealousy at a time like this, but it was there anyway. "A man?"

She bit her lip and crossed her arms, as the rain pelted the top of the umbrella. "I have to go. Take care of yourself."

He pressed the handle of the umbrella into her hand and stepped back and away from her. Now, he felt the cold rain digging into his head and neck. "Ditto," he said.

"Eli, I'm sorry."

But he was already walking away.

———

Eli was drenched by the time he got back to his car. He pulled the burner phone out and looked at it. There were no texts or missed calls from Mom. He dialed her number, and it rang six times before he gave up.

"Damnit," he whispered. Then he called Dale's burner.

"Hey," she answered, and Eli could hear the tears in her voice.

"What's wrong?" he asked.

"It's not working," she said. "It's just killing her."

"We have to give it time," Eli said, hating himself and knowing his words would not comfort her any more than they did him.

"Another two weeks of this mess and Bella is going to wither away. The nausea is just . . ." Her voice broke, and Eli grimaced.

"Don't quit, honey," he said. "We can't quit."

"I'm not *quitting*. I'm just venting to my husband, who is in Washington working while I take care of everything here."

"We agreed that it was pointless for us both to be there, and you know I'm working on something that could help Bella."

"Right. Your conspiracy theory." She sighed. "You're chasing windmills."

Eli closed his eyes. "I don't think so. Anyway, I'm not going to stop until I learn the truth. And I can't quit my job, Dale. I'm the chief of staff to the president."

"And I was one of the most powerful attorneys in Washington and Virginia. I took a leave of absence and am on the cusp of losing my law practice."

He opened his eyes. The rain was coming down so hard now that he could barely see out the windshield. "Look, I'm coming to Houston this weekend."

A long pause and then her voice, cold and firm. "Don't bother. We'll probably be home by then anyway."

"Dale—"

"I'd rather cancer kill her than this poison, do you hear me?"

Eli said nothing. For several seconds, the only sound on the phone was his wife's labored breathing. Then, as Eli said "Yes," the line went dead.

He set the burner down next to his smartphone and leaned back in his car seat. It was raining too hard for him to go anywhere.

Truth be known, he wasn't sure where to go. Home felt like a ghost town without Bella and Dale. His relationship with SK Moss was long over. The president was dining with representatives from the United Nations. Eli had endless paperwork to digest on his desk, but he wouldn't be able to focus.

He snatched the burner phone and again dialed his mother. Five more rings and no answer. Eli gripped tight to the device and held it to his chest. He tried to think.

What more can I do?

But he was stymied. He couldn't talk to anyone else without showing his hand, and he didn't know who, if anyone, he could trust. He gritted his teeth, feeling restless and on edge. How much time did they have left? He thought back to his wife's broken voice. *It's killing her . . .*

Eli sighed and looked out the window with a blank stare.

The rain showed no signs of letting up.

26

The two women sat in the front seat of the Mustang, windows rolled down, smoking unfiltered Camels. Despite the cool air, Foncie could smell the salt spray. She peered over the steering wheel at the dark waters of the gulf. They were in a mobile home park off Highway 98 between Destin and Panama City. It had taken an hour from Niceville to get here, and they'd made a stop.

A pint of George Dickel sat between them. Foncie had bought the liquor on the way, as Candy said she needed something to take the edge off. The last living relative of Mary Frances Bruce grabbed the bourbon and twisted off the top. She took a short sip, wincing as she swallowed. The cigarette dangled out of the corner of her mouth.

Foncie was withholding the meth until the woman told her everything. So far, Candy had registered nothing other than needing a drink and a smoke. Foncie could have pressed. Gotten aggressive. Made more threats. But she'd learned over her years as an investigator that sometimes time and space were better. Many times, people *wanted* to share their story. They just had to get in the right frame of mind. So, despite kidnapping Candy Bruce, Foncie had barely said a word since leaving the Whataburger in Niceville.

Foncie felt the burner phone vibrating in her jeans pocket and sighed. Eli had called twice, which either meant he'd learned something . . .

. . . or that he was being impatient.

Probably the latter, she thought. Then another idea popped into Foncie's mind that made her feel sad and bittersweet. *So much like his father . . .*

"Something wrong?" Candy asked, taking a long drag off the Camel and blowing smoke out the window.

"My son," Foncie said. "Let's just say patience isn't his best trait."

Candy snorted. "I've never known any man to have that quality."

"My son is different than most men," Foncie said. "He's waiting for something from me."

"Ah," Candy said. "And I'm assuming that whatever he's waiting for has something to do with me."

Foncie looked at the woman, who continued to stare out at the gulf. "For a meth head, you're smarter than you look."

Candy sipped the bourbon that she continued to hold in her left hand. "There was a time when . . ." She trailed off and blew more smoke out the window. "What does it matter?"

"It matters to me," Foncie said. "You see, my son's daughter, my granddaughter, has cancer. She has masses in both her lungs, and her doctors have given her a death sentence." Foncie hesitated and puffed on her own cigarette. *Now or never,* she thought. In her two prior conversations with Candy Bruce, she'd danced around the subject and gotten nowhere. *Ain't no time to dance now.* "My son believes that your mom had access to a medication that cured her cancer . . . and that she was murdered because of it."

Candy sucked in a breath but said nothing.

"I've investigated the police file and read the articles about your mother's death. She was run over by a dark sedan less than a mile from her home. *Your home.* It was seven thirty at night, so just past dusk in the summer. Her dog was also killed. It was a yellow Lab."

"Julio," Candy whispered, pressing the George Dickel to her lips. "Julio Jones Bruce. Mom was a huge Bama fan."

"Roll Tide," Foncie forced the words out of her mouth and tried not to vomit. While her ex-husband and only son were staunch Bama fans, Foncie bled orange and blue, and, after the Lord's Prayer, Foncie's favorite memorized lines were Auburn's creed, especially the last seven words: *I believe in Auburn and love it.*

Christ, the things we do for our children.

Candy smiled, but her face was sad. "I never cared much for football or the Alabama–Auburn rivalry. But Mom did. She loved that dog, and so did I."

"How old were you when it happened?" Foncie already knew this information, but it didn't hurt to keep her talking.

"Twenty-eight." Candy's voice was distant.

"You lived right down the street from your mom, didn't you? With your husband, Jack?"

Candy nodded and took another pull from the pint.

Foncie grimaced. The goal to keep her talking had backfired. "His name was Wilkins. Jack Wilkins. When did you change your last name back to Bruce?"

Candy blew smoke into the car, and Foncie almost admonished her but held her tongue. "About a year after the divorce. Just didn't want any reminders."

"Did he hurt you? Hit you? Cheat?" Foncie pressed.

"He didn't do any of those things," Candy said. "Jack was a good man. Not great, but solid. It wasn't his fault. We wanted a child, and I couldn't produce one. We had thought of adopting, but my mom and his parents discouraged it. *Keep trying,* they all said." She sighed. "I started drinking heavily and taking Xanax for anxiety. Jack tried to be supportive, but we eventually stopped trying. Then Mom died, and I just . . . quit." Tears formed in the corner of her eyes. "I quit everything. I went to rehab for the first time a little while later, but that only introduced me to more drugs." She took another hit from the cigarette. "Jack filed for divorce about a year later. I was thirty years old, and I'd lost every dream I ever had in life."

"What became of the police investigation of your mom's death?"

Candy shrugged. "They quit too. No leads. No evidence. It just . . . looked like a random accident."

"But it wasn't," Foncie offered, her voice soft. "Was it?"

"No," Candy said. "No way."

"The police file says that interviews were requested of you several times, and that you refused to answer questions. Why is that?"

Candy turned her head toward Foncie. Candy's eyes were red, her lips a grayish purple. When she'd laughed earlier, Foncie had noticed that she was missing some teeth. Methamphetamine was one of the worst drugs out there. Highly addictive and capable of as much damage as crack cocaine or narcotics. Meth was cheaper and easier to manufacture, which only compounded its devastation.

"How do you know that?" Candy asked. "No charges were ever filed. I was told that the file would be confidential."

"You were told wrong," Foncie said. Being an investigator in south Alabama for thirty years had yielded her plenty of contacts in the Mobile Police Department and the Baldwin and Mobile County sheriff's offices. "The file disappeared. There is no file."

"But you said—"

"I said I *investigated* the police file. My investigation revealed that it was gone. All my information comes from the articles . . . and from an old friend who agreed to talk with me on condition of anonymity."

"And your old friend said the file was gone."

Foncie nodded. "And that you would never agree to an interview." She flung what was left of her Camel out the window. "Now, I'm assuming the reason the file disappeared is the same as why you wouldn't meet with the police."

"Why would you assume that?"

"Because it makes sense, Candy. Did you know your mom had taken a drug that had made her cancer go away?"

She looked out the window and smoked.

"Candy, please. Did you know? Had you ever gone to the farmers' market in Gulf Shores with her? Did you see her buy medication from a man there that said his concoction could help shrink or cure her cancer?"

Candy took another sip of Dickel. When she spoke, her voice was low. Almost a croak. "Do you know how much danger you are in?"

"I know, Candy. And I don't care. My granddaughter's life is at stake."

Candy smirked. "Do you know how many hundreds of thousands of people have cancer? Your granddaughter is no different than anyone else."

The slap came faster than anything Foncie could have expected. All of a sudden, she saw her right hand twisting and moving with speed toward Candy's face. She connected with the woman's left cheek, and the sound reverberated in the Mustang. Candy dropped her cigarette out the window and yelped. She would have dropped the bourbon, but Foncie snatched it from her and slammed it down into the drink console.

Candy grabbed for the door handle, but Foncie was too fast. She placed the tip of the GLOCK's barrel on the woman's forehead. "I wouldn't do that. You see, *I'm* losing patience now. And you're a meth head that no one gives a damn about. I could blow your brains out and throw you into the gulf, and no one would ever give a rat's ass." Foncie smelled bourbon and Candy's stale scent. "I'm tired of playing. Did you know your mom was taking a medication that cured her cancer?"

"Yes," Candy said.

"How?"

"She told me. Hell, she told everyone. Momma liked her secrets, but her favorite saying was 'I probably shouldn't tell you this, but let me tell you anyway.'"

"Where did she buy it?"

"Like you said. The Gulf Shores farmers' market."

"Did you ever go with her?" Foncie removed the gun from Candy's forehead an inch but kept it pointed at the woman.

"Once," she said. "One time."

"Did you see the man who sold the cancer drug?"

"Yes."

"Describe him."

She sucked in a breath. "He was foreign. Not sure exactly how. Light-brown skin. Dark-black hair. A big man. Not fat, just large."

"Go on. What else do you remember?"

"Just that Mom acted weird around him . . . and that he was a bit unusual. His cart was in the back of the market. He advertised herbal remedies. Arthritis anti-inflammatory natural supplements and such. Mom said you had to know what to ask for if you wanted the . . . you know."

"The cure for cancer?"

"That's not what he called it."

"Oh, did he have some type of code name?"

"I can't remember that part. Just that there was a name of some kind."

"What about this man? Did he have a name?"

Candy blinked. "It was also unique. I can't remember the whole thing."

"What do you remember?"

Candy Bruce rubbed her bloodshot eyes. She glanced at Foncie, and her gaze registered a fear that had nothing to do with the gun being pointed at her. "What are you going to do with this?"

"Doesn't matter," Foncie said. "If you don't give it to me, you're gonna be swimming with the sharks."

"I don't believe you'll kill me."

"People will do crazy things for the ones they love," Foncie said. "I don't want to hurt you, but I don't have many options here." She again pressed the barrel on the woman's forehead. "What was his name?"

Tears slid down Candy's cheeks. "They made me promise not to tell."

"Who's *they*?"

"I don't know. I just . . . a couple of days after Mom's death, some men came to my house and said they were with National Security or something like that. They asked me a lot of the same questions that you have."

Foncie felt her stomach tighten. "What happened?"

"They gave me $250,000 and made me sign a nondisclosure agreement with respect to the man that Mom bought her medications from." She swallowed. "They also made me promise to not talk with the police about my mom's death."

Oh my God, Foncie thought, anger and exasperation rising within her. "Candy, didn't you think . . . didn't you know that these were the people who murdered your mom?"

"I didn't want to believe that. I thought maybe it was a coincidence. I was hard up for money. I just . . ." She trailed off and then let out an anguished sob.

Foncie dug the gun into Candy's temple until she yelped in pain. "Just do it," Candy said, her voice monotone. "Pull the trigger and end my misery."

Foncie shook her head. "I won't be doing you any favors. You said the men that paid you off said they were with National Security."

"Yes."

"Did they say anything else?"

"Just that the man from the farmers' market was a threat to the United States and they asked me to tell them everything I knew about him."

"Did you tell them his name?"

Candy wiped her nose and nodded. "Only what my mom called him."

"What did she call him?"

"I'm a dead woman walking the minute I tell you."

Foncie gritted her teeth. "You just asked me to blow your brains out. Seems like you're screwed either way." She leaned closer to the woman. "Come on, Candy, do a good deed. What did your mom call this man?"

Candy Bruce closed her eyes. "Mato," she said. "She called him Mato."

27

"Mato Nakai." Foncie whispered the name. They had driven from the beach to a Waffle House, and she had her laptop out on the booth's counter and a steaming cup of black coffee to the side of it.

"Does that sound right?"

Candy shrugged. "When am I gonna get the goods?" She pointed to Foncie's jacket, where she still kept the baggies of meth.

Foncie had been searching names and hit pay dirt within thirty minutes. A missing-persons notice in the classified ads of the Mobile *Press-Register*. The date of the article was July 18, 2017. Mary Frances Bruce had died three weeks earlier on the last week in June that year. *Maybe it took a while to find him . . . Could someone have tipped him off? Maybe after Mary Frances Bruce died in a suspicious accident, he went into hiding. Regardless . . .* She pointed at the article and sipped her coffee.

"This has to be him."

"Why are you talking to yourself?"

Foncie glared at the other woman. Candy was drunk and, by the looks of her twitchy neck and shaking hands, she was about to go into methamphetamine withdrawal.

"I'll be right back," Foncie said. She strode to the restroom and locked the door. She removed the packages of meth and poured the drugs out into the toilet. Then she flushed. She threw the containers into the garbage, and then she relieved herself.

Finally, after washing her hands, she pulled out the burner phone and dialed the number.

Eli answered on the first ring. "Mom?"

"Mato Nakai," she said. "That is our man from Mobile. Mato . . . Nakai." She spelled the name and told him she'd call him tomorrow. "Don't do anything stupid, son. Just sit tight and I'll check in with an update as soon as I know more."

"Why are you so sure it's him?" he asked.

"Because Mr. Nakai disappeared in July 2017. Three weeks after the murder of Mary Frances Bruce." She paused. "And because Ms. Bruce's daughter went to the Gulf Shores farmers' market with her mother, and she remembers that Mary Frances called her supplier 'Mato.' He had a name for his cancer drug, but she couldn't remember what it was."

Silence and then a whistling through teeth. "My God."

"And that's not even the worst of it." In a hoarse whisper, she told her son about the men from *National Security* who'd paid Candy Bruce a visit and a bunch of hush money. When she finished, Foncie looked at herself in the mirror, cringing at the wrinkles on her face and around her eyes. *I'm too old for this shit.*

There was silence on the other end of the burner.

"Son? You there?"

"I'm . . . here. I just . . . *can't believe it*. Candy Bruce was . . . *bribed?*"

"That's what she told me."

"Is she credible?"

"On the surface? No. She's a meth addict with a dump truck full of problems."

"But . . . do you believe her?"

Foncie again stared at her bloodshot eyes in the mirror. "Yes, I do. Every damn word."

For a few seconds, the only sound was his breath, which sounded ragged. Heavy. *He's in shock,* Foncie thought. *Join the frickin' club . . .*

"What are you going to do now?" Eli finally asked.

"Headed home to check on the horses, but I'll be back at it first thing in the morning, doing a deep dive on Mr. Nakai and trying to find any living relatives. Can you hold tight awhile longer? I've almost got it."

There was no answer.

"Eli?"

"Be careful, Mom," he breathed.

"You, too, son. We're swimming in dark water."

28

Eli clicked End and set the burner down on the table. A smile came to his face despite the chill he felt in his bones. *Swimming in dark water . . .* One of his mother's oldest sayings.

He glanced at the clock above the kitchen sink. It was just past one in the morning. How long had he sat in his car in downtown DC? Watching the rain fall and feeling completely lost.

He wasn't sure, but he didn't feel much better now that he was home. They had a name for the mystery man. And a witness who said she was bribed by men from *National Security*? That sounded a lot like federal operatives to Eli. Again, SK's cautionary question played in his mind: *"Do you know how powerful the Department of Defense is?"*

Jesus . . . Christ, Eli thought. They were getting closer to the truth. *Then what?*

Do we disappear like Mato Nakai? Or do we go the way of Mary Frances Bruce?

He stood and paced around the breakfast nook. The house was eerily silent. If the government was hiding the cure for cancer and they had killed Mary Frances Bruce and Mato Nakai . . .

What's going to happen to me? To Mom? To Dad? Dale and Bella?

Eli wanted to talk with Lionel. Needed to see his friend. Lionel would know what to do. My God, he was in the same boat. He had terminal cancer. Then he remembered their last conversation. Lionel's cancer had stabilized. His prognosis was improved. Not the same boat at all . . .

Eli stopped walking and peered down at the table. Paranoia had set in. Could his oldest friend already know about Mato Nakai's cure? Eli was chief of staff, but that didn't mean he attended every meeting with the president. Far from it. Lionel had participated in many briefings with the top brass of major government departments without Eli present, including the DOD. *And I've been gone a lot . . .*

Eli rubbed his neck, which was covered with goose bumps, and thought about an old saying he'd heard once. Not his mother's, but it came to his mind in Foncie's voice:

You're not paranoid if they're really after you.

29

General Kyle Randolph had heard enough. He thanked his team leader for the information and terminated the call, which had been on speaker. Then he peered at the other two people in the room. "What do you think?" he asked.

Robert Bellamy cleared his throat and leaned his meaty forearms on the table. "Seems pretty obvious based on the bugs we have in Mr. James's kitchen. The man's gone rogue. He has made himself, and apparently his mother, a direct threat to the national security of the United States." Bellamy paused. "I don't see how we have a choice. We have to eliminate the threat."

Randolph moved his eyes to the director of the FBI. "How about you?"

Beth McGee released a deep sigh. "General, I agree in principle with what Robert said. But we are talking about the chief of staff to the president of the United States. Lionel Cantrell's best friend and the only person who knows that the president is dealing with his own cancer diagnosis. This . . . is a delicate situation. I would not say that Mr. James has gone rogue . . . yet. He is investigating a tip he received from someone, and it's pretty obvious who that must have been."

Randolph nodded. "Agreed. However, his inquiry has gotten a lot farther than anyone else who's looked into it. As Robert pointed out, the recordings make it clear that his mother spoke with Candace Bruce last night."

"She's a topflight PI who has helped her son and Lionel for years dig up dirt on other politicians and foils. I'm not at all surprised that she got this far. But what does that mean? Even if she has the name of Mato Nakai, how can she or Mr. James use it?"

"We paid Ms. Bruce off," Randolph barked. "She signed an NDA. Her disclosures to Ms. James, whatever they may be, violate our agreement."

"And are a direct threat to national security," Bellamy added.

"Gentlemen, we can't just eliminate the mother of the chief of staff to the president. And certainly not the chief of staff himself."

"Why not?" Bellamy asked her. "Given what's at stake."

"Because," she said, pursing her lips, "I'm not sure we want to poke the bear here. Seems like a diplomatic tactic might work better. Eli James is a political survivor. If he knew his career hung in the balance, then perhaps he would back off."

Bellamy snorted. "You really think Eli James is a bear. He doesn't have any real power. It's all attached to Cantrell. He has little in the way of family or friends. If an accident were to befall him, I doubt anyone in DC would give a damn."

"I think someone in New Mexico might," McGee snapped. "Especially if something happened to Mrs. James."

Bellamy rolled his eyes. "Give me a break."

"Desperate times call for desperate measures," McGee said. "I think you should talk to Mr. James, General. Assure him that the rumors his mother may have uncovered are just that. Rumors. Another ridiculous conspiracy theory with a little smoke but no fire. If he pushes you, tell him the FDA tested the drug developed by Mato Nakai, and it had no more therapeutical value than a placebo."

"What about Candace Bruce's disclosure of the payoff?"

"I think you can chalk that up to the absurd ramblings of a person with a serious drug problem. She was hooked on Xanax and alcohol then, and our sources say she's worse off now."

Randolph rubbed his chin. "You think James will back off?"

"No," Bellamy said. "But, unless Lionel Cantrell has an attack of conscience, I don't see how he can hurt us. Screaming conspiracy with Candace Bruce as his eyewitness will make him look like a fool."

"*Exactly,*" McGee said. "General, the key here is the president. As long as the president doesn't disclose anything to his best friend, there is no way that Eli James can hurt us without crippling his own political career."

"What if he doesn't care about that anymore?" Randolph asked. "What if his daughter's diagnosis changed him?"

McGee smirked. "A tiger doesn't change his stripes. Eli James is no martyr."

"All right. I don't think we act on Mr. or Mrs. James," Bellamy said. "At least not yet. But Candace Bruce and James's parents are fair game. All three are expendable."

McGee said nothing, and Randolph knew her silence was acquiescence. "I think there's someone closer to home who needs to hear from us as well," the general added. "A certain lobbyist who needs a lesson in keeping her mouth shut."

McGee and Bellamy remained quiet.

Silence is acquiescence, Randolph thought again.

30

Foncie made one stop on the way home.

"You've got to be kidding," Candy said.

"This place will help you," Foncie said, staring at the sign on the building, which read **Pensacola Recovery Center**.

"I gave you what you asked," Candy said. "Now give me the meth."

"I flushed the drugs down the toilet of the Waffle House," Foncie said, digging into her purse and bringing out a wad of cash. She placed the money in Candy's lap. "That ought to get you in the door. If you need more . . . and you will . . . call this number." Foncie gave her the number to her office landline at home.

Candy gazed out the windshield. "And what if I take this money, get me an Uber, and spend the rest on meth?"

"It's a free country," Foncie said. "You've helped me, Candy. At great risk to yourself. I'm just trying to do the same for you. You're an addict, and the PRC . . ." Foncie pointed at the door. ". . . is an excellent place to start over."

"How would you know?" Candy asked, her voice bitter.

Foncie turned and glared at the other woman. "Because I've had my own struggles . . . and the people here helped me."

Candy said nothing. Her bottom lip began to tremble.

"All right then," Foncie said, patting her knee. "Go on. Good luck to you."

Candy sighed. "Well . . . thanks, I guess."

Once the door was shut, Foncie put the car in gear and eased out of the parking lot. Her last image of Candy Bruce was of her standing and gazing at the front door of the Pensacola Recovery Center.

———

An hour later, Foncie saw the green sign indicating FAIRHOPE CITY LIMITS. She was ready to be home. She needed a shower and to see her horses. Most of all, she needed to rest. Exhaustion had crept in on the way home, and she was having a hard time keeping her eyes open.

She planned to sleep for four hours, go for a morning ride, and then do a deep dive into the life of Mato Nakai. Perhaps he had surviving relatives that knew of the miracle drug. An old friend? A day job? There had to be something. She'd come too far to lose the scent now. She pulled into her garage and glanced at the clock on the dash. It was 3:09 a.m.

I am definitely too old for this shit.

She clicked off the ignition and opened the door. Her legs felt wobbly as she got out of the Mustang. It wasn't until she was standing that she realized what was wrong.

She always left one of the two overhead lights on in the garage when she departed the house. She tried to alternate, so as not to burn out both of them, but she always turned one of them on.

Foncie didn't like to enter the house in the dark.

She reached for the GLOCK, but it wasn't there. She'd put it back in the glove compartment after dropping Candy off. She grabbed the door handle but felt cold steel on her neck.

"Ms. James, I'm not here to hurt you, but I will if you force my hand."

Damnit, Foncie thought. She was so close. She should have been watching her back.

"Who are you?" she asked, keeping her voice calm. She knew she could elbow him, but she wasn't sure if he was alone.

"A friend," he said. "I know what you've been doing, and you are in grave danger."

"You're going to have to do better than that, *friend*," Foncie said, turning full on to face the man. In the dark, it was hard to see anything but his black hair.

"My name is Jalen Nakai. Mato Nakai . . . was my father."

31

Sarah Kate Moss kept a gun in the top drawer of her bedside table. When she heard the doorbell ring, her first instinct was to check for the weapon. Then she checked her alarm clock.

It was 4:30 in the morning. Her alarm wouldn't go off for another thirty minutes. She climbed out of the bed and threw on a robe. Then she grabbed the handgun and walked toward the front door.

"Who is it?" she asked.

"SK, it's Thad Raleigh. Please let me in."

Thad? What could the commissioner of the FDA want with her at this hour? And what could possibly warrant an in-home visit?

SK felt cold and vulnerable in her pajamas and robe. Still, she opened the door a crack and saw Thad's grim face. Behind him, she recognized another face. It was Robert Bellamy, the former director of Homeland Security. SK let the door fall open, and she took several steps backward.

Jesus Christ, she thought, as Thad and Bellamy entered her apartment followed by three others, two men and a woman, all of whom were wearing dark suits and grave expressions.

SK led them into the kitchen. "Coffee?"

"No, thanks," Bellamy said, his tone gruff. "Ms. Moss, we have reason to believe that you may have disclosed information that has endangered the national security of the United States."

SK sank into her seat. Eight hours ago, Eli James was placing the handle of his umbrella into her hand, effectively ending their relationship. She'd then had drinks with a political staffer for a senator from Kansas. He'd been cute and she'd given him her number. She'd checked the box of being seen out with a man other than Eli. *Moving on,* she had thought . . .

"That's preposterous," SK said, forcing strength into her voice. "What's this about?"

"SK," Thad said, taking a seat next to her and leaning an elbow on the table. "We know you are close with the chief of staff . . . Mr. James."

"So what? My professional relationship with the chief of staff has been *very* beneficial to my employer."

"I know," Thad said. "I know that. This isn't about your job, SK."

"Ms. Moss, Bella James, the daughter of the chief of staff, has cancer. We are concerned that you may have disclosed classified information regarding cancer trials and treatment to Mr. James."

"Why would you think that?"

"We aren't the ones answering questions, Ms. Moss. You are. Now, what have you told Mr. James?"

"Thad, this is ridiculous."

But the FDA head stood and walked away. Bellamy took his place in the seat next to her. When he spoke, his breath was bitter. "Ms. Moss, this is a very serious situation, and we need your cooperation. We've been led to believe that you have, in fact, provided Mr. James with classified information. If that is true, then you are guilty of violating federal law."

SK felt her heart beating fast in her chest.

"And we know your and Mr. James's relationship was a bit more than professional. So why don't you cut the crap and tell us what you've told him." He paused. "Then we can decide whether to arrest you."

"I'd like to speak to an attorney," she said.

Bellamy leaned back in his chair. "It would be a lot easier if you just cooperated."

SK looked past him, but she didn't see Thad Raleigh anymore.

"He's gone. And if he's ever asked, he'll deny ever being present for this meeting."

"What about the video cameras outside the building?"

"The manager will find that they are not currently operational."

SK bit her lip to keep it from trembling. "Are you threatening me?"

"Call it whatever you want, Ms. Moss. But I'm not leaving here until you tell me everything you have told Eli James."

"And what if I won't talk? I have rights." Her voice cracked on the last syllable.

"I think you'll find that when a matter is deemed to involve national security, we have a certain amount of . . . leeway . . . that we don't have in other matters." His eyes didn't waver as they bored into hers. "Now, were you aware that the chief of staff's daughter was diagnosed with cancer?"

SK peered down at the table. "Yes."

"And did Mr. James ever ask you about cancer treatment or anything to do with cancer?"

SK closed her eyes and nodded. "Yes."

32

Foncie packed a travel bag while Jalen Nakai scoped the rest of the house.

"How much time do we have?" she asked.

"I learned about your investigation earlier today. I'm assuming they already know."

"They?"

"The people who killed Mary Frances Bruce . . . my father . . ." He sighed. "And many others."

"Suffering pooch," Foncie managed, blinking as adrenaline flooded her body. She knew it was possible that this man was wrong. Paranoid after losing his father. She could wait things out. Would "they" really kill the mother of the chief of staff to the president? She pulled out her burner phone, realizing that questioning Jalen Nakai's paranoia was hypocritical, given the steps that she and Eli had already taken to hide what they were doing. She zipped up her bag and stood. Her legs felt stronger, her mind calming. She thought of Candace Bruce's story. The payout the woman had received after her mother's suspicious death. Was it over the top for her to be running with the son of Mato Nakai?

Hell no, she thought, as she tiptoed toward her kitchen.

The house was dark. She had not turned on any lights at his direction. Now, as she walked around her sparse accommodations with the duffel bag draped over her shoulder, she wondered if she'd ever see this place again.

My horses . . .

"What's our plan?" she asked, not seeing him but feeling his presence somewhere close.

"I parked a half mile away. You have a neighbor with a barn close to the road. I pulled my car behind it."

"So, we go on foot to your vehicle?"

"Unless you have a better plan. I'm a cop, but I can't say I know this area very well."

"You're a *cop*?"

She heard him suck in a breath and could feel his frayed nerves. "Yes. Biloxi PD."

Foncie let out a breath she was holding. "That barn belongs to the Rowes. They're friends of mine. We can leave out the back of my house, and there's a grove of trees that we can follow almost to the road. The last few hundred yards are over a weedy clearing."

"Okay. Makes sense."

"There's one stop I need to make on the way."

"Ma'am, we don't have time—"

"I don't care. You're welcome to leave at any time. I didn't ask you to come save me, and for all I know, you may have led 'they,' whoever the hell 'they' are, right to my freakin' doorstep." She poured herself a glass of water from the sink and took a long sip. Her throat was dry, but her mind was clear. "One stop, and it'll be quick."

———

Five minutes later, Foncie stood in the stable next to Winston. The horse was a brownish red Thoroughbred that she'd purchased eleven years ago. Arthritis had set in over the past couple of years, so their rides had gotten shorter. His life was nearing its end, and Foncie knew that she wouldn't be too far behind.

Or ahead, she thought, as she glanced behind her to the stall door and to the man standing guard by the door. She whispered into her boy's ear, telling him that Hannah Rowe would be watching over him now and that she'd take good care of him.

Foncie would leave word for Hannah tomorrow that she was taking a lengthy trip.

She wiped a tear, knowing that this wasn't a trip. She peered around the stables, which were her favorite place on earth. The only place where the world made perfect sense.

"I'll see you at the end of the Rainbow Bridge, big boy," she said, kissing his cheek. "And if you get there first, I'll come running, you hear?" She stroked his neck and walked outside.

"Ready?" Jalen asked.

Foncie James pulled the GLOCK out of her jacket. "As a bride on her wedding day. Let's get on with it."

33

Eli rose early and went to the gym. Twenty-Four Hour Fitness was a bare-bones facility a mile from their house in Arlington. Eli averaged three workouts a week, even during difficult times, and since returning from Houston, he was off schedule.

After a full body-weight circuit and thirty minutes of interval training on the treadmill, he was drenched in sweat, but his muscles felt pumped and his mind engaged. When they'd first bought the home, Eli and Dale would go together, each doing their own thing. They'd come home and eat breakfast afterward, and when they were trying to have a baby, they'd end up in the bed after a quick joint shower.

"Sperm travels faster in the morning," Dale would say, and then, after they'd finished, she'd lie on her back with her legs pulled up, willing Eli's boys to swim even faster.

As he refilled his water bottle at the fountain, Eli couldn't help but smile at the memory. They'd tried so hard for so many years to have a baby.

But they'd been successful only once. Eli ground his teeth when he thought back to his conversation with Dale last night. *It's killing her . . .*

He ran his hand under the fountain and splashed the water on his face. Then he turned to see a man in a suit blocking his path.

"Mr. James, I need you to come with me."

"Who are you?"

"I'm General Kyle Randolph's administrative assistant. The general is waiting outside for you."

Eli wiped his face with a towel, trying to feign nonchalance. The former chairman of the Joint Chiefs of Staff and onetime secretary of defense wanted a word. No big deal. Eli was the chief of staff after all.

Eli took a pull from his bottle. "After you."

———

A couple of minutes later, Eli sat in the back of a Cadillac Escalade. The temperature inside the vehicle matched the cool of the morning air, and Eli's sweat had dried. When he breathed in, though, he smelled his own body odor. A mixture of bourbon, sweat, and morning breath. Not the most pleasing of aromas. But if the man sitting next to him was uncomfortable or irritated by the scent, he wasn't letting on.

General Kyle Randolph wore his green US Army uniform. Four silver stars adorned both sides of his collar. Eli wondered if he'd ever seen Randolph when he wasn't in uniform. The two men had spoken only a few times over the years, and Eli hadn't gotten the feeling that the general thought much of him.

"Mr. James, I'm glad to see you are starting your day with exercise," Randolph said.

"I'm glad that you approve," Eli said. "What's this about? Has something happened?"

"Mr. James, as you know, I still work closely with the Defense Department, and we've been given reports that you have done quite a bit of non-business-related traveling lately. To Mobile almost a month ago. Then to Houston with your wife and daughter."

Eli almost snapped "That's none of your business" but stopped himself. He was a public figure, right hand to the president. He was allowed a private life, but not much of one.

"We understand from the president that you are having some personal problems. Your daughter . . ." He trailed off, waiting for Eli to finish an answer he no doubt already knew. In the back of his mind, Eli again wondered about Lionel. All the meetings that Eli wasn't privy to.

"Bella has lung cancer," Eli said. "We've been seeking second opinions and treatment options. She is currently undergoing a trial in Houston."

Randolph made a tent with his hands. "I see. So . . . that's why you went to Mobile."

Eli held his eye. "Yes. My father is a physician. He is one of the finest ER doctors in the Southeast. Any time we ever had a health crisis, I've sought his counsel."

"I'm sorry," Randolph said. "Cancer is an awful condition. I can't imagine what you and your wife are going through."

Eli looked away. The sun was rising over the barren brick building. He glanced to the front seat to the clock on the dash. It was 5:45 a.m., and one of the most powerful humans in the world was talking to him about his daughter's health. Something was off here. Eli could feel both phones in the pockets of his joggers.

Been watching me, have you?

"You are obviously familiar with the president's history of cancer, aren't you?" Randolph's tone gave away nothing.

"Of course," Eli said. "I took Lionel to his chemo sessions back when he was in the Senate. He beat it . . . and now he's helping me with Bella."

"He is?"

"I mean, he's been supportive. Granting me leave to go with my wife to explore options."

"I see," Randolph said. "That's good." He paused. "Have you noticed anything different about the president's health in the past few months?"

"No," Eli lied. "He's lost a little weight, but that was planned." He forced a chuckle. "So he'd look better on TV."

"Right," Randolph said. He smiled, but there was no humor in his eyes. Like his tone, his gray irises gave away nothing. "Well, we just like to keep tabs on the cabinet. Your recent travels and activity have been a bit unusual, so I just wanted to personally check in on you." He again hesitated and turned to face Eli. "You are an important person, Mr. James. The president depends on you. By extension, so do the American people."

"Yes, sir," Eli managed, not sure what to say to that.

Randolph glanced up to the front seat and gave the driver a nod. Seconds later, Eli's door was being opened.

"Have a nice day, Mr. James."

"Thank you," Eli said, stepping out of the Cadillac and breathing in the fresh air. He turned to say something else, but the door was already closed. A second later, the SUV was pulling out of the lot.

"That was weird," he whispered, knowing that the meeting meant one of two things:

Either they know about Lionel's recurrence . . .

Eli took a deep breath and exhaled as he strode toward his vehicle.

Or they're onto me . . .

As he climbed into his car, the burner phone began to vibrate in his pocket.

He snatched it out of his pocket. "Hello, Mom?"

Eli listened and gripped the wheel tighter. "What?" he breathed. Then, "Oh my God."

34

Frank James often wondered if God had forgotten about him.

Or perhaps the good Lord had written him off a long while ago, and it was the other guy who wasn't paying attention. Frank sat up in the bed and gazed to his left, where a woman more than half his age lay naked on her stomach. Somehow, after their tussle in the sheets, Frank had managed to steal all the covers during the night.

Classic, he thought, rubbing the whiskers of his beard and rolling off the bed to his feet. He gazed down at the woman, who had a tattoo of a purple flower at the small of her back just above her perfectly toned ass, and thought that perhaps he had it wrong.

Maybe the devil was just enjoying the show.

He made himself a cup of coffee in the Keurig machine. As the appliance of modern convenience gurgled out a ten-ounce french roast pour, Frank walked up the steps and opened the door. He stepped out onto the deck of his pride and joy, a Sea Ray cabin cruiser he'd purchased five years ago after selling both his homes. He peered out at the harbor and breathed in the salt air. The sky was overcast, and most of the boats, like his own, were still docked. Their owners were likely still slumbering away far from the confines of their vessel.

But not Frank James. He'd been divorced now for almost fifteen years. And outside of practicing medicine, which he still loved, and chasing pussy, which he had always loved, the ocean was his heart. He wasn't sure whether he would like living in his cruiser, but he was enjoying the adventure. And his alternative living arrangements certainly didn't hurt his chances of bringing ladies home with him. They did hurt his chance of keeping a woman, which made the whole situation the perfect way to live out his remaining years.

The sun had yet to rise but would do so soon. One habit that Frank had never been able to kick was waking up early. It didn't matter if his shift ended at midnight or if he drank into the wee hours of the morning, he always woke just before the sun.

Like a fucking rooster, he thought, rubbing his neck. His head was clear, which was also rather odd. Given the amount of whiskey he'd enjoyed last night at AJ's and the shots from the bottle he and Shayna had done when they got back here, he ought to have a raging headache.

But the hangovers had stopped years ago. He figured his tolerance was such now that he simply didn't suffer them anymore or, more likely, he no longer recognized the symptoms.

He trudged back down the steps and grabbed his coffee cup. The cabin consisted of a tiny kitchen with a sink and microwave and table for two. Then there was a narrow opening with a bathroom and, past that, the bedroom. Frank took a sip of coffee and leaned against the hallway wall. He was due at the hospital at 7:00 a.m., and the clock on the microwave said it was just after five, so there was a little time to chill out.

Frank had given up full-time ER work five years ago, but he still pulled two weekend shifts a month at Sacred Heart Hospital. He was seventy-five years old. Long in the tooth to still be working, but what else was he going to do? He still enjoyed the challenge of treating patients, albeit in briefer pockets of time now. And, of course, working was a great place to meet women.

He gazed at the beautiful creature on his bed, wondering how a woman like Shayna could end up here. She was smart. Pretty. Employed as a nurse for several years. And married to a man whose job required a lot of travel. They had a kid, who was spending the night with a friend.

Shayna had shared some of the details of her life with Frank during their shift together yesterday.

And, because he enjoyed her company, he asked her to meet him for a drink. She said she might just do that, and the proposition was a win-win for Frank. If she showed up, he'd have a chance to lay a married woman and a coworker, both of which were special treats that almost alleviated the need for a Viagra.

Almost.

And if they didn't hit it off, he'd still have the rest of the night to prowl. But things had gone well. Frank took a sip of the scalding hot coffee. *Very well.*

He watched her slow and steady breath, sleeping like a baby, and thought of her husband somewhere on the road. Perhaps they had an open marriage, and he was waking up next to his own colluder. Or maybe he was a staunch conservative who wasn't adventurous between the sheets. Or, more likely, maybe he just was never home, and Shayna was lonely. Frank sipped his coffee, acknowledging that he didn't give a shit.

I'm going to hell, he knew, looking down at the floor. *Enjoy the show, motherfucker.*

He turned and walked back into the kitchen. He'd left his phone on the counter, and he grabbed it as he plopped down in a chair. He had three missed calls and a voice message from a number he didn't recognize.

Frank sighed, figuring it was another real estate prospector who wanted to know what he was going to do with his condominium properties in Panama City. While he now lived on a boat, he still owned several waterfront condominiums and was part owner in a hotel. He was getting at least two calls a week from strange numbers in unusual places. He was about to click on the message when he heard three hard raps on the door upstairs.

His stomach tensed, as he glanced through the hallway to the woman still lying naked on his bed. He had never been confronted by an angry husband, but he was certainly due for a scene like that. For a man like him, long past his bedroom prime, it was amazing how many young women with rings on their fingers ended up in his bed. The fact that he had lots of cash, an always-full bottle of 100 mg Viagra, and a devil-may-care attitude probably helped his chances, but he figured the real reason was far simpler.

Like him, all they really wanted was a night of sex with no consequences.

He set down his cup and strode back to the bedroom. He opened the top drawer of the built-in dresser, pulling out the SIG Sauer 9 mm piece that was his customary concealed carry. He trotted up the steps and cracked open the door, gripping tight to the weapon with his other hand.

No one was there. He opened the door wider and stepped out onto the deck. Light was beginning to filter through the clouds, the first vestige of sun. Frank squinted and saw a woman sitting on the hull. She wore tight jeans and a black shirt, and her brown hair was up in a ponytail.

She waved at him.

He took a couple of cautious steps toward the woman, still holding the gun in his left hand. "Can I help you?"

"Are you Dr. Frank James?"

"Who wants to know?"

"You're not going to shoot me, are you?" Her voice was singsong. She shook her brown hair loose from its elastic and her thick locks fell to her shoulders.

"Depends," Frank said, taking another step. "You're trespassing. And you haven't said your business."

"Is your boat for sale?" She winked at him.

"No. What's this about?" He thought again to the voice message on his phone and the missed calls. The message had been short. Maybe only ten seconds. Most of the spam messages were much longer.

"Everyone has a price, don't they?" She loosened the top two buttons of her shirt.

Frank forced a smile. "Are you . . . going to make an offer?"

She undid another button. He could now see her cleavage. And that she wasn't wearing a bra. Frank took another step forward. He was three feet away from her.

"Maybe," she said. She unfastened the last two buttons and slipped off the shirt. In the dawn's early light, all Frank could make out was the shadow of her breasts and the outline of her nipples.

"Spectacular," he said, but the tingle he would normally feel in this type of situation was absent. "But you'll need to do better than that." In the background, Frank could hear his cell phone ringing. He glanced behind him to the door, which he'd left half-open. It was closed now, and a man stood in front of it. He held a pistol pointed at Frank's chest. "What the—?"

But Frank James never got the rest of his last words out.

35

After eight rings, Eli slammed the burner phone down on the passenger seat. "Damnit, Dad." He gripped tight to the steering wheel of the rental, a 2023 Chevy Impala. He wanted to put his foot all the way on the floor, but he kept the cruise control at seventy miles per hour.

He'd left his normal cell phone at home and his Range Rover at the Whole Foods store a few miles from his house. He'd taken a cab to the airport and then ridden a shuttle from the terminal out to the rental car area.

At around 7:30 p.m., after renting the Impala with the fake ID and credit card he'd utilized for certain . . . *shadier* purchases on the campaign trail, he'd started driving. He'd now been on the road for almost twelve hours, and he still wasn't all that close to his destination. Eli turned the radio to a classic rock station, but he wasn't able to listen to the music.

He grabbed the phone and again tried his father. Eight more rings. No answer.

Probably just doesn't recognize the number and is screening the call . . .

But Eli wasn't so sure. His mom's call had spooked him. Her fear. The fact that she'd left her home in the middle of the night. Abandoned her horses to go with a man whose father might have discovered the cure for cancer.

He forced himself to take a deep breath. He wanted to call Dale, but he knew he had to ration how much he used the burner. He'd need to replace it once he got to where he was going. And maybe buy a few more. Eli smoothed his hair behind his ears. He'd always been good in a crisis, but this was getting ridiculous. He again tried to reach his dad.

This time the phone rang once and went straight to voicemail. *Please be okay,* he thought. He'd brought danger on both his parents by involving them, but he hadn't had a choice. But his mother was now on the run, and his dad, who'd always been an early riser, wasn't answering his calls. As the sun began to peek over the pine trees to the right of the interstate, Eli saw the green sign that said **WELCOME TO ALABAMA THE BEAUTIFUL**. Normally, the sight would have given him a warm feeling of home.

Now, he was scared to death.

36

General Kyle Randolph took the call on his secure phone in the back of the Escalade. "Is it done?"

"Yes." A female voice, and Randolph knew it was his best operator.

"Drowning?"

"So unfortunate," she said.

"Are you sure there were no witnesses?"

"Positive. There was hardly any light, and Dr. James was the only owner who spent the night in his boat."

"Did he have any visitors?"

"He did, but we watched her leave. She looked around for a while but made no calls. She must not have heard anything and probably assumed he just went to work."

Randolph nodded. "Good work. And what of Mr. James's mother?"

"Not at home this morning, but our crew is on it."

"Keep me posted." Randolph ended the call.

As the Escalade pulled into Joint Base Andrews Naval Air Facility, Randolph made another call. "Is he still off the grid?" the general asked, forgoing pleasantries.

"Yes. He apparently drove to a Whole Foods near his home, and our crew lost him."

"How is that fucking possible?"

No answer.

"Tell me what we know," Randolph barked.

"He did not report for work today, and the White House says he has taken a private day to be with his family."

"Have you spoken to our folks in Houston?"

"Yes, and it's status quo there. Only the wife and daughter."

As his car came to a stop, Randolph held up his hand to the driver to wait before letting him out. "Stay after it. I want him located as soon as possible."

Randolph terminated the call and gazed out the window. They had driven out to the runway to inspect a new aircraft the navy was considering putting into operation. The general had a folder with all the specs next to him on his seat, but his mind was still on Eli James.

Unless he's found someone else who can manufacture the cure, he's chasing a rainbow . . .

Still, Randolph was concerned. This was his operation. His detail. As he stared out the window, he thought back to the origins of Project Boomerang.

Seven and a half years ago, while acting as secretary of defense, he was asked to attend a top secret meeting with FBI Director Beth McGee. The conference was held in a classroom at the FBI academy in Quantico, Virginia. McGee, who'd only been at the top Bureau post a few months at the time, needed advice on a delicate matter.

At the request of the FDA, McGee had dispatched Bureau operatives to Mobile, Alabama, to investigate a man named Mato Nakai, who had been rumored to be peddling a product at farmers' markets that some purchasers were calling "the cure for cancer." One particular patient of Nakai's, Mrs. Mary Frances Bruce, had been quite vocal in spreading the word of Nakai's discovery. Initially, the FDA had asked McGee to get involved, because they suspected Nakai was a fraud. But upon investigation and testing of the medication in question, it appeared that Nakai's drug might well be a miracle of modern medicine.

On the surface, the news seemed wonderful, and Randolph even said so, but Director McGee quickly changed his viewpoint by describing the potentially disastrous consequences of the drug's discovery, as well as the endless array of problems with introducing it to the world. First and foremost, more testing was needed. Sure, the initial studies were incredibly positive, but it typically took years for a new drug to be approved because there needed to be more trials. Second, assuming those tests were consistent with the preliminary results, which pharma company would be chosen to manufacture this wonder? Or would it be a free-for-all? Could Big Pharma be trusted with such a miracle, or would they destroy each other, the biggest companies eating the others? The answer to that was a definite no. Big Pharma could not be trusted, so the only logical and equitable plan would be for the government to produce and distribute the drug . . . but how and when would they—rather, *we*—do that? Third and perhaps most concerning, McGee informed him: Assuming the drug was, in fact, the cure for cancer, could the United States economy survive such a discovery? The oncology market was a multi-billion-dollar-per-year industry and growing exponentially. The boomerang would instantly make much of the oncology industry obsolete. The sudden loss of jobs, careers, and money would be staggering and could cripple, if not destroy, the nation's economy. And none of this even began to consider the impact of the discovery around the globe. Until these questions could be answered and concerns alleviated, McGee had argued that the boomerang was a threat to national security and must be kept secret.

"What do you think we should do?" she'd asked Randolph after presenting her thoughts.

The general, who agreed with all her concerns, asked for some time to stew on a possible solution. That was Randolph's specialty as a field commander. Planning. Figuring out an enemy's weakness and exploiting it. Discovering the quickest and swiftest way to achieve victory and then executing. Randolph was the most decorated and popular American soldier since the days of Norman Schwarzkopf and Colin Powell. He'd commanded troops during the Gulf War in the 1990s and the war on terror after 9/11. But those days were long since over, and the four stars on his uniform represented the past, not the future.

Project Boomerang would be his parting gift to the country he loved.

Two days after the meeting with McGee in Quantico, he brought the FBI director to the Pentagon, outlining his plan and who he thought should be involved. He wanted his old friend, Robert Bellamy, on board, because Bellamy was a Homeland Security lifer who would understand better than anyone the concerns that McGee had mentioned. The commissioner of the FDA also needed to be part of it, as testing of the drug would be necessary, as well as an eventual rollout plan. And finally, the president would have to know.

Though there were reservations, all the original members of Project Boomerang agreed with Randolph's suggested course of action. They agreed that his plan was "for the good of the country," and "in the interests of national security." Finally, they all insisted that it should be Randolph who would lead the mission.

And I've done so. I have done everything asked of me.

Randolph blinked and rubbed his face, trying to bring himself back to the present. He knew, without a shadow of a doubt, that he had done the best he could do. *They came to me . . .*

As with all successful military campaigns, there had been casualties. Dr. Frank James became the latest this morning.

General Randolph sighed and grabbed the folder with the aircraft specs.

There will be others.

37

The Beau Rivage Resort and Casino was a spectacular, albeit gaudy, structure that was nestled on the edge of the Gulf of Mexico. During his first years as an attorney in Alabama, Eli had been on the executive committee of the Young Lawyers Section of the Alabama State Bar and had participated in several "meetings" at Biloxi's crown jewel. The business of these get-togethers normally lasted no more than two hours, with the rest of the event nothing more than a tax write-off boondoggle.

Eli had enjoyed himself on these excursions, and, if he'd been in a better frame of mind, he might have felt some nostalgia as he gazed up at the gold-lettered sign at the top of the high rise. "The Beau," as everyone called it, was a great place to catch a buzz, lose a wad of cash, and perhaps shack up with a willing woman. Eli had done his share of all three as a young lawyer.

Now, though, as he strode through the doors of the casino, his senses were on high alert, and the past was the furthest thing from his mind. He headed toward the first group of elevators with his head down. He wore a pullover, slacks, tennis shoes, and a Nike cap. He figured he looked like any number of men staying at the Beau for a weekend of golf, gambling, and booze. He stepped inside the elevator and clicked on the third floor. A minute later, he was walking down a long carpeted hallway. He stopped at room 217. He started to knock, but the door opened before his knuckles touched wood.

A dark set of eyes stared back at him. "Mr. James?"

"Yes."

"Come in."

The door shut behind him, and Eli saw his mother sitting on one of the two double beds. She rose to her feet, clutching her arms tight to her chest. "Hey," she said, her voice etched with fatigue.

"Hey, Mom. You okay?"

She nodded and leaned into him. Eli had rarely, if ever, seen his mother shaken.

"There were people who came to my house. They had guns. If it hadn't been for him . . ." She gestured toward the other person in the hotel room and trailed off, walking back to the bed and sitting.

Eli turned to the man standing by the door. "Eli James." He extended his hand.

"Jalen Nakai." They shook, and Jalen lowered his voice to a whisper. "Your mother is lucky to be alive. As we were leaving, they showed up."

"Tell me," Eli said.

"There is a cure for cancer," his mother told him.

Foncie's resigned tone sent a shiver of fear up Eli's spine. That should be good news. Cause for celebration. Why would it be muttered in despair?

"Go on," Eli said, looking from Foncie to Jalen.

"My father was a pharmacologist," Jalen said, leaning his back against the door. "He studied at Auburn and was at the top of his class. Auburn has one of the best pharmacy programs in the country. For many years, he worked in Opelika as a pharmacist at different hospitals and even for the university for a while. But . . . he eventually got fed up with the racket."

"The racket?"

Jalen sighed. "The ridiculous insurance situation that makes paying for a prescription like the Wild West. Use this manufacturer's coupon and a four-hundred-dollar medicine costs twenty bucks. Enter this authorization code and get eighty percent reimbursed by Blue Cross. Instead of a medicine having a uniform price, it's like playing the stock market to try and get the lowest price possible. My father got sick of it all. He'd also done a residency at MD Anderson in Houston, and he knew there were many medicines that were on the cutting edge of cancer treatment that patients weren't being given access to. He'd been dabbling with some of those drugs and had come up with his own version."

Eli felt his heartbeat pick up speed. "That he sold at farmers' markets?"

Jalen nodded. "We moved to Mobile about twelve years ago. I was in high school. Dad took a job with CVS, but started working at farmers' markets on the side, selling his cancer medication under the table."

"Isn't that illegal?"

Jalen rubbed his hand over his face. He had long dark hair that he'd put up in a ponytail and brown eyes. He wore jeans, boots, and a short-sleeve button-down with the shirttail out. "Who knows? Farmers' markets have become a haven for all kinds of gray-market products and even some heavier-duty drugs. It's hard to draw the line sometimes where legal ends and illegal begins. Dad packaged his drug as an 'herbal supplement' and made no guarantees or assurances that it would do anything beyond make a person feel better."

"But it did a lot more than that," Eli said.

Jalen nodded. "The results were amazing. Better even than Dad expected. So many of his customers would come back six weeks later and say that they'd had a clear PET scan or that the tumor in their chest or colon or wherever had shrunk or evaporated completely."

"How is that possible?" Eli asked, genuinely curious. He took a seat on the edge of the other double bed in the room. He felt like he'd just entered the twilight zone.

"The pharmacology is complicated, and I don't understand it myself. I just know he called it 'the boomerang' because it returned a person to their state of health before they had the disease."

"Candy Bruce knew it had a funny name," Foncie chimed in. "Her mom took the medication and was killed in a suspicious car accident."

"It was no accident," Jalen said. "She was murdered. And I'm pretty sure my dad was too."

Eli felt the hairs on his arms tingle. "I'm sorry," he managed. "What do you mean by *pretty sure?*"

Jalen walked a few steps into the room, staring at the wall. "Dad just . . . disappeared. It was mid-July, almost eight years ago. Dead of summer. He was hitting several farmers' markets along Highway 30A, and he was supposed to meet with a manager at the famous Modica Market in Seaside. This guy knew the Modica wouldn't sell it, but he wanted to go in with Dad on a food truck at Seaside or Seagrove that would have been a front for the treatment." Jalen crossed his arms and looked down at the carpeted floor. "But Dad never showed. He was last seen in Grayton Beach. He'd eaten dinner at the Goatfeathers bar. A half dozen oysters on a half shell, fried shrimp, and a Corona."

"How do you know the order?"

"I went down there and investigated myself when the police didn't show much interest. Dad ate at Goatfeathers quite a bit. The bartender remembered him." Jalen chuckled, but it was a bitter sound.

"Did you check in with the Modica Market guy?"

"Of course. I combed 30A for two weeks looking for any trace of him. He left Goatfeathers at around nine fifteen p.m. on July twenty-seventh and was never heard from again."

Eli found himself staring at the carpet. He knew the 30A area of the Gulf Coast pretty well. He and Dale had taken Bella there a few times when she was younger for spring break and once for the Fourth of July. Beautiful beaches, incredible food, and a fairly wealthy clientele. Not exactly where you expected someone to disappear. But . . . between the towns on the famous stretch of road, there were a number of swamps and county roads and wildlife refuges. "What do you think happened?" he asked.

"I think they followed him out of the restaurant, ran him off the road, and executed him. They disposed of his body and the car somewhere in that area . . . or perhaps they took him farther away."

"What kind of car?"

"Ford F-150."

Eli looked up from the floor. "How could a pickup just disappear?"

Jalen squinted at him. "You'd be surprised at the talents of those in the highest branches of the United States military."

The hairs on Eli's arms were standing up again. "You really believe that the US government has deliberately covered up the cure for cancer?"

Jalen Nakai didn't hesitate. "Yes, I do. And my dad paid for coming up with his miracle with his life." He nodded at Foncie. "As did Mary Frances Bruce and . . . many others."

"How many?"

Jalen shrugged. "Conservatively . . . at least five human beings who wouldn't stop asking questions."

"Jesus." Eli whistled between his teeth. "Jalen, if all this is true, how are you still alive? And what about the rest of your family? It seems like they would all be at risk."

Jalen put his hands in his pockets and looked up at the ceiling. "My mom died of breast cancer when I was in middle school. I have no other family. I was just out of high school at the time of Dad's murder." He shrugged. "I think they sized me up as a stupid kid. Not a threat. And . . ." He smirked. "I haven't continued the family business."

"Have you thought about it?"

"Every day. It was my father's passion. His dream was to help other families never have to go through what we did with my mom. Unfortunately, the government raided our house and took all Dad's computers and files on the drug. And I'm no genius like Dad was."

Eli sighed. "My daughter has lung cancer. It's terminal."

"Foncie told me. I'm sorry."

Eli stood and gazed at Jalen. "If the boomerang was still available, would it help my daughter?"

Jalen nodded. "It would cure her. And millions of others. There is not a doubt in my mind."

Eli glanced at his mother, who sat on the edge of the other bed, arms crossed tight, rocking back and forth as she listened to every word. "Jalen . . ." He struggled for the right words and then just spit it out. "How do I get my hands on the boomerang?"

Jalen Nakai's stare turned stony: "Ask your president."

PART FOUR

PRESIDENTIAL COINCIDENCE

Highway 30A is a madhouse. It is the first week in March. Spring break for thousands of kids, and the blacktop between Seaside and Seagrove mirrors a teenage Bourbon Street. Eli sits on a wooden bench behind a place called Bud & Alley's. The spot is perfect to view the sunset, and Eli gazes at the orangish-red hue and then out to the emerald green waters of the gulf. Beyond that, he sees the spot where the green turns a deep shade of navy. Light to dark.

"We're in the dark water," he says.

"Yep." *His mother's voice is monotone. Still in shock. She's been trying to reach Dad, but he isn't picking up. Eli stopped calling after the meeting with Jalen Nakai.*

He's gone, *Eli thinks, just like his mother would have been if Jalen hadn't picked up her scent before they did. He wants to stop at his father's boat, but he knows that such a move is too risky. And possibly fatal . . .*

Will they kill me too? *Eli wonders.* The sitting chief of staff to the president of the United States?

"Only one president of this country has ever died of cancer," *Foncie says, peering out at the gulf.* "One. The others that had it all died from something else."

"Could just be a coincidence," *Eli says, but he doesn't believe it. Not anymore.*

"*Right.*" *Foncie's voice drips with sarcasm.* "*Jimmy Carter had metastatic melanoma all over his damn body and he was alive for almost a decade after his diagnosis. He was one hundred when he died.*"

"*They say he was given Keytruda.*"

Foncie scoffs. "*That's not what I think.*"

"*The boomerang?*"

"*Damn skippy.*"

Eli watches the horizon until the sun dips below it.

"*You know what you have to do.*" *Foncie's voice is stern. The same tone she used when she told him that he wasn't going to quit the basketball team in eighth grade.*

Eli feels his mother's eyes on him, but he doesn't look at her. "*Yep.*"

38

The cancer was gone.

President Lionel Cantrell could hardly believe his ears. "Are you sure?" he asked.

"Your colonoscopy showed no indicia of a tumor, and the PET scan registered zero activity. Your initial PET in October had several hot spots, but there is nothing now. Congratulations, Mr. President."

"Thank you, Dr. Gleason."

The physician gave a knowing smile. Trey Gleason was the oncologist assigned to him by Project Boomerang. "I'm happy for you." Then he nodded at the other person in the room. "General."

Kyle Randolph nodded back and shook Gleason's hand.

"We'll schedule another scope and PET in three months," the doctor said, walking toward the door to the office. "Assuming those scans are clear . . . and they will be . . . then we can cut the follow-ups to every six months. That work for you, Mr. President?"

"Of course," Lionel said.

Gleason left, and Lionel turned to Randolph. "I can't believe it."

The general slapped him on the back. "The country is safer with you healthy, Mr. President. Always remember that." He paused. "But there is something . . . or rather someone . . . we need to talk about."

Lionel tensed. "Okay."

"Your chief of staff, Mr. James, has been off the grid of late.'"

"He's dealing with a personal situation," Lionel said.

"Yes, I know. Unfortunately, his daughter's cancer may make him more curious as to your recovery. I have a feeling that he'll be asking for your help very soon regarding cancer treatment options."

Lionel raised his eyebrows. "Why?"

"You know about his relationship with Sarah Kate Moss." A statement, not a question.

The president didn't bother to respond to it.

"Ms. Moss may have filled Mr. James's brain with illusions of some kind of conspiracy to hide a miracle cancer drug." Randolph crossed his arms, and his blue-gray eyes narrowed. "It is amazing what secrets are shared between political . . . bedfellows."

"What are you saying, General?"

"It is our belief and understanding that Mr. James is spending his personal leave chasing these conspiracy rumors . . . and that what he finds might lead him directly back to you. Especially given today's report from Dr. Gleason."

Lionel sighed. "If he does, I won't say anything about the boomerang."

"I hope not, Mr. President." Randolph grabbed the doorknob.

"General?"

Randolph looked at Lionel over his shoulder.

"Where is he now?" asked the president.

The general squinted. "I don't know."

39

Eli crossed into Virginia at sunrise.

He'd bought several more burner phones and took one of them out now. He pulled into a convenience store and dialed his mother's number.

"Where are you?" he asked.

"Lake Charles, Louisiana. About to pass into Texas." Foncie's voice was hyper, amped up. "You?"

"Virginia."

"Have you called her yet?"

Eli closed his eyes and leaned his head against the steering wheel. "About to now."

Before leaving coastal Florida, they'd each bought laptops with cash, and Foncie had looked up the contact information they needed while Eli thought it through and tweaked his plan.

This is crazy, he thought. *What if we're wrong? What if Lionel can't . . . or won't help?*

He leaned back in his seat and gazed over the access road to the interstate, where cars were traveling bumper to bumper in and out of the state of Virginia. He knew he was stalling. Once he made this call, the die would be cast. *No turning back . . .*

Eli closed his eyes and thought about his father. Frank James had missed a lot of Eli's childhood events. He'd been addicted to work and booze, and those vices led him to stray with other women. He hadn't been Ward Cleaver by any stretch.

But Frank had taught Eli about competing in an uncertain world. *Control what you can. Don't waste time or energy worrying about the rest.*

And his eternal wisdom on conflict: *Don't bring a knife to a gunfight.*

Eli thought back to their last encounter at the Donut Hole. Frank's bloodshot eyes. The smell of bourbon on his breath. Chugging coffee and blinking, trying to give his son the best advice he could.

"What are they afraid of?" Eli whispered his father's words as he took out his phone. So much work and sacrifice had brought Lionel and him to the White House. So many late nights. Risks that had to be taken. Leaps of faith.

Dirty deals . . .

Promises they couldn't keep . . .

Eli sighed. It was bound to end at some point. There would have been a *now what* moment coming down the pike in any case. Either after Lionel's death from colon cancer or their loss during the next election. Eli hadn't thought too much about it, because the idea scared him to death. But what *would* he do once Lionel Cantrell's presidential term was over? Where would he go when his friend lost the presidency . . . or his life?

Long-term planning had never been Eli's strong suit. Crisis management, on the other hand . . .

He finally dialed the number for the MD Anderson residential suites. When the operator answered, he spoke fast and didn't have to fake the nerves he felt: "Yes, I'm trying to reach my wife, Mrs. Dale James. She's in suite four. There is something going on with our phones. I can't get my daughter on her cell either. Could you have her come down to the front desk? I need to give her an important message."

There was a pause for a few seconds, as if the dispatcher had to ask someone a question. Then she was back. "Of course, sir. I will ring her room now. Did you want to hold or call back?"

"I'll wait, thanks," Eli said, putting the burner on speakerphone and clutching it to his chest. His knuckles rested on his heart, and he could feel the rapid beats. Outside the windshield of the Impala, a man in a suit was striding toward a BMW. He'd just made a pit stop for coffee and what looked to be a box of doughnuts. Eli imagined that he was a young attorney going to a hearing or a deposition. That would fit. He glanced down at his phone. His wife was one of the best litigators in the country. A world-class arguer, and Eli had been the victim of many of her rants, almost all of which were logical, well reasoned, and dead on the money. Had he *ever* won a marital spat?

I need to win this one, Eli thought, and then another Foncieism came to him: *This one and one more will make two.*

"Hello. Eli? Are you okay?"

The sound of his wife's voice sent a wave of emotion through Eli's chest. When was the last time they'd spoken?

"No," he said, hearing the fatigue in his voice.

"What's wrong? You haven't responded to any of my calls or texts. I almost called the White House . . ."

Eli cringed. "Please tell me—"

"I didn't."

Silence for several seconds. "Eli—"

He cleared his throat and felt his eyes dampening. He tried to control his breathing but was having a hard time.

"Eli, what is it?" Dale's voice had softened.

"When it comes to the health of our daughter, do you trust me?"

For several seconds, there was nothing. No sound. Then, finally, a sigh. "Yes."

Eli let out a breath he was holding. "Good. Just go with me on these next few questions, okay? Don't respond with questions. Take off your lawyer hat for a moment, and just give the information I'm asking for. Okay?"

Another pause. "Okay."

"Have you and Bella made friends with anyone at MD Anderson? Another patient? A family? An employee?"

"Well . . . yes. I guess. Everyone in the complex kind of knows each other. Misery loves company, you know?"

"I know."

"There's another teenage girl who's going through a leukemia trial. Her mom and I have had dinner a couple of times together, and the girls have grown pretty close. Her name is Rachel. I'm not sure of her last name."

"That's good," Eli said. "That's perfect. So going to her room would not be unusual for you."

"No. Eli—"

"Just hear me out. No questions yet." He bit his lip and forced himself to continue. "You're being followed. I'm not exactly sure by who, but I know that you are. Go to this woman's room and ask to borrow her cell phone. Tell her yours is broken or make up something. Then call me back in five or ten minutes on this number." Eli read off the digits and waited.

"Eli, I have a burner phone, why don't—?"

"I don't want the folks who are watching you to see you use it right now. It will arouse suspicion."

"But—"

"I'll explain everything when you call back."

———

The sound of Dale's soft crying was almost more than Eli could bear. "Oh my God," she said, her voice brimming with exasperation and fear.

Eli glanced at the clock on the dash. It was 7:43 a.m. He'd managed to explain their predicament in fifteen minutes. He knew Lionel was meeting with several foreign heads of state today, but those conferences wouldn't start until eleven. Typically, the chief of staff would help with the preparation, but nothing had been typical since Bella's diagnosis. It would take him every bit of an hour, maybe an hour and a half, to fight the morning traffic, park, and get to the president's office. And that didn't account for any interruptions. He didn't have much time, but he knew he couldn't be impatient right now. Everything about his idea hinged on Dale. Just as in the election . . . she was his secret weapon.

"We need a plan," Dale finally said. Gone were the fear and trepidation in her voice. Her tone radiated confidence and a tinge of anger. "But I bet you already have one."

Despite the sadness, fatigue, and guilt he felt, Eli managed to smile. This was the Dale he needed. "I do, but I need to know something first."

"What?"

"How is Bella?"

A choked sigh. "Weak. She's lost at least twenty pounds. The trial medication has made her so nauseated she hasn't been able to eat much. She gets fluids every day, but she's had a really hard time holding down solid food."

"Is the treatment working?"

"Who the hell knows." Dale spat the words. "Her scans have been stable, meaning the tumors haven't gotten any worse."

"But not any better either."

"Right. And who's to say if we'd done nothing, that they'd have gotten worse? It's all—"

"Bullshit," Eli said. He'd heard Dale tell the story of her father's hopeless fight against cancer many times. "The treatment trial's over this week, right?"

"Thursday," Dale said. "Three days."

"Well, Bella's ends today. Can she travel?"

"Eli—"

"Is she up for a trip?"

Another sigh. "By car or plane? And how long?"

"Car." He paused. "About twelve to fourteen hours."

Eli heard the whistling of air through teeth. "Good grief, Eli. Where . . ." But her voice trailed off, and Eli knew that she understood what he was asking. "I think so," she said. "We'll probably need to break it up into two days."

"You'll want to do that anyway."

For several seconds, the airway was silent. Eli could hear his wife's breathing. When she finally spoke, the fear was back in her voice. "Eli, are you sure? I mean, I've been thinking about it myself the last few weeks, but . . ."

"You've always wanted to go back," he said, unable to keep the bitterness out of his voice. "You spent more time growing up in Alabama, but New Mexico will always be home. Your brothers will help. They worship you." Eli closed his eyes as he heard his wife's soft sniffles. "The whole Gutierrez family. Your aunts, uncles, cousins." Eli sighed. "They love you like their own, and they love Bella. If I don't make it—"

"Don't you dare talk like that." Dale snapped back to life.

"Just being realistic. I don't have the energy for pity. You're a lot closer to Albuquerque than I am, and you have one of the most street-smart people in the world on her way to help you get there." He opened his eyes and squeezed the steering wheel.

"Eli, no. Foncie can't stand me, and I can't say that I feel that much different about her. She's weird and she makes me and Bella nervous."

"We need all hands on deck, honey, and Mom is one of the most skilled investigators I have ever known. If you don't believe it, ask Isaiah Blankenship. The thing is, her job depends on her not being seen. She'll get you there."

"But how? If I'm being followed, how can Bella and I just get in the car with Foncie and head west?"

Eli squinted at the traffic out on I-95. "I doubt there are many eyes on you. Jalen Nakai said he saw approximately six operatives at Mom's house the night it was raided. I'm guessing that there will only be half that on you."

"So what do I do?"

Eli took a deep breath. Then, for the next few minutes, he explained where he wanted her and Bella to go . . . and what he needed her to do before they arrived.

When he finished, there was a long pause. Finally, Dale sighed. "Are you out of your ever-loving mind?"

"Mom will take it from there."

"Oh, great," Dale said. "Mom will take it. Eli, are you fucking crazy? You are a politician, not an undercover spy."

"I'm a piece of shit, Dale. A bankrupt husband and a mediocre father. But I'm a decent problem-solver, and this was Mom's idea. It will work. You'll lose the crew, and Mom will get you to Albuquerque."

"And then what? It's not a stretch for us to go to New Mexico, Eli. Hell, it's almost predictable. Based on all you've said, once you talk with Lionel, the shit is going to hit the fan. They'll be waiting on me when I get there."

"No," Eli responded with absolute calm. "They won't. You're going to disappear."

Dale said nothing, but her breathing had become labored.

Eli ignored the fear and doubt circling his brain. "I'm going to need some help here too. An escape hatch . . . a diversion . . ."

"Eli—"

"Dale, do you understand what I'm asking you to do?" His voice had risen, and his own heart was pounding. "I would never, and I mean *never*, suggest this under any other circumstances, but we don't have a choice."

Eli closed his eyes and heard his father's gravelly voice in his mind: *What are they afraid of?*

"It's good that your family is in New Mexico," Eli continued. "I know they'll help . . . but they aren't enough. We need protection." He waited a moment. "Dale?"

"I'm here . . . and I understand."

Eli nodded to himself as his wife put voice to his high-stakes gamble:

"We need Nester."

40

Eli parked the Impala a couple blocks from the White House. He took out his briefcase and left his duffel bag in the car. The sun hit his face as he stepped onto the sidewalk and gazed past the stoplights to the Washington Monument. The air was cool but warming by the second with a gentle breeze off the Potomac.

Spring had come to the nation's capital. Hints of green had returned to the trees and the grass. Moreso than the turn of the year, the beginning of spring was, at least to Eli, a time for hopeful optimism, but he was feeling anything but positive right now.

This is nuts, he thought, walking briskly down Pennsylvania Avenue. He was a bit surprised that he hadn't already been intercepted by General Kyle Randolph and a team of dark SUVs.

I have done nothing wrong. No crime has been committed. I need to walk in here like I own the place.

Eli strode through the employee entrance to the White House and passed through the security checkpoint without a hitch. None of the Secret Service officers seemed concerned with him, and he rode the elevator with a couple of aides who were talking about a show they were watching on Netflix.

Reflexively, Eli reached in his pocket for his iPhone but felt one of the burners instead. His smartphone was likely still at home on the kitchen counter. *Or in the hands of General Randolph . . .*

Eli shook off the thought as he exited the elevator. He walked to his office as if nothing was unusual and placed his briefcase on the visitor's chair while he stared out at the Washington skyline. He picked up the landline to call the president's receptionist, but then hung up. *Better to catch him with no warning.* He walked toward the Oval Office and heard a voice from behind him.

"Mr. James?"

Eli recognized the voice but didn't stop walking. If anything, he picked up his pace.

"Mr. James, I need a word."

Eli reached the president's door and glanced at his assistant. "Is he with anyone, Alison?"

Alison Barnes had been with Lionel since his time in the Senate. She stopped typing on her computer and raised her eyebrows. "Eli . . . uh . . . no. I'm sure he'd love—"

"Good," Eli said, grabbing the doorknob just as he felt a firm hand grasp his shoulder.

"We need to talk." General Randolph peered at Eli with emotionless eyes.

"And we will," Eli said, wriggling out of Randolph's grasp. Now he stepped forward into Randolph's personal space, forcing the general to take a step back. "But I work for the president. Not you. And I owe him a report."

Randolph said nothing, and for a moment the two men just stared at each other.

"Where have you been?"

"None of your damned business," Eli said. Then he turned and opened the door, slamming it shut before Randolph could say anything else. As he took a few cautious steps into the Oval Office, he found his old friend pacing behind his chair and studying a yellow notepad. Lionel looked up from the page, and, after a second's hesitation, smiled. "Elijah Longstreet James," he said, his voice a tad hoarse. "It's been a minute. How are things?"

"What do you mean?" Eli kept his eyes on the president as he took a seat in front of the desk.

"How are you? How's Bella? You've been gone for almost two weeks."

"Bella's trial is almost over. She's lost about twenty pounds. Can't hold down food. She's a shell of her former self."

"I'm . . . sorry." Lionel flung the pad on the desk and rubbed his face with his hands. Then he sat in his chair and crossed his legs. "And what about you?"

"What *about* me . . ." Eli spoke with deliberate calm. He forced his breathing to be measured and slow and took in everything. The mood in the room was somber, the tension obvious. His oldest friend, the man that Eli had groomed to be president, who Eli had spent countless hours with in boardrooms, courtrooms, and bars, was uncomfortable in his presence. Lionel's face no longer looked thin and gaunt. His weight looked to be back to the baseline before his October diagnosis.

Lionel cleared his throat and looked down at the desk. "Look, Eli, it's good to see you, but I'm meeting with the prime minister of—"

"Canada. I know. The meeting's not for another fifteen minutes. What's the deal, Lionel?"

The president crossed his arms and frowned. "I'm confused, Eli. What—?"

"You have metastatic colon cancer. We both had hoped that you would beat it, but your prognosis was dire. Two years is what your doctor said, and you had already lost fifteen pounds with treatment at the time of the inauguration." Eli hesitated. "But *look* at you."

Lionel held out his palms. "The first round of radiation and chemo shrank the tumor and stopped the spread. I'm having a good run of luck."

"Luck? You've gained all your weight back. You don't look sick at all."

"Cancer doesn't always act like we expect. That's one of the first things my oncologist said during my initial bout. It's unpredictable."

"Bullshit," Eli said, rising from his seat. "You're not a good liar, Lionel."

The president rocked in his chair but maintained eye contact. "I'm not lying. Listen, Eli." He stood. "I know things are tough for you right now. If you need more time. If you need anything, I'm here."

Eli paced around the desk to the window, not looking at his oldest friend. "You're holding back on me."

Lionel chuckled, but Eli could hear the nerves behind the laugh. He knew Lionel Cantrell better than anyone else in the world did. Better than Lionel's wife. There was a reason that the soon-to-be president had trusted only one person with the news of his recurrence of cancer. *What do I do, Eli?* Lionel had asked in October. Eli had broken down their options with concise clarity. *We can get off the board and swim back to shore with our tails between our legs* . . . At that first alternative, they both had shaken their heads. *Or we can ride this wave all the way to shore* . . .

"We've come too far to jump off," Eli whispered. "You remember when I told you that?"

Lionel sighed. "Yeah, man. We were at a fundraiser in Huntsville. Sitting in one of the private rooms at . . . what was that restaurant?"

"Cotton Row," Eli said without emotion. "On the square downtown. The food was fabulous, and then we went to that office building nearby where the money was being moved. Fifty grand in one night, as I recall."

"I remember. Another winner from my future and now current chief of staff. The event . . ." He sighed. ". . . and the advice. You were right, Eli. We rode the wave out, and my cancer has gone away with treatment. As always, your counsel was sound. Thank you."

Eli continued to stare out at the skyline. "The women were nice in Huntsville too . . . as I recall. Young married girl for you, right? So excited to meet the future president that she took off her panties."

"You made out okay, too, didn't you?" Lionel's voice was low now. He was getting angry.

211

Good, Eli thought. "Yep. Mine was older. Less innocent. Using me just as much as I was using her." He hesitated. "I saw your girl after she left your room. I was down in the lobby, and she was waiting for an Uber. She had a blank look in her eyes . . . and tears. Buyer's remorse, I'm sure. Your dick for her soul was not a winning hand."

"Well, it worked out okay for me," Lionel growled. "Look, I'm busy, and I think you need to take a—"

"There's a cure for cancer," Eli said, turning to face the president. "A man named Mato Nakai . . . a pharmacologist from Mobile, Alabama, who once worked at MD Anderson came up with it. For a couple years, he sold it in farmers' markets across the gulf coasts of Florida, Louisiana, Mississippi, and Alabama. Unfortunately for him, some of his patients talked about him and his miracle drug too much. One of them, a lady named Mary Frances Bruce, was killed in a faked hit-and-run accident while out for a walk in her blueblood Mobile neighborhood. Her daughter Candace was paid a sizable amount of money to not cooperate with authorities. Mato Nakai disappeared on Highway 30A a couple weeks later. He'd just had oysters and beers at Goatfeathers and was never seen again." Eli snapped his fingers. "Gone."

Lionel blinked his eyes, his face twisted in confusion. "I don't believe it. How . . . did you learn all of this?"

"I have pretty reliable sources in the world of pharma."

"SK?"

"Let's just say I got a tip from someone who cares, and our investigator did the rest."

"Our inve—" Lionel stopped and his eyes widened. "Foncie?"

Eli nodded. "Same woman who uncovered that Isaiah Blankenship was a sexual deviant during his college days."

"She's good," Lionel conceded. "But, Eli . . . come on, man. No one wants there to be a cure for cancer more than me, but give me a break."

"I don't think I will." Eli stepped closer. "I think you already know. You can't bullshit a bullshitter, and you can't con a con. Why is General Kyle Randolph so interested in my comings and goings? Why did my mother have to flee her home before assassins showed up at her door?" Eli clenched his jaw but could no longer keep his emotions in check. "Why's my dad, Dr. Frank James, *dead*?"

Lionel's face had gone pale. He sank into his chair. He opened his mouth, but no words came out.

The phone in the Oval Office buzzed. "Mr. President, just a reminder that your meeting with the prime minister starts in ten minutes."

"O-okay," Lionel managed, gazing at the phone.

Eli glared down at him. "What are you really taking, Lionel?"

"I . . . I don't know what you're talking about."

"Oh, come off it. I've had a bunch of time to think over the last month, and I've done a hell of a lot of cancer research. My week at MD Anderson was spent peppering those oncologists with every conceivable question. My conclusions are the same as anyone who has ever studied cancer treatment on this planet. Unless you have a surgical option, there is no cure. You're going to die from it. The tumor may shrink some. The growth may slow. But it doesn't just go away."

"I didn't say mine was gone, Eli. Just that I'd responded well to treatment. You're crazy, man. You need to take a permanent leave of absence."

Eli shook his head. "If you don't tell me what you're taking or give me every bit of information you currently know about what you're not sharing with the American public, then I'm going to sink this ship. I'll tell *everything*, you hear me, Lionel? Not just your Huntsville fling, but all the affairs and one-night stands you've had. How about all the coke we did in law school? All those campaign-finance laws you broke on your quest to the White House? I'll tell the world that your biggest financial contributor was the Scourge of New Mexico—Nester fucking Sanchez." Eli leaned so close to Lionel that he could smell the president's aftershave. "You'll be impeached within a month."

"You're bluffing," Lionel said, his voice toneless.

"You've got two hours."

Lionel scoffed. "The prime minister of Canada—"

"Can go fuck herself. If I don't have the same medication you're taking in one hundred and twenty minutes, I'm going to blow you out of the water."

"Eli, I can't . . ." He stopped himself. "I don't have anything to give you." The president's voice shook.

Eli put both his hands on Lionel's face. "You're lying. *I know you are.*" He let go and walked around the desk. When he reached the visitor's chair, he turned around. "If you tell General Randolph about my threats . . . if I get detained . . . if I get hit by a car . . . if a bolt of fucking lightning strikes me down from the sky, then separate packages will be delivered to Fox News and CNN that have every one of our secrets exposed."

Lionel stood on shaky legs. "You're blackmailing me." He snorted. "The president of the United States."

Eli smirked. "You'd be a second-rate ambulance chaser if it weren't for me, Lionel. The only reason you're sitting in this office is because of my blood, sweat, and tears and the efforts of my incredibly well-connected wife. You owe me." Eli gripped the back of the chair. "This is *Bella*, for God's sake! Your goddaughter. I kept your secret about having cancer. I told no one. I won't tell anyone about this either. I'm not interested in saving the world." Eli let go of the chair. "Only my daughter."

"Can you give me more time?" Lionel asked.

"How long does it take to grab a pill bottle?"

Lionel squinted at Eli.

"Mato Nakai called it 'the boomerang.' I'm not sure what you and General Randolph call it, but, in two hours, you're gonna give it to me. Do you understand?"

"Eli, please—"

"Handle your meeting with the Canadian prime minister. I'll be in my office. Remember what I said. If you are late or if something happens to me . . ." Eli put his palms together and then spread them. "Boom." He walked to the door and grabbed the handle.

"You're fired," Lionel said. "Today is your last day. I'll have our PR folks say it's for personal reasons."

Eli looked at him over his shoulder. "That's fine. But I'm not leaving the White House without the medication you're taking. If I don't get it, you'll be a whole lot worse than fired. Think *ruined*."

"No one will believe you."

Eli glared at the president. There was fifteen feet between them, but it felt like an abyss. "Do you really want to find out?"

41

The George Bush Intercontinental Airport in Houston, Texas, was hopping at just past noon. By the time Dale and Bella reached gate 32, they were both exhausted. They'd had to stop several times during the walk, as Bella's stamina was low. An airport employee had offered a wheelchair, but Bella had refused.

Now, as they sat in rubber-backed chairs and gazed out at the planes circling the runway, Bella finally croaked out the question that Dale had been asking herself ever since she'd started packing their suitcases.

"Mom, what are we doing?"

Dale glanced at her daughter. Bella wore a cap to cover her now-bald scalp. Gone were her curly blond locks, which she'd gotten from Dale. But her brown eyes, which she'd inherited from her father, still shone, though the light behind them seemed dimmer. Fear and pain had replaced the fire that had once burned within. The desire to succeed had been replaced by the fight for survival. Dale swallowed and touched Bella's neck. She forced her voice not to crack. "We're going home."

"But my trial isn't over. Why are we leaving now?" Bella had asked the same questions when they were leaving the room, and Dale had blown her off, saying something had come up with another possible treatment option. It wasn't exactly a lie, but it sure as shit wasn't the whole truth either.

We're running.

"Mom?"

"There are only a couple of treatments left, and we . . . have a better option."

"In Virginia? Come on, Mom. If that were the case, why did we come here? I'm sick, but I'm not stupid. You put both our cell phones in the luggage that we checked. Something is clearly going on. Tell me."

Dale looked away and glanced at her watch. They'd arrived at the gate at 11:07 a.m., and it was now 12:10 p.m. She'd been hyperalert since leaving the residence parking lot. She'd noticed the black Escalade that had followed them to the airport car rental area, but since dropping off the sedan, she hadn't seen anyone who looked suspicious. Not on the shuttle to the airport. Not in the security checkpoint line. Not in the foot traffic through the terminal.

She had to admit that the plan seemed to be working.

"Mom?"

"Bella, something's . . . going on, okay?" She looked at her daughter, and Bella's eyebrows were raised.

"What?" Bella asked.

"Are you hungry?"

"Mom?"

"Come on. Bring your bag."

Dale hustled toward the nearest bar. A place called the Hubcap Grill and Beer Yard. She looked over her shoulder to make sure that Bella was following, and her daughter rolled her eyes at her but continued to pull her luggage forward. Dale found a seat in the second row of chairs. She set her bag at her feet and placed her elbows on the green counter. Bella groaned and did the same. "Mom, come on. The smell of this place is going to make me gag."

But the scent of beer, hamburger meat, and onions smelled far nicer than any air that Dale had breathed in a while. She looked around the place, knowing that she was a few minutes early. A waiter stopped by and asked them if they wanted anything. Bella reluctantly ordered fries, and Dale asked for a beer and a burger.

This is pretty close to exactly what we'd be doing if we were really waiting for a 4:00 p.m. flight, Dale told herself, trying to relax. A minute later, a cold pint was placed in front of her, and Dale took a slow sip of the local IPA. She hadn't called into the office today, which was a first. She'd now been gone approximately a month, and she knew her leave of absence was about to be permanent. But none of that mattered anymore.

She did, however, make one call. Five minutes after hanging up with Eli, she dialed Nester. He answered without bothering to say hello—as always, frugal with his words.

"Are you okay?" His voice was soft. Almost a whisper. Nester rarely raised his voice. When he was upset, he only became more deliberate. He liked to describe himself as a "dog that bites, but doesn't bark."

"No," she had said. "We need your help. I . . . need you."

There had been almost fifteen seconds of silence, and Dale had almost asked if he was still there. Then, finally, he'd said, "Tell me."

And so she had.

"Santi will meet you at the New Mexico border."

Dale's eyes watered with tears at the mention of her stepbrother. "Thank you. And for Eli? He'll need more help than us."

Silence had followed, which Dale finally broke. "Nester, if Eli makes it to Albuquerque, he'll be bringing something far more valuable than a presidential pardon."

"So you say."

"Have I ever lied to you?"

"No." He'd said it with no hesitation. Then, after several heartbeats, he added, "I'll send help." Then he'd ended the call, and Dale was left to ponder if her old friend was being truthful.

Or if he planned to throw her husband under the bus.

No, she thought now as she drank another sip of beer. The pint glass was almost empty. *Nester would not take advantage of us.* She drank from the mug again, draining the last of the beer. *He is my—*

"You girls up for a road trip?" The voice that interrupted her thoughts was raspy and unmistakable. Dale looked at Bella first, whose eyes had gone wide.

"Nan—?"

Foncie quickly covered Bella's mouth with her hand.

Dale fought back tears as she forced herself not to hug the woman standing next to her. Foncie had her long silver hair tied up in a bun and was wearing a recently bought Houston Astros cap. She wore jeans and a gray hoodie and could probably have passed for midfifties instead of early seventies.

"You're a sight for sore eyes," Dale managed.

"Nana, *what*—"

"I'll explain everything in the car, honey. After your food comes, I want you to eat as much as you can, you hear?"

They both nodded.

"We have a hell of a long drive ahead of us, and we won't be stopping at a Bojangles anytime soon."

Dale doubted there were any Bojangles this far west, but she didn't dare correct her mother-in-law. "Okay," she said.

"I promised my son I'd get you to Albuquerque, and by God, that's a promise I intend to keep."

"Albuquerque?" Bella asked, her voice wistful.

Foncie nodded and then looked at Dale. "I've been watching you since you got past security. From what I can tell, no one's following."

"Good plan," Dale said.

"So far, so good," Foncie grunted. "In fifteen minutes, I want you to pay and then walk toward the exit. I'm driving a gray Ford Explorer. I'll pick you up just past the cabstand."

"Thank you, Foncie."

"I haven't done anything yet."

Dale touched her hand. "Yes, you have."

Foncie James squinted at Dale and squeezed her hand with both of hers. "Job's not finished. Did you call your friend?"

"He's sending my brother to meet us at the New Mexico state line. We'll have an escort from there on."

"I ain't worried about us."

"He's going to help Eli too."

"You sure?"

"He's never lied to me." She hesitated before meeting Foncie's eyes. "And he's never let me down."

"Well . . . good." Foncie gave Dale's hand another squeeze and let go. Then she touched Bella's cheek. "You ready?"

Bella smiled wide, showing her teeth. Dale couldn't remember the last time she'd seen her daughter's eyes light up like they were now. "You know it."

"Hell, yes," Foncie said. "See you in fifteen," she said to Dale. Then she leaned forward so that only Dale could hear. "Help or no help, my son is going to need a miracle to get out of DC alive."

Dale held her fierce gaze. "He has something better than a miracle. He has Nester."

42

Exactly one hour and fifty-seven minutes after their conversation in the Oval Office, Eli heard three sharp knuckle cracks on his office door.

"Come in."

As the knob turned, Eli half expected to see General Kyle Randolph and a team of uniformed soldiers. Instead, the president of the United States peeked his head in the opening. "Now a good time?"

Eli nodded, and Lionel shut the door behind him.

"How did it go with the Canadian prime minister?"

Lionel smiled, but there was no humor in his face. "Just another photo op. Otherwise, pure-grain bullshit."

"Your specialty," Eli said.

"*Our* specialty," Lionel corrected.

Eli shrugged. Nothing to argue there. "Did you bring it?"

Lionel reached into his pocket and pulled out two orange pill bottles. He walked over to Eli and set them on the desk between them. "Bella should take one a day. I normally take it at breakfast, but I've waited until dinner a couple times depending on my schedule. Once the tumors are gone, she'll need to cut back to a maintenance dose of one every three days."

Eli could feel his heart pounding in his chest. *Once the tumors are gone* . . . "So this is really it? I . . . can hardly believe it."

"Me neither," Lionel said, taking a seat in one of the chairs in front of Eli's desk. Eli also sat. For several seconds, neither man spoke.

"I'm sorry," Lionel said. He wiped at his eyes and leaned forward on his knees.

"Me too," Eli managed. The room felt cold. Like something was dying. *Something is,* he thought.

"They gave me a nine-month supply, and that's almost all I have left. So . . . around seven months of it." He paused. "I held back about a week's worth to give you a little time."

"Before what?"

"I tell them."

"Them." Eli spat the word. "They, them, their. Who *are* they? Is it Randolph? Someone higher?"

"Randolph is the leader, but . . . I'm pretty sure there are others in the Defense Department."

"Jesus H. Christ. Lionel . . . pretty sure? You're the president, for God's sake. Shouldn't you know who's keeping you alive?"

"I know. I . . . know."

"How long do you have to take it?"

Lionel whistled through his teeth. "They haven't told me."

"This is the cure for cancer." Eli pointed at the bottles on his desk, feeling ridiculous. He opened one of them. "If this is just a boatload of Viagra, I'm going to be pissed."

Neither man laughed.

The capsule was white. Nondescript. Completely ordinary looking. Not unlike the magnesium muscle relaxer that Eli sometimes took after working out.

"How can I be sure that this is the real deal?" Eli asked. "For all I know, you've told Randolph, and this is just some placebo."

Lionel shook his head. "No, that's the real McCoy. If I'd told Randolph, you would be in DOD custody as we speak. I did speak with the general a few minutes after our last exchange and reassured him that you are not a threat . . . that you'll be leaving your position to be with your daughter and Dale during this difficult time."

"Well . . . thank you," Eli said. "Do you think he believed you?"

Lionel stretched his arms over his head and sighed. "Honest? I don't have a clue. That man is hard to read. Look, Eli, this whole thing has been a mind-fuck for me. I wish I had given the medication to you sooner. I was just scared. I . . . *am* scared."

"Can I ask you something?"

Lionel shrugged. His body language reeked of resignation.

"Why you?" Eli asked. "And how did they even find out you had cancer? Wouldn't that be a violation of HIPAA?"

Lionel smirked. "With respect to the second question, I have no idea. Randolph said that in matters of national security, they have a lot of leeway. As for the first question, they felt that my death from cancer would cripple the country." He paused. "There's not a lot of faith in our vice president."

At this, Eli actually laughed, despite the tension in the room. "You've got to be kidding. You've been gifted the fountain of youth because Yancey's an idiot?"

"It seems so."

"Who else?" Eli asked.

"What do you mean?"

"Who else has been given this miracle?" Eli nodded at the medication.

Lionel held out his hands. "I don't know. All I know . . . is that it *is* a miracle. My cancer is completely gone, and I'm glad that my goddaughter will benefit from it." The president reached into his suit jacket and pulled out a pint of Jack Daniel's Black. He unscrewed the top and took a long sip. Then he extended the bottle across the desk. Eli grabbed it and pressed the glass to his lips. He winced as the whiskey burned his throat going down.

"I love you, brother," Lionel said, his voice cracking. Tears in his eyes.

Eli nodded and drank another long sip. His eyes were hot. "I have to get out of here." He peered at his desk. "None of this matters a bit unless I can get it to Bella."

"Where are you going?"

Eli managed a grin. "Better for you not to know."

"Doesn't matter," Lionel said. "I have a pretty good idea." He paused. "And so will they." He cocked his head toward the door.

"I need you to get me out of here."

"Why can't you just walk out? You haven't done anything illegal . . . I mean, other than blackmail the president of the United States."

"Tell me exactly how it went with Randolph."

"I told him that all you did was ask me what I knew about a possible cure, and I said that I knew nothing. That you had pressed me about my improvement and that I stood my ground and stressed that the chemo and radiation is all I've done. Then you said you were leaving your position to be with your family." Lionel paused. "That was it."

"That won't stop him," Eli said, standing and crossing his arms. "I'm surprised he hasn't already taken me into custody."

"Eli, about your dad . . . Are you sure?"

"He hasn't answered any of my calls in days. I've reached out to a couple of his friends and neighboring boat owners, and they haven't seen him in at least a week. He's . . . disappeared." Eli peered at the president. "Just like Mato Nakai and Mary Frances Bruce. Just like I will if I can't get out of DC."

Lionel shook his head.

"Are you still flying to Japan this afternoon?" Eli asked.

"Diplomacy never stops," Lionel grunted, nodding. Then he looked at Eli. "I'll be gone a week."

"When do you leave?"

Lionel glanced at his Rolex. "Not for another four hours. I'm supposed to have cabinet meetings until then."

"Cancel those," Eli said, pacing back and forth behind his desk. "Is the Secret Service in with Randolph?"

Lionel blinked. "Honestly, I don't know. No agent has been present for any of my dealings with him, but that doesn't mean anything."

"The Secret Service is your detail. They should be separate, and I would think the fewer people that knew about this secret, the better."

"That's . . . a reasonable assumption."

Eli thought about it for another second and made his decision. "Call Alison and tell her that you're going to the VA Medical Center to make some unannounced drop-ins on patient soldiers to show your support for their efforts. Have her round up your Secret Service detail."

"Eli, I can't just—"

"You're the president of the United States, and this is something you should have done already. That's the attitude I want you to convey. That you need more of a presence over there. You are, after all, the commander in chief of the military. What could be more presidential than a photo opportunity with wounded soldiers?"

"I agree with that, but—"

"Do it." Eli pointed at the phone on his desk. "Now. Tell her you want to be gone in five minutes."

Lionel sighed and picked up the phone. He barked out instructions to Alison Barnes.

"Now what?"

"We wait here. You don't leave my side. If Randolph peeks his head in, you tell him that we, me and you, are dropping in on the VA hospital."

"Eli, I can't just tell General—"

"Yes, you can, Lionel. You're the president of the fucking United States." Eli felt a lump in his throat, but he forced the emotion back. "We got here together. Me and you. If you get me out of DC, I'll never roll on you, Lionel. But . . . if I don't, then—"

"You're changing the rules of the game," Lionel said, slamming his fist down on the table. "You said if I brought you the medication that you'd keep your mouth shut."

"It doesn't do me any good unless Bella gets it."

"That's not fair."

"No, it's not."

Lionel started to say something else, but three loud knocks on the door stopped him cold. Eli pocketed the pill bottles. Before he could say "Come in," the door opened, and Edgar Sams, the head of the Secret Service detail, stepped into the room. "We're ready, Mr. President. A team has gone ahead to make sure the area is secure."

"Good deal, Edgar. Thank you. Uh, Mr. James is going to be accompanying me on this trip."

Edgar glanced at Eli and then back to the president. "Yes, sir."

"All right then," Lionel said. He stared at Eli with sad eyes. "Let's roll."

43

Kyle Randolph sat in the back of the Escalade. The general hated surprises, and he'd just been given another big one.

"General, are you still there?"

"I'm here. Are you sure?"

"Yes, sir. The president has called for an impromptu trip to the VA Medical Center to visit with wounded soldiers. Mr. James, the president, and the Secret Service are leaving the White House now."

"Why is Mr. James going on this excursion?"

"I don't know, sir."

Randolph closed his eyes.

"General, what are my orders?"

"Follow, but at a safe distance."

"Ten-four."

Randolph ended the call and then glanced out the window. *It could be nothing at all. One last event together . . .*

His team in Houston said that Mrs. James was flying home to Virginia this afternoon. Early, but not too early. The girl wasn't doing well with the trial. Mrs. James had quit her job, and Eli was leaving his. It all made sense, given the circumstances. Their only child was dying.

The president had assured him that all was well, the secret intact. Eli James had peppered him with questions, but the president hadn't broken.

Can I trust him?

Randolph chuckled to himself. He didn't trust anyone, much less a career politician like Lionel Cantrell.

His driver looked at Randolph in the rearview mirror.

What is James up to?

Randolph reran his tense exchange with him earlier that morning. The defiance in the man's tone and body language. Eli had been an excellent lawyer. He'd guided Lionel Cantrell's career all the way to the White House. And, based on their questioning of Sarah Kate Moss, he hadn't been given much of a tip on the boomerang before he tracked down Candace Bruce. What else had he learned? They'd gotten to his father, but his mother—the investigator—was in the wind. Eli had left his cell phone at his home in Arlington and had managed to walk into the White House without any of their operatives seeing hide or hair of him in over three days.

He isn't going to quit.

The game they were playing was dicey. Randolph couldn't simply have Eli arrested or detained. He'd committed no crime. And while Eli's father might be a casualty, Eli himself was the chief of staff to the president. Not exactly famous, but not someone who could just disappear without the world taking note.

What if he goes to the press with what he's found out so far? Randolph had thought through this possibility a lot, and, while it would require a response, he didn't think James would get far with a media campaign.

That's not what he's after, anyway.

Eli James was no crusader for justice. He wasn't trying to bring the cure for cancer to the general public.

He's a father trying to save his daughter's life.

Randolph whistled through his teeth.

Which makes him a dangerous man . . .

The driver looked at him again in the mirror, seeking direction.

"Keep following the motorcade," Randolph directed him. "We're going to the VA Medical Center."

44

As the presidential caravan pulled in to the hospital's visitor entrance, Eli gripped Lionel's forearm and whispered into his ear. "After we're ushered inside, I'm going to receive a call on my phone that's an emergency. I'll tell you and then I'll get an Uber to pick me up so as not to be a distraction to you or the Secret Service. If anyone asks—and you and I both know who *anyone* is—I left the hospital shortly after arrival. Do you understand?"

Lionel nodded. "Eli—?"

"If I don't make it to where I'm headed . . . if something happens to me along the way and I don't ever arrive, then that envelope with all of the skeletons gets delivered to the news stations."

"You told me if I got you out of DC—"

"That was then," Eli snapped. "This is now. If anything interrupts Bella's treatment, you're going down."

"You can't keep changing the rules. Besides, bringing me down would only destroy your credibility. No one will believe that a terminated employee with an axe to grind and his own hefty closet full of skeletons is telling the truth."

Eli swallowed, and his mouth felt dry. "I resigned."

Lionel smiled, but there was no humor in his eyes. "This is Washington, Eli. The narrative changes in the blink of an eye, and once you go rogue, General Randolph will do everything in his power to destroy your name."

Eli scoffed. "Bigger fish have tried."

"No. You're wrong about that. Kyle Randolph is a great white shark. He's motherfucking Jaws."

"Mr. President, are you ready?" The driver had rolled down the barricade that separated the front and back seats. Eli glanced out the window and saw the team of suited-up agents ready to escort them into the VA Medical Center. Inside the door, there were more agents.

"One second." Lionel glanced down at the floorboard. "I won't say anything to Randolph or anyone else until I absolutely have to. I'll try to buy you some time, but Eli . . ." He trailed off, and his voice cracked. "This isn't going to end well for you."

"Nothing that ends ever ends well," Eli said, feeling emotion in his own voice. Adrenaline and fatigue fought a tug-of-war in his veins, and he knew he had to stay hyperalert.

"Mr. President?" the driver asked again.

"Good luck, Eli."

Eli nodded. "Ditto."

"All right," Lionel said, his deep voice filling up the interior of the limousine as he looked at the driver. "Let's do it."

45

At 6:35 p.m., Kyle Randolph waited outside of gate 21 of the American Airlines terminal of Reagan National. The 737 that Dale and Bella James were slated to be on from Houston had landed minutes earlier, and passengers were beginning to filter out of the long tunnel from the plane to the gate. Randolph felt a tightness in his chest. He was agitated. Frustrated. Angry with himself. *I should have detained the SOB at the White House.*

He shook his head and focused on the people arriving from Houston. He would have expected mother and child to have flown first class. If so, they would have been some of the first off the plane. But as the waves of men, women, and children strode out of the narrow opening embarking on the next adventure of their lives, there was no sign of Dale and Bella James.

Maybe the girl got sick. She could be in the bathroom. Mrs. James might be waiting until everyone is off the plane.

It was plausible. Cancer treatment was awful, and Bella had been suffering from nausea from the trial. That was one of the reasons Dale had given for their early departure from MD Anderson. The side effects had been brutal.

Randolph glanced at his phone and thumbed a quick text. **Anything?**

Seconds later, he saw the dots indicating a response was on the way. When it came, the general ground his teeth as he read the message he expected.

Nothing, sir. Status quo.

Randolph put his phone back in his pocket and went over the facts in his mind. He'd followed the presidential caravan to the VA Medical Center and watched Eli James be escorted into the hospital with the president. However, an hour later, when the president's entourage exited the building, the chief of staff was not with them. According to the Secret Service, James received an emergency call a few minutes after arrival and said he was leaving the hospital via Uber. If that was true, and with all the cars coming in and out of the VA . . .

. . . *it would have been impossible to see him go.*

Since then, the general's efforts to locate the chief had been unsuccessful. Currently, Eli James was not at home or at the White House. His Range Rover was still parked at a Whole Foods about a mile from his house.

The general had suspected the call James received was from his wife telling him that she and Bella were on a last-minute flight home. Mrs. James had, in fact, booked the trip from Houston earlier this morning.

Again . . . it was plausible. But if Eli was picking his family up at the airport, then why hadn't he Ubered to Arlington to get his car? Would he really drive a rental? And why the hell did he abandon his car at a grocery store in the first place?

To evade me, Randolph thought. It was the only logical explanation.

He probably still has the rental from wherever he's been. He probably drove it to the White House this morning.

Randolph rubbed his chin, continuing to watch the passengers disembark. He glanced at his watch. 6:40 p.m. The president was leaving for Japan in less than an hour and would be gone a week. His phone vibrated. He snatched the device from his pocket and glared at the screen.

We're checking all the cars waiting in the arrival pickup area, and there is still no sign of Eli James.

Randolph typed a quick response. 10-4. Keep watching.

He again glanced at the tunnel and saw that the traffic had died down. The flight attendants were now coming out of the tunnel. Randolph walked toward them and pulled out his credentials. Three agents stationed at other areas of the gate followed in behind him.

The plane's crew, a young blond woman with green eyes, an older Black gentleman, and a plump redheaded man, looked surprised and irritated at being stopped. "I'm sorry for the intrusion," Randolph said, "but did you see this woman and her daughter on the airplane?" He flashed them photographs of Dale and Bella James. "The daughter probably looks different now. Thinner and with no hair. She would have been wearing a cap. Their tickets were for first class."

All three shook their head.

"Two of the seats in the first-class cabin were empty," the Black man said, rubbing the stubble on his chin. "Weird. Pay that much money for comfort and then not show up."

"Yeah," Randolph said. "Weird. Thank you for your time."

The general strode to the information counter, showed his badge, and asked the woman behind the counter to call Houston and ask about two passengers that were scheduled to be on the flight but had not disembarked.

We should have watched them closer, Randolph thought, but then shook off the unhelpful second-guessing. There was no reason to think that Dale and Bella James would not be on the plane. They had packed their luggage. Driven their rental car to the airport. Checked their bags and gone through security. How could anyone expect them not to get on the plane?

There has to be an explanation. Perhaps Bella got sick at the airport and wasn't up for the flight. That made sense. Again . . . plausible. They were probably either still at George W. Bush or back at MD Anderson. Those would be the first calls he made after getting confirmation.

He watched the woman behind the counter. She'd dialed a number, asked about Bella and Dale, and was now waiting. Finally, she put her hand over the receiver. "Houston says that neither woman's boarding pass was scanned at the gate." She paused. "They weren't on the plane."

"Thank you," Randolph said, already walking away and pulling out his cell. He had another text from the agents outside.

Still no sign of the chief of staff. Was his family on the plane?

He thumbed no and called his team leader in Houston. He gave specific instructions to scour the American Airlines terminal and the entire airport. He also instructed her to call MD Anderson.

As he ended the call, Randolph trusted his instincts. His next call was to Edgar Sams with the Secret Service. "Edgar, this is General Kyle Randolph. I have a matter of the utmost national security that I need to discuss with the president."

A pause, then Sams's gravelly voice: "Air Force One is fueled up and ready to depart to Tokyo. The president is already on board, and the crew is making final preparations. Takeoff is imminent."

"I'll be at Andrews in thirty minutes," Randolph said, now running back to his ride. "I have to talk to the president before he leaves." He paused. "I need you to stop that plane."

Randolph ended the call without waiting for a response. He picked up his pace.

The situation was spiraling out of control.

"Damnit, Lionel," he panted through clenched teeth. "What have you done?"

46

What have I done? Lionel asked himself, massaging his temples with his thumbs.

"The general said we have to wait," Edgar Sams's voice was firm. Authoritative. "He said it was a matter of—"

"National security." Lionel almost spat the words as he gazed at his watch. It was seven o'clock. Approximately five hours since he'd last seen Eli. His friend had received his fake phone call, said he had to go, and was walking down the corridor of the hospital at a furious clip the last Lionel had seen of him.

Elijah Longstreet James . . .

Lionel closed his eyes, thinking of his friend. He had hoped to give him a week, but he hadn't even made it a day. Not even a half day. In truth, Lionel was amazed that Eli had gotten as far as he had.

He heard a rustling and a smattering of voices outside the conference room. The sheer size and stature of Air Force One never ceased to amaze Lionel. This was the first trip he'd been able to take on the plane with Vanessa, and he'd been looking forward to giving his wife the grand tour. Alas, Kyle Randolph and *national security* had foiled his plans.

The door swung open, and the former chairman of the Joint Chiefs of Staff barged in. "Edgar, please give me a minute with the president alone."

Edgar Sams rose and strode out of the room. Then Randolph walked in and circled the long rectangular table. Lionel recalled his analogy for Eli:

Motherfucking Jaws.

"The James family is MIA, Mr. President. We lost contain on Eli shortly after your entry to the VA Medical Center. His wife and daughter were scheduled on the four p.m. flight from Houston to Reagan National, but they never got on the plane. Their luggage arrived. So did their cell phones. But they didn't."

Lionel couldn't suppress a smile. *Smart,* he thought.

"Do you find this amusing?" Randolph asked, approaching and taking the seat next to Lionel.

"Intelligent is what I find it," Lionel said, looking the general in the eye. "And sly. And . . . ambitious. Three qualities that my former chief of staff and his wife have in spades."

"Clearly they have something to hide." Randolph's tone was quiet and menacing. "Have you been lying to me, Mr. President?"

Lionel glanced down at the mahogany table. "He blackmailed me. I . . . had no choice."

Randolph crossed his arms. "Yes, you did. You don't think I could handle a little shit like Eli James? Let me guess, he threatened to tell the world about your various and sundry affairs and one-night stands on the campaign trail? Or maybe your cocaine habit in law school?"

Lionel raised his eyebrows, feeling his heart begin to pound.

"We know everything, Lionel. *Everything.* And we know all that needs to be known about Eli James too. We could have quashed any blackmail attempt. Please tell me you aren't that stupid."

Lionel looked past the general to the far wall. The airplane was huge. The conference room was huge. The country was huge. Everything was so fucking big.

And I'm nothing but a puppet for this sonofabitch.

"Eli James is my friend. Bella James is my goddaughter."

"Don't make this about nobility. I'm not stupid."

"I'm not either. And you're probably right. If Eli came forward, I'm sure you could drown him in a sea of counterallegations and make him look like a rogue employee out for revenge." Lionel paused, and then he glared at the Defense Department stalwart. "But my wife would know. And my children eventually would too. Vanessa knows how close Eli is to me. If he came forward, the country might not believe him . . . but Vanessa would."

Randolph pushed himself off the table. "Enough of your reasons. We're wasting time." He glared down at the president. "Did you give Eli James the contents of the medicine box?"

Lionel glared back at him. "Yes, General, I did."

47

As the headlights of the Explorer flashed on the green sign, Dale felt a wave of relief wash over her.

WELCOME TO NEW MEXICO
LAND OF ENCHANTMENT

"Hot diggety damn," Foncie said, rapping her knuckles on the steering wheel. "So where are the dark SUVs and the chopper?" she asked, moving her calloused right hand through her hair to clear the frizzy bangs from her eyes. "Goddamnit," she whispered, repeating the gesture until her vision was clear.

"Nester is subtler than that," Dale said, feeling herself smiling despite the danger they were in. She couldn't wait to see her family. On her work trips to handle Nester's legal business, she hardly ever had time for a visit. Her mother had died years ago, but her stepfather's family remained a huge presence in Los Lunas: Her stepbrothers Santiago and Amos. Uncle Ralph and Uncle Leonard. All the cousins. The Gutierrez clan loved Dale James like she was blood, and she loved them back.

She wiped at her eyes and glanced behind her shoulder, where Bella lay on her side across the entire back seat. Sleeping soundly. They'd gotten fast food in Amarillo, and Bella had eaten a few fries, but that was it. Since then, she'd been snoozing while darkness covered the plains.

The bare flatness of the land never ceased to amaze Dale. In Virginia and Alabama, the verdant, mountainous topography was such that you could only see a little way in front of you. But here, in Texas and now New Mexico, a person could see for miles in every direction. It was a shock if you weren't used to it.

Now, though, all you could make out were scattered lights as far as the eye could see. Almost as if their car were a meteor moving through a vast galaxy.

"Earth to Resting Bitch Face," Foncie rasped. "What's the plan? Where's your brother?"

"I don't know," Dale said, snatching her phone from the drink console. "Do you have to be so crude?"

"Yes," Foncie said, without explanation.

Dale had received no calls, texts, or messages since talking to Nester that morning. For a moment, she wondered if her blind trust in him was foolish. He was, after all, a criminal.

When was the last time she'd seen him for something other than business? Their twenty-year high school reunion had been six years ago. Nester had not attended any of the activities, but she'd met him briefly after the reception. In a suite in the same hotel as the party. They had spoken for no more than five minutes. And before that?

Dale couldn't remember, but it had probably been right after college. More than twenty years ago. Sure, there had been phone calls, letters, and texts. But their last meaningful personal conversation had occurred more than two decades ago.

And yet, she knew . . . *knew* Nester would be there for her.

As the interstate added a third lane and the neon hue of a gas station came into view, Dale saw a flash of light and looked over her shoulder. A truck was behind them, and its brights were on. She watched as the vehicle moved into the left lane and pulled even with the Explorer. The interior light in the cab of the pickup came on.

When Dale saw him, an audible sob escaped her lips. The man behind the wheel had thick jet-black hair and a sleek build. He glanced at her and mouthed the words "*We've got you.*" His eyes were kind and as dark as his hair.

"La Bamba," Foncie said. "I hope he's with us."

"That's my brother," Dale said, her voice cracking. "Santiago Gutierrez. We call him Santi." She crossed her arms over her chest and mouthed "*Thank you*" to Santi.

"I'll call him handsome," Foncie said. "Watch out, now. We've got another truck incoming on the right."

Dale jerked her head and squinted. The driver of this vehicle had short brown hair, broad shoulders, and a crooked grin. He mouthed the word "*Sissy.*"

"*Amos . . .*"

Amos Gutierrez blew her a kiss and fell in behind them, as Santi sped up and got in front.

"Well, I'll be damned," Foncie said as Dale wiped fresh tears from her face. "We got us a convoy."

———

Two hours later, about an hour from Albuquerque, they pulled in to an all-night Allsup's convenience store. Dale staggered out of the Explorer on shaky legs. Since crossing into New Mexico, she'd been on an adrenaline high, but now she felt anxious and afraid. Guilt permeated her being. When was the last time she'd spoken to her brothers? *Too long . . .*

As Dale rounded the back of the SUV, she stopped.

They were both leaning against the tailgate of Santi's truck. Amos wore a black Gold's Gym tank top with faded jeans. His arms were huge, biceps bulging, but his face carried his patented crooked grin, and his buzzed haircut highlighted his large ears. *So cute.* Amos was the perennial prankster, who'd once put dye in her shampoo bottle, turning her blond hair jet black, but he had a soft heart and had been inconsolable when she'd left New Mexico for college. Next to him, his older brother Santi, wearing the khaki uniform of the Los Lunas Police Department. Arms crossed, squinting at her. His dark eyes and lashes had always made him so handsome. He'd been a quiet, smart boy. Wise beyond his years. Somewhere, in a box at their home in Arlington, she had the letters he'd written to her in college.

Now they were middle-aged men. And Santi a cop, of all things.

Dale forced her feet to move forward. Her eyes stung with tears, and her lips trembled. Foncie and she had been driving for fourteen hours, with four stops for Bella to become violently sick. She was *so tired*. As her legs began to give, she lunged forward, and her brothers caught her. For a moment, they shared a group hug, and Dale cried into Santi's shoulder.

"I'm sorry," she croaked. "I—"

But before she could say anything else, Amos lifted her off the ground. "Shh, sissy." He set her down, and then Santi put his hand around her neck and leaned his forehead into hers. It was something he had always done. "It is good to see you. *Sorry* is something you never have to say to us."

"Thank you," she managed. "Thank you so much." Relief washed over her like a hot shower. It had always been like this with the Gutierrez family. When her mom had married Jerry, the family had accepted her as one of them. No questions. No passive aggression. No jealousy. They called her *sister* or *sissy*, and that was that.

"Are you hungry?" Santi asked, his face breaking into a grin as he gestured with his head toward the front door of the Allsup's. "You know you want one."

Dale couldn't help but laugh.

"I don't know about her, but I could eat the hide off a mule's ass." Foncie had come around the Explorer after starting the gas pump. Next to her, Bella was rubbing the sleep out of her eyes.

"Allsup's has its world-famous burrito, but sissy always preferred the chimichanga," Amos said, stepping forward.

"It's a gut bomb," Santi added.

"My gut's made of steel," Foncie said. "I'll take one of each." She extended her hand. "Foncie James. Thank you for the escort."

"You're welcome, Auntie," Amos said, and Foncie wrinkled her face and glanced at Dale. On the drive, Dale had explained that her family would treat any relative of hers as their family too. Amos walked over to Bella and put his hand on her shoulder. "Don't feel so good, huh?"

Bella shook her head, looking down at the asphalt.

Santi had walked over and stood next to his brother. "You're beautiful like your mother."

Bella rolled her eyes. "I'm skinny and bald." Her voice was scratchy from lack of water.

Santi leaned down and kissed Bella's bare head. "No, niecey." He rubbed the spot he had kissed. "You are beautiful, and you are going to get well here." He turned to Dale. "Just like your mom did."

Dale wiped her eyes. Santi had always been so wise. Dale had not been physically sick, but her heart had been severely broken when she and her mom moved to New Mexico. But then they joined the Gutierrez family. *And I healed.*

"Well, I'm ugly all day," Foncie barked. "Let's get on that chimichanga." She strode past them to the door, and Santi glanced at Dale with eyebrows raised.

"She's a piece of work," Dale whispered.

"I like her," Santi said.

"Me too," Amos said, grabbing Bella by the hand and leading her forward. "Now, you don't have to eat anything here. We can get you something bland. Maybe some pretzels."

"Goldfish?" Bella suggested.

"They got it all here. This is the best convenience store in the world."

Dale started to follow, but Santi grabbed her by the hand. "No one has been following us. We've been keeping a close eye, and we have spotters behind and in front of us."

"Thank you."

"You're safe, sister. No one will find you where we are taking you."

Dale swallowed. For a few moments, the family reunion had taken her away from the danger they were in. Now it all came crashing back. She hadn't heard from Eli since this morning. How had it gone with Lionel? Did he have any leads? Could it be possible that there was a cure for cancer that Lionel had been taking? Had Lionel given it to Eli? Was he on his way to meet them?

She sighed, feeling gooseflesh on her arm. Or had it gone badly? Was Eli in the custody of the FBI?

Or has he disappeared? Like Mary Frances Bruce. Mato Nakai . . . and his father.

"You okay?" Santi asked. "You disappeared there, for a second."

"I'm worried about my husband."

Santi glanced to the store, and a wry grin formed on his face. "He's going to be fine."

"He's surrounded in DC. I just don't see how he can make it out of there without being seen."

Santi touched her shoulder. "Help is on the way."

48

The storage closet smelled of cardboard boxes and ammonia. Eli sat with his back against a cinder block wall. Arms wrapped around his knees. His eyes had adjusted to the darkness, and he stared at the doorknob. Since stepping inside this sanctuary approximately fifteen hours earlier, he'd seen it turn only twice. Both times, a nurse had not even fully stepped inside. They'd grabbed the medicine or device they needed without even a glance at the back of the closet where Eli crouched in plain sight. Now, Eli heard nothing but the occasional beep of an empty IV or other monitor in a patient's room.

His back ached from sitting, and his butt was numb from the cold tile. Occasionally, he got up and paced the small confines of the closet, but that had made him dizzy and claustrophobic. Now, he simply sat and tried to keep his mind calm.

He'd initially gone in with the president to meet the first patient. Her name was Kim Beech, and she'd been a medic in Afghanistan. A young woman in her late twenties. She'd lost her left leg when a roadside bomb detonated. She'd been surprised to see Lionel, but her eyes also seemed glazed over with what had to be pain medication. She'd been admitted a week ago, and they were still waiting for her to be stable enough to go to the rehab wing. Eli had been hyperalert, listening but also contemplating his move. As they were walking out of the room, he pulled out his burner and faked being suddenly agitated. He'd run his hand through his hair and told his dead phone, "I'll be right there." Then he'd turned to Lionel and whispered "I have to go" in his ear. After that, he'd found Edgar Sams and said he had a family emergency and would take an Uber. Sams had nodded without any questions. The group had continued to the next patient's room, and Eli hadn't looked back.

He'd ridden the elevator back down to the visitor's entrance, and he'd started to hail a cab. An Uber would be less conspicuous, but his burner didn't have that capability. Then he realized he'd need to leave the hospital via a less traveled area. Randolph probably had people watching the facility. He went down to the basement, which connected to the parking garage, and saw several cabs. He could pay cash and get out of there.

But where would he go? It was foolish to think that he could just be dropped off at his rental car a couple blocks from the White House. He could try it, but his gut told him that was a fool's errand. He'd be seen. Randolph had probably already located the Impala and, if he hadn't, he'd have an army watching for Eli. Now that he had the boomerang in tow, he couldn't risk being detained before getting out of DC.

So he'd gone back inside the hospital. When he saw the storage closet, he'd peeked his head inside, thought about it for a few seconds, and made his decision. It had felt right at the time. *Dale will call Nester, and he'll send people to help. They'll call me on the burner, and we'll need somewhere to meet.* The VA Medical Center was a landmark that would be easy to find.

Plus, the story he told Edgar Sams should have Randolph looking anywhere but here. It was a good plan. In a crisis, it was oftentimes better to stay still and let others become impatient and make mistakes.

But it's all for naught if no one comes to deliver me to Bella . . .

Eli wondered about Nester. The man was utterly devoted to Dale, but would he help Eli? With Eli running for his life, he could no longer be of any service to Nester. The pardon that Eli and Lionel had promised was now a pipe dream. Eli had thought this through, and he knew what his play would be if he made it to New Mexico. If Lionel was right and the pill bottles in Eli's pocket truly contained the cure for cancer, then Eli could give Nester something better than a pardon.

Lifetime leverage.

He just had to get to Albuquerque alive and with the medicine.

But honestly . . . why would Nester help me? When I'm out of the picture, he can have Dale to himself. He sighed. *Dale won't throw me under the bus.*

Eli took out his phone and glared at the screen, willing it to ring. It was 5:17 a.m. He'd left the closet only a few times to use the bathroom, which was two doors down. He needed to go again, but he'd been fighting the urge, hoping he'd hear something. *Dale will come through . . . she always does. If Nester leaves me high and dry, Dale will never forgive him. Surely, she's told him enough about what I'm doing to pique his interest.* Eli forced himself to take a deep breath, slowly exhaling, as he tried to control his thoughts. He couldn't afford to think negatively.

He also couldn't afford to wait to pee any longer or he was going to wet his pants. He pulled himself to his feet and reached for the knob just as his phone started to vibrate in his other hand. He stared at the screen, wondering if he was hallucinating. The area code was 505.

New Mexico.

He answered the call.

"Yeah," Eli croaked.

"Where are you?" The voice had a Mexican accent and sounded vaguely familiar.

"VA Medical Center in DC. I'm in a storage closet on the basement floor."

Several seconds of silence. Then the voice again. "Smart. I'm . . . about twenty minutes from you. I'll call again when I'm closer."

"Wait—"

The line went dead. Eli's heart was racing. He felt a weird mixture of relief, anxiety, and fear. He tried to control his breathing.

It was good to hear a familiar voice, but . . .

. . . what in the hell is going on?

49

Panic was not a word in General Kyle Randolph's vocabulary. He would never use it to describe his state of being. Nor would he even conceive that such a thing as a panic attack could happen to him. He'd fought in wars. He'd sent men and women to their death in order to protect the United States of America.

And he'd ordered the murders of Mary Frances Bruce, Mato Nakai, Dr. Frank James, and other citizens in the interest of national security. But now, having lost containment of the entire James family and having been told that the contents of the medicine box were in the rogue chief of staff's possession, Randolph felt his grip slipping. He tried to control his thoughts, but they were a whirlwind of possibilities, none of them good.

Dale and Bella James were gone. The trail was lost and would not be found. He'd assumed that the flight Dale booked that morning was one that she and Bella would actually be on.

When you assume, you make an ass of you and me.

The hoary cliché remained as true as ever.

He *had* assumed, and it had cost him.

And now it might cost the country . . .

Randolph ran his fingers along the four silver stars on both sides of his collar. He'd done so many things in his life, but Project Boomerang was, without a doubt, his most important mission. In the years since he'd cofounded the initiative, as director, he'd tasked himself with putting together a Special Forces unit to handle the dirty work when situations became risky.

For seven and a half years, he'd done his duty, fulfilling the obligations of his post. The boomerang had remained a secret while Beth McGee, Robert Bellamy, and the FDA had tried and failed to come up with a rollout plan or any way to prevent an economic meltdown if the cure for cancer were given to the world.

Now, Randolph knew, the cover-up had grown bigger than the cure itself, making it more vital than ever that the secret be protected.

Randolph rolled down the window of the Escalade and breathed in the cool, damp air. No, he was not panicking. His resolve was only growing stronger as he focused on the battle at hand.

Eli James was last seen with the president inside the VA Medical Center. Again, assumptions were made. Since James came in with the president, it followed that he'd leave with the president.

But he hadn't. Eli had taken an Uber or a cab or had left the hospital on foot, and he was nowhere to be seen. They'd found the Chevrolet Impala that he'd rented and were now aware of the fake ID and alias credit card he'd used to reserve it. The sedan had been parked a couple of blocks from the White House. Randolph had since made a few calls and had frozen Eli's credit cards, including the alias, so he couldn't take another Uber or rental, though he could still pay for a cab with cash. Time was of the essence.

And it might already be too late.

The general's black Cadillac Escalade was idling in the front parking lot of the VA Medical Center. Randolph had been rethinking another assumption he had made.

That Eli James had told the truth.

He'd advised both the president and Edgar Sams that he was leaving the hospital, but what if that was a ruse? Sure, Eli had to run if he was going to get out of DC, but maybe he'd told Edgar and Lionel what he wanted everyone to know.

Maybe he's still in *the hospital.*

He'd dispatched a team a few minutes ago. Given that it was still predawn and visitation wouldn't begin for hours yet, they should be able to scour the hospital in no time.

Randolph burped and covered his mouth. He had heartburn and indigestion and felt as if he might puke. For seven and a half years, he'd guarded Mato Nakai's secret invention with his life. The cure had been given to only a handful of people. The decision to allow access to Lionel Cantrell had been a calculated one based on the fear of Vice President Yancey coming into power. How could anyone have known that the one human aware of Lionel's diagnosis would come up with his own cancer crisis? Things would have been so much easier and predictable if Lionel had told only his wife about his recurrence.

But Lionel was a politician, and his bread had been buttered by the scheming of Eli James.

Randolph lifted his walkie-talkie: "How's it going?"

Static and then his team leader's shrill voice. "We've covered the first four floors and seen nothing suspicious. We're going to the basement now, but it looks clean."

Randolph covered the receiver with his hand and sighed. "All right, keep me posted."

"Ten-four."

Damnit. Randolph would need to call an emergency meeting with Beth McGee and Robert Bellamy, first thing in the morning. It didn't matter whether they caught Eli James. Things had gotten out of control. The president had caved. Hard decisions needed to be made.

Randolph visualized the smarmy sonofabitch in his slick custom suit. How could that career politician get the jump on him?

"Where are you?" Randolph whispered, staring out the window at the dark hospital.

Where the fuck are you?

50

Eli was moving.

He'd gone to the bathroom five minutes after the call he received, knowing he might have to hold it for a long time once he left the medical center. But when he peeked his head out of the men's room, he saw uniformed soldiers striding down the hall to his right.

Eli's stomach clenched. He glanced to his left, seeing no people and an exit sign. He knew he couldn't hesitate; nor could he stay where he was. He eased the door shut and walked as fast as he could toward the exit, pushed through the door, and got his bearings. He was in a foyer that had a vending machine and a kiosk where patrons could insert their parking stub and pay for the time they'd been in the lot. Another door led to the parking garage; he scanned the area past the glass, looking for more soldiers but not seeing any. He pulled out his phone and dialed the 505 number that had called him.

"Almost there," the familiar voice answered.

"Almost ain't good enough. They've found me. I'm in the parking garage. Basement level."

"I'm two minutes out. There should be a loading area down there. Head that way and you'll see me."

"Wait, how—?"

"You'll know."

"I'll know what?"

But the call had ended. He looked around the area and saw a ramp on the far side. He glanced behind him and saw no one coming. Then he walked out the exit and into the garage. After a few strides, he started to run.

———

"Nothing on the basement floor," the team leader's voice sounded through the walkie-talkie. "We'll check the parking deck next and then . . ." She trailed off.

"That'll be it," Randolph completed her thought. He continued to gaze out the window, seeing a couple of delivery vehicles pulling in to the garage as well as a few cars. Nurses and staff reporting for their next shift. The day was about to start.

And Eli James was still missing.

Damnit, Randolph thought, picking up his phone and finding the confidential number for the director of the FBI.

———

When Eli saw the eighteen-wheeler with the electric-blue trailer and red, white, and blue logo, he understood. And he knew.

Without a shadow of a doubt, he knew.

"I'll be damned," he whispered as he slowed his run to a jog and then a fast walk. A man had stepped down from the cab and was limping toward the back of the truck. He glanced at Eli. "Hey, *mijo*, can you help me?"

"Y-yeah," Eli managed, following the man as he unhooked a couple of clamps and opened the back of the trailer. Then he dropped a ramp down onto the pavement. He walked up the ramp into the bed, and Eli did the same. Once they were inside the trailer, the man pointed at Eli. "You stay here. I'm going to take down a couple of cases for show, and then we'll be out of here."

"Ralph?"

"In the flesh," Ralph Gutierrez said, holding out his palms. Dale's stepuncle was maybe five-four and weighed well over two hundred pounds. He had a long forehead and a big nose, and his black eyes were huge and sorrowful. His facial expressions reminded Eli of a hound dog from an old Disney movie. For as long as Eli had known him, which stretched over twenty years, Dale's oldest uncle had worked for Pepsi.

"The accommodations aren't all that comfortable in here," Ralph told him. "But after we drive awhile, I may let you up in the cab." He paused and held up his index finger. "Maybe."

"There are federal agents looking for me here."

"They aren't going to bother an old fat man delivering Pepsi to the hospital."

Eli started to say something, but Ralph was already limping back down the ramp with two cases.

"I'll be damned," Eli said again, relief now replacing shock as he hunkered down in the pitch-dark trailer.

51

Beth McGee stood with her arms folded at the head of the table. "Are you *fucking* kidding me?"

Randolph gave his head a jerk. "I wish I was." He peered at her. "But I'm not."

"Eli James is in possession of the boomerang." Robert Bellamy's voice sounded defeated. "The president actually gave it to him." He scratched the back of his neck. "I knew we shouldn't have trusted him."

"Oh, really?" Randolph asked. "I don't remember you telling me not to pull the trigger."

Bellamy let his hand fall to the table. "I warned you of the risk with Cantrell. I . . . we . . . should have seen this coming."

"Easy to say after it's happened," Randolph said. "And the risk with Lionel was never that he'd spill the beans. The risk was—"

"Nester Sanchez," McGee interrupted. "Folks, this second-guessing isn't helping. We have a five-alarm, DEFCON-1 emergency here. We have to act swiftly and without further mistakes."

Bellamy grunted and nodded. "Agreed. What's our play?"

McGee was now pacing the floor, hands folded into a tent against her chin. "James has stolen confidential information and materials that endanger the national security of this country. He has blackmailed the sitting president of the United States in order to steal them." She glanced at Randolph. "He's done enough already to be charged with several federal crimes." She snapped her fingers. "And if his wife is in on it—and, judging by her sneaky actions today, she most definitely is—she, too, can be charged as a conspirator."

"Beth," Randolph said, nodding along with her reasoning. "That's all well and good, but we're talking about the cure for cancer that he's stolen, here. There's also the issue of the actions that we've had to take these last seven and a half years to keep the drug a secret." He sighed. "The whole situation is a powder keg."

"That's true, but we can't sit idly by and let him get away with what he's done."

"Why not?" Bellamy asked, and Randolph and McGee both jerked their heads toward him in surprise.

"What?" Randolph asked.

"Why not?" Bellamy said again, rubbing his hands together. "So Eli James has stolen the cure for cancer. So he blackmailed the president. So what? He's not on a crusade to bring this medicine to the world. He's only trying to save his daughter. He's also a career political animal, and his wife is a respected attorney. Both of their careers are at risk."

"So, are you saying to not even pursue them?" McGee asked.

"No. We have to find them. But after that, I say we negotiate."

McGee was shaking her head with ferocity. "No. Too dangerous. We're too late in the game to be talking. Too many casualties already."

For several seconds, silence filled the conference room. Randolph stood and looked out the window at the skyline of the nation's capital. The sun had begun to rise on another day. In thirty or so minutes, it would be full in the sky. Randolph thought of Bella James. She'd not done well with her trial at MD Anderson. Chronic nausea from the get-go. Lost weight. Likely a broken spirit. He glanced down at the sidewalk and saw a few people walking. In a half hour, the pedestrian areas would be full of traffic. People going to work. To school. Men and women with children. For a cancer patient with a stage-four diagnosis, how many more orange sunrises would he or she see in the east? And what would that person . . . or her family . . . do to change the inevitable outcome? And once in possession of a game-changer . . . a lifesaving medication . . . was there any chance they would voluntarily give it up?

"I agree with Beth," the general finally said. "We have to extinguish the risk. But first we have to find them."

"Well, that shouldn't be too hard," Bellamy said. "Given where Dale James grew up and her close relationship with Nester Sanchez . . ."

"Shouldn't be too hard," Beth repeated, her tone dripping with sarcasm. "Nester Sanchez is under investigation for at least fifteen federal crimes, and we have yet to apprehend him. New Mexico is his stronghold. He's a human trafficker, for God's sake! You think he'll have any trouble hiding a family?" She'd stopped pacing and joined Randolph by the window. "You realize what we're facing here?" She'd lowered her tone to just above a whisper.

"Afraid so," Randolph said.

"You think Eli James has figured it out?" Bellamy asked, fear now palpable in his voice.

Beth scoffed and rolled her eyes at the Homeland Security lifer. "There's not a doubt in my mind."

52

The trailer was pitch dark. Eli had no idea of the time. He figured they'd been driving for at least twenty-four hours, but he'd dozed off some so it could be longer. There was a light switch, and he'd turned it on a few times, but seeing the stacks of Pepsi cases only made his anxiety worse. He preferred the darkness.

There was also hardly any sound. The trailer was well insulated, and other than the occasional honk or the sound of a diesel engine, he could hear nothing but his own breathing. His butt was numb from sitting on the hard floor of the trailer, and, every hour or so, one of his feet would go to sleep, and he'd have to shake it awake. And while the piss bucket that Ralph had provided was at the other end of the trailer, Eli could still make out the faint scent of urine in the uncirculated air. One positive was that the trailer was not refrigerated. He was grateful to not be freezing his ass off.

He wondered where they were. He'd never driven from Washington to Albuquerque, New Mexico, but he knew it had to be at least a whole day, and that was with no breaks. Oklahoma? Texas? Maybe closing in on Albuquerque? His stomach growled, and he wondered when Ralph would stop again.

Once outside of DC, Ralph had pulled in to a rest stop and checked on Eli while changing the license tag from a fake Virginia one back to New Mexico. Since then, other than a few gas stops, where Eli had stayed in the trailer, their only respite from the road so far had been a truck station just outside of Memphis, and that had been hours ago. Ralph had ordered burgers, fries, and diet Pepsis from the all-night diner, and they'd eaten the meal in the cab of his rig. Eli had remembered that in his few encounters with Dale's eccentric uncle, Ralph would never let anyone drink anything but Pepsi products. *Loyalty,* he'd thought then and considered it again now as the rig continued to rumble down what Eli assumed was Interstate 40.

Loyalty was the preeminent trait of the Gutierrez clan. To family. To their jobs. To everything they held dear. Once Ralph's brother Jerry had married Dale's mother, Dale had become one of the clan, and they would do anything for her. *Anything* . . . no matter the cost.

And while Jerry had passed several years ago, his brothers, Dale's uncle Ralph and uncle Leonard, looked upon Dale as their own.

Dale's stepbrothers, Santiago and Amos, were also good men to have on your team, and Eli had always enjoyed their company. Amos was into bodybuilding, and his muscles were ripped. He was an excellent mechanic, and he could fix almost anything. He was also a jokester who made everyone laugh. Santi, the older of the two, was more cerebral. Quiet, soft spoken, and smart. He'd gone into law enforcement and was a sheriff's deputy with the Los Lunas Police Department.

Sure, the family did the bidding of Nester Sanchez. Everyone in Los Lunas had to kiss the ring. But Ralph Gutierrez wasn't solely here because of Nester. This was a family endeavor.

After finishing their meal, the old man and Eli had argued about whether Eli could use the bathroom inside the convenience store. Eli said he was happy to continue pissing in the bucket, but he wouldn't be shitting in it, and he doubted that PepsiCo would like that either. Ralph had finally relented, and Eli's five minutes inside the Love's restroom had been his only freedom since leaving the VA Medical Center in DC. Otherwise, he'd felt like he was in a moving prison. He would have much preferred to ride shotgun for this trek, but he understood Ralph's concerns.

Surely, there was a federal manhunt underway for him now.

How will Randolph play it? Eli wondered, thinking through the possibilities. There could be a nationwide search happening right now with an APB for every sheriff's department and police precinct across the country. He imagined the headline:

"Eli James, disgraced former chief of staff to President Cantrell, on the run from the law after blackmailing the president into giving him property deemed of the utmost national security of the United States."

He shook his head. *No.* Too risky.

Eli could call a press conference and tell the world he was holding the cure for cancer and that the president himself had been saved by the magic drug. He might sound crazy, but the story would sell. The FDA would have to respond, and he could imagine that Randolph and everyone else involved in the cover-up would have their assholes puckered up tight.

Eli scratched his neck and peered down the rows of Pepsi products. The smarter play would be to send in Special Forces to take him and his family out. Clean disappearance. It'd worked before.

But, unlike Randolph's three earlier victims, the James family weren't sitting ducks. They had foreseen the danger and sought protection. Eli returned to his dad's final question:

What are they afraid of?

Eli imagined Randolph convening his team and mulling the situation. Perhaps they had already brought Lionel in. He figured his old friend would break sooner rather than later. In fact, once Randolph learned that Dale and Bella weren't on the plane from Houston, Eli figured the general would call for a full-court press, which would include interrogating the president and hunting down the James family, starting with Eli. Randolph had clearly come around to suspecting that Eli hadn't left the VA hospital—that's why the agents had shown up just before Ralph Gutierrez saved the day with his Pepsi truck. But when they didn't find Eli, Randolph would know where they were going. Lionel had predicted the inevitability of this conclusion, and he was right.

So . . . Randolph knows we've run to Nester . . . and that scares the hell out of him.

Eli started to smile, but the grin wouldn't come. Instead, he felt a cold chill run up his arms as the rig begin to slow.

It should also scare the hell out of me.

In the run-up to the election, Eli had promised Nester a pardon in exchange for his financial support. He'd stressed the need for patience after Lionel's inauguration. But now, with Eli and Dale on the run . . .

. . . all bets are off.

Eli let out a breath he didn't realize he'd been holding. *Nester Sanchez will help us because of Dale, and only because of her.*

The irony was thick. Eli had always hated Dale and Nester's relationship. He'd spent his marriage feeling jealous and afraid of what they had.

And now it might save us all.

As the truck came to a stop, Eli moved his hand to his pocket and felt the pill bottles. He had another chip to play, aside from Nester's loyalty to his wife.

I'll give Nester something better *than a pardon.*

Eli nodded, forcing himself to believe.

As the trailer door slid upward, Eli saw the light at the end and then Ralph. "You hungry, *mijo*?"

"Starved," Eli croaked, his voice hoarse and dry.

Ralph gestured. "Come on."

Eli's legs were shaky as he walked through the stacks to the end of the trailer and down the ramp. When his feet hit the concrete, his eyes adjusted to the new landscape. Last he'd been outside, it had been nighttime in Memphis. Nothing but interstate and darkness. Now all he saw was bright sunshine and brown in every direction with mountains as the backdrop. "Where are we?" Eli asked, seeing that they were in the parking lot of a restaurant. The sign on the front read SOPAS.

Ralph chuckled, but it was forced. Eli sensed the old man's nerves. "Home."

Eli's heart rate accelerated. "Are Dale and Bella in there?" He cocked his head at the building and moved his eyes around the empty lot.

This isn't right, his instincts screamed.

"You'll see them soon," Ralph said. "But first, let's eat." He grabbed Eli by the elbow, but Eli didn't budge.

"Ralph, what's—?"

"He just wants to talk."

Eli glanced at the sign and then back at Dale's uncle. "Is my family safe?"

Ralph Gutierrez put both hands on Eli's shoulders. "Yes. And so are you. Do you think I would lead my niece's husband to slaughter?"

Eli didn't answer. He knew Ralph wouldn't, but he still felt anxious.

"He just wants to talk," Ralph repeated. "That's reasonable, no? Given what he has risked, and . . . what he has lost."

Eli let out a ragged breath. Finally, he nodded as Ralph nudged him forward.

As they started to walk to the door, Ralph whispered, "All that being said . . . I do hope you have a plan."

53

Nester waited for them in a booth in the back corner.

Eli had met Nester Sanchez only once. It had been Dale's ten-year high school reunion from the Menaul School in Albuquerque. That was also the last time he'd seen Ralph and the Gutierrez family. Dale had made numerous visits, but the reunion had been Eli's only taste of New Mexico. And while his interactions with the family and Dale's other friends had been warm and friendly, his brief encounter with Nester had been anything but. "I hope you are enjoying your stay," was all Nester had said, while piercing Eli with his golden brown eyes. Since then, all of Eli's communications with Nester had been through Dale.

Now, over fifteen years later, Nester appeared as if he had barely aged a day. He wore a khaki button-down, faded jeans, and brown work boots. His jet-black hair was matted with a hat imprint and sweat; a red "Menaul Football" trucker cap lay next to the napkin dispenser. Never in a million years would a person believe that the man seated at this booth was one of the most powerful landowners, business tycoons, and criminal overlords in the world.

"And that is his secret," Dale always said. *"The people love him because he's one of them."*

Eli knew different. It was the perception that Nester wanted to create. The Beast was much more than a people's champion. He was a chameleon. A copperhead snake. A man who had shown no qualms about killing men, women, and children to reach his goals. You didn't rack up fifteen federal felony charges without a conviction by being popular and cooperative.

You did it by being ruthless and aggressive. By using people.

And by holding business partners to their promises . . .

As Eli approached the booth, he felt the hair on his arms and the back of his neck standing up. He saw no other patrons in the restaurant. In fact, aside from Nester, the only other person in the building was a woman wearing a Sopas T-shirt and a nervous smile.

"Can I get you gentlemen something to drink?" the waitress asked as Eli took his seat across from Nester and scooted to make room for Ralph. He was boxed in now, but that was okay. He'd been a salesman his whole life; hell, he'd had to make a hell of a pitch and throw in some blackmail to get Lionel Cantrell to give him the boomerang. He figured this meeting would be similarly tense.

"Pepsi for me," Ralph said.

Before Eli could say anything, Nester laughed.

"What?" Ralph asked. "I like Pepsi. I want . . . a Pepsi."

"And if drinking a Coke would give you the fountain of youth and a good-looking *chica*?"

"I'd still order a Pepsi," Ralph said. "Youth is overrated, and good-looking women are expensive and more trouble than they're worth. Give me a Pepsi and Pornhub." The old man grunted. "And the Paramount channel. I love me some *Yellowstone*."

Nester laughed, but his eyes had shifted to Eli. "I bet you're glad you spent that trip in the trailer instead of the cab."

Before Eli could respond, the waitress cleared her throat. "Um, sir, what would you like to drink?" She was looking at Eli. She was still blushing, and Eli wondered how many times Ralph had produced that reaction.

"Coffee," Eli said. "Black. And some water."

"Be right back," she said, speed-walking away from them.

"Please." Nester waved his hand across the table, set with chips, salsa, and guacamole. "You must be hungry. Enjoy." He took a chip and dipped it in the salsa. Then he grabbed a plastic container of honey and squirted some of it on the top and popped the chip in his mouth. "A little sweet to cool off the spice," Nester said, nodding at Ralph. "His brother taught me that."

Eli took a chip and scooped up some salsa. He put it in his mouth and immediately wished he'd heeded Nester's recommendation.

"Hot, huh?" Nester chuckled as he waved at the waitress. "Hurry, Jeralyn."

Eli's mouth was on fire, and he grabbed the water as soon as the glass was set on the table.

"The salsa here has some bite, but I love it," Nester said. "Pops—that's what Dale called her stepfather, Jerry—and I would meet here for lunch before he passed. He was a unique man. Always wore a big watch on his left wrist." Nester touched his own silver timepiece. "Pops gave me this when I graduated from the University of New Mexico. He was like a second father to me. I think of the Gutierrez family as my own."

"And we feel the same," Ralph said. Eli turned and saw that the older man's eyes were growing misty.

"Where . . . are we?" Eli asked, coughing as he talked, still trying to get over the heat of the salsa.

"Bosque Farms," Nester said. "About five miles from Los Lunas. Twenty from Albuquerque."

"What time is it?"

"It's a little before seven." Nester made another chip with salsa and honey and handed it to Eli. "Go on. Try it."

Eli did as he was told. As he crunched, he had to admit that the honey took the edge off the salsa, and the concoction was delicious. If he weren't so nervous that he could barely breathe, he would have enjoyed it.

"The restaurant's official hours begin at eight," Nester continued. "But Jeralyn opened early for me."

Eli looked at the woman again and realized that she must not just be a waitress but was rather the manager or owner. He turned to Nester. "Is my family safe?"

"Very," Nester said. "And so are we. Ralph was not followed, and there are ten armed men and women guarding the restaurant as we speak."

"That's good," Eli managed, meeting those copper eyes. "Thank you."

"I hope you don't mind, but I ordered huevos rancheros for each of us with a mixture of green and red chile." He chuckled. "Christmas, as we like to call it."

"*Perfecto*," Ralph said, taking a long sip of Pepsi.

"That's great," Eli said.

"Uncle, would you mind waiting by the door for a few minutes?" Nester asked. "I'd like to speak with our guest alone."

"Of course," Ralph said, sliding out of the booth and grabbing his glass of Pepsi.

"Thank you," Nester said, putting both hands on the table and studying Eli. "You have some explaining to do."

"Wouldn't you prefer to have Dale here?" Eli asked. "That way the conversation is privileged."

Nester frowned. "You are being pursued by the United States government. You have put your family . . . and me . . . in grave danger. You have essentially destroyed any chance of me obtaining a pardon from your president, which was the sole reason I donated millions of dollars to his campaign. I don't like to be disappointed, Eli. Since I seriously doubt confidentiality is going to save you or me under these circumstances, I want to hear it from the horse's mouth. What the hell is going on?"

Eli decided to forgo any bullshit. He reached into his pocket and pulled out one of the two pill bottles. "This medication was given to me by the president of the United States. Lionel Cantrell was diagnosed with stage-four metastatic colon cancer in October, and after taking this medication for not even two months, he's in complete remission. Bella has stage-four lung cancer. After learning there might be a miracle drug the government covered up, I hired an investigator and did a deep dive." Eli paused. "And what I found could destroy this country."

Nester picked up the container and twisted the top. He looked at one of the white capsules. "Are you saying this is the cure for cancer?"

"Yes."

Nester blinked, returning the pill to the bottle and resealing it. "How can you be so sure?"

"Because the United States government has killed at least three people to keep this medication from the general public." Eli quickly recited how Mato Nakai had formulated the drug and sold it to people at farmers' markets across the Gulf Coast, eventually reaching Mary Frances Bruce, who made the mistake of talking about the miracle cure.

Nester made himself another sweet-and-spicy chip and peered down at the table as he chewed. "Why should I believe you?"

"Because I have skin in the game. The third person they killed was my father. They almost killed my mother. And they would have taken me out if Ralph hadn't shown up. Dale's lost her job and her career. I've lost mine." Eli could feel himself losing his composure. His voice shook, but he forced himself to speak clearly. "But we will not lose our daughter. I came two thousand miles to give Bella this medication."

Nester drank a sip of coffee. "And you're confident it will work."

"It has to," Eli said through gritted teeth.

"And what happens when it is gone? Then what?"

"Then we make them give us more."

"*We?*" Nester grinned, but there was no humor in his eyes. "You and me? A team, are we?"

"And Dale," Eli said. "Yes, we're a team. You provide us protection, and we give you the greatest bargaining chip in the history of the world." Eli squinted at him. "Better than a pardon. Better than anything I could possibly give you. This could give you absolute immunity. The ultimate leverage."

Nester took a sip of water and squinted at Eli. "The cure for cancer, huh?"

"It's bigger than that." Eli felt adrenaline and caffeine fueling his body as the ramifications came pouring out of his mouth. "The government has been hiding this medication for eight years because a cure would cripple the billion-dollar oncology industry and destroy the United States economy. For no reason other than pure greed, millions of patients have died after having their bodies ravaged by chemo and radiation when that little pill . . ." Eli pointed at the bottle. ". . . could have saved their lives. What the former chairman of the Joint Chiefs of Staff and whoever else is in on this with him have done is an act of treason against this country and an act of war against the rest of the world."

Nester pushed himself back from the table. His hands gripped the sides of it as he glared at Eli. "This is . . . preposterous. Outrageous." He slid out of the booth and stood, placing his hands on his hips. "Why should I believe this lunacy?"

Eli wasn't having it: "I've told you why."

"You're a desperate man at the end of your rope. You know I could kill you with the snap of a finger. You're selling me a story and buying yourself time."

Eli scooted out of the booth and held out his hands. "That's all true. But the story I'm selling is one hundred percent fact. And if the media ever gets wind of it . . ." Eli brought his palms together, making a loud clap. *"Boom."*

Nester rubbed the back of his neck, as Jeralyn emerged through the kitchen with their plates of food. "Are we still eating?" she asked, looking from Nester to Eli and glancing behind her shoulder, where Ralph stood at the door. Eli followed her eyes and saw that the old man's face had gone pale.

"I don't know," Nester said, continuing to pierce Eli with his golden brown eyes. "I don't trust you."

"You don't have to. Just let Bella take this medication. The results will speak for themselves."

"And if they don't?"

"They will," Eli said.

Nester crossed his arms. "I want to believe you, Eli. I really do. And I hope and pray that Bella gets well. But, if this is true, then your friends in Washington aren't going to go peacefully."

"No, they aren't."

"They'll come for you and, by virtue of that, me. You've subjected my world to great risk."

"What I've done is given you incredible leverage over the most powerful country in the world. In weaker hands, I agree that the exposure would be too much." He took a step closer to Nester and spoke in a tone just above a whisper. "But you're King fucking Kong."

"Gentlemen?" Jeralyn's squeaky voice broke through the tension.

Nester scoffed. "You're kissing my ass."

"I'm telling it like it is. The United States government was already scared to death of you. And now I've given you a nuclear warhead."

Nester peered past Eli to the door. After a few seconds, he waved Ralph toward them.

"Nester—"

"Come," Nester interrupted, winking at Jeralyn and sitting back in the booth. "Let's eat."

"Nester?" Eli stood lock still, unsure if he'd made the sale or not.

"I like that," Nester finally said, as Jeralyn put the steaming plate of huevos rancheros in front of him.

"What?"

"King fucking Kong."

54

The Tamaya Resort sat on the banks of the Rio Grande and was framed by the Sandia Mountains. The property sported the Twin Warriors Golf Club, horseback riding, and numerous hiking trails through the brush and along the river. It also had event spaces for weddings. Dale had considered getting married here after she and Eli became engaged, but she'd chosen a location in Alabama instead. The hotel grounds were on land owned by the Santa Ana Pueblo and, while it had become a Hyatt property, the tribe still controlled the majority of the operation.

In addition to the hotel and golf course, the property also included storage facilities, barns, and other outbuildings on 550 acres of sovereign reservation land. Which made it an ideal place to hide someone.

As the sun began to sink behind the Sandias, Dale James stepped out of the metal shack and sat down in a wooden rocker. She wore a cap with her hair tucked through the back and the green collared shirt and khaki work pants of the stable staff. She felt like she had entered some sort of alternate reality, which she guessed she had. For twenty years, she'd dressed in dark pantsuits and skirts, litigating cases in courtrooms all across the country. Now, she had the odd sensation that she'd traveled through time and was working at a summer camp. She hadn't looked at a phone or a computer in days. At first, she found herself digging in her pockets and purse for the device that wasn't there, but she was slowly weaning herself off it. Now, she gazed up at the orangish-red sun and closed her eyes, breathing in the desert air and praying that she'd hear something from Eli soon.

They had been in New Mexico for almost three days now, and there was no word other than a cryptic update from Santi that "they are on the way." Her brother had asked for their burner phones on arrival, saying he was following Nester's instructions and that the devices would be returned in short order. Dale hadn't liked that, but she and Foncie had handed them over. She knew her old friend craved control, but she hadn't come to Albuquerque to trade one prison for another. Not being able to call her husband bothered her. Not having any independence was nerve racking. Part of her still wondered if she could trust Nester, but the other side countered with a rather obvious and frightening question: *What choice do we have?*

She felt a hand on her shoulder, and her eyes shot open.

"Easy," Foncie rasped. "It's me." She pointed toward the sandy dirt road leading to the stables. "Someone's coming."

Dale blinked as the Pepsi truck rolled up the blacktop toward the stables.

"I haven't seen any vending machines up this way, have you?" Foncie asked.

Dale shook her head, but her heartbeat began to speed up. She walked toward the truck as it pulled to a stop in front of the shack.

The driver, a short, plump man with dark hair that was receding at the temples, plopped down from the cab and gave a weary smile.

As she'd done when she first saw her brothers, Dale's bottom lip started to shake. "Uncle Ralph?"

The old man had tears in his eyes. "I wish Jerry could be here to see this. He loved your mother and you so much. For you to come home . . ." He wiped his eyes and glanced at the mountains. The sun had almost disappeared behind them.

Dale ran toward him and flung her arms around her uncle.

"When can I see everyone?" she asked.

"Soon, niecey. We'll have to be careful, but . . . soon." He paused and then grinned. "I have a surprise for you." He walked toward the back of the trailer and unchained the hitch. He rolled up the door and yelled. "All right, *mijo*. Trip's over." Ralph rolled his eyes at Dale. "He's a cranky one."

Dale gasped as Eli emerged from the darkness of the trailer. He eased down to his bottom and then hopped to the ground, stumbling a bit on shaky legs. Then he looked at Dale with bloodshot eyes. Eli typically was clean shaven, but his face was covered with stubble. He wore suit pants and a button-down with the shirttail out. He carried his wrinkled jacket in his hand. He looked awful . . . but also wonderful.

"Hey," Eli said, his voice hoarse.

"Hey."

"You look like a dog's unwiped ass," Foncie's rasp rang out from behind them.

"Mom?" Eli gasped, and his eyes filled with tears.

Foncie walked toward them and kissed Eli's cheek and ruffled his hair. "Glad you could join the party." She turned to Ralph. "Thanks for getting him here. I'm—"

"Beautiful," Ralph interrupted, his puppy dog eyes wide.

"That'll work," Foncie said. "You can also call me Foncie." She spat on the ground and shrugged. "Either one."

Dale stared at Eli. She still hadn't touched him. She wanted to, but she felt an invisible force field keeping her feet in place. Finally, she frowned and crossed her arms. "Did you get it?"

Eli squinted and reached into his pocket, pulling out two pill bottles. Next to Dale, Foncie whistled through her teeth.

"Where's Bella?" Eli asked.

———

Thirty minutes later, Eli and Dale sat on opposite sides of Bella's bed. Foncie stood in the doorway. Ralph had taken his Pepsi truck back to the distribution center and had returned to the reservation in his pickup. His son, Jeffie, who Dale had only barely known growing up, was with him, and they stood watch outside. Eli held a pill in his hand while Dale had the glass of water.

Bella was sitting up, and it hurt Eli's heart to look at her. She'd lost almost forty pounds. *She can't weigh over ninety*, he thought, extending the capsule to her.

"Dad?" Bella's voice was weak. "Where have you been? Are . . . you okay?"

"I brought you some medicine," he said.

Bella started to shake her head. "I can't do any more meds, Dad. The trial at MD Anderson almost killed me."

Eli glanced at Dale. His wife had told him that she had said nothing to Bella about a possible curative drug. Dale hadn't wanted to get Bella's hopes up.

But the time for sugarcoating things was over. "Bella, honey, this medication is different. This won't just help you. It will cure you."

Bella actually laughed at that, and then started coughing.

"That happens a lot," Dale whispered. "Her lungs . . ." She trailed off for a second, trying to keep it together. "You just have to let her cough it out."

Eli nodded and waited as Bella hacked, sniffled, and finally grew quiet.

"I'm not joking, honey," Eli said. "Your godfather had a recurrence in October. He had metastatic colon cancer and was given two years max. He took these pills for a few months and—" Eli snapped his fingers. "The cancer went away, and he's in full remission."

Bella's tired eyes widened. "Did he give you this?"

"Yes," Eli said. "But there are people who are angry that he did."

"And that's why we're here," Bella said. "We're on the run." She squinted. "We're outlaws."

"Don't worry about any of that, honey," Dale chimed in. "We're safe here. Just take the medicine."

Bella held the pill up to her face and shrugged. "It can't be any worse than the trial." She placed it in her mouth and took the glass of water from her mother. As she swallowed her first dose of the boomerang, Eli closed his eyes and said a silent prayer. *Please, God, let this medicine heal my daughter.*

"How often—" Dale started.

"Once a day," Eli said, opening his eyes. He grabbed a couple of saltine crackers he'd placed on the bed and gave them to Bella. She took a small bite, and a tiny smile came to her face.

"How did you do this, Dad?"

Eli glanced at Dale. "That's classified, honey."

"You could tell me, but you'd have to kill me," Bella said, a tease in her voice that warmed Eli's soul.

He forced back tears. "Something like that."

———

Eli watched his daughter fall asleep, holding her hand the entire time. Then he walked his mother from the shack to the stable. The night air was cool, and the temperature must have dropped almost fifteen degrees since the sun went down.

"I love it here," Foncie said wistfully. "I'm envious of Dale for growing up in a place like this."

"It sure is horse heaven," Eli agreed, opening the barn door and letting Foncie inside. "Still, I bet we can arrange sleeping quarters for you somewhere else. They could probably get you a room in the resort or at least a shack like ours."

"Are you kidding? I love it in here. Half the time, at home, I'd spend the night in the stables. I love the smell of hay and horse manure and horse hide and leather and hell . . ." She took in a deep breath. ". . . all of it. If I live the rest of my days right here with these animals, I'll be happy as a clam."

They stopped at a tiny office just big enough for Foncie's cot. There was a counter with a sink and a coffee maker. "I got water, hot coffee, and horses, and that's more than enough for me."

"Good night, Mom." Eli started to walk away, but felt his hand being gripped tight.

"I'm proud of you." Foncie's voice was stronger, the rasp temporarily gone. Eli knew his mom's voice got deeper when she was trying to keep her emotions in check. "I'm sorry about your daddy."

"Me too." He looked at her. "He gave me some good advice the last time I saw him."

"Oh, yeah, I know. That's why I sent you there. I figured he'd probably know something, and sure as shit, the name Mary Frances Bruce turned the tide. We found what we were looking for."

"Yeah, there was that . . . but the last thing he told me was something simpler." Eli sighed and gazed around the barn. "He basically told me to come here."

Foncie leaned in and kissed his cheek. "You remind me so much of him."

"Thanks," Eli said. "I hope I remind you a little of you too. I wouldn't be anything at all without you."

For a moment, they just looked at each other, and finally Foncie grinned. "Maybe a little."

Eli chuckled and turned to leave.

"Hey, boy," she said.

He looked at his mother over his shoulder. "Yeah?"

"This ain't over."

He grimaced. "No, ma'am." Then he sighed.

It's just beginning.

PART FIVE

ARMAGEDDON

Beth McGee understands the impact, but she wants it driven home. "I need you to repeat those numbers, Thad."

She sits at the head of a table in the basement of the Pentagon. The four people in the room are the only current members of Project Boomerang. When the initiative was founded, Dr. Thad Raleigh was the chief medical officer of the Food and Drug Administration, and he now serves as the FDA's commissioner.

He fidgets in his seat and looks again at his laptop. "Oncology medicine alone is responsible for over $200 billion in annual sales revenue, and that number is expected to exceed $300 billion in a couple of years and is trending toward a trillion in five. Cancer medication makes up almost a quarter of drug sales."

McGee crosses her arms. "And . . . if there was a single medication that could cure cancer . . . ?" *She trails off, and the question hangs in the air.*

"Well . . . presumably . . ." *Thad fumbles on his laptop, but it is obvious that he isn't looking at anything.*

"It would all be gone," *McGee says.* "Right?"

"There would be a charge for the new drug . . . but you are basically correct."

"And what about oncologist salaries? Chemo nurses and techs? Radiation therapists? Where do those jobs go?"

"Well . . . there will still be a need for . . . some of those jobs."

McGee's eyes meet General Kyle Randolph's. The updated numbers have confirmed all their worst fears—as if they needed confirmation. She stands and folds her arms. "Folks, let's forget about the loss in revenue, which we all agree would cripple the United States economy. How do you think the citizens of this country . . . and the people all over the world . . . are going to feel if they find out that this miracle drug has been out there for over seven and a half years, and the US government has been hiding it from them?"

The silence in the room is deafening. McGee growls at Randolph. "Tell them, General."

"It'll be Armageddon."

55

The Albuquerque International Balloon Fiesta began on the fourth day of October. While the mass ascension wouldn't start until after sunrise, the gates opened at 3:00 a.m. For as long as Dale had been a member of the Gutierrez family, they had gone to the fiesta and had typically arrived early. Some of her fondest memories of those high school years were parking in the fairgrounds and walking across to where the multitude of aircraft and their crews were readying for the big adventure. There had been food trucks and hot chocolate galore, and the smell of piñon coffee mixed with breakfast burritos was one of the most pleasant aromas she had ever known.

As she walked through the entrance at just after 4:00 a.m., Dale breathed in the scents she remembered as a teenager and felt a rush of gratitude as she glanced at Bella, who was taking it all in with excited, albeit sleepy eyes. During her nearly seven months of taking the boomerang pills, Bella had gained back half the weight she'd lost, and her face was pink with health. Her stamina was still a tad low, but it picked up by the day.

Was it possible that Bella could be in remission? That she might be cured?

Nester had arranged PET and CT scans for tomorrow morning at an oncology center in Santa Fe. Since starting the boomerang medication, Bella had not seen a doctor. *Too risky,* Nester had warned. As powerful as he was, he knew that the government had eyes everywhere, and any type of cancer hospital would be staked out. He'd set up a fake name and credentials for Bella and chosen a trusted couple to take her in for the tests. "Always better to hide in plain sight," he'd advised, explaining that it would be next to impossible to keep any kind of private testing secret. Dale and Eli would arrive separately from Bella, and Nester promised that an oncologist would see the family together as soon as he had the results. And while he believed in his plan, Nester would have a security detail there in case things went awry.

Which they could, he had warned. Dale wondered if that was the reason he'd relented to her request to take Bella to the balloon fiesta today.

Dale grabbed her daughter's hand and squeezed. *What if something happens tomorrow? What if they find us? What if I don't see her again?*

"Mom, you're hurting me." Bella's voice broke through Dale's nightmarish thoughts, and she loosened her grip.

"Sorry," Dale said. "Just excited to be here."

"Are Santi and Amos coming? Or Uncle Ralph? What about the cousins?"

"Not today, honey. It's just us."

"Okay," Bella said, but the disappointment in the girl's tone made Dale smile. Since their arrival in New Mexico, Bella had become close with her family. Because any of the Gutierrez clan would be fair game for the government to attack, they were all hiding out on the reservation as well. Jobs and lives put on hold. At least fifteen human beings affected by Eli and Dale's decision to go rogue with the cure for cancer. The stables at the Tamaya had become like a smaller reservation inside the bigger one, and each night, with the barn doors closed, they ate together, laughed, argued, tossed a football, and made the most of their forced fellowship.

When she allowed herself a few seconds not to worry about the future, Dale enjoyed the respite from reality. But it was Bella who was truly thriving.

The camaraderie. The sunshine. The horses. Perhaps even the chile beans. Or maybe it was just knowing that this small band of brothers and sisters and cousins and uncles would all die for her. Any one of them. That type of devotion was rare and couldn't be faked. If you wanted to boil it down to one word, it was love. While the drug ridded Bella's body of her cancer cells, the unconditional love of the Gutierrez family was cleansing her soul.

And mine too.

"Mom, why are you crying?"

Dale looked at her and then peered into the distance at the multitude of balloons preparing for takeoff in a few short hours. She wiped her eyes. "I guess I'm just happy to be here, honey." She studied the crowd. Their driver was standing over by a breakfast truck, and she saw two other familiar faces from the Tamaya. Nester said he would have them well protected, and, despite the number of people, she felt safe.

"Can I get a breakfast burrito?" Bella asked. "You've always said the ones here are the best."

"Of course," Dale said, pointing to the nearest stand. "Let's do it."

A few minutes later, they were both holding the steaming rolled goodness of a sausage, egg, and cheese burrito. Dale washed hers down with coffee, while Bella sipped from a Dr Pepper.

"OMG," Bella said, after swallowing her first bite. "You weren't kidding. This is incredible."

Dale grinned at her, feeling another wave of gratitude. The girl's blond hair had come back in curls, but her locks were covered by a baseball cap. The spark in her eyes, which had all but gone out after the trial at MD Anderson, had returned. Once she'd regained some strength, Eli and Dale had told her everything. Bella needed to know the danger they were in, but also the incredible gift she'd been given. Predictably, she'd asked a lot of questions. "Does this mean I can't go to Belmont? What about my friends? Our house in Virginia? Your job, Mom?" But after a few minutes, the girl's maturity and intelligence had shone through. "What if this medicine actually works? What if it does heal me? What about all the other cancer patients? The ones at MD Anderson and in Virginia . . . and everywhere?"

Dale had glanced at Eli. The questions were valid, and Dale had begun to think about them more and more as she saw her daughter's improvement.

"I stole this medication, honey," Eli had said. "The government doesn't want anyone to have it . . . unless healing that particular person is good for America."

"I don't understand. How could curing cancer, the worst disease in the history of the world, somehow be bad for the United States?"

Eli had gritted his teeth and shared a look with Dale. "Unfortunately, honey, some people in very high places of our government seem to think so."

"What it boils down to," Dale had chimed in, "is money. Curing cancer will mean a great loss of revenue to the United States, and believe it or not, the folks your father is talking about don't think the benefit is worth the financial cost."

Bella opened her mouth in horror. Then she scowled at Eli. "You've got to be kidding me. Does LC feel that way?"

Eli had gazed at the ground. "No . . . I don't think he does."

"But he's the president. Couldn't he do something to help?"

Eli had offered his daughter a weak smile as he rolled the pill bottle in his hand, then handed it to Bella. "He already has."

For several seconds, Bella had waited for more of an explanation, but neither of her parents had anything else to offer. Finally, she whispered under her breath, "This seems . . . so wrong."

Dale had eventually ended the conversation, as she often did, with a proclamation. "Let's just see if it works."

And tomorrow we'll find out, she thought, taking a sip of scalding coffee and scanning the crowd. Many young families had brought lawn chairs and were already staking out the best place to watch the mass ascension. Dale had a towel that she would spread out on the ground when the balloons began taking off, but she hadn't wanted to bog them down with anything else in case they had to make a run for it. Even thinking such a crazy thought—*having to run for it*—was surreal, but it was what it was.

Dale walked closer to the balloons and saw a spot on the grass that would give them a nice view. She laid the towel down and waited while Bella sat. Then she did the same, with Bella holding her coffee until she was comfortable. She took the java from her daughter and toasted the girl's soda. "To the balloon fiesta," Dale said.

"To my cancer being gone," Bella said.

"Amen," Dale added, taking a drink and closing her eyes for a second. *Please, God, let it be so.*

"Mom, can I tell you something?"

"Anything," Dale said.

"I'm scared."

Their eyes locked, and Dale forced her voice to be strong. "Everything is going to be fine," she said, trying to sound convincing. "We have a good plan, and you're feeling better, right?"

"It's not the scans I'm worried about. What if they find us?"

Dale took a bite of her burrito and forced herself to chew it slowly. She took in the cool fall air. Finally, she spoke while gazing out at the balloon park. "They won't."

"How can you be so sure?"

"Because I believe in Nester."

"What's the deal with him? He's doing all of this stuff for us, but I haven't seen him yet. Have you?"

Dale shook her head. She had spoken to Nester on the phone at least twice a week since their arrival, but they had yet to meet face to face. She had to admit that she, too, was curious about that, but she hadn't pushed it.

"Nester is a very cautious man. He has many enemies, so he has to be careful about being visible. I'm sure we will see him soon."

In truth, Dale was anything but confident of what she'd just said. Nester was her friend, but he was also ambitious. Was it possible that he might betray her for personal gain? Wouldn't the United States government accede to his demands if he gave them the James family on a silver platter?

Dale couldn't fathom such a thing happening, but it would be naive not to at least consider the danger. She and Nester had shared something so intense during their high school years, but that was eons ago. Dale had married Eli. She'd moved on. But Nester had not taken on a partner. And she was unaware of any serious relationships.

Even now, he seemed to trust only her. He'd insisted on her being on his legal team, even though he'd hired some of the best criminal defense lawyers in the country. Nester's inner circle was small, and Dale knew that she had a special place in it.

But will that be enough in the face of what the government might offer? Absolute immunity? A pardon? Millions . . . or billions?

"You really trust him?" Bella asked, her voice soft.

"Yes," Dale said with no hesitation.

There were several minutes of silence as they both finished their food and wadded up the packages into tiny balls to be thrown away later.

"Can I ask you something else?"

Dale looked at her. The girl's voice was timid. Almost a whisper. "Of course."

"Are you and Dad okay?"

Dale peered at the balloons. "Yes. Your father and I are both totally committed to seeing that you get well."

Bella rolled her eyes. "That's not what I meant. You guys aren't sleeping in the same room, and he just doesn't seem like himself. Dad's always been kind of loud and funny, and he's so quiet now." She paused. "I know you were having problems before my diagnosis. I'm not an idiot. I just thought things would get better here, but . . ."

As her daughter's voice trailed off, Dale gazed upward at the dark sky. Soon, the sun would begin to rise, but now, just before dawn, the world was as black as her thoughts. Even the stars were covered with clouds. Finally, she sighed. "Adults can make a mess of things sometimes, Bella. Your father and I . . ." Now it was she who trailed off. Dale, too, had thought that maybe their marriage might improve in New Mexico, but the crisis had focused everything on Bella and survival.

Eli James is at his best in a crisis.

How many times had she heard Lionel say that over the years? And it was true. Her husband had withdrawn into himself, as if he were preserving energy for the coming storm. *Which might begin tomorrow . . .* Intimacy was probably the last thing on his mind, but maybe she was reading him wrong. There had been several moments over the last few months when Dale had wanted to touch her husband, to hug him or to kiss his cheek or even just to hold his hand, but she found that she just couldn't make the first move. She wondered if Eli had felt the same thing; she knew he was also recovering from grief.

"Your father has been through a lot," she admitted, continuing to stare at the dark sky. "He has really struggled with his dad's . . . your grandfather's death. He feels responsible." She hesitated, feeling her own wave of guilt. "And it's tough for him here. He's . . . never felt comfortable around my New Mexico family . . . and my friendship with Nester." She trailed off.

"He's jealous of Nester."

Dale finally looked at her, and Bella's eyes were raised. Dale averted her gaze.

"I'm right, aren't I?"

"Maybe," Dale said, sighing. "Probably."

"Do you still love him?"

Dale felt a pang in her chest, and she studied the ground. The question was ambiguous as to which "him" Bella was talking about, and Dale wondered if that's how her daughter intended it.

Dale wiped a tear from her eye and looked at her daughter. "Yes," she finally said. She waited for the girl to ask the follow-up question that would clear up the ambiguity, but it never came.

Instead, mother and daughter continued to stare at the sky.

Eventually, the first hint of light began to rise in the east.

56

As the bloody sun began to rise over the Sandias, Eli crouched by the bank of the Rio Grande, waiting.

Not for the first time, he wondered how he'd gone from the president's chief of staff to an outlaw working with the most legendary New Mexican criminal since Billy the Kid.

The voice came from behind, but Eli didn't turn. They'd met in this exact spot at 5:30 a.m. every week for the past six and a half months. He rose and waited for Nester to join him.

"Everything is set up for tomorrow," Nester said, his voice typically soft, the cadence melodic.

"Ralph's going to take us?" Eli asked.

"Part of the way. He'll pick you up at the stables at sunrise. We have a spot just outside of Santa Fe where you can wait, and then another of my associates will bring you to the clinic approximately two hours after Bella's scans."

Eli frowned, thinking. "You're sure your doctor's on board."

"Yes. Dr. Baca is a personal friend. I've made significant contributions to her clinic, and she will do what needs to be done."

"What have you told her?"

"I've given her copies of the reports that you gave me. She should be able to compare what she sees tomorrow with them."

"Thank you," Eli managed.

Over Nester's shoulder, three armed men waited under a copse of manzanita. The Beast's detail.

"How much do you have left?" asked Nester.

"About a week's worth. If the tumors are gone, then it should last longer. Maybe a month. But that's it."

Nester squatted and picked up some pebbles on the ground. He skipped one across the river's surface. "The government has reached out to my people."

Eli's stomach clenched. "When?"

"Yesterday." Nester skipped another stone. "They want a meeting." He hesitated. "With you."

Eli nodded. He'd expected such a move eventually. Nester had too. "What do you think?"

"I think you should hear what they have to say."

"How would we set that up?"

Nester stopped skipping stones and put his hands in his pockets. "We would pick the time and the location."

"And one other condition."

"What's that?"

"I speak only with the president."

Nester chuckled. "You know he's just a puppet. General Randolph is pulling the strings."

"I know, but I don't trust them."

Now Nester full-out laughed. "And you trust the president? The man you had to blackmail to save your daughter? His own goddaughter? Come on, *mijo*. You can't be that naive or stupid."

"He's my friend. I think he'll help if he can."

"Don't be a fool, Eli. None of them will help. They all want you and your family to disappear. Even your precious president."

Eli gave his head a jerk, knowing Nester was correct about Randolph but unwilling to believe his old friend would want him, Dale, and Bella dead. "Do you think it's a trap?" he asked.

"I don't know. It could be. But here's the thing. I am good. My people are loyal. But I can't hide you here forever. The government is offering a fortune for information about you and your family, and to pull off tomorrow's appointment, I had to push the boundaries of my network. While Dr. Baca is a friend, the facility is huge, and Carmen can't control every employee there." Nester shrugged. "I think it's time."

"For what?" Eli asked.

"To play the game."

Eli walked a few steps away. He'd learned that Nester liked to talk in riddles, but it was still frustrating. "Can I ask you something and get a straight answer?"

Nester said nothing.

"In all the time we've been here," Eli continued, taking the other man's silence as acquiescence, "you have yet, to my knowledge, to see Dale. I meet with you once a week, we see each other quite a bit, but you only talk to Dale on the phone. Why is that?"

"Because I respect the covenant of marriage." He squinted. "And I know what will happen if I see Dale again."

"That confident in yourself?"

Nester took a step toward him. "I know what I want. Do you?"

Eli felt a wave of anger roll through him. He clenched his fists, then opened them. "I want my daughter to be healthy and safe. I haven't thought anything beyond that." Eli studied the brown water of the Rio Grande, trying to keep his emotions in check. He sensed Nester come closer.

"You asked if I think it's a trap. You *know* that whatever they offer will be a trap." Nester's tone had grown softer, but if anything, more intense. "You are a walking grenade. The government will never let you live."

"You sound happy about that," Eli said.

"Just being realistic."

"And what have they offered you, Nester? The moon? The stars?" Eli gestured toward the river. "The Rio fucking Grande?"

"I have not had any talks with them beyond their request to meet with you."

Bullshit, Eli thought, but if he were honest, he didn't have a clue what Nester Sanchez was up to. The Beast was as hard to read as a champion poker player.

Eli crouched and picked up a handful of pebbles. He jiggled them in his hand and brought them to his nose, smelling the dirt. He had an image of Maximus doing the same thing in the movie *Gladiator* before each of his battles.

The bullets are about to start flying.

"What do you want me to do?" Nester asked.

Eli flung the rocks into the water and stared into the eyes of the Beast. "Set it up."

57

Beth McGee watched the balloons ascend into the air from the window of the penthouse suite of the Albuquerque Marriott Pyramid North. The iconic downtown hotel had served as headquarters of Project Boomerang since a week after the James family had fled to New Mexico. Beth had spent the first week in Albuquerque supervising the mission. Since then, she'd checked in once a month but had otherwise stayed in DC and let her field agents do their jobs.

Tracking down a family under the protection of Nester Sanchez was next to impossible, and there had been no breaks in the case in the last seven months.

That is, until this morning.

"Play the pertinent part of the tape again."

She heard a clicking sound behind her and then a voice that had clearly been altered to sound like a machine voice. "Bella James will be at the CHRISTUS St. Vincent Cancer Center in Santa Fe tomorrow morning. She is checking in under an alias with fake parents."

There was static, then an agent's voice. "Who is speaking?"

More static.

"Please, sir. Who is this?"

Silence.

"Is there anything else you can tell us?"

"She will be . . . well protected." The call ended then.

Beth turned to face the people in the room. General Kyle Randolph leaned against the bar, holding a cup of coffee. Below him was Robert Bellamy, seated on a couch with his legs crossed. They looked to her because she was now in charge. As Eli James had committed federal crimes on US soil, Beth had asserted the FBI's jurisdiction and marshaled the full might of the Bureau's resources in a thus-far unsuccessful effort to take the former chief of staff into custody. But while James had stolen top secret information and blackmailed the president, bringing him to justice for these offenses wasn't Beth's top priority.

Preserving the sanctity of Project Boomerang was.

And the buck stops with me. She gazed at Randolph, then Bellamy. The only other person in the room was the agent who'd played her the tape. Beth looked at her. "Please wait outside, Gina."

Once the door was shut, Beth studied the general's gray eyes. "Is your team ready?"

"Yes," he said, his tone self-assured.

Beth rubbed her hands down her pant legs. "Robert, any thoughts?"

Bellamy leaned his meaty forearms onto his knees. "Only that we can't waste this opportunity. Seven months without a tip or a break, and this caller gives us the mother lode."

"Any idea who it might be?" Beth asked. "Or whether it's legit."

"No . . . and no." Randolph had set his coffee down and was staring at the floor. "The beginning of the call set up a delivery of the reward money via wire transfer to an offshore account in the Bahamas. Half was transferred this morning as a down payment, with the rest due if the information is useful. Sounds . . . pretty smart. My guess is the caller is an employee or perhaps even a physician at CHRISTUS, but who the hell knows? Everyone has a price." He shrugged. "I think we have to treat it as real. And if it is . . ."

"It might give us the leverage to put the genie back in the bottle," Bellamy said, resting his chin on his fists.

"Why would Nester take such a risk?" Beth asked, thinking as she talked. "Allowing Bella out in public gives us a chance to expose his whole operation."

"Oh, I don't know," Bellamy said, sarcasm seeping into his tone. "Because he's sitting on the cure for cancer, and he wants to see if it's real. Maybe that? And until this particular phone call . . ." He pointed a chubby finger at the speaker on the table in front of him. "We haven't so much as sniffed a clue as to the James family's whereabouts. Hell, I'm half convinced that Nester is the one behind the call."

"I thought of that myself," Beth said, letting out a breath she hadn't realized she'd been holding. "But why would he want Bella caught?"

"To trade Eli for the girl," Randolph said.

"We would need a lot more than that," Beth said. "Eli gives us next to nothing if Nester still holds the secret."

Randolph shrugged. "Just trying to get at a possible motive for Nester to be playing us."

"No," Bellamy said, sarcasm gone. "Nester gains nothing by giving up the girl. The call is either a hoax, or it is legit. Or . . . perhaps it *is* Nester, and he wants us to put the full weight of the government behind apprehending Bella in Santa Fe tomorrow while she actually goes to another location." He raised his eyebrows.

Randolph snorted. "We have a big operation, but to put agents in every single cancer center in New Mexico . . ."

"And we'd have to go broader," Beth said. "At least the Four Corners. He has free rein in all four states."

"There's no way." Bellamy sighed.

For almost a minute, the room was quiet. Beth turned to face the window again, peering up at the hundreds of balloons that blanketed the morning sky. She bit her lip, thinking of her mother, who'd died at seventy-four of breast cancer. Then she thought of Eli and Dale James, hiding somewhere, hoping that their daughter would be cured of terminal lung cancer. And then Bella. Eighteen years old. A good soccer player. A gifted singer and dancer who had a scholarship to Belmont University in Nashville.

Beth had never let herself think too deeply about the ramifications of their actions, but the more she learned about this fugitive trio and their extended family, the harder she was finding it to keep it all business. She'd been on board when these decisions were made eight years ago; when the discovery was fresh, they'd treated it as akin to nuclear technology. They'd eliminated threats. Killed people in the name of national security. In a way, it hadn't seemed real. It was simply the job, and Beth was determined to do what needed to be done. But this felt different. This wasn't simply pushing a button or sending in a team. This could get messy, and if she were honest, she was beginning to have second thoughts about the entire operation.

We could just let it go, she thought. *Pack up our things and let it the fuck go. If they ever say anything about the cure, we just deny it. Deny, deny, deny. Let things simmer down and die out. If Nester and the Jameses can't produce more of the boomerang, then what's the harm of them having it?*

Beth leaned her head against the cool surface of the window. *They won't go away. Eli James is too smart and stubborn for that, and Nester Sanchez will never let it go.*

"We have to assume the call is real," Randolph finally said.

Beth closed her eyes. "I agree. General, assemble your team."

"I said they're ready," Randolph said.

Beth turned to face him. "We take the girl alive." She glanced at Bellamy. Took their silence as assent.

"What if her real parents are there?" Bellamy asked.

"Eli James is expendable. If we have a shot, we should take it," Randolph said, popping his words like machine-gun fire. "But like Beth says, we have to be careful with Bella. Ditto with Dale. If either is harmed . . . or killed, then . . ." The room again fell silent. Finally, Bellamy pushed himself off the couch, cleared his throat, and said what they were all thinking. "The fallout would be a PR nightmare that could expose our whole operation. We could lose everything."

Beth McGee felt nauseated. "And that might not even be the worst part." She studied the two men. "We would also feel the full wrath of Nester Sanchez."

58

Dale and Eli waited in Dr. Baca's private office. The lights were off, and the door was locked. Eli glanced at the time on his burner phone. 10:37 a.m. Any minute, they would see Bella and the doctor and—once more—receive the results that would define the rest of their lives. He took a deep breath and exhaled.

The trip this morning to the CHRISTUS St. Vincent Cancer Center had already been quite the adventure. Ralph had driven them to an Allsup's just past the Kewa Pueblo reservation in a rental Toyota Camry. While Ralph filled his vehicle with gas, Eli and Dale went inside to the restroom and exited the other side, where a navy BMW 6 Series sedan was waiting. Eli opened the back passenger-side door for Dale and walked around the vehicle, scanning the convenience store lot for any signs of trouble. There were none.

When he'd climbed inside and shut the door, he was surprised to see a young man wearing a white physician's coat behind the wheel.

"Dominic Baca," the driver said, his voice measured as he sized them up in the rearview mirror, holding his gaze on Eli. "Menaul, class of 2000. I was a year behind your wife."

"Oh my God," Dale said, leaning forward so that she could see him better. *"Dom?"*

A grin spread on the man's face as he nodded. "Dale Davis. Captain of the cheerleaders. Valedictorian. Girlfriend to the baddest man on the planet, and I don't mean Mike Tyson." His grin widened. "Prettiest *chica* to ever set foot in Menaul."

"Jesus Christ," Eli whispered under his breath. "What is the deal with that school?"

"Your wife used to sneak vodka shots before history class, and I'm pretty sure the teacher knew it but was holding out hope that you might need *extra credit* in his class." He winked at Dale. "No such luck."

"Dom, you're a doctor?"

The smile slowly dissipated, and Dom shook his head. "I'm a pharmaceutical sales rep. But my mom is one of the best oncologists in the state of New Mexico . . . and I believe she's seeing a new patient this morning."

"Thank you," Dale said.

"Why are you doing this?" Eli asked. "Surely, your attachment to your alma mater doesn't go this far."

"No, *señor*, it doesn't. But when Nester says jump, I say how high."

"Why is that?" Eli asked as the BMW hurtled down I-25 toward Sante Fe. "Are you afraid of him?"

"Yes," Dom said. "As you should be too. But that's not entirely it. Nester and I played football together. We've been friends since high school. When Rachel . . . my wife . . . died, I got messed up on drugs. My mom and dad were at a loss as to what to do, but Nester made me see things different."

"How did he do that? If you don't mind me asking."

"I kinda do mind, but I'll tell you anyway. We went up to the Sandia Peak back when High Finance was still the restaurant at the top."

"I loved that place," Dale said.

"Me too. Now there's a more modern spot called Ten 3 at the top of the peak, which is also cool, but I miss High Finance. Anyway, he bought me dinner, and after it was over, we went and looked out at the view. Then, out of nowhere, he punched me in the stomach and kneed me under the chin. I was seeing stars and, the next thing you know, he's dangling me over the edge of the peak by my pant leg. I weighed close to two hundred pounds then, but Nester held me like a sack of flour. He was laughing at me. Calling me a pussy. Saying that he might as well let me go, since I'd quit on my life." Dom's head gave a jerk. "I screamed for help, but no one came and, if anyone had heard me, they would have seen Nester and walked away. He asked me again and again, '*Do you want to die, motherfucker?*' I screamed no over and over again. For a moment he let go, and I thought I was gone, but he'd just shifted his grip for a second to the other leg. He'd thrown me up, not down." Dom paused. "That one second changed my life. He pulled me back up and bear-hugged me and told me that I was his friend, and that it was time for me to get the fuck over it." Dom's voice shook as they passed a green sign that read SANTE FE, 22 MILES. He nodded to himself. "I reconciled with my parents the next day, went to rehab, and voilà. Here I am."

"Here you are," Eli had said, biting his lip hard. He'd wanted to say *Just another one of Nester's bitches,* but swallowed the comment. He'd had all the Nester-worship he could stand, and he still wasn't sold. Had Nester really helped this man? Or had he simply abused him and brainwashed him into servitude?

"My mom is already at the clinic," Dom said. "When we get closer, I'm going to ask you both to duck down out of sight while I park in the physician's lot in the garage attached to the facility. I'm going to drop you off right at the door, where my mom will be waiting. She'll take you up the employee elevator to her office, where you'll wait to see her and your daughter with the results."

Eli nodded along with the game plan, which had worked like a charm thus far.

Dom had dropped them off at 10:00 a.m., and Eli and Dale hopped onto the sidewalk and through a door being held open by a petite woman wearing a white coat. Once they were in the elevator, she'd given a tense smile. "I'm Carmen Baca. Bella is out of her PET scan and is waiting with her . . . other parents in one of our patient rooms. When I have the results, I'll peek in and give her the go-ahead, and she'll take a restroom break. Except, instead of going to the bathroom, she'll come to my office, where you two will be waiting. Once we're in, we'll only have a few minutes to talk. I've seen the prior reports, so I know what we're dealing with. Two tumors, one in each lung. Inoperable. Incurable. Terminal. Correct?"

"Yes," Eli had croaked as the elevator had opened.

Now, in the darkness of the small office, they waited. The room smelled of spearmint gum, and Eli could hear Dale's breathing. He felt his heartbeat thudding in his chest. He glanced at his phone. But before he could see the time, the door swung open.

For a few seconds, Eli could see nothing, and then a desk lamp was turned on, and he could make out his daughter standing with her back against the now-closed door. She was wearing a blue LA Dodgers cap, a gray T-shirt, and jeans. "Hey," she whispered, stepping forward so that she stood between her parents. The three of them stared at Dr. Carmen Baca, who was sitting in her desk chair, rocking back and forth, arms folded, face pale. She looked almost . . . angry.

"What's wrong?" Dale asked.

"Nothing," the physician said. She handed Eli a stack of papers. "These are the three reports. CT of right lung. CT of left lung. PET scan." Her voice was matter of fact, giving away nothing. With the faint light from the desk lamp, Eli couldn't see the page.

"Do you mind if I turn on another light?"

"No need. You can read the reports later. The impressions for all three are very short and basically say the same thing."

"Which is?" Dale asked.

Dr. Baca swallowed. "No evidence of carcinoma."

59

Eli leaned against the wall to steady himself. He was crying and looked away so that his wife and daughter couldn't see. He felt a hand on his shoulder. He turned and looked at Bella. He took her cap off and put his hands on her cheeks.

"Thank you, Dad." Tears streaked her face, and Eli wiped them with his thumbs. He nodded but couldn't speak. He glanced at Dale, who had sunk to her knees. She was shaking, and Bella leaned down and wrapped her arms around her. Eli knew he would break completely if he saw his wife's face. Instead, he tried to focus on Dr. Baca, who was talking almost as if to herself. "I just don't understand *how* this could be. I have never seen anything like it. What treatment has she received?"

"The less you know, the better," Eli said. "Now how do we get out of here?"

Carmen Baca blinked, and then she was back. "Bella will come with me and will leave with the Arruzas. You stay here with the lights off. I will be back in a few minutes and will take you to my car myself." She hesitated. "I'll drive you out of here."

"Thank you," Eli managed.

She touched his arm. "I'm happy for you, Mr. James. I'm happy for your family. But I must say, I am completely perplexed. What I'm seeing on these scans is an impossibility. I just . . . don't believe it."

Eli wiped tears from his eyes and peered at his beautiful daughter. "Believe it," he whispered, saying a silent prayer as Bella stood and gave him a hug.

"See you this afternoon," Bella said, kissing his cheek. "We have some celebrating to do, right?"

"Right," Eli managed.

"Let's go, Bella," Dr. Baca said, peering at Eli. "I'll be back as soon as I can."

Then, seconds later, they were both gone, and Eli and Dale were left alone in the dark office.

"Well . . . ," Eli started to say, but the words wouldn't come. He was exhausted. In his mind, while listening to the news from Dr. Baca, he'd imagined his own father standing in the corner of the room. Whistling. When he was doing an important surgery, Frank James always whistled. He did it to relax and project confidence. Both in himself and his nurses and the patient.

Eli hadn't allowed himself to mourn his father. Not while Bella's life hung in the balance. He started to lose it again, but then gritted back the tears. *This isn't over,* he told himself. *Not until we're back at the reservation, and even then* . . . He thought of the meeting the government wanted and Bella's dwindling supply of the boomerang. Then he glanced at Dale, who was staring at him. Eyes focused and hyperalert. He knew she was thinking the exact same thing.

It's far from over.

60

General Kyle Randolph surveyed the entrance to the lobby of the CHRISTUS St. Vincent Cancer Center and spoke into a handheld device. "Do we have the subject in sight?"

"Affirmative, General. The girl is in the lobby. Jeans, Dodgers cap. She's with a couple that appear to be posing as her parents."

Randolph was in a BLACK HAWK helicopter high above Santa Fe. Far enough away to not be visible or audible, but close enough to drop in, if need be. It had been a while since he'd flown in a chopper. The flight and the adrenaline of right now brought him back to Afghanistan. He was in his element. A field commander stalking his prey. It was what he did best.

"Did the couple park their car in the lot?"

"Yes, sir. The vehicle is a Honda Accord. We have a team watching it and officers stationed at every exit. What are our orders?"

Randolph gazed out of the aircraft's window at the vast brown landscape below. "Have you seen any sign of trouble?"

"None, sir."

"All right, then. Let's wait until they are outside the clinic. Then take custody of the subject and bring her to the rendezvous point." Randolph licked his lips. "Tell your people to expect resistance and retaliation and to be ready to return fire at will."

A pause over the line.

"Do you understand, Captain?" Randolph barked.

"Yes, sir. But, General . . . do you really think . . . *he's* here?"

Randolph let out a ragged breath. "Yes, Captain, I do. You have your orders."

"Ten-four."

Randolph leaned forward and patted his pilot on the right shoulder. "Let's get closer. We'll need to move soon."

"Yes, sir."

Seconds later, the BLACK HAWK dived into its descent, and Randolph's ears buzzed to the sound of the throttle. The plan would work. He knew it in his bones. In his balls.

They would not only reclaim the boomerang and eliminate the threat posed by the James family.

They would also obtain leverage with Nester Sanchez. The kind of pressure to flush him out into the open.

And when that happens . . .

Randolph felt his pulse quicken.

. . . we kill the Beast.

61

Eli paced the inside of the dark office. "Something is wrong," he finally said. "Dr. Baca should've returned by now."

Dale was sitting on the floor with her back against the wall. Since the physician's departure, neither had said a word. The tension in the close quarters was palpable. They'd been gifted a miracle. Their daughter was healthy. But now they were both scared to death the gift would be snatched away.

Dale pushed herself off the ground. She took out her phone and glanced at the screen. "It's been almost ten minutes." She peered at Eli. "You're right."

Eli started to say something but felt his own phone vibrating in his pocket. He snatched it like a lifeline and read the number on the screen. He showed it to Dale. "Should I—?"

"Answer it," she said. "Has to be one of our people. Click the speaker button."

Eli did as she instructed. "Hello," he said.

"The mission has been compromised."

Eli's stomach clenched into a knot as he recognized the voice of Nester Sanchez. "What do you mean? What do we do?"

Dale had flipped on the lights, and they were staring at each other. "Nester, talk to me," she said.

"They are here, and they are going to try to take her."

"Oh, hell no, they're not," Dale said. "Over my dead body."

"Nester, you have coverage, right?" Eli asked, hearing the plea in his voice.

"I do, but I don't want to risk Bella's safety." There was a beat of silence, and Eli glanced at Dale, whose face had turned pale white. When Nester's voice came back over the line, it was softer. "I am going to create a diversion. I am sorry, Dale, but your uncle agreed to do this."

"Agreed to do what?" Dale asked, her voice rising.

"Get downstairs to the basement parking garage and find the car you came to the facility in. Can you do that?"

"Yes," Eli said. "Nester, what about Bella?"

"The diversion will allow us to get her out. I promise."

"What are you *talking* about?"

"It is hard to defeat an old man with a death wish," Nester said. "Stay away from the lobby. In a few seconds, all hell is going to break loose . . . and hell will be driving a Pepsi truck."

"Nester?"

"Go," Nester commanded. *"Now."*

62

Ralph Gutierrez had always loved the Chicago Bulls. When he had finally gotten cable, in the late '80s, the best thing about having it was WGN. The Chicago network. Home of the Bulls and a fella named Michael "Air" Jordan.

Ralph was a lifelong chain-smoker. He'd been a short, chubby kid, and not much had changed as an adult. His father had beaten him as a child. Abuse was a way of life in their family. His brother Jerry, the oldest, took the brunt of it. Leonard, the baby of the siblings, was mostly spared, and Ralph was thankful for that. Leonard had joined the air force. He'd gotten out of the land of entrapment. The sign welcoming people to the state said ENCHANTMENT, but Ralph knew different. New Mexico was like a big spiderweb lined with black tar. Once you were tangled up in it, there was no escape. But Leonard had. So had Dale. Ralph was thankful.

He knew he could've felt bitter, but he didn't.

Not even about his ex-wife, Deborah, who'd cheated on him throughout their miserable marriage. He'd loved her. Hell, he still loved her. Couldn't help it. When a Gutierrez loved you, it was for life. He loved his father too. Despite the beatings, he worshipped the man. And even now, even with just a few seconds of life left, he had the odd thought that he hoped his father would be proud of him.

He also hoped he would go to heaven. He knew Jerry was up there, but Ralph wasn't sure if he'd make it. He'd done some bad things. Nothing too criminal, but when you worked for Nester Sanchez . . .

Ralph took a long sip of Pepsi and peered at himself in the mirror. Tears streaked his big eyes, and he chuckled. He'd always been a crier. Could never get through even the simplest of prayers without tearing up. Weddings. Funerals. Jeffie's first day of kindergarten. Didn't matter. It was always Niagara Falls.

Would he miss this world?

He was nodding. Yes, he would. He'd miss his son. He'd miss his FaceTime talks with Leonard, who now lived overseas. And he'd miss his niece Dale and his great-niece Bella. He'd miss knowing how this story was going to end.

Ralph burped and peered around the inside of the truck. How many deliveries had he made in his life? The number had to be in the thousands. Now, he'd make his last.

He'd always loved westerns and superhero movies.

Maybe that's what had drawn him to Michael Jordan. His Airness was like a real-life superhero. So fucking cool.

Ralph Gutierrez had never been cool. He wasn't a badass, nor did he think he was anyone's hero. He was a small, fat man who'd driven a Pepsi truck most of his life. He was dying of stage-four lung cancer. He could probably have mentioned that to Dale. Hell, maybe he could even have stuck around to see if they could get more of the miracle medication that Bella was on. He could've done those things, but he didn't want to.

He was tired. He missed his brother. He'd endured all he needed to in this world.

He squeezed the wheel and shifted the truck into drive. He'd pulled off along the curb a half mile from the facility. From this vantage point, he had a straight shot toward the front doors of the clinic.

And plenty of blacktop to hit the far right of the speedometer.

His phone dinged, and a text popped up. It was one word, and it came from the biggest badass he'd ever known.

Now.

Ralph tugged on his cap. Then, thinking of an old Sylvester Stallone movie he'd loved, he turned it around on his head. He fiddled with the radio in the truck until he found his playlist. The song he wanted was first.

"Sirius" by the Alan Parsons Project. The Bulls intro song from the Jordan era.

Ralph Gutierrez pulled at the chain around his neck until he touched the cross. He brought the gold to his lips and kissed it. Then he pushed Play, and the greatest guitar riff in the history of the world began.

Visions danced through his head like a slideshow. Of Jeffie at his high school graduation. Deborah on their wedding night. Leonard the morning he left for the air force. Ralph closed his eyes and saw his family. But as the song roared on, another image gripped him.

Funny, the things you think about when you're about to die.

Jordan with the ball in his hand. Dribbling down the court. Taking off from the free throw line. Soaring toward the basket. Flying . . .

"I was Ralph Gutierrez," the old man said out loud.

The song had reached his favorite part. Ralph screamed and mimicked the announcer's iconic team introduction as he'd done a million times before and floored the Pepsi semi, its eighteen wheels screeching forward.

"AND NOW . . ."

63

"We're going to either need to go in or abort, General. The subject did not come inside and has returned to the patient area with her fake parents."

"Then go, goddamnit!" Randolph screamed, as the BLACK HAWK swooped down and the CHRISTUS St. Vincent Cancer Center became visible. "I have air coverage. Whatever it takes, get the girl, do you hear me?"

"Ten-four."

Randolph started to cut loose another obscenity but stopped when he saw what was happening on the land. His crew was going in, but they weren't the only ones. He gripped his handheld as he stared at a Pepsi truck streaking down the main drive.

It's not slowing down.

"Captain, there's a delivery vehicle—"

"We see it, General. Holy—" His voice abruptly cut off as the eighteen-wheeler crashed head-on into the front doors of the clinic. Seconds later, an explosion of fire and gas lit up the midmorning sky, and the helicopter veered hard left to avoid the fallout.

"Captain!" Randolph screamed. "Captain!"

Nothing.

"General, what do you want me to do?" the pilot yelled.

Randolph was breathing hard, but his thoughts were crystal clear. "Put me on the ground."

64

The force of the explosion nearly took Eli to his knees, and he and Dale grabbed each other to keep from falling.

"Jesus Christ, what was that?" she asked.

"Our diversion," Eli said, glancing up and half expecting the concrete roof of the garage to collapse on them. He saw men and women running up the exit ramp, and a few of them were wearing uniforms. Were they security guards employed by the facility? Or soldiers working for Kyle Randolph?

Eli wasn't sure of anything. There were also people sprinting toward their vehicles, and cars backing out of places and peeling toward the exit. Eli heard screams, the screeching of tires, and panicked voices. It was a madhouse.

"Come on," he said, as they crouched low and edged down the sidewalk a few feet. "Do you see the car?"

"No," Dale said. "Wait, is that it?" She pointed to her left. "Last space in the second row."

Eli scanned the lot. It was a parking lot for oncologists, so it was littered with BMWs and expensive cars. He followed Dale's finger, saw the car, and then a hand sticking out of the window. Waving.

"Yes!" he said.

"*Dom*," Dale gasped.

"Let's go." Eli grabbed her hand, and they ran toward the vehicle. Halfway there, he saw the headlights flash and heard the engine of the German luxury car roar to life. Dale got in the back seat, and Eli climbed in after her.

"Shit's gotten real," Dom said, eyes wide, voice high pitched.

"What now?" Eli asked.

"We follow the train of rich doctor cars out of here. Both of you duck down."

As the BMW lurched forward, Eli and Dale crouched low in the back seat floorboard. The blare of sirens became louder as the car ascended the ramp.

"Jesus, Mary, and Joseph," Dom said.

Eli peeked out the window, and his breath caught in his throat. The clinic was a ball of fire and smoke. "Is our daughter still in there?"

Dom didn't answer as the car picked up speed. There were dozens of police vehicles, and fire trucks were racing toward the building as the BMW passed in the opposite direction.

"We can't just leave her!" Dale screamed.

"We aren't!" Dom yelled back. "You'll see." He turned the wheel hard left and followed the fire trucks back toward the inferno. Then he veered to the right. The visitor parking lot was a chaotic mess as people were trying to get out of the facility. Eli saw one vehicle rear-end another. Then, in the distance, he saw people, employees and patients alike, running across the grass, escaping the fire on foot.

"Oh my God," Dale screamed. "Eli—"

"I see," he interrupted. "Dom—"

"I've got them," the driver said. "We'll pick them up on that access road. Look!" He pointed over the steering wheel. "There are several cars doing the same thing."

Eli peered through the windshield, watching a woman open the back seat of a waiting car, which peeled off the road.

"Dom, Bella is wearing jeans and—"

"I know," he interrupted. "My mom is right next to her." His voice was shaking, his breath coming out in spurts. Eli guessed Dominic Baca was on the verge of hyperventilation.

And I'm not far behind, Eli thought, as he forced a ragged breath out. Carmen Baca must have taken it upon herself to get Bella out.

"There she is," Dale said. "Don't hit them, Dom!"

The BMW slid to a stop, and Dom rolled his windows down. "Get in!"

Eli opened the back door, and, when he saw Bella's brown eyes widen, his heart swelled in his chest. *So close.*

"Bella, get—"

But his voice was drowned out by the roar of a helicopter propeller. "Jesus Christ!" He leaped forward and covered Bella with his body.

"Get in the car, Mr. James!" Dom's scream was faint under the roar of the chopper engine. When Eli looked up, he was staring at a BLACK HAWK hovering a few feet off the ground near them.

"Eli and Bella James. Lie on the ground with your hands behind you." The voice blared through a microphone, but Eli still recognized it. *General Randolph.*

He turned and saw Dale, leaning her head and chest out of the car. "Come on," her lips said, but Eli heard nothing. Next to him, Dr. Carmen Baca was on her knees, holding her hands over her ears. The sound of the chopper was deafening.

"Now, Mr. James," Randolph's voice said.

Eli turned and saw that the chopper was on the ground, and the door was opening. Beyond it, a black Cadillac Escalade raced toward them. Without hesitation, he grabbed his daughter around the waist and walked her to the car, where Dale pulled the girl inside.

"Mr. James, you are under arrest. Please put your hands behind your back and kneel on the ground."

Eli turned to Dr. Baca, crawling toward the car. He helped her in.

"Mr. James, we will not hesitate to fire."

"*Go,*" Eli mouthed at Dom, moving his arm in a circle. "*Now.*"

Eli turned to his wife and daughter. Dale was screaming "No," but the car spun its tires in reverse. He dropped to his knees and put his hands behind his head as the BMW sped away.

"Follow them!" Randolph screamed, turning to the BLACK HAWK. Then he pointed his gun at Eli. "It's no use," he shouted above the engine roar at Eli. "We've got you now. All of you."

Eli closed his eyes. They had been so close. How could Dom Baca get his family to safety with a BLACK HAWK helicopter on his tail?

He felt handcuffs locking around his wrists and hot breath in his ear.

"It's over," yelled Randolph.

"No, it's not," Eli managed, unsure if the general could hear him and not caring. "The person you fear most in the world knows your secret. Do you think he's going to let it go?"

"He will once we have your wife and daughter in custody, which shouldn't be—" He broke off, and Eli opened his eyes. He saw the BLACK HAWK stalling in the air.

"Why aren't you following?" Randolph yelled into his handheld device.

Static and then Eli heard the pilot's voice, which dripped with fear and awe. "General, I don't think that bird's with us."

"What are you talking about?" He turned to where the BMW had left, and Eli did the same.

"Sweet Mother of God . . ." Eli gasped.

A hundred feet above the ground hovered an Apache attack helicopter. The craft had been painted jet black, and its windows were tinted.

"That can't be," Randolph said.

And yet it was.

Machine-gun fire exploded from the front of the Apache, and Eli turned to see the BLACK HAWK lit up on its front and side.

"I'm hit!" the pilot's voice screamed through Randolph's handheld. "I'm setting down."

More gunfire punctured the pavement, and one of the black Escalades that was approaching stopped, disabled.

Eli felt himself being grabbed and cold steel pressed to his temple.

"Not quite over, is it, General?" he spat.

"Fuck you," Randolph growled in his ear. Then, using Eli as a shield, he backed away from the Apache. When Randolph reached the grounded BLACK HAWK, he opened the door and pushed Eli inside. Then he leaned forward and snatched the PA microphone from the front of the cab, glaring at the black Apache. "Mr. Sanchez, if you are in there, you listen and listen good. You have acquired stolen property that belongs to the United States, and you are harboring fugitives who have committed treason against this country. We will not stop. Not until we have what's ours. This is America, sir."

Seconds later, the ground lit up with gunfire from the Apache. When the dust cleared, a voice that Eli knew well rang out from the attack craft.

"This is New Mexico, General. Around here, the sky—and everything else—belongs to me."

65

Eli had no idea where he was. He'd been blindfolded on the ride from the CHRISTUS medical center, and now he was in a room with cinder block walls and a metal door. *A prison? Army barracks?*

He didn't have a clue.

His stomach churned, and he thought he might be sick. The trip to wherever he was now had been a bumpy one, and having his eyes covered had made it all the worse. He'd been given no food or water in the few hours since he'd been placed in this stale cell.

He hoped Dale and Bella were safe and believed that they were. Nester had disabled Randolph's BLACK HAWK, so Dom Baca should have been able to get out of there without being seen or caught.

Where are they now?

Eli leaned his head against the cinder block wall and thought of his mother. He hoped she wouldn't be too upset. Bella was safe and free of cancer. Their plan had worked. Eli would be a casualty, but that was okay. Probably inevitable, anyway.

I give Randolph zero leverage, Eli thought. That's why, in the seconds when a decision had to be made with Randolph's BLACK HAWK hovering above them and no sign of a rescue, Eli had sacrificed himself.

It was the right play. Bella was safe. Dale was too. They still had the boomerang, and they even had a physician with them who could explain the miracle. Trading Eli for Dr. Baca was actually an upgrade.

He couldn't help but smile. He figured that Nester also knew this. Plus, with Eli and Dale estranged, Nester would benefit from Eli being out of the way.

The gamble had paid off.

He let his back slide down the hard surface of the wall until his bottom touched the concrete floor. The power of the United States government had been on full display today. They'd somehow found Bella. They'd employed what must have been a SWAT team or some top secret Special Forces group to go in and detain her.

And they were defeated by one man . . .

Eli closed his eyes. His mind raced with thoughts and images of the past few months. SK Moss. What had happened to his former lover? Would she suffer from the fallout of this debacle? And what of Jalen Nakai? Had Nester made any progress tracking him down? And Uncle Ralph . . .

Who saved all of our lives.

Finally, in the darkness and solitude of the cell, he allowed his mind to think of his father. There had never been an official declaration from Destin. Eli had followed the news since arriving in New Mexico. Finally, a missing-person report had been filed, but that was it.

But Eli knew. He'd known from the get-go. Frank James was gone, his body likely at the bottom of the Gulf of Mexico. And if that were his final resting place, it was fitting. *Dad loved the salt water and the Gulf Coast.*

Eli wiped tears and took his mind back to Dr. Baca's office.

Where all their hopes and dreams had ridden on the results of three scans.

How many people had felt the exact same way in waiting rooms and doctor's offices across the country and the world? Your entire existence hanging on a radiologic impression. Eli had experienced the utter hopelessness of knowing that, with Bella's stage-four diagnosis, he and Dale would never hear anything that would manage their fears and anxiety. But today, in the minutes before Dr. Carmen Baca had opened the door, he'd felt what so many cancer patients and families never feel:

Hope.

Seconds later, he'd heard the words he'd dreamed in his mind for over six months.

"No evidence of carcinoma," he whispered.

Eli took a deep breath and exhaled.

There is *a cure for cancer,* he thought. *There has been for eight years. Eight years . . .*

He gritted his teeth, thinking of all the human beings who had lost their lives when they could have been saved by the boomerang. Mato Nakai should have a place at the Nobel table with Albert Einstein and Marie Curie. He should have been at the *head* of that table of geniuses who'd changed the world for the better.

Instead, he disappeared on Highway 30A between Grayton Beach and Seaside, Florida.

For what? *Greed. Money. National fucking security.*

"What bullshit," he said, speaking louder, his voice defiant.

Why do we kill our miracles?

66

The barn was lit by candles. The smell of hay and horse manure was thick in the air.

Dale took no notice as she stroked her daughter's curly hair. Bella leaned against her body, and Dale could feel the girl's heartbeat. Since arriving back at the reservation, the Tilt-A-Whirl in Dale's mind, body, and heart spun on like none she'd ever experienced.

Gratitude.

Grief.

Joy tinged with regret. But most of all . . .

. . . loss.

The price for today's miracle had been high. *Too high,* she thought, hearing the sniffles of her daughter mixed in with the others.

"Will you . . . tell it again?" Foncie asked. She was sitting next to them. Her silver hair tucked inside of a green Tamaya Resort baseball cap. Foncie wasn't overly emotional, but the tears on her cheeks told the story.

Bella cleared her throat and described the moments outside of the CHRISTUS medical center.

"My boy is a hero," Foncie said, nodding to herself, not wiping her tears. "I will miss that Ralph. He was such a character."

Dale closed her eyes. She had found it impossible to look at her family since their return. She knew they were all here, and she hated what she'd put them through.

"I'm sorry," she finally said. "If we hadn't come . . ."

She felt a warm, strong hand on her neck. ". . . you would be dead, sissy." It was Amos. "Uncle Ralph would not have wanted that."

"He's up there with Dad now," Santi said. "And Mama Bev. That's what he wanted." He cleared his throat. "He wanted to go out in a blaze of glory."

"Well, he sure as shit did," Foncie said. "I'll miss that funny bastard."

There were a few laughs, but they were drowned by more sniffles. "He died a hero," Foncie continued. "Just like my . . ." But she couldn't finish as her lip began to quiver.

"They won't kill him," Santi said. "They'll try to use him, but it would be foolish to kill him."

Silence filled the barn, and Dale opened her eyes. They'd taken a roundabout way home from Santa Fe, changing vehicles several times, arriving at the Tamaya just after dark. It was late, but none of them had mentioned sleep.

Dale wondered if she'd ever be able to sleep again.

What now? she thought. Bella was healthy, but nothing was over. They were still almost out of the medication. A deal had to be reached, but was that possible?

Nester had held off the wolves today, but Dale knew they wouldn't quit.

The quiet was broken by the barn door sliding open. Santi, Amos, and Foncie shot to their feet. Guns out, pointed at the opening.

When Dom Baca peeked his head in, there was a collective sigh.

"Might want to knock next time, chief," Foncie said. "We've all got itchy trigger fingers around here."

"Sorry," he said.

"Are you okay?" Dr. Carmen Baca asked her son. She had been sitting in the corner of an empty horse stall. She came to him.

"Fine," he said. "I have a message." He looked at Dale.

"What?" she asked.

"He wants to see you."

67

"The situation is out of control." Beth McGee chose her words wisely as she moved her eyes from General Kyle Randolph to Robert Bellamy.

"That's a bit of an understatement," Bellamy said, peering at the floor. "It's a raging shitstorm. Have you seen some of the cell phone videos? Jesus God, General, what the hell were you thinking?"

Randolph cleared his throat. The man's typically unflappable demeanor remained in place, but his gray eyes were bloodshot. "I was attempting to secure the target. We were not expecting a Pepsi truck to hit the front entrance of the facility going almost one hundred miles per hour and detonate a series of onboard explosives." He paused, and Beth could hear his teeth grind. "We were also not expecting Nester Sanchez to have a fully equipped Apache attack helicopter."

"You had a team of Rangers, SEALs, and Green Berets," Bellamy fired back. "Don't you guys train to deal with the unexpected?"

"Of course we do. Today just got away from us."

"There are at least fifty human beings, most of them civilians, who are being treated for serious injuries." Beth kept her tone matter of fact. "There are five confirmed dead, and that number is expected to rise. Questions are pouring in from all quarters, the big one being what you were doing in a BLACK HAWK helicopter and holding the former chief of staff to the president at gunpoint."

"Easy to resolve," Randolph said. "We make Eli James the scapegoat. He has illegally given information of the utmost national security to a known fugitive and one of the most dangerous humans in the civilized world. In our attempts to apprehend James and Sanchez, one of Sanchez's men drove a truck loaded with dynamite into the CHRISTUS medical center in Santa Fe, killing and harming innocent citizens of New Mexico. It's a PR nightmare for the Beast, and it's not only a reasonable story: *it's also the goddamn truth.*" He slammed his fist down on the table.

"General, we both know it's more complicated than that. There is no proof that the driver of the truck was linked to Nester, though there is a link to the James family, as Ralph Gutierrez was Dale's stepuncle. So, best case, the scapegoat is still Eli or the James family. But if that *information* that Eli James allegedly has given Nester somehow gets out into the media space?" She waited. "Do I have to go on? And in terms of PR nightmares, what about the president? This *was* his chief of staff. His best friend. Who's now gone rogue, and whose hands are all over this attack. We gave Lionel Cantrell access to the boomerang in an effort to make damn sure Governor Yancey didn't become president. What if Lionel is impeached? What then?"

"Oh, come on, Beth. The president can wash his hands of James. Lionel Cantrell is slippery as a minnow. He'll wiggle out of this, and he'll have our help. We will control the narrative, starting with prohibiting the use and disclosure of those videos."

"They confirm what we've suspected for years. Nester has an Apache. What else does he have?" Bellamy asked. "How can one man hold off the Special Forces of the United States?"

Randolph sighed and pushed himself off the couch. "It was *one* skirmish. One day. He won't be able to do it again. And if we could ever just go all in, we would destroy him."

"Are you sure about that?" Beth challenged. "How do you take down a chameleon? Do we even have an accurate photograph of him after high school? The reaction here in New Mexico has been anything but anti-Nester. If anything, the confrontation seems to have only added to the man's lore. We can't blame this incident on Nester. We have to make it about the James family . . ." She sighed. ". . . and you."

"Me?" Randolph asked.

"At least in the public eye, there has to be some type of admonition. Nothing substantive, but a public slap on the wrist."

"You've got to be kidding."

"General, you turned Santa Fe, New Mexico, into a war zone. CNN, Fox News, and every local media outlet in the country has a correspondent there now. The president is set to give a press conference in a few hours in front of what's left of the CHRISTUS cancer center. Governor Florez will be by his side. They are going to do just as you said. Call out Eli James, the James family, and Dale's uncle Ralph as having committed terrorist acts on American soil, but they are also going to publicly reprimand your maneuvers as foolish and over the top."

Randolph couldn't believe it. "This is your doing, isn't it?"

"It's what's best for the country. You would do it yourself in a heartbeat to me if it meant preserving national security."

"And how will the president and the governor handle the questions about the Apache attack craft that fired on my chopper?"

Beth sighed. "They will say that an investigation is ongoing and that no definitive determinations have been made. However, the preliminary report will be that the confrontation between two US Army helicopters was . . . friendly fire caused by the chaotic aftermath of the truck's crash into the center." She swallowed. "And poor decision-making in the heat of the moment."

Randolph glared at her and then at Bellamy. "Did you know about this?"

"Yes," Bellamy said. "And I agree with Beth. There's a lot of heat, General. Frankly, I doubt anyone is going to buy the friendly fire story, but none of the videos have captured the audio from the Apache all that well, so . . ." He trailed off and rubbed his hands down his pant legs. Then he stared at Randolph. "I don't see how we can admit to the American people that a four-star general and living legend of the United States military was outmaneuvered by a common civilian who has somehow acquired a goddamn attack helicopter. *Do you?*"

Randolph opened his mouth, but no words came out. His hands were shaking. Beth had never seen the man so angry and frustrated.

"General, this is just a public admonishment," she said, choosing her words carefully. "It's nothing. We just need to address your involvement for PR purposes. You are still the leader of Project Boomerang, and we all have faith in you." But Beth knew that affirming her belief in the general only made it sound like the opposite. She licked her lips. "Let's get back to brass tacks. This mission was supposed to be stealth, and it has become anything but." Beth paused and crossed her arms. "Questions are being asked. Questions that we don't want to have to answer. And I doubt they are going to stop. We have to put out this fire before it's too big to control."

"Agreed," Bellamy said. "Surely we can make a deal. We have Eli James."

Randolph shook his head, his face still flushed. "Not enough."

"Maybe not," Beth said. "But we have to try. Assuming the boomerang worked, and Bella's scans were clean—"

"Of course it fucking worked," Randolph said.

"What I'm trying to say is that the James family has presumably achieved its objective. Like you've always said, Robert." She turned to the Homeland Security operative. "This was never about saving the world for Eli James. It was about saving his daughter. He's done that."

Bellamy nodded, then sighed. "If only it was Eli with whom we were dealing."

"But it's not," Randolph chimed in. "Regardless of whatever bullshit story the president and governor tell the country, the Beast is dealing the cards now. And Nester Sanchez doesn't give a damn about Eli James." He rubbed the back of his neck. "I guess we'll see how much Mrs. James cares about her estranged husband."

"Do we agree that we need to make a deal?" Beth asked.

"Yes," Bellamy said. "As soon as possible. We'll need to be careful with the terms, but I think we can contain the damage. The genie may not get put back in the bottle, but perhaps we can put her on a desert island where she can't do any harm."

Beth thought she understood the analogy. She studied Randolph. "General?"

"Dealing is a mistake. The only way to put out this fire is to do something we should have done a long time ago."

Beth creased her eyebrows. "What might that be?"

"Kill the Beast," Randolph hissed. "Nester. The James family. All of them. Use the carrot of a deal to bring them out, and then wipe the world clean of them."

Beth blinked at him. "I don't agree with that approach."

"Me either," Bellamy said. "Look, Kyle, no one wants Nester Sanchez gone more than me, but you saw what he did today."

"One day. One skirmish."

"He's the Scourge of New Mexico for a reason," Bellamy fired back. "There aren't just videos of what happened. There's word of mouth. Beth is right. His legend has grown. He's fucking Spartacus with a splash of Robin Hood, Josey Wales, and John Dutton thrown in. We can't win a guerrilla warfare battle against this man. It'll be a mini Vietnam."

"Not if we assassinate him," Randolph said. He was now staring out the window, and Beth followed his gaze. The sun was beginning to rise a brilliant and firestorm red over the Sandias. *The Land of Enchantment,* Beth thought, wondering how such a beautiful place could be the setting for such tragedy and bloodshed.

Beth approached Randolph, speaking softer. Almost a whisper. "General, we know that yesterday was tough for you, but we can't solve this situation with an emotional reaction. Now is the time to be cold blooded."

Randolph turned to her. His eyelids were as red as the sun. "Nothing is more ruthless and to the point than putting a bullet in that SOB's head."

"We don't have the time or the resources for that," she said. "You're outvoted, and we are moving forward with a deal. Do you understand?"

Randolph said nothing, looking away.

Beth decided to take silence for agreement. "Given the situation, you both know who we have to involve." She hesitated. "Not just for the press conference this afternoon but also to help us behind the scenes."

Bellamy nodded, but Randolph was shaking his head. "No," the general said. "We can't trust him. Not after what he's done. He has conflicting loyalties, and they'll rear up again."

"Maybe so, but we don't have a choice." She took out her phone. "Yes, put me through to the White House."

"Beth, he'll only make it worse," Randolph pleaded, but Beth waved him off.

"Yesterday afternoon, a terrorist act played out on American soil that involved a retaliation and reaction by a four-star general and former secretary of defense and chairman of the Joint Chiefs of Staff. Innocent civilians were killed." Beth turned back toward the window. "We need the president."

68

Lionel Cantrell gazed at the makeshift stage that had been placed in front of the ruins of the CHRISTUS cancer center. The smell of smoke still permeated the chilly, dry air, and the president folded his arms across his chest. At his press secretary's direction, he'd dressed in jeans, a white button-down, and a brown leather bomber jacket. Aviator sunglasses covered his eyes, and if his old friend from Lick Skillet were here, Eli would be ribbing him for dressing like Maverick from *Top Gun*. According to the PR folks, he needed to look like a strong leader, working hands-on at the scene, and the clothes gave that impression.

Whatever, Lionel thought. He felt ridiculous.

He was standing in a tent to the side of the stage and flanked by at least seven Secret Service agents. At the podium was Governor Abigail Florez, a tall, striking woman with black hair and dark eyes. Eli had spoken to Abby, as she was known in political circles, only a few times, but he'd always been impressed with her passion for New Mexico. A fire that was on full display now.

"We will not tolerate terrorism in our home!" Her voice was strong and exuberant. "The attack on this place of healing yesterday was a senseless act of violence, and I am honored that our president has flown down here to survey the damage and help us find an explanation and a solution."

What have you gotten us into now, Eli? Lionel thought, only half listening to the governor's spiel, which she'd gone over with him a few minutes earlier with FBI Director Beth McGee listening in. The director had revealed herself to Lionel as a member of Project Boomerang during a terse meeting at the tarmac when Air Force One had landed in Albuquerque earlier this morning. She'd laid out her damage-control strategy, which Lionel had to admit seemed sound.

In a few moments, he'd take the stage and tell the American people that his best friend had lost his mind in the wake of his daughter's illness and had presumably involved a family friend in an act of violence on this fine establishment. Eli James was a federal employee who was being investigated for suspicious activity in recent months, and General Randolph received a tip that morning that led him to travel in a helicopter to Santa Fe. Unfortunately, the general and his team arrived too late to thwart the attack and, in the aftermath, appeared to have been involved in a friendly fire incident. The investigation was ongoing, and no definitive conclusions had been reached. He would close by assuring them all that the president of the United States stood with Governor Florez and New Mexico.

He clenched his fists as the governor recycled a stump speech on her efforts to clean up her state and how yesterday's attack would not derail her work.

From what Lionel had seen on video, his oldest and best friend had faced down General Randolph and protected his daughter and wife from harm, then dropped to his knees and taken one for the team. The hair on Lionel's arms had stood up when the Apache came on screen and opened fire on the BLACK HAWK.

Friendly fire, my ass.

The name Nester Alejandro Sanchez would not be mentioned by either Abby Florez or him today, but Lionel felt the presence of the Beast everywhere. Signs saying THE SKIES BELONG TO NESTER, I AM NESTER, and IN NESTER WE TRUST were held by patrons who had gathered in front of the stage and throughout the once-intact campus of the CHRISTUS St. Vincent Cancer Center. Word of mouth was strong, as was the video evidence. The Apache appeared to have been spray-painted black, and though voices couldn't be heard on the clip, several people confirmed that Nester Sanchez had defied a four-star general and fired on the sonofabitch.

Was New Mexico about to be the site of a full-on insurrection? Surely not, given the top secret information that Nester Sanchez now possessed. Regardless of the bullshit spouted today by the president and governor, there would have to be another cover-up: the Apache had fired by mistake. It was all a big misunderstanding.

Deny. Deny. Deny.

He'd have to appear strong and decisive. He knew the speech would be televised and shown on every news outlet in the country. He'd also meet with the victims. He'd have sit-down discussions with the mayor of Santa Fe and Governor Florez. The photo ops, starting right now, would be important. The mood somber. Serious. Faces stoic. Body language and words screaming, "*We're going to do something about this.*" Abby Florez was carrying off that vibe now, and the president was on deck.

But Lionel knew what was about to happen. If Randolph and McGee had custody of Eli, they had nothing. To come to terms with Nester Sanchez, Dale James was the trading card they needed, with Bella a distant second.

Eli was expendable. Nester had the high ground, and an all-out war against him would result only in loss of life and the inevitable disclosure of the most egregious lie the American government had ever told its people.

There would be no war.

Instead, a deal would have to be made. Yet another soul-stealing agreement to hide the miracle that had saved his and Bella James's life.

As Governor Florez began her introduction of him, Lionel closed his eyes, wondering if the country even had a soul anymore.

69

Dale felt her heart racing as she gazed at the front door to Donaldson Hall. While the Menaul School had undergone significant renovations and added new structures, this particular building, with its red adobe columns, looked the same to her. She felt goose bumps on her arms, and her heart rate began to accelerate. It would have been emotional and moving if she had been coming only for a reunion. But given the events of the past twenty-four hours . . . and the person she was meeting inside these doors . . . the moment felt mostly surreal.

And overwhelming.

Dale wiped her eyes and took a deep breath. She peered to her right and gazed at the sun, which shone crimson above the Sandia Mountains. She exhaled and forced her feet to go up the steps. How many times had she burst through these doors as a teenager? Often laughing. Sometimes crying. Stressed because she was running late? She smiled. That had been a regular occurrence.

This humble structure had been her happy place when she'd moved from Alabama to New Mexico. It hadn't been initially. She'd been scared. Terrified of this new chapter in her life. She'd wanted to go back home. But then she'd met a boy, and her stars had realigned.

Now, for the first time since her return, she would see the man the boy had become. The man they called the Beast on television and even in the halls of the Pentagon.

She opened the door and gazed straight ahead. The door to the chapel was open. The lights were off. She walked through the opening and saw a figure sitting in the second pew. His back was to her, and he didn't turn.

Dale again had to force her legs to move. She walked down to the right and then across in front of the stage. In the darkness, she couldn't make out his face. Just the shadow of the man. When she approached, he clicked a lighter, and she saw them.

The golden brown eyes of the lion.

Her lip started to tremble, and she hung her head. "Hey," she said.

Then she felt his strong hands on her shoulders. "I have missed you," he whispered in her ear. "Please, sit down."

She did as he asked and, for almost a minute, neither of them spoke. Dale had done nothing but practice what she was going to say since Dom had burst into the barn last night, but she found that her brain was scrambled. Awash in stress and flooded with memories.

"Why did you pick this spot?"

"Why do you think?"

Dale closed her eyes and opened them. Her mind had gone back almost thirty years. School was out for the day. They'd sneaked into the chapel. The lights were off just as they were now. They'd fumbled in the blackness like teenagers do. Giggling. Breathing hard and heavy. He'd struggled to unsnap her bra, and she'd finally done it herself. The smell of his sweat from football practice mingled with grape bubble gum and pubic hair. It was so wrong. In the house of the Lord. She would surely go to hell. But she didn't care. She was sixteen, and so was he. It was the '90s. Long before cell phones transformed the world. The act hadn't even lasted a minute. It was wonderful and awful. It felt great, but it also hurt. She was proud of herself and ashamed. If life itself could be boiled down to fifty-seven seconds, she'd experienced every emotion. The highest of highs and the lowest of lows.

And it was all right, because she loved him, and he loved her. And that was all that mattered in the world in that moment.

"I have thought of you often," Nester said softly. How could a man so dangerous, so feared, be so soft spoken? "And of the time we shared here."

"Me too," she said.

"It almost killed me when you married him." The voice quieter still, but Dale felt the hairs on the back of her neck lift. "I couldn't handle it." He paused. "I still . . . have a tough time with it."

Dale sighed. "I'm sorry." She didn't know what else to say. She'd loved Nester with her whole heart, but she knew she couldn't live here. She'd heard Pops and Uncle Ralph warn repeatedly that New Mexico was the "land of entrapment." They'd both encouraged her to get out.

So she'd taken the scholarship offer from Alabama. She'd studied law. And she'd met Elijah Longstreet James.

And fallen in love all over again.

"I know," Nester said. "It's okay."

"I love you," Dale said. "But I also love him. Despite everything he's done, he is my husband, and I don't want him to . . . d-die." She let out a choked sob after getting out the last word.

Nester stood and walked down the aisle, now facing the stage with his back to her. "They want a meeting," he said. "Originally, they wanted it with Eli." He turned to her. In the darkness, she couldn't make out his face. "Now they want you."

"Who?"

"Beth McGee. The director of the FBI."

Dale crossed her arms. She had never met the head of the Bureau before, but she'd heard that Beth McGee was a no-nonsense leader. "What do you think?"

He shrugged. "Before yesterday, I would have said that there was no harm in hearing them out. Especially considering that Bella's supply of medication is dwindling."

"But?"

"But that was before yesterday. And that was before they wanted to meet with you."

"You were okay with Eli getting hurt," Dale said.

"Yes," Nester said without the slightest hesitation or guilt in his tone.

Dale wasn't surprised. Bullshit was Eli's stock and trade, but it was a foreign commodity to Nester.

"I didn't think they would harm him then. Now, I'm not so sure. They are desperate and worried. Yesterday didn't go as planned. We had a counter, and it was a bit more . . . explosive than they bargained for."

"Uncle Ralph . . ." She looked at the floor.

"I will miss him greatly, and I know you will."

For several seconds, the chapel fell quiet. Dale found herself feeling calmer and wondered if it was Nester's presence or perhaps the Almighty that was making her heart rate and thoughts slow to a manageable level.

"What do you think I should do?" she finally asked.

"What do you want?" Nester asked. "Do you want a happy family again with Eli and Bella?" He paused. "Or something different?"

"It's bigger than that, and you know it," Dale snapped. She had never had any problems holding her own with Nester, and she would stand her ground now.

"Not to me, it isn't."

"You're lying," Dale said.

"I never lie, Dale. You know that."

"You're simplifying then." She shrugged. "I get it. You're decisive. You don't have problems making tough choices." She stood and walked down the aisle, not stopping until she could see his golden brown eyes.

"That's because I always choose what's best for me."

"I don't believe that. I think that, at least in your mind, you believe that you are doing the right thing. *Always.*"

"You glorify me." He jerked his head. "Like they do. They call me nicknames. They think I'm a monster. Anyone could become what I have. You have to work, and you have to know what you want. I have no trouble with either."

"What do you want now?" Dale asked.

"I'm looking at her."

She blinked and crossed her arms. "Nester—"

"You are the only woman I have ever loved. I will treat you better than Eli James. I would never cheat on you." He again put his hands on her shoulders. "He doesn't deserve you."

Dale was shaking her head. She knew she should've been surprised, perhaps even angry, that Nester knew of Eli's infidelity, but she wasn't. "Things are more complicated than they seem. Eli isn't solely to blame for our problems." She could hardly believe her own ears, but the words had come from her mouth. "And even if he were, he's still Bella's father." She put her hands on his face. "I have to do everything I can to save him. *I have to.* Bella would never forgive me."

Nester studied her. "If you meet with Director McGee, you'll have to do it under my safeguards. And even then, I can't promise that something won't happen. I did everything I could do to make yesterday safe, and things still backfired. I hate to say it, but that could happen again."

"When do they want to do it?" Dale asked.

"As soon as possible," Nester said. "Their people asked for tomorrow morning."

"Then set it up," Dale said. "I've thought about this situation a lot, and they have to be scared. Things could get incredibly complicated for them." She licked her lips. "They probably want a deal as much or more than we do."

"I would agree with that."

"And meeting with me makes more sense than Eli anyway. Even if Eli hadn't been taken by Randolph yesterday, I would have still wanted to be the point person."

Nester leaned into her. "Why is that?"

"Because I can not only speak for my family, but, as your lawyer, I am able to speak for you." She hesitated. "If you want me to."

Nester leaned back and scrutinized her. Finally, he took both of her hands in his and kissed them. "Okay."

"Okay what?"

"You can speak for me."

"Thank you," she managed, feeling a croak in her throat. "I won't let you down."

"I know you won't," Nester said, whispering into her ear. "You never have."

Dale closed her eyes. "What are your terms?"

Nester ran his nose along her neck and then pulled back a few inches. For the next minute, he told her his conditions.

When he was done, she took a step back from him. "Nester—"

"I've told you what I want," he interrupted, his voice low, but now there was a menace in his tone. The eyes of the lion shone on her. Then he let go of her hands and strode toward the exit.

"Where are you going?"

Nester stopped but did not turn around. "The meeting will take place tomorrow."

"Have you decided where?"

He nodded, but still didn't turn. "The Sandia Peak."

Gooseflesh broke out all over Dale's body, but she managed a smile. "Are we riding the tram? Like we used to."

"If they want the meeting, they'll have to ride it." He looked at her over his shoulder. "We'll arrive by alternate means."

She nodded, following the wisdom in the plan. "Makes sense."

"That doesn't mean it will work. Yesterday taught me a valuable lesson. One that I had forgotten, but always seems to come back to me when you are around."

"What's that?"

"I can't control everything. Despite my best efforts . . . something could go wrong."

Dale cleared her throat, unsure how to respond.

He peered at the floor. "Will you do me a final favor?"

She snorted. "Don't make it sound like that."

"Look, the government will have to make you disappear, and I'm not talking about killing you. They'll want to keep tabs on their investment." He paused. "Today could be our last time together."

Dale felt the steady thud of her heart. "What do you want?"

As he walked back toward her, she felt a wave of fear run through her. And, if she were honest, a tingle of anticipation. He leaned forward until his lips grazed hers. Their eyes met, and then she closed hers.

"To go back in time," Nester finally whispered.

70

"Absolutely not." General Kyle Randolph's voice shook with intensity. "That is insanity, Beth. We cannot negotiate with this monster."

"We have no choice," Beth McGee said, her tone stern and unwavering. "You are outvoted and need to stand down."

"If we do this, the United States will be at the mercy of Nester Sanchez."

"Here's a news flash, General. We're already at his mercy. At least we'll get something for being his bitch. Perhaps if you had handled things differently at CHRISTUS . . ."

Randolph glared across the hotel suite at her. "This is the president's fault. Not mine. If he had listened to me, Eli James would have been nothing but a fly on a boar's ass."

"Spilt milk, General. We need to clean up this mess. I believe that Dale James and I can reach a compromise that protects all our interests."

"You're crazy."

"No, I'm practical."

Randolph turned to Robert Bellamy. "Come on, Robert. This is lunacy. We can't trust these people."

"I agree with you," Bellamy said. "But I also see Beth's point. In purely practical terms, we can't get to Sanchez. Let's make the deal. Then afterward . . ." He trailed off.

"Afterward, he'll disappear," Randolph said. "We'll never get this close again. We could use this opportunity to get him out in the open, and once we take him out—"

"Too risky," Beth said. "Look, I'm all for extinguishing a threat, but are we certain that things will be better here without Nester? At least he's a single entity. Or would you prefer working with the cartels, the Catholic Church, and the Pueblos?"

Randolph scratched his neck. "None of those groups of people attacked a United States aircraft with an Apache attack helicopter, nor are any of them aware of the most explosive secret in American history."

"Lots of folks are calling him a hero," Beth said. "All you did was burnish the legend of Nester Sanchez."

"People." Bellamy raised his arms. "Beth. General. We aren't getting anywhere. Beth, let's negotiate this truce tomorrow. If they will agree to the terms you mentioned and Nester's conditions aren't too high, then I'm all for it." He paused and looked at Randolph. "As a temporary solution."

Randolph peered up at the ceiling in disgust.

"General, there's no other way," Beth said. "The president's damage-control speech was pretty good today in Santa Fe. Did you see it?"

Randolph gave a pained nod.

"He played ball and deflected the blame onto Eli. You saw the headlines on CNN and Fox this evening."

"*Rogue chief*," Bellamy said. "Not bad. As good as we're gonna get." He scoffed. "A hell of lot better than 'botched mission.'"

"Fuck you," Randolph said.

"No thanks."

They were face to face in the living area of the suite, and Beth cringed at the swordfight happening in front of her. "Gentlemen, put 'em back in your pants. We have serious business to discuss."

They turned to look at her. Bellamy's face was as red as Randolph's bloodshot eyes.

"Tomorrow, I will make a deal to secure the safety of our country and the global economy. As Robert said, whatever peace I negotiate might be temporary." She knew she had to give Randolph something, so she dangled the carrot of a future attack on Nester.

"You're really going to take the tram?"

"Yes. With twelve of my best agents."

"Weak," Randolph said.

"It is what it is," Beth said, but he was right.

Randolph walked to the door. "Good luck, Madam Director."

"Thank you," she managed.

Once he was gone, Beth turned to Bellamy. "I'm worried. The incident at CHRISTUS really did a number on him. You don't think . . . ?"

The Homeland Security operative gave his head a jerk. "The general's solid. He may not agree with the plan, but he'll help you execute it." He hesitated and squinted at her. "I'm more worried about you."

"Why?"

"What if you're walking into a trap? You don't really think he'll approach this in a straightforward manner, do you?"

She turned to the window. The sun had set, and darkness had come to Albuquerque. Finally, she spoke the one prevailing thought she'd had since Nester's people had responded to her request for a meeting with his conditions.

"No. But what choice do we have?"

71

Eli was jarred awake by the clanging sound of the cell door opening.

"Good morning, sleepyhead."

Eli rose up out of his cot and swung his legs over the side until they touched the cold concrete. "Lionel?"

"In the flesh," the president said, as the fluorescent lightbulb on the ceiling flipped on.

Eli squinted at his old friend, trying to adjust to the light. Edgar Sams, the head of Lionel's Secret Service detail, set an aluminum chair down beside the president, and Lionel sat in it. Sams took a step back but did not leave the cell.

"At ease, Edgar," Eli said. "I'm not armed."

Sams did not smile or even acknowledge Eli.

"You look like shit," Lionel said.

"Thanks," Eli managed. "You look . . ." He sized up his old friend, who wore a pin-striped navy suit, red tie, and white shirt. ". . . like the president of the United States."

Lionel spread his arms. "How is Bella?"

Eli smirked. "I'm sure you already know."

Lionel peered down at the floor. "I'm glad," he whispered. "I really am."

"I bet."

"Despite what I may say in public, Eli, I still consider you my friend."

Eli continued to stare at the ground. He'd had a lot of time to think over the past twenty-four hours, and he'd anticipated that the damage-control efforts of the White House and the Pentagon would paint him as the scapegoat for the chaos in Santa Fe. Finally, he squinted up at the president.

"Let me guess. You're telling the public that I've gone rogue. Lost my mind. In an estranged marriage. Daughter with cancer." Eli paused. "You've washed your hands of me and my family."

Lionel grimaced.

Eli shrugged. "Hell, I don't blame you. It's the right play. If I'd been in your cabinet . . . wait, I *was* in your cabinet." He sighed. "I digress. Anyway, I would have done the same thing. Happy to be your scapegoat, Lionel . . . as long as my daughter and wife are safe and Bella continues to have access to the boomerang."

The president leaned forward in his chair. "You aren't pulling the strings here, Eli."

"That's right, Mr. President. I'm not. That man happens to be a whole lot smarter and meaner than I am."

A sad smile came to Lionel's face. "Meaner . . . maybe. Smarter? Not a chance. Eli, you've always been two steps ahead of trouble. It's why we got as far as we did. And it's why you were able to get out here with Bella. You went to the one place and sought protection from the one man the government couldn't control."

Who are they afraid of? Eli heard Frank James in his mind again and looked away.

"You remember that class we took third year of law school? It was a civil procedure motion clinic with Professor Weglage."

Now it was Eli who smiled. "How could I forget? Weglage was one of my favorites."

"Mine too. Do you remember how we started off every mock hearing?"

Eli grinned. "'Assuming our motion for trial by battle is denied . . .'"

Lionel chuckled.

"We thought the olden-days rules were so awesome, we always requested it during the clinic. I think Weglage enjoyed it."

"He loved it," Lionel said. "Weggie was a history nerd."

"What brought that memory on?"

The smile left Lionel's face. "Because that's what this is, Eli. That's what the incident in Sante Fe was. It's trial by battle. The Boomerang crew doesn't care about bringing you to justice in a courtroom. They don't care about justice at all. They want to take you out, brother. They're using General Randolph and whoever he employs as their champion."

"And mine is Nester Sanchez." Eli nodded. "I just . . . at this point, I would think that Randolph would want to make a deal."

"Not sure if *want* is the right word, but that's in the works."

"When?"

"Today."

Eli felt his pulse quicken. "What can you tell me?"

"Director McGee will break it down for you on your way."

"On my way where?" Eli stood, and Edgar Sams took a step forward. The Secret Service agent was close enough to touch Eli now.

"I'm not at liberty to say," Lionel said, holding a hand up to Edgar, who took a step back.

"Then why are you here?"

"To see my friend," Lionel said, his voice cracking as he extended his hand. "One last time."

"What are you talking about?" Eli asked, ignoring the proffered hand.

Lionel took a step forward and then put his arms around Eli, wrapping him in a bear hug. Eli felt hot breath in his ear. "Whatever happens today . . . it's still a trial by battle." The president stepped back and wiped a tear from his eye. "Lick Skillet forever."

———

In the hallway, General Kyle Randolph was waiting.

"What did you tell him when you hugged him? We couldn't catch that on camera."

Lionel held the general's eye. "That I loved him." He started to brush past the general, but Randolph blocked his path.

"Please make way for the president." Edgar Sams's deep voice rang out in the tight corridor.

"It's okay, Edgar. What do you want?" Lionel snapped. He was exhausted. Physically and emotionally.

"That wasn't part of the deal," Randolph said. "You said you wanted to see him, so we allowed that. Whispering secrets wasn't part of our arrangement. Now, I'm going to ask you again, did you give anything away?"

Lionel glared into the four-star general's gray eyes. He was growing tired of the roleplay. "How could I? You have provided no details about today's meeting and next to nothing about Project Boomerang other than providing me access to the medicine box." He took a step forward, invading the other man's space, but Randolph didn't budge. "And I didn't *ask* for this meeting. I am the president of the United States. Commander in chief of the Armed Forces. And I *told* you I wanted to say goodbye to my friend." He paused. "And that's what I did. Now, I'd like you to get out of my way before I provide Edgar with different instructions."

"This is your fault," Randolph said.

Lionel blinked. "Partly. I'll take responsibility for my actions, but not the ones you think. I should have been the one to take you down, not Eli. If I had behaved like a true patriot, like the person the American people thought they were electing, I would have exposed the boomerang from the beginning."

"And we would have *disposed* of you."

Lionel squinted. "Right. And dealt with Vice President Yancey?"

"If you had threatened the national security of this country, you would have forced our hand. Just as Eli James has done."

Hatred burned through Lionel's veins. For Randolph. For the government. But mostly, for himself. "I should do something now, but I can't. By taking part in this cover-up, I have no choice but to see it through. Otherwise, everything I've worked for my whole life will be ruined." He swallowed. "I won't let you do that to me. I won't let Eli do it either. I won't be destroyed."

Randolph took a step back. "Well . . ." He winked. "I'm glad we understand each other." As he attempted to push past Lionel, the president caught him up under the arm and leaned forward.

"It's ironic," Lionel said.

"What is?" Randolph asked.

"That you think Nester Sanchez is the monster. The Beast. The Scourge. The Lion." He scoffed. "*You're* the monster, Kyle." Lionel had never called the general by his first name, and it caused the soldier's face to flush red. "*I'm* the monster," Lionel said, letting go of the other man's arm and stepping back, holding his arms out wide. "We . . . the government that's supposed to be of the people, by the people, for the people . . ."

Lionel let his arms fall to his side. "*We're* the monster."

72

Kirtland Air Force Base was located on Wyoming Boulevard in southeast Albuquerque. Less than a half hour drive from the temporary Project Boomerang HQ at the Pyramid Marriott. A thirty-minute helicopter ride from the governor's mansion in Santa Fe.

Twenty-five miles to the Sandia Peak Tramway.

The mood in the conference room was edgy. "Governor, we appreciate you being here." Beth McGee sat at one end of the table. Her voice was scratchy, her throat sore. She'd barely slept last night, her mind racing with questions, possibilities, and alternatives.

Abigail Florez, who two years earlier had been elected to her second term as governor of New Mexico, shrugged. She crossed her legs and folded her arms tight across her chest. "I don't like this, Director. What's happening in my state." She glanced at General Randolph, who sat in the middle of the table. "The tragedy at CHRISTUS. I want it to stop."

"It stops today," Beth said.

Governor Florez inclined her head but said nothing.

"What do you think of the meeting spot?" General Randolph asked.

"Nester craves control, and he's very good at exercising it."

"Can you break that down for me, Governor?" Robert Bellamy asked.

"He means what the fuck are you talking about?" Randolph said.

Florez stared at the general. If she were upset or flustered, she was doing a good job hiding it. "Unless you have access to a helicopter, there is only one way up the Sandia Peak."

"The tram, which he has insisted that we take," Beth said. "Do you expect trouble with that? Will he try to sabotage us? I know that tram has had incidents before."

Florez rubbed her chin with her fist. "I think that's unlikely. I suspect his goal is to prevent an ambush. What does killing you do to serve his purposes? It will only hurt his reputation and bring negative press to New Mexico."

"He didn't seem to care about that at CHRISTUS," Randolph snapped.

"Our people feel differently about that," the governor fired back. "The way we understand it, you tried to apprehend a young woman getting cancer treatment, and your ambush backfired. Nester is seen as her defender here. Her protector." She put her hands on her hips. "And, at least here in New Mexico, no one is buying that friendly fire bullshit. They know the truth just as I do."

"Good grief," Randolph said, chuckling. "I'm sure that's the propaganda he's putting out."

"The line between propaganda and truth can be pretty blurry," Florez said. "What is it that Eli James stole that makes him such a danger to this country? That's the key detail that the president and all of you have yet to reveal."

"That's classified, Governor," Randolph said.

"Let's stay on task," Beth said, putting both palms on the table. "Governor, Nester Sanchez has in his possession an Apache helicopter. Putting aside how he, as a civilian, could have somehow purchased this craft, are you aware of him having any other munitions?"

"No," Governor Florez said, recrossing her legs. "I'm not aware of that. But I would almost guarantee that he does."

"Why?" Randolph asked.

Florez rolled her eyes. "You guys are truly amazing, you know it. You come down here and literally have no clue or appreciation of what's really going on. Of who Nester Sanchez is, what he's done, and just how powerful he's become."

"Then why don't you tell us?" Bellamy said.

"I will. In the last seven years, crime in Albuquerque is down fifty percent. *Half.* Crime in Los Lunas is nonexistent. Same for Rio Rancho, Bernalillo. In fact, the entire state of New Mexico's crime rate is down thirty percent, which is unheard of."

"Sounds like great fodder for a campaign commercial," Randolph said.

"I wish I could take credit for it," she said, emotion creeping into her voice. "I work hard. I've lived here all my life, and I love this state. It is my home and always will be. But this is not my doing, and the improvements don't stop at crime. Enrollment in our colleges is up. Graduation rates have increased. Hospitals are being renovated. Roads, highways, and interstates have improved. New neighborhoods are being built. Auto plants and manufacturing centers. We have a Facebook office in Los Lunas. Amazon's coming. The infrastructure of this state has never been healthier or stronger than it is now. *I wonder why that is.*"

Silence filled the room, and the governor stood. "We used to have a lot of gang violence, and I'd be lying if I said the gangs had gone away. The Brew Town Locos are as strong as ever despite being investigated by your department, Madam Director." Florez gave an exasperated sigh. "The Mexican cartels are strong too. The Pueblos haven't gone anywhere, and the Catholic Church is still kickin'. And for years, these groups took from the people. Scared them. Intimidated and bullied and didn't care. But now . . . *no more.* And what or who do you think it is that has led to these changes? *Me?*" She snorted. "The state government? Local governments try hard, and so do we, but we can't do it alone. And for years, the federal government has turned its back on the Land of Enchantment."

"Governor—?" Beth began.

"Let me finish," she snapped. "When Albuquerque was burning, where were you guys?" She put her hands on her hips again. "Playing your fiddles in Washington." Her voice had dropped to just above a whisper. "You all need to hear what I'm about to say. The gangs. The cartel. The Pueblos. The Church. They don't answer to me." She put her thumbs on her chest. "And they don't answer to you." She pointed to Randolph. "But they do answer to Nester."

"Are you saying that New Mexico, for all intents and purposes, is a dictatorship?" Randolph asked. "No one should have that kind of power in this country."

Florez chuckled, looking around the room. "What a bunch of hypocrites you all are. Talking about power and how best to use it. Coming to my state and causing a tragedy that killed five civilians and then not telling me, the governor of this state, the real reason you're here." She made for the door.

Beth got up from her seat to intercept her. "Governor, please. I understand your frustration."

"Do you? Because I don't think anyone in this room is listening. You're calling a man public enemy number one who's done more good things for this state than anyone in the last fifty years."

"He's a murderer. A ruthless killer." Randolph's voice reeked of self-righteous arrogance, and Beth wanted to gag.

"And you aren't?" Florez pointed at Randolph and then stared at Beth. "Good luck today, Director."

"Governor, is there anything else you can tell us? Please. We are in uncharted territory here. We do not want to escalate a military conflict on your state's soil."

"Too late," Florez said. "You've already done that. You came into Nester's home and drew first blood."

"We don't want to make things worse," Beth said.

Abigail Florez moved her eyes to each of the power brokers in the room, holding on to Beth's. "You really want to help?" She leaned forward and whispered loud enough for them all to hear. *Do what he says.*

73

The hangar was nothing more than a large barn. If you were looking at it from the road, you'd think it contained horses. Or maybe chickens. Or perhaps even a couple of tractors or similar equipment. There were farms throughout Los Lunas with barns that housed exactly that.

"Unbelievable," Dale said, staring wide eyed at the Apache and then moving her gaze to the other items in Nester's vast arsenal, which were equally impressive. She was in awe. "How—"

"I've been building this for most of my life," Nester said.

Dale gazed through the barn door at the fading light of the moon. It was almost dawn. In thirty or so minutes, the sun would begin its ascent. *What will this day hold?* Dale wondered. Regardless of what happened, she knew one thing for certain.

Nothing is ever going to be the same.

"Are you ready?" Nester asked.

"The meeting's not till eight. Where are we going?"

Nester squinted at her. "Higher ground." He glanced at the two other people who had made the trip. "You'll be safe here. I'll have someone pick you up this evening and bring you back to the reservation."

Foncie's face was pale in the faint light. She looked older. Tired. During the car ride from the Tamaya, she'd barely spoken. "Thank you for letting us be here. And for all you've done for my son and his family." She paused. "And for me."

"You're welcome," Nester said.

Bella was shaking, but she stood tall and straight. "So you're him?"

Nester took a step closer. He wore a black T-shirt, corduroy pants, and work boots. A red cap saying "Bosque Farms" covered his head. He could have literally been anyone in Los Lunas, Rio Rancho, Bernalillo, or Albuquerque. But he wasn't.

"I'm him," he said. "And I am so pleased to finally see you in person. Your mom . . . and your dad have told me much about you."

"Will you bring my dad back?"

Nester frowned. "I learned long ago, Bella, not to make promises unless I was sure I could keep them. But I will promise this. I'll do my best." He nodded at the Apache chopper. "That has normally been sufficient."

Bella hugged Dale. "I love you. Please come back. And . . ." Her lip trembled.

"I'll get him, honey," vowed Dale.

"Take care of yourself, girl," Foncie said, surprising Dale by putting her rough hands on Dale's shoulders. "The luckiest day of my son's life was when he married you." She kissed Dale's cheek. "Love you, daughter."

That was it.

Dale had been keeping things together, but to hear a salutation her own mother and her stepfather had used a million times come out of her mother-in-law's mouth was too much. Her eyes watered, and she covered her face with her hands.

"Mr. Sanchez," Foncie began, but Nester quickly cut her off.

"Please. Here, people call me Nester."

"Nester, then," Foncie said. "I, uh, I'm not the most Christian of women. I use profanity as a second language, and I doubt the good Lord listens much when I talk to him, but um . . ." Her voice shook, but she didn't break. ". . . but I also believe in leaving everything on the field, and there's this passage from the Bible that I, uh, kind of love. It's about a horse. Do you mind if . . ." She trailed off and looked away.

Nester reached out his hand to Dale, who took it and clasped her other hand to Bella's, who grabbed Foncie's hand. Nester's free hand took hold of Foncie's other hand, and they formed a circle. Nester turned to Foncie and nodded.

"Dear Lord, thank you for my granddaughter's health. Thank you for Mr. Sanchez . . . Nester . . . and for my daughter-in-law, Dale, and for my son, Eli. Please be with Dale and Nester and Eli today. I pray that you will help them and guide their way. I pray that you will help them be like the horse in the thirty-ninth chapter of Job." She paused and, when she spoke again, her voice was stronger, the rasp barely present. *"It laughs at fear, afraid of nothing. It does not shy away from the sword. The quiver rattles against its side, along with the flashing spear and lance. In frenzied excitement . . ."* Foncie's voice finally broke, and for a moment the only sounds in the barn were their respective sniffles. Finally, Nester broke the quiet with his melodic voice:

". . . *it eats up the ground,*" he said. Then Foncie and Nester said the next verse together: *"It cannot stand still when the trumpet sounds."*

"Amen," Foncie said. She cocked her head. "Know your Bible?"

Nester bowed. "I'm a good Catholic. Like most of New Mexico."

Foncie chuckled and wiped her eyes. She peered up at the Apache. "Are you taking this badass bird?" Then she turned and pointed to the rear of the barn. "Or that scary-as-hell-looking motherfucker in the back?"

Nester's golden brown eyes gleamed with a hint of mischief. "What did you say about leaving everything on the field?"

Foncie whistled under her teeth. Her face grew paler, but she managed to grin. "I'm glad you're on our side, you magnificent bastard."

"I like you, too, Ms. Foncie." Then he turned to Dale. "Ready?"

She nodded and kissed Bella's cheek. "I'll bring your dad back," she whispered.

74

When the blindfold was lifted, the tram had already moved a hundred feet off the ground, making Eli's stomach jump and head spin. As his legs wobbled, a strong hand grabbed his arm.

"Are you okay?" a woman asked.

"What is this?" Eli blinked to adjust to the light as the tramcar continued to ascend the mountain. *Sandia Peak,* he answered his own question.

"Oh, just headed to a little family reunion. I don't believe we've officially met, Mr. James. I'm—"

"Beth McGee," he interrupted. "I know who you are." Eli scanned the enclosure. In addition to himself and Beth, there were at least ten and maybe more armed agents in the car. "I take it this isn't a sightseeing expedition."

"Your friend Mr. Sanchez has asked us to join your wife at the top of this mountain. We come by tram, and we assume that he will be arriving by way of his favorite toy."

Eli glanced down at the ground, which was getting farther away by the second. He'd ridden the tram with Dale during his lone trip to New Mexico for her tenth reunion. Ralph had taken them to the top to eat at High Finance, which was an awesome spot. It had been dark during the ride, and Eli, who was scared of heights, hadn't minded the trek. Now, though, in the light of morning, Eli's stomach felt queasy as the tramcar ascended. He tried to focus on the mountains and forced himself not to look down. He shivered. The temperature outside couldn't be much over forty-five degrees and would get colder as they went up. He wanted to cross his arms to warm himself, but his hands were cuffed behind his back.

"I guess it's too late to ask for an alternative meeting spot," Eli said. "I hate roller coasters, airplanes, and any kind of object that moves in the air." He again shivered. "And it's also cold as hell."

"No, not too late to ask," Beth said. "Just irrelevant. Your protector set these conditions."

I hope he knows what he's doing, Eli thought. Even if Nester arrived in his helicopter, he couldn't control everything. What would stop Randolph and his goons from sending in a bomber or helicopter of his own to ambush them?

"If it makes you feel any better," Beth said, leaning down and removing a blanket from a duffel bag and throwing it over his shoulders, "I don't much like this either."

They studied each other, and Eli could see the determination in the woman's dark-green eyes. "What happened to General Randolph? I thought killing the miracle was his detail."

Beth held his stare. "We don't see it that way, Mr. James. And General Randolph is still very much involved in this operation." She paused. "But I'm in charge now."

Eli shook his head. While he hated the hero worship of Nester Sanchez, he'd seen firsthand what the man was capable of. Setting the terms for this meeting was one more example. "I think you're about to find out who's in charge."

Beth pursed her lips. "We'll see."

75

Kyle Randolph stormed into the air traffic control room with his fists clenched. "I want four Ghostrider fighter jets right now."

"I'm sorry, General," the controller said. "I'm on strict orders to clear the airspace for the next hour. No planes from the air force base are available."

Randolph clenched his teeth and strode toward the controller, who was standing by his post. "I'm not going to ask you again, sir. I am the former chairman of the Joint Chiefs of Staff, secretary of defense, a four-star fucking general, and the most decorated living military officer of any kind in the world. I am your superior officer, and I am demanding that you release four jets to me and my team. The director of the FBI and her crew need coverage on the Sandia Peak."

"No, sir. They don't."

"Are you *arguing* with me?" Randolph grabbed the other man by the collar. "I promise you that you will never work in the air force again."

"I don't answer to you, General. And I have my orders."

"*What?*" Randolph shook him and finally let go. He looked around the room, where every eye was now on him.

General Forrest Hawkings, the base commander, entered the room and crossed his arms, and Randolph breathed a sigh of relief.

"General Hawkings, I need four airplanes from your base. Your controller here—"

"Has strict orders from me not to release any aircraft for the next hour."

"What?" Now Randolph moved on Hawkings. "Need I remind you that I outrank you?"

Hawkings scratched his face with his hand and then rubbed his bald head. He looked Randolph dead in the eye. "My orders come from the president of the United States."

76

Sandia Peak rose to just over 10,300 feet. The tram followed an almost three-mile ride up the mountainside. If the national security and future of the country didn't literally hang in the balance of the meeting she was about to have, Beth McGee might have enjoyed the experience. But her nerves were fried, and the cold wasn't helping. Her ears were also popping, and she'd forgotten to bring gum.

She straightened her pants and tried to keep her mind on the task at hand. As expected, the top of the peak appeared to be a ghost town. There were no workers or employees that she could see anywhere. But she wasn't so naive as to think that Nester Sanchez didn't have someone up here watching. She peered at the building that housed the restaurant, which carried the cutely descriptive name: Ten 3. She'd sent a group of soldiers to scope out the area upon arrival, but they'd detected no signs of life anywhere.

She glanced at her watch. It was 7:53 a.m. The meeting was scheduled to begin at 8:00 sharp, and there was still no sign of them. Her phone buzzed in her pocket, and she stared at the screen, which indicated the call was from General Randolph. She clicked on it. "Hello?"

"You're crazy to not have aerial coverage."

Beth gritted her teeth. "That was Mr. Sanchez's first condition, General, and I am here to make a deal. I trust you tried to secure a plane anyway and were told where to go."

Silence on the other end of the line.

"I thought so. Kyle, when this meeting is over, I'm going to request that you take a leave of absence. Your behavior this week has been abhorrent."

"We're both in too deep for that, aren't we? Unless we're going to start telling *all* of our secrets?"

She glared at the phone and clicked End. *No time for that.*

7:55 a.m. *Where are they?* She glanced at Eli James, who was bouncing on his toes, clearly cold despite the blanket draped over his shoulders. "Your friend is about to be—"

But her voice was drowned out by an almost foreign sound ringing out from what must be hundreds of speakers on top of the peak.

Music. Loud music that Beth McGee . . . recognized. She could barely hear herself think, the volume was so high, but she knew this song. She knew it like the back of her hand. She'd graduated from Virginia Tech University, and this was the tune that played when the team took the field.

"Enter Sandman," by Metallica.

Beth felt gooseflesh on her arms, and then she saw it. Rising up from the northern crest of the peak like a spray-painted black phoenix from the ashes, the AH-64 Apache showed itself.

Beth could barely hear herself think, which she assumed was the point. Between the metal and the engine roar, she had no chance of barking any last-minute instructions to her team.

All they could do was wait as the Apache circled the mountain and hovered, showing no signs of setting down. Beth cocked her head, confused, but then it dawned on her.

Air coverage . . .

Given the stunt General Randolph had just tried to pull, the Beast's instincts were sound.

But if he's not in the Apache, then—

"Jesus H. Christ," Eli James whispered next to her.

Beth's breath caught in her throat, and for a few seconds, she was transfixed by a childhood memory. She must have watched the movie *Red Dawn* a dozen times as a kid, and the scene that terrified her the most was when the tiny band of American high school guerrilla soldiers were resting by a mountain and were attacked by a Russian helicopter swooping out of the sky and heading straight for them, firing on them at will.

Now, standing just a few yards from the edge of the Sandia Peak, Beth felt like one of those teenagers in the film as the camouflage-colored Mil Mi-24 helicopter gunship, code-named the "Hind" by NATO, closed in on them. Manufactured by the Soviet Union in the early '70s and still active in at least thirty countries, the Hind could be used for heavy fire support and was able to transport up to eight passengers. Russian pilots nicknamed it "the flying tank," and Beth thought that was a spot-on description.

As she gazed at the Apache continuing to circle from a safe distance away and then watched the Hind touch down on the mountaintop, Beth remembered Governor Florez's guarantee that Nester Sanchez likely had more munitions.

Does he ever . . .

Beth took a deep breath and glanced at her watch, as the thwap of rotor blades and the blare of Metallica rocked her eardrums.

7:59 a.m.

Right on time.

77

From inside the gunship, Nester pointed out Eli on the ground. When Dale saw him, she breathed a deep sigh of relief.

Eli was standing next to a woman wearing a black pantsuit, presumably Beth McGee, and flanked by at least a dozen armed soldiers. He had something bulky draped over his shoulders, but he appeared safe and unharmed.

Dale yelled to be heard above the music and the roar of the rotor. "Quite an entrance!"

Nester shrugged and spoke into her ear. "There's a method to my madness." He leaned forward, touched the pilot on the shoulder, and made a slashing gesture at his neck. The pilot grabbed her phone, clicked a button, and just like that, the agonizingly loud music stopped. Seconds later, the engine was cut, and the rotor began to wind down.

"Are you sure you want to do this?" Dale asked. "The terms you've requested . . . they're . . . surprising."

"I know what I'm doing."

"I hope so," she said. "And I hope they agree."

Nester said nothing for several seconds. Then he nodded toward the window. "Do you see the picnic table?"

"Yes." Dale squinted to the left of where McGee and Eli were standing. There was a wooden table with a bench on either side a few feet from the cliff edge atop the peak.

Nester scooted forward and grabbed the microphone in the middle of the console of the pilot's deck. "Director McGee, Mrs. James is about to exit the helicopter. If a hair on her or Mr. James is harmed, I will unleash the full power of this machine as well as the one circling this mountain and wipe the world of you and your soldiers. Do you understand?"

Dale saw the director look at one of her subordinates, who handed her a megaphone.

"We understand. And if I am hurt in any way, then the United States is prepared to order martial law in the state of New Mexico. Are we clear?"

"Crystal," Nester said. He turned to Dale. "Are you ready?"

She felt butterflies in her stomach and acid in her mouth. She also felt another emotion as she again gazed through the windshield at her husband: guilt. "Can I ask you something?" She was staring out at Eli.

Nester said nothing.

"In the chapel at Menaul, when you said you wanted to go back in time—?"

"Dale—"

"Let me finish. Why did you stop? You gave me a peck on the lips and took me for a walk around the school when you could've . . ."

He turned her face to his. "I . . . can be a monster, Dale, but not with you. Never with you."

She wiped her eyes. "Thank you."

He gave a swift nod, and his eyes grew hard. "It's time to go to work, Counselor." He pointed toward the window. Beth McGee was already sitting at the picnic table.

She bit her lip. "All right then."

The copilot exited the cockpit and opened the hatch. Dale started to climb out but felt Nester's hand grab hers. She looked at him.

"Do you trust me?"

She managed a smile. "Always."

78

Now that they were finally here, it was amazing how quiet it was. The silence was almost eerie, Beth McGee thought, looking into the eyes of Dale James across the picnic table. Getting her bearings, she glanced to her left and saw that Eli and the team of agents guarding him waited a good thirty yards away. Over Dale's shoulder was the green-and-brown-camouflage Hind and, in the distance and still very much visible, the black Apache.

"No use beating around the bush," Beth said, propping her elbows on the wooden surface. "I think we both have something the other wants."

Dale nodded. "I want my husband back. Now. Today. And I want a lifetime supply of the boomerang for my daughter with specific instructions on the dosages, if any, she should take now that her tumors are gone. And I want whoever is behind this cover-up to leave me and my family alone. Forever. Those are my conditions."

Beth tapped her fingers on the wood. "And, in exchange for that, your family, Mr. Sanchez, and Dr. Carmen Baca will all agree to never breathe a word of the boomerang's existence to another living soul?"

Dale shrugged.

"We'll insist upon a vow of silence, Dale. Surely, you expected that."

"I did, but . . . what I didn't expect were Nester's terms, which, if you agree, might make all of this superfluous."

Beth raised her eyebrows. "Go on."

"Mr. Sanchez will agree to a vow of silence provided that the government agrees to my conditions and . . . the boomerang is made available to everyone in the world within the next week. There doesn't have to be any confessions regarding how long it's existed or anything else that you and your cronies did to keep it secret. But the boomerang has to be released to the public, which would, of course, include Bella and anyone else with a cancer diagnosis."

Beth stared out over the peak and blinked. It was said that you could see four cities from here. If she saw a yellow brick road leading to Oz, she couldn't have been more surprised than she was right now. "What else does he want?"

Dale glared at her. "Nothing."

Beth crossed her arms and forced a chuckle. "This is some kind of joke, right?"

"Wrong. No joke. These are our terms. Leave my family alone. A full and free supply of the boomerang indefinitely to Bella, with instructions. And release it to the world within seven days."

"Dale, that's impossible."

"No, it's not. It's actually quite easy. You've been aware of the drug for almost a decade. You obviously know how to manufacture it. You know how effective it really is, and you won't have to apologize for anything and no one will ever mention the atrocities the United States government has inflicted on its own citizens. As long as you do the right thing and release this miracle to the whole world."

Beth bit her lip and stared at Dale James. *What is this?* She felt like she was about to step into a trap.

"Why does Nester Sanchez give a damn whether we release this medication or not? How does that benefit him?"

"I don't know," Dale said. "I'm just telling you my client's terms." She pursed her lips. "Is the government in or out?"

"This is preposterous," Beth said. "I mean . . ."

"Forgive me, Madam Director, but what's preposterous about asking this government to open up the medical miracle of the century to all people afflicted with cancer?"

Beth turned and looked at Eli James and her team of soldiers. She thought of calling Robert Bellamy and getting his thoughts, but she knew what he would say.

If we agree to these terms, then what have we been doing the past eight years? Nothing has changed. The cure for cancer will cost the United States economy approximately $300 billion in revenue, countless jobs, and will cripple the nation to the point that we will be vulnerable to attack. Releasing the boomerang is, was, and will always be a national security concern of the highest order. DEFCON-1. Armageddon. The end of days.

Beth peered out over the peak. Anger swelled within her as the realization of what was happening came to her. She turned toward the helicopter gunship with its armored fuselage. Nester Sanchez hadn't made this offer because he wanted to save the world. He made it . . .

. . . because he knew we'd refuse.

The Beast. The Scourge of New Mexico. The Lion of Los Lunas. The monster who had somehow acquired the two most lethal attack helicopters ever made and whose ownership of New Mexico rivaled Napoleon's of France had offered terms that would save a billion people.

And we said no.

The United States of America. Land of the free. Home of the brave. One nation. Under God. With liberty and justice for all. *We're the greatest country in the history of the world . . .*

. . . and yet the Beast would save the world . . .

. . . while we watch it burn in the name of money.

Liberty? Freedom? Democracy? She swallowed, and it tasted of bile. Justice wasn't red, white, and blue.

It was green.

She turned to Dale James. "No," she said.

Dale stared at her. "No what?"

"The United States cannot agree to those terms."

Dale shook her head, disgust in her expression. "All you have to do is the right thing . . . what should have been done all along . . . and you're really saying no."

"Things aren't as simple as you're making them sound."

"Oh, yes they are," Dale said. "This is about money and nothing else. Money and fear."

"How about I propose a counter?" Beth asked, clearly hoping to steady the ship and get back on course.

Dale held out her palms.

"You and your daughter will enter the witness-protection program tomorrow. Bella is allowed to keep the medication she still has, but there won't be any additional meds provided." She creased her eyebrows. "Your husband will plead guilty to charges of treason against the United States of America, several counts of murder and conspiracy to commit murder with respect to the tragic events at the CHRISTUS medical center, and be sentenced to life in prison at ADX Florence maximum security prison in Colorado. The Gutierrez family of New Mexico and Mrs. Foncie James will not be affected provided that they keep their mouth shut, but their activities will be monitored. Same for Dr. Carmen Baca as long as she also remains quiet. As for Mr. Nester Alejandro Sanchez, he will receive a full pardon from the president of the United States as to all pending charges against him." She hesitated. "These concessions are obviously predicated on complete silence with respect to the boomerang."

Dale was shaking her head. She looked sadly at Beth. "I thought you wanted to make a deal."

"I do."

"It doesn't sound like it."

Beth narrowed her gaze. "You're a lawyer, Dale. This little caucus essentially amounts to a mediation without a mediator. We had to start somewhere."

"You should've accepted my offer." Dale glared at Beth. "Nester asked for nothing but the release of a medical miracle. We asked for nothing but our lives back."

"I can't do that," Beth said. "*We* . . . can't do that."

"Well, I don't have any other terms." She stood from the table. "I'll either be right back or he'll speak from the chopper." She started to walk away, but then turned and stared at Beth once more.

"Really? Do you have children, Beth? Have you had anyone in your life affected by cancer?"

Beth crossed her arms and held Dale's gaze. "I'm just doing my job."

———

Once Dale was back inside the helicopter, she didn't have to say anything.

"Let me guess. The response was a resounding and unequivocal no."

Dale nodded. Then she recited McGee's offer.

"Her proposal is obviously refused," Nester said, rubbing his hands together. "Here are my new terms. I want a full pardon of all pending charges as well as absolute immunity for any future crimes. I want their drones removed from the Four Corners; I don't want to be watched, followed, or tracked in any way whatsoever." He hesitated, making a tent with his hands. "And I want $500 million." He leaned back in his seat. "I don't expect that these terms can be met overnight, so they have a week. But that's it."

A sad smile crept across Dale's face. "You knew they were going to say no."

Nester's face remained stoic. "*Sí.*"

"And so now you think they'll be more inclined to accept what you really want."

"Guilt and shame can be a powerful motive to go above and beyond," Nester said.

She turned to leave, but his voice stopped her.

"I would not agree to witness protection if I were you," he said. "I can protect you better than them, and once you're in their program, there's no guarantee I'll be able to find and help you." He blew into his clasped hands. "As for making Eli the scapegoat, that's . . . up to you."

Dale felt the weight of the world on her shoulders. "You can't defend us indefinitely."

"I will."

"I can't let you. I won't put my New Mexico family in that kind of danger forever. The best part of their deal is they'll leave us alone."

"Do you really believe that?" He shook his head. "Dale, I love you, but you have always been too trusting. I will get my money, my pardon, and immunity. But will they leave me alone? Perhaps . . ." He shrugged. ". . . for a while. But remember what they have already done."

Dale closed her eyes. She felt numb. Fatigue was setting in. She was so tired of running. She wanted to believe there was a way out. She started to try to put those thoughts into words, but Nester interrupted her. "Do what you want," he said. "I will support you regardless . . . even if I don't understand."

"Thank you," she said.

Dale took a deep breath and again departed the helicopter. She strode toward the table where Beth McGee waited. She recited Nester's new terms and added, "That's not a counter, Beth. That's a final."

The director whistled through her teeth and then ran a hand through her hair. "Steep. Very steep."

"You could've just done the right thing."

Beth ignored her. "And what about your family?"

Dale bit her lip but maintained the director's gaze. "Before I can consider any kind of witness protection, I'll need to talk with my husband and daughter, but . . . I am leaning on agreeing as long as you leave my New Mexico family, Foncie, and the Bacas alone. And provided that Eli is allowed to go with us."

Beth stood and came around the table to Dale. "I know that this situation is impossible for you."

Dale scowled at her. "Do you?"

Beth nodded. "Believe me, it's impossible for me, too, although I don't have the personal stake you do." She hesitated. "Dale, you know that it's a shitstorm down there. We must have a scapegoat. Someone to blame all of this mess on. It can't be Nester, and the United States is not going to fall on its sword."

Dale felt hot tears in her eyes as she thought of everything that had happened since Bella's diagnosis. The incredible ordeal the family had been through. The sacrifices, both personal and professional. And as much as she had lost . . .

Eli has lost more . . .

. . . and if we accept these terms, he'll lose everything.

"It's so ironic," Dale said, gazing up at the clouds. She thought of how Bella had described the situation when Eli had broken everything down for her.

It's so wrong.

"Dale—"

"My husband . . ." Her lip was trembling. ". . . is a hero. He risked his life to save our daughter's. Bella would be dead if Eli didn't do what he did."

"With all due respect, ma'am, he blackmailed the president of the United States of America. He stole top secret information and contraband that are critical to the national security of this country. And he brought everything he'd stolen to the most dangerous man in America."

"I helped him do that," Dale snapped.

"Maybe so, but Mr. James knew what he was doing." Beth softened her tone. "I think he saw this coming, Dale. Why else would he give himself up two days ago. No one was more politically savvy in Washington, DC, than Eli James." She started to reach out to touch Dale's arm, but Dale flinched.

"If you touch me, you gutless bitch, I'll throw you off this mountain and tell Nester to unleash the full power of those two attack helicopters on your agents."

Beth held up her hands and took a step back. "All right. Let's keep things civil. If the bullets start flying, we're all dead." She cleared her throat. "If you give us Eli and agree to go into witness protection with your daughter and mother-in-law, then I think we can concede to all of Nester's terms."

"I have one more," Dale said, wiping her eyes and hearing the cold in her own voice.

Beth crossed her arms, waiting.

"A lifetime supply of the boomerang for Bella."

The director stared down at her feet. Then back at Dale. "If I can agree to that condition, will you agree to give us your husband?"

Dale let out a sob. "I can't speak for him."

Beth McGee took a small step forward. "Dale, off the record, everyone in our . . . *project* . . . knows what Mr. James's motives have been from the start." She licked her lips. "To save his daughter. *Your daughter.*" She again hesitated. "What I'm offering will guarantee that his . . . and your . . . efforts will not have been in vain."

"And he'll go down in history as a murderer. A criminal. A combination of Benedict Arnold and a no-account killer."

The director's eyes softened, as did her tone. "But Bella will live."

Dale folded her arms against her chest. She peered across the space and saw Eli staring at her. Her legs felt wobbly, and the world was beginning to spin. She couldn't speak. She could barely breathe.

"It may take some time to put together the package that Mr. Sanchez has requested."

Dale blinked, snapping back to it. "He'll give you a week. Nothing more."

Beth licked her lips. "Okay. I think we can do that. Do we have a deal with respect to you and your family?"

Dale gazed at Eli across the top of the peak. Her lip began to tremble again.

"Mrs. James, I can't leave without at least that part sewn up. Do we—"

"Yes," Dale said, turning to her. "But only if you agree to Nester's terms." She crossed her arms. "It's a package deal."

Beth took a step forward and spoke in a low, conspiratorial voice. "The money is not a problem, nor is the pardon. Removing the drones and the heightened scrutiny that Mr. Sanchez has received in the Corners will be challenging, but with a pardon, no pending charges, and Governor Florez's support, I think we can weather that storm." She paused. "But absolute immunity is next to impossible to promise. I'm willing to make that pledge. However, it will have to be a handshake deal, as the country would never understand such a move if it were documented. Will he . . ." She nodded at the gunship. ". . . be okay with that?"

"I think he will," Dale said. "As long as you're satisfied with a handshake agreement by him to stay quiet on the existence of the boomerang."

Beth nodded. "We would have to accept that."

"And that any breach of this verbal contract means that all bets are off."

"Yes," Beth said. "I think we're almost there. Now . . . will you and Bella agree to enter witness protection with your husband going to prison for the rest of his life?"

Dale flinched and felt a wave of nausea roll through her. She was beginning to lose her grip. She couldn't look at Eli. She grasped the picnic table so hard her fingers hurt.

"Mrs. James?" Beth extended her hand gingerly. "Do we have a deal?"

Dale finally looked over at Eli and choked back another sob. She shook her head. "I promised my little girl that I'd bring her daddy home."

"I can't do that," Beth said. "I'm sorry."

"Then no deal."

"Dale—"

"I am not breaking my promise to Bella. Eli is leaving with me on that chopper, or no fucking deal." She bit her lip to keep it from trembling. "Please. Let him come with me and give us a week. Then we can set up an exchange," Dale said. "Eli for the money and pardon. You get what you want, none of the terms change, and everyone is happy."

"If I do that, then I have no leverage."

"You had no leverage to begin with. The man in that helicopter doesn't give a damn about Eli, and you know it." She leaned forward, speaking in a loud whisper. "We've done a good job of cutting the bullshit. Can we keep it that way?"

The director took a few steps toward the edge of the mountain and placed her hands on her hips. For a moment, Dale had the odd and ridiculous thought that the woman might jump.

"You need a week to comply with Nester's demands anyway. Give my husband that time to be with his family . . . and to say goodbye."

Beth sighed and turned to Dale. "All right. He can leave with you, and we'll set up a meeting where Eli is returned to our custody in exchange for our wiring the money to Mr. Sanchez and confirming his pardon. You and Bella will enter witness protection the following morning, and your daughter will be provided the boomerang for the rest of her life." She approached and extended her hand. "Do we have a deal?"

Dale glanced again at Eli, feeling the fissure growing. Her chest was on fire. She grimaced against the pain.

"Mrs. James?"

"Yes," Dale finally said, shaking the director's hand. "Deal."

79

Eli kept his eyes closed during the helicopter ride. He felt sick to his stomach, as the Hind's every sudden movement caused him to flinch.

Dale gripped his hand with both of hers as if her life depended on it. He wanted to tell her to ease up a little, but he wouldn't dare. He couldn't remember the last time she'd touched him.

The buzzing whir of the chopper was deafening, and Dale had yet to say anything to him other than "I'll tell you everything when we land."

Eli had nodded and then shut his eyes tight as the helicopter departed the peak. He'd hoped to at least flip the bird at Beth McGee while they were leaving, but as soon as the aircraft lifted in the air, he couldn't handle the motion.

About five minutes into the flight, Dale leaned her head onto his shoulder and began crying. He felt her heart beating hard against his own chest. Could smell the fragrance of her shampoo. He wasn't sure what was about to happen, but he was grateful to be here and not in the custody of the government. For the second time in the last few days, he felt hopeful.

But as the chopper touched the ground and the engines were cut, Eli knew the good tidings wouldn't last. As he heard the door open and what sounded like several people exiting the craft, he didn't want to open his eyes. He wished he could live in this moment a little longer.

"Eli." Dale's voice sounded tired and weak in the cabin. She coughed and cleared her throat.

Eli rubbed his face with his hands and got his bearings. They were alone in the cabin of the gunship, having landed in what looked to be a cavernous barn with some kind of retractable roof that must open to allow the aircraft to come and go.

Eli managed a chuckle. "Has anyone seen Nester and Batman in the same spot?"

Dale didn't laugh. "I did my best." Her voice shook.

"I know."

"I . . . this is going to be hard."

"Everything about the last seven months has been hard. Just spit it out."

Dale touched his face. "Look at me."

Eli turned to her, and she brushed her hand over his hair. The silence now seemed louder than the roar of the helicopter, and Eli felt the uncanny sensation that something was dying.

"Let me get through it all before you ask questions," she told him.

"Okay."

Then, in the close confines of the Hind's passenger compartment, she laid out the deal.

———

Dale's heart was about to explode by the time she finished. Eli kept his promise, which somehow made it worse. He hadn't asked a single question or said even a word.

"That's it," Dale croaked. "That's everything."

Eli gazed away from her, his body language belying nothing.

"I'm sorry," Dale said. "She wouldn't budge and . . . I knew . . . I knew . . ."

"You knew I would want you to go through with it," Eli said, continuing to stare out the window. "And you were right."

"Eli—"

"Where are we?" he asked.

"Los Lunas," Dale said.

"Are we going back to the reservation?"

"I think so," Dale said. "Probably by car later today."

"I hope so," Eli said. "I've grown to like that place." He frowned. "Will you ask Nester if Mom can . . . ?" He gritted his teeth, and the tears in his eyes were like gasoline poured onto the fire in her chest. She knew he was trying to keep it together.

"Yes. I'll make sure that Foncie can stay on the Santa Ana. She can probably work at the Tamaya and give horse tours."

Eli wiped his eyes. "Thank you."

For a few seconds, the silence hung in the air like a thick fog. Dale wanted to comfort him, but she was having a hard time reading him. Was he angry? Frustrated? If so, he had every right to be.

"Are you sure about witness protection?" he finally asked.

"No," Dale said. "But I don't want to put my family at risk forever. They've already given so much, and Uncle Ralph . . ." She trailed off.

"I understand. I just don't trust the feds, despite having been one."

"I don't either. And neither does Nester. We'd no longer be a threat in witness protection because they'd always know our whereabouts."

"Doesn't sound like much of a life."

"It's better than the alternative."

Eli pressed his head against the armored wall of the cabin. "You're right."

Dale couldn't stand it any longer. She had to get out. She wanted to scream. To run. To be anywhere other than here. The pain had become unbearable. "I'm going to go," she said. She reached for the door, but Eli's voice, strong and firm, stopped her.

"You did exactly what needed to be done." He turned and looked at her. "Don't ever regret it."

80

Beth McGee stared at the two other men in the penthouse suite of the Pyramid Marriott. She felt grimy. Dirty. And not from her trip up and down the Sandia Tram.

"How soon can we get the money?" she asked.

"A couple days," Robert Bellamy said. "Our operation has a heavy war chest, and there is almost no price too big for pharma to keep the boomerang off the market."

Beth bristled.

"Something wrong, Madam Director?" he asked.

"No," she lied. She wouldn't be opening up her soul to anyone in this room. "And the pardon?"

"Almost anytime," Bellamy said. "The president wants to cooperate."

"Of course he does," General Kyle Randolph said through clenched teeth.

"So that leaves the exchange." Beth peered around the room. "I'm thinking a public place, preferably large. I go in with everything needed for the money wire. Once Mr. and Mrs. James arrive, I ask Dale to confirm that the money is in Nester's account. Then I leave with Eli."

"That sounds reasonable," Bellamy said.

"No," Randolph said. "That's not sufficient."

"What do you mean?" Beth snapped.

Things were edgy in the room. Volatile. They needed to be cold blooded, but she felt like the mood in the room was anything but.

"You're making a handshake deal with the most dangerous human being in America. You're also giving him half a billion dollars and pretty much a green light to rule New Mexico as he sees fit."

"Your point?" Beth asked.

"If you're going to make a handshake deal with the devil . . . you need to shake the devil's hand."

Beth put her hands on her hips. "He'll never agree to that."

"I bet he will," Randolph said. "He doesn't trust us. Is he really going to send in the woman he loves to make this deal all by herself?"

"He did this morning."

"While he watched from an armored gunship with aerial coverage from the most lethal attack helicopter in the world."

"He'll never agree to a public meeting," Beth said.

"He dictated the terms of the last meeting," Randolph said. "We're doing almost all of the giving here. We should make the rules this time."

Beth stared into the general's gray eyes and then turned to Bellamy. "You agree?"

The big man grunted. "Why don't we offer a choice? A private meeting under his parameters with Nester and Eli James, or a public exchange with Dale James and her husband?" He hesitated, nodding. "Let Nester choose."

"General?" Beth said, expecting resistance.

But Randolph surprised her. "I . . . actually . . . kinda like that. Good idea, Robert."

"What about shaking hands with the devil?"

Randolph rubbed his chin. "I like the idea of giving him the option. He'll have to decide what's more important to him."

"Protecting his face or his woman." Bellamy grunted again. "What do you think, Beth?"

She turned back to the window and studied the lights of Albuquerque. "All right then," she finally said. "Let's set it up."

81

As the sun set on his last day of freedom, Eli walked along the banks of the Rio Grande with his daughter. The week, as he'd expected, had flown by, but he'd made the most of it.

No regrets. He'd taken horse rides with his mother. He'd enjoyed his meals with Bella and Dale.

And each day had wrapped up with a stroll along the great Rio Grande with his daughter.

"I wish we could just stay here," Bella said.

Eli stopped and gazed at the brown water. Then the purplish-red sun, which had nearly dipped behind the Sandias. "I never thought I'd say this . . . but me too."

"I wish you and Mom . . ."

Eli closed his eyes, knowing where she was going. "Yeah. Well . . ." He started to say "me too" again, but he stopped himself. He didn't want to leave any negative impressions with his daughter. "I know your mom loves me, and she knows that I love her. Life is just . . . complicated, and some mistakes are too much for a person to forgive."

"Are you scared?" Bella asked.

Eli looked at her as the last vestiges of light left the sky. "No."

"Not even a little?"

Eli put his hands on Bella's shoulders. "When I thought that you might die, I was scared. Prison." He shrugged. "It can't touch me."

"I love you, Dad."

Eli hugged his daughter tight to his chest. "Can I tell you something?"

"Anything."

"Remember when you were in middle and early high school? When we'd get to the soccer field early on Saturdays for your warm-up, and you'd let me kick the ball with you."

Bella's eyes filled with tears, and her body began to shake.

"Yeah, me too," Eli said. "I missed so much of your life, honey, but those Saturday mornings. Most of them at least. I was there."

"I know."

"Remember the song you would play in the car on the way . . . and on your earbuds when you'd get to the field? On one of my weekends home, we binge-watched *Cobra Kai* and the *Karate Kid* movies, and you loved that—"

"'You're the Best,' by Joe Esposito," Bella said, smiling despite her tears.

"That's the one." Eli scratched the back of his neck and sighed. "God, I loved watching you play. I wish so much that I'd been a better father."

"Dad, you—"

"Please, Bella. Hear me out. I was gone too much and I know it. But . . . we had . . . moments."

"We had more than that."

Eli bit down on his lip. "I just want you to know that even though it didn't always seem so, I loved being your dad. I lost my way somewhere along the path to the White House with Lionel, but the last seven months have helped me find it." He grabbed hold of her hand and leaned forward and kissed the tears that were falling down her cheeks. "I have had a wonderful life and too many blessings to count. Your mom. Nana. The time we've had together these last few months. This past week . . ."

Bella finally collapsed into his arms, and Eli hugged her tight to him as he breathed in the wind coming off the river. He remembered how she would fall asleep across his chest in the rocking chair when she was a baby. He whispered directly into her ear and hoped his words would live forever in her heart.

"I love you, too, Bella. You were the best thing that ever happened to me."

82

El Pinto was an Albuquerque institution. The restaurant had opened in 1962 and was consistently voted one of the region's best sites for authentic New Mexican food. Located on Fourth Street on historic Route 66 and known for its homemade salsa, sauces, sopapillas, and green chiles from the Hatch Valley, the place had always been one of Dale's favorites.

Through the windshield of the armored SUV, she gazed at the front entrance, trying to concentrate on her breathing. Other than the driver, the only people in the vehicle were Eli, Nester, and she.

"The director is waiting in the garden," Nester said, his soft voice providing little comfort. "I trust you remember the way."

"Yes," Dale said, letting out a ragged breath.

"You'll make sure that Bella and Dale make it to the witness-protection drop-off in the morning," Eli confirmed.

"You have my word," Nester said. Then he turned to Dale. "You have the burner on you?"

"Yes. In my pocket. On silent."

"Good. Put it on the table and tell the director why. I will text you when I receive confirmation that the money has been wired and the pardon has gone through. Then . . ." He shrugged.

"I leave and Eli stays."

"Correct. But if at any point that phone starts to ring—"

"We end the meeting . . ." She glanced at Eli and then back to Nester. "And run."

"Sir, it's seven fifty-seven," the driver barked from the front seat.

"All right," Nester said, rubbing his hands together. "Go time."

"Thank you," Dale said, turning and hugging him.

"If something happens to us tonight . . . ," Eli started.

"I'll take care of her," Nester said. "Bella will always be safe."

Eli extended his hand, and Nester shook it.

"You remember that . . . thing . . . you wanted me to try to track down?" Nester asked Eli.

Dale tilted her head and moved her eyes from Nester to Eli.

"Did you find him?" Eli asked.

"Him? Who?" Dale asked.

Nester nodded. "And then some."

Eli's eyebrows rose. "Will you do it?"

Nester shrugged. "Maybe."

"What the hell are you two talking about?" Dale asked.

"Nothing," Eli said, grabbing the door handle. "Let's roll."

83

Beth McGee ordered a margarita, but she had yet to touch it. Outside in the garden, the air was cool but pleasant. She checked her phone for the time, and it was 8:01 p.m. *Late,* she thought, but then her face tensed as she saw them.

Walking in together as a couple, per her own instructions.

As Dale and Eli James sat down across from her, the director dialed a number, which was picked up on the first ring. "They're here," she said, moving her eyes from Dale to Eli. "Wire the money."

Beth watched them as the waitress took their orders. Eli ordered a Dos Equis amber and Dale a margarita. As they waited for their drinks, Beth ate a chip with the homemade salsa. Then she looked at Dale. "The money should be en route."

Dale took out a burner cell phone and placed the device on the table, nodding at it. "Waiting for confirmation."

"Of course," Beth said.

The drinks were placed on the table, and Beth stared at hers.

"Did you ever think about doing the right thing?" Eli asked, taking a long sip of beer. "I mean, even for a second."

Beth blinked but held his gaze. "I believe I am doing what's best for the United States of America."

Eli shook his head. "Not what I asked."

Beth saw the screen on the burner phone light up. Dale leaned forward and inspected the text.

"Do we have confirmation?" Beth asked, feeling her heartbeat accelerate. *Almost there.*

"Yes," Dale said. "And the pardon?"

"Is being faxed and emailed from the White House to the number and address you provided as we speak. You should be receiving word . . ." The screen on the burner again lit up, and Beth pointed at it. ". . . now."

Dale glanced down at the burner and then back up at Beth. "Got it."

Beth leaned back in her chair and placed both hands on the table. "All arrangements for you and Bella to enter the witness-protection program have been made. As I understand, we will be meeting the two of you tomorrow at a location in Bosque Farms."

"Sopas," Dale said, peering at her drink but making no move to drink it.

"At that time, I'll have two bottles of the pills along with dosage instructions and a number for you to call if and when you need a refill." She paused. "But you shouldn't."

Dale nodded and bit her lip.

"Well . . . is there anything else?" Beth asked. She moved her eyes from one to the other.

"No." Dale's voice cracked ever so slightly.

"Then, Mrs. James . . . you are free to go."

Dale was staring at her drink. Her hands were shaking.

Eli touched his wife's shoulder, and Dale closed her eyes.

"Mrs. James?" Beth asked again. She started to say something else, but then she saw the burner on the table light up again. This time, however, it wasn't a text message.

It was a call.

84

As soon as Dale saw the burner vibrate on the table, she shot to her feet. "Eli!"

"Down!" Eli cried almost simultaneously, dragging Dale to the floor and covering her body with his. "Stay low and *move*."

Above them, Beth McGee was stammering, "What is going on? What—?"

But her voice was drowned out by the rapid patter of machine-gun fire. McGee crumpled to the ground, holding her chest.

Jesus, no! Dale thought, feeling herself pulled forward by Eli. Smoke filled the air, as did the screams of the patrons. Dale began to cough and couldn't stop.

"We have to go." Eli's voice, right in her ear. Strong. Firm. Calm. *Always best in a crisis . . .* She let him pull her forward into a hallway as more gunfire lit up the room.

"Where are they?" A male voice. "Where did they fucking go?"

"They have to be here somewhere, General."

General? Dale blinked but had no time to process the information as Eli pushed them forward through a door on their hands and knees.

"In here!" A plump man wearing an apron motioned with his hands. "In here!" he repeated. Eli stood and pulled Dale with him as they reached the man. Scanning around the space, Dale saw stoves and a sink. *Kitchen . . .*

They noticed that other patrons were running past the man in the apron.

"There's an exit out the storage closet," the man told them. "Go!"

"He may have men stationed there," Eli said. "We should—" But more machine-gun fire muffled his voice, and Dale dropped to the concrete floor. Again, all she could see was smoke. But as it cleared, she saw something that took her breath away.

"Eli!"

He was on the ground, blood pouring from his left shoulder and abdomen.

"Eli!"

He blinked up at her and motioned for her to come close.

"Crawl back to that storage closet and get out of here."

"But you said—"

"There's no other way. Go!"

"Not without you."

"Please go," he said, grimacing in pain. "It's been at least two minutes. It's about to happen."

"What's about to—"

Loud static blared from the restaurant's stereo system. The kitchen went pitch dark. There were several nervous yells, but the gunfire had stopped.

When the opening chord of "Enter Sandman" blared out of the restaurant's stereo system, Dale felt the hair on her arms stand up.

"Go!" Eli screamed above the music. He started to keel over, but she caught him and pulled him close to her. She kissed him hard on the lips. Tears streamed from her eyes.

"Take care of Bella." His voice was weaker. Fading. He pushed her toward the storage closet, and Dale scrambled backward. As she made her way to the closet, she turned to look over her shoulder, but she couldn't see him anymore.

As gunfire again lit up the kitchen, the sparks provided enough illumination for Dale to reach the closet. She found the exit trapdoor with her hands and crawled through it until her hands touched gravel, then grass. It was almost as dark outside as it was in the restaurant.

She rose and heard sirens in the distance. Getting closer, but too far away. She wasn't sure whether to be relieved or more afraid.

Fuck! She turned back to the door she'd just exited through. *I can't just leave him.* She sucked in a breath and swallowed as the sirens got closer.

"Mrs. James," a male voice spoke from somewhere behind her. She turned and peered at the shadow of a tall man. As he stepped into the faint light coming from headlights in the parking lot, she looked into his gray eyes. And registered the assault rifle in his hands.

"I don't believe we've had the pleasure," the man said. "General Kyle Randolph."

Dale opened her mouth . . . but the words wouldn't come.

"Let's go back inside, shall we?"

"Why?"

"Because you're going to help us." His voice was an eerie calm. Almost monotone.

"Help you . . . what?"

Randolph shoved her toward the door and slid down a pair of night-vision goggles over his eyes. "Put the genie back in the bottle."

85

Kyle Randolph knew it wouldn't take long, and he trusted his instincts. He couldn't strong-arm the air traffic controllers or the base commander at Kirtland into following his orders, but his Special Forces unit didn't ask questions.

Robert Bellamy had stayed neutral when Randolph ran the idea by him. *"I'll keep my mouth shut, but it's your ass if it doesn't work."*

Classic Bellamy. That was fine. He could handle the Homeland Security bulldog. It was McGee who'd become a thorn. Project Boomerang came with casualties. They'd known that from the beginning, and yet she'd come to question it.

And now she is one . . .

As was Eli James.

He reentered the garden from the hallway outside the kitchen, his eardrums aching from the god-awful heavy metal. He'd cuffed Dale James and now gripped her around the waist. He'd slung the M4 over his shoulder but kept the barrel of the GLOCK 17 at her temple.

The music abruptly stopped, but the lights remained off.

"You need to let the woman go, General." His voice was gentle. Melodic. Nonthreatening. Randolph blinked, but even with his goggles on, he saw no one.

"To whom am I speaking?"

"Don't you know?"

"Let's quit with the games. Turn the fucking lights on, or I'll put a bullet in her head."

"I don't think you will. If you do . . . you will have nothing that I want."

Randolph looked around. He saw the body of Beth McGee lying motionless under a table. Arms folded over her chest.

Where is my team?

"Game's up, asshole. You're about to be surrounded by a combination of the baddest men and women that the US Armed Forces have to offer."

"Really?" The voice had an annoying singsong quality to it.

Randolph put the barrel of his pistol across Dale's throat and pulled back hard on it, choking her. The only sound in the garden was of her gagging. "Not so funny now, is it?"

"General, I believe that the Madam Director hit some type of emergency signal before she was shot. Can you hear the sirens?"

Randolph chuckled. "I'm a four-star general and the most decorated soldier in this country. Local cops don't concern me." He pressed harder on Dale's throat, causing her to moan in pain.

"She is no good to me dead," the voice said.

Three of Randolph's special operators edged their way through the opening, joining him, each wearing night-vision goggles. Randolph eased up on Dale's throat. He held up a finger and moved the gun in a circle. The men began to filter into the darkness.

"Nester! There're three—"

Randolph's pistol wrist clamped hard onto her throat, cutting off the air supply.

"That wasn't very smart, Mrs. James." He kept the pressure up, making Dale choke for air. "Time's running out, Sanchez. Wouldn't it be better to turn yourself in?"

"For what? I have a full pardon from the president of the United States for all crimes that have ever been charged against me." He paused. "I am not the criminal here."

"What's he talking about, General?" one of his soldiers asked.

"He's trying to distract you. Just *follow* orders." Randolph felt adrenaline raging through him. He could hear those sirens now. They were close. He needed to do something. "Just remember, Sanchez. This was your fault." He moved the GLOCK's barrel to Dale's abdomen. "You hear me? Your fault."

Then he pulled the trigger.

86

The world had slowed down, the seconds moving in smaller increments from Eli's position on the floor. When he'd heard General Randolph's voice moving past him in the dark kitchen, he'd felt a tiny spark of energy. But when the gunshot rang out, followed by his wife's scream and the lights flicking back on . . .

A surge of power roared through his core. It was as if he'd been electrocuted—chest-paddled back to life.

An old image filled his hazy mind. It was from the movie *Creed*, which he and Bella had loved: Adonis on the canvas saw the image of his father Apollo and got up to fight.

Fight.

More images replaced the fallen fighter: Mom and Dad at law school graduation. Bella and him kicking the ball around on a Saturday morning. Election night, hugging Lionel. Dale on their honeymoon, slipping off her bathing suit in the Caribbean . . . then later, in the bedroom, her scent on the sheets. On his clothes. In his veins . . . Ralph Gutierrez in his Pepsi truck . . .

Eli blinked. He felt no pain. He rose and leaned against the wall. He pulled out the burner phone he'd packed without telling anyone, putting it on speaker, and dialed the only number he knew by heart.

911.

Then he pushed through the door and staggered into the garden.

"Emergency dispatch, what is your emergency?" A monotone female voice filled the room.

"My name is Eli James," Eli declared, glaring into the steely eyes of Kyle Randolph. "Former chief of staff to the president of the United States. I am here to report multiple murders at the El Pinto restaurant perpetrated by General Kyle Randolph, who just shot my wife."

"Have you lost your fucking mind?" Randolph asked, eyes wide, face pale. One arm was wrapped around Dale's neck, and the other held a pistol to her head. Dark-red blood covered her midsection.

"I'm gonna keep going, Kyle."

Gunfire erupted from the darkened rear of the garden.

"Jefferson? Rodriguez? *Nichols?*" Randolph listed the names but got no response as at least ten unfamiliar men emerged from the shadows. All held semiautomatic weapons and wore jeans and hoodies.

Eli could hardly believe his eyes.

"*Which one of you is . . . ?*" General Randolph stammered.

"I am Nester," one of the men said. The general's eyes darted to him.

"I am Nester," another said, and Randolph wheeled toward the voice, still holding Dale, his arms shaking.

"I am Nester," a third man echoed.

"You're all fucking crazy," Randolph spat, finally turning back to Eli, desperation oozing from his stare.

"Give it up. Game's over. You lost," Eli managed to tell the general.

Randolph stood, frozen, still holding the limp body of Dale.

"Sir, are you still there?" Emergency Services asked, and Eli stared at his phone.

"Still here," Eli said, clearing his throat and taking another step toward Randolph. "And here to tell you . . . and the world . . . that there's a cure for cancer. They call it the boomerang, and General Kyle Randolph, the former chairman of the Joint Chiefs of Staff, has conspired with high-ranking officials in the FBI and the Pentagon to cover it—"

But he never got the rest of it out. In his mind, the seconds were passing in quarter increments now. He saw Randolph's face registering defeat. The hand holding the GLOCK rising to meet him. Dale falling to the floor. The blast from the muzzle.

Eli fell to his knees, as the shot from Randolph's gun connected with his right shoulder. The phone dropped from his hand. As he started to fall, he heard machine-gun fire strike Randolph's body from seemingly every direction.

Seconds later, he was staring into the golden brown eyes of Nester Sanchez. "Hold on, brother," he said.

"Dale," Eli gasped. "Focus . . . on . . . Dale."

"She's going to make it," Nester said. "Just stay with me."

"Hello, this is Emergency Services. Sir, I'm still here. Are you okay? We've tracked your location to the El Pinto restaurant, and paramedics and police are on their way."

Eli reached for his phone but couldn't find it. He stared at the ceiling and wondered if he'd already died.

Beth McGee was up somehow, holding Eli's phone in her hand.

Eli tried to stand, to lunge at the director, but Nester's voice soothed him. "It's okay," he said. "She was with us in the end. She shot the bastard too."

Eli again stared up at McGee, who wore an odd smile on her face.

"It's muted," she said. "911 didn't hear any of it." She limped forward and crouched down. "You conned him." She shook her head.

"And so your precious boomerang remains a secret," Nester said.

But Eli couldn't hear them well, now. The power surge that had driven him was fading. Almost out. He struggled to breathe.

"Eli?" Nester's voice was a million miles away.

Eli reached with his hand but saw that his arm wasn't really moving. He smelled salt water. Felt it in his nose. He was walking down a sandy beach. A man was approaching him. Sunburned skin. White hair.

Eli closed his eyes as the light flickered out.

87

When Dale awoke, she was in a dark hospital room. For a moment she thought she was alone, but then she saw a shadow by the door. She tried to speak, but her mouth was too dry. The shadow moved closer, and she saw his golden brown eyes.

"You're going to be okay," Nester said. "You lost a lot of blood . . . but they were able to save you."

Dale felt so weak and foggy. Flashes from El Pinto came into her mind, but it seemed like a bad dream. "How long—"

"You were in surgery and ICU for twelve hours, and now you're in a room." He leaned down and kissed her forehead. "The worst is over. You'll be here for a few more days to make sure you don't get an infection, but they were able to get the bullet out."

"Bella?"

"Fine. With Ms. Foncie and your brothers at the reservation."

Dale looked at the window. "What hospital are we at?"

"Presbyterian," Nester said.

"Is Eli still here or has he been discharged?" She continued to stare at the window.

Nester said nothing.

Finally, after a few seconds, Dale turned to face him.

Nester's face had always been difficult to read, but it wasn't now. The sadness in his eyes and in his slumped shoulders was palpable.

"Just tell me," Dale said.

"He's dead."

88

At 7:30 a.m., four days after the shoot-out in Albuquerque, Beth McGee entered the Oval Office. She wore a sling over her right arm, and her ribs were bandaged underneath her sweaterdress. For a person still recovering from bullet wounds to her left shoulder and ribs, she thought she was doing pretty well, though any type of sneeze or cough brought tears to her eyes, it hurt so bad. She sat in one of the chairs facing the antique desk.

The president had his back to her and spoke while looking out at Pennsylvania Avenue. "How are you feeling?"

Beth grunted. "Physically, I'm in some pain but improving. Mentally, psychologically, emotionally, I really don't know. Ask me in another month. Or a year. I'm still processing."

"We don't have that kind of time."

"I was being facetious, Mr. President. I'm sorry."

"He wants a meeting."

Beth almost asked who, but decided against it.

"When?"

"Tomorrow morning. Sandia Peak." Lionel turned to her. "He asked that you come alone." He paused. "He trusts you."

Beth nodded. "I'll be there. Is there anything else, Mr. President?"

"Yes, there is." Lionel walked around the desk and took a seat in the other visitor chair. He leaned forward, resting his elbows on his knees. "Do you think Bellamy knew about Randolph's plan?"

"Yes." Beth didn't hesitate. The president had spoken with her in the hospital, and she had privately disclosed to him the other members of Project Boomerang.

"Can you prove it?"

"No."

"So, he has to stay on . . . for now."

"For now," Beth agreed.

"And Thad Raleigh?"

"Absolutely didn't know."

"And what of Randolph's Special Forces team?"

"Instruments only. They knew nothing of the content of our initiative. They simply followed the general's orders."

"Well, now they answer to me," Lionel growled. "And so do you." He rubbed the back of his neck. "Project Boomerang must remain top secret and confidential."

Beth grunted her agreement. "General Randolph was wrong about a lot, but he was right about one thing. Never mind the drug. If the American people discover what we've done to suppress it, it'll be Armageddon."

"Even if we could figure out a rational way to deliver the boomerang to the world, we've waited too long."

Beth said nothing.

Lionel sighed. "Goddamnit."

"Mr. President—"

"All right, then. Project Boomerang will remain top secret, classified, and confidential." He ground his teeth together. "But it will no longer be under the umbrella of the Department of Defense. It is now an *executive* initiative. Do you understand?"

"Yes, sir."

"I am in charge, and you report to me."

"Yes, sir. But Mr. President, with all due respect, what happens if you are not reelected?"

"You better hope the fuck I am. I'm going to insist that you stay as FBI director beyond your term. After the events in Albuquerque, the narrative has made you a hero and Randolph a maniac who went on a revenge mission to assassinate Nester Sanchez. You have me and Governor Florez to thank for that."

Beth nodded. She wasn't sure she'd ever seen Lionel Cantrell so angry. Unhinged, almost. So different from his usual smooth and unflappable demeanor. "I'm grateful, sir."

"You should be." He let out a bitter chuckle. "Crazy as it sounds, I think the American people will embrace an extended term for a *hero* like you." He spat the words. "Ironic, isn't it?"

Beth said nothing. She'd felt a lot of shame, guilt, and regret over the past few days. An ass-chewing from the president seemed appropriate and perhaps a step in the right direction.

"Take away the cover-up mess that makes everything impossible now," Lionel started, putting his hands on his hips. "Do you still believe a release of the boomerang would cripple the United States economy?"

Again, she didn't hesitate. "It would be devastating and insurmountable. Additionally, even without the catastrophic financial loss, a fair and equitable rollout of the medication is next to impossible and, in the hands of Big Pharma, would be an unadulterated disaster. Each global-release scenario that we've gamed turns quickly into a chaotic nightmare. Kyle and I always agreed on the reasons for keeping the medication secret. We just differed on our methods of protection."

Lionel scoffed. "All of those *reasons* . . . and yet what do you call what happened in Albuquerque? How would you assess your efforts up to this point?" When Beth didn't respond, Lionel pointed at her. "I'd call it, and them, an unadulterated disaster."

"We made mistakes," Beth said, looking at the floor.

"*Mistakes?* Through inaction, you murdered countless innocent American citizens, without remorse. And you had zero problem taking extreme measures when Eli James fled to New Mexico with my supply of the drug."

She gave a slow nod and raised her head to meet his glare. "That's all true, sir. But I am not a liar. I intended to follow through with our promises to Mr. Sanchez and the James family, and I didn't anticipate that the general would go rogue." She rubbed the bridge of her nose. "I should've."

"Shoulda, woulda, coulda." Lionel finally rose from his chair, glancing toward the outer door. "Nester trusts you because you saved his life."

"No," Beth said. "If he trusts me, and I tend to doubt that, it's because I took a bullet and joined his team in gunning down General Randolph when the shit hit the fan." She snorted. "But I didn't do anything. The hero at El Pinto was Eli James." She paused. "He conned Randolph, saving his wife and giving us an opening to take the general down. It was brilliant."

Lionel walked back to the window, and Beth noticed that his shoulders were heaving.

"Mr. President, are you okay?"

Lionel Cantrell choked out a sob. "Eli James was my oldest and best friend."

"I'm sorry, sir."

He held up a hand but didn't look at her. "Good luck tomorrow."

89

This time, the meeting was held in the cabin of the Hind helicopter gunship. The weather outside was frigid. Much colder than the last time, and Beth was grateful for the warmth. Nester sat several feet away from Beth and wore a cap pulled low over his brow. Aviators covered his eyes.

"The terms of our arrangement are obviously going to have to change," Nester said. "I do not believe you were behind what happened at El Pinto . . . but nevertheless, the conditions were breached."

"I understand," Beth said, trying to control her breathing.

He crossed one leg over the other. "First, the easy stuff. I keep the money you wired, and the president has obviously already executed my pardon."

"Obviously," Beth agreed.

"With respect to the James family, I want two changes. As I'm sure you understand, after the ambush that took the life of Eli James, we have no trust in the government. Witness protection is out. Bella and Dale James will stay here in New Mexico. They will be left alone. Once she heals, Dale will be my legal representative on all matters, legal or otherwise. All federal contact with me goes through her."

"That's reasonable."

"And Bella James is allowed to finish high school in Albuquerque, and she will not be given a second's trouble." Nester paused. "You will also follow through with giving her a lifetime supply of the drug."

Beth rubbed her chin. "Also reasonable." She reached into her pocket and pulled out two full pill bottles.

He took the medication from her.

"Is that all?"

"One more thing. Have you decided how you are going to spin the event at El Pinto?"

"Yes, we have," Beth said. "We are pinning all of it—the murder of Eli James, the shootings of me and Dale and other innocent civilians, the hijacking of the restaurant, et cetera—on Randolph."

Nester was nodding. "That's good." He squinted at her. "And Eli?"

"He'll get barely a mention. A victim of Randolph's wrath. Nothing more."

Nester stared out the window. "We both know that the man is an American hero."

Beth cocked her head. "I wouldn't go that far. Look, Mr. Sanchez, we did the best we could. Randolph is the easy out now. Are we good?"

"Yes. I believe so, but I am curious. With General Randolph gone, who is in charge of keeping the boomerang a secret? You?"

Beth shook her head. "I am still heavily involved, but Project Boomerang is now being led by the president of the United States."

A wry grin played on Nester's lips. "Interesting."

"Is there anything else?"

He smiled. "One thing. I could mention our handshake deal for absolute immunity, but your folks have already tried to kill me. Here is my proposal. Instead of calling it absolute immunity, let's refer to it as 'fuck around and find out.'" He lowered his voice. "You tell your president that if the government fucks around with me, the James family, the Gutierrezes, the Bacas, or any employee, friend, or close acquaintance of mine, he'll find out fast that such an action was a drastic mistake."

"Is that a threat?"

"Yes, obviously. You leave me alone, I leave you alone. It's that simple." He held out his hand. "Are we clear?"

Beth McGee leaned forward and shook his hand. "Yes, we are."

Nester touched his pilot on the shoulder, and seconds later, the door to the cabin opened.

"I think that concludes our business, Madam Director."

Beth scooted toward the door but stopped before descending the steps. She turned and gazed at the man they called the Beast. "You know, I just realized something."

Nester said nothing, his expression curious.

"You ended up with everything you wanted."

He edged closer to her and lowered the aviators a fraction of an inch. His brownish-gold eyes gleamed in the morning light. "I always do."

90

Bella held the dirt in her hand and peered down at the coffin. She'd watched as her mother and grandmother had taken their turns. Both had come back and sat down under the tent, too emotional to talk.

Now it was Bella's turn. She held her hand out and let the dirt slowly slide from her fingers. Tears filled her eyes, but she felt strong.

She peered down at the casket as the last of the dirt fell from her grasp. "I love you . . . and I'll never forget what you did for us."

———

Thirty minutes later, Bella and Dale entered the gates of Menaul School. They parked behind the football field, which doubled as the soccer pitch, and they walked past the bleachers and onto the grass. Dale carried a backpack with a soccer ball, cleats, and shin guards.

"So, this is where I'll play," said Bella, lacing up her soccer cleats.

"Yep."

Bella took a deep breath. "Do you mind if I start?"

"No. Do you mind if I watch?"

Bella shook her head and hugged her mother.

"Don't overdo, okay? It's been a while."

But Bella ignored her and trotted out onto the field. As she did some stretching, she also ignored the men watching them from both ends of the field. She'd grown used to the constant supervision provided by Nester Sanchez's security team. It was just part of her life now.

Finally, feeling loose, Bella jogged the length of the field twice. As she broke a sweat, she put her earbuds in and played the song she and her father loved.

"You're the Best," by Joe Esposito.

As the guitar strings announced the tune, Bella started to dribble the ball toward the far goal, her legs moving steadily and then picking up pace. By the time she reached midfield, she felt like she was flying.

When she got within twenty yards of the goal, she began to cry but managed to focus on the ball, kicking it as hard as she could into the net. She closed her eyes and breathed in the desert air.

Thank you, Dad.

PART SIX

THE WORLD GOES ROUND

The president feels bile in his throat as he looks around the huge ballroom. The gala is a fundraiser for cancer research. How many of these events are held each year? This one, though, is the granddaddy of them all. A mandatory public appearance for him.

Lionel shakes hands. Smiles. Even says a few words to open the evening.

When it's his turn to talk, he gazes out over the audience and delivers his milquetoast remarks. We have to do more. We are winning this battle. Our research scientists are the best in the world. Blah, blah, blah. *He sits at the head table and gazes around the room. He can't help but wonder where it all goes.*

Twenty thousand dollars a table.

A silent auction with hundreds of items that'll raise another hundred grand.

A raffle that'll bring in even more.

Where does the money go?

Lionel wants to walk outside and puke, but he doesn't. Instead, he stays and listens and does his duty.

There is a speaker who says she has "beaten" cancer. A radiation oncologist raves about new techniques. A pharmacologist mentions a breakthrough medicine that can reduce tumors by half if a patient has the right set of genes.

Applause follows.

Tears are shed.

And the night ends with a vow from the leader of the organization that they must do more. And with everyone's donations, they will.

More checks are written.

The oncology pot grows.

And the world goes round and round.

91

Nester had just finished his morning workout when he received the call.

"Hey," Dale said. "Amos's wife, Gloria, met with Dr. Baca yesterday to go over the results of her scans." A pause. "She has breast cancer. Stage four."

Nester petted Dog behind the ears, and the brown pit bull licked his hand. He took a sip of coffee. "Okay. I was planning to go today anyway." He walked out onto his patio and peered up at the yellowish-orange sun rising above the Sandias.

"Just wanted you to know."

"Thank you."

He clicked End and made a call of his own. Fifteen minutes later, a black Bronco picked him up, and he brought Dog along with him.

Dog, like Nester, loved the desert.

The ride took about an hour, and the last fifteen minutes was off road, but he eventually saw the trailer in the distance.

The scene reminded him of one of his favorite shows, *Breaking Bad*, which had been filmed outside of Albuquerque.

But they weren't making methamphetamine in this trailer.

We are making a miracle.

The Bronco came to a stop, and Dog hopped out and scampered off. "Watch for snakes, *chico*," he yelled after him. *And they better watch out for you.*

He grabbed a small duffel bag and walked to the front door of the double-wide. He knocked once, then entered.

Jalen Nakai looked up from a microscope and smiled. "Morning."

Nester nodded, and then stared at the other man in the room, who looked like a gray-haired *viejo* version of Jalen.

"Is the first batch ready?"

Mato Nakai stood from his microscope and went over to a counter by a sink. He opened a drawer and pulled out several pill bottles. He handed them to Nester, who peered inside the clear containers. The capsules looked identical to the ones that Bella was taking.

Nester put the bottles in his bag. "Where is he?"

"Out walking." Jalen cocked his head toward the door. "He should be back soon."

"Thanks," Nester said. "Both of you. Good work."

"No, sir," Mato said. "Thank *you*. We are doing a good thing here."

Nester nodded. "It's a start."

As he walked down the steps of the trailer, he saw a figure approaching in the distance with Dog close on his heels. Nester strode toward the man, stopping a few feet away. For a long few seconds, they stared at each other. The desert air was heating, and the man had sweat rolling down his face and neck. He wore jeans and a long-sleeved shirt, his thick hair covered by a ball cap.

Finally, Nester smiled. "Methinks that death has served you well."

Eli James smiled back. "Methinks you're right."

THE END

AUTHOR'S NOTE

On March 31, 2017, my wife and I waited in a tiny patient room for test results that would define the rest of our life. Dixie had a tumor in her right lung that had spread to the lymph nodes. Mucinous adenocarcinoma, the same condition that Bella James is afflicted with in this story. My beautiful bride had endured a grueling three-month chemo and radiation regimen that caused her to lose over forty pounds. All in the hopes that the tumor would shrink and there would be no further metastasis.

Now we would see whether the torture worked. The paralyzing fear and anxiety felt by Eli James during the "Waiting Room" scene of this story is what I experienced then. The world, at least in my mind, had pressed pause.

In those precious seconds, I envisioned my father, Randy Bailey, standing against the back wall of the room. Arms crossed and whistling. Like Eli, Dad was always at his best in a crisis. Four weeks earlier, Dad had lost his own battle with lung cancer. Surgery hadn't been an option for him. Now we would find out if it would be for Dixie.

I held my breath when Dr. Waples walked into that cramped room, smiling big and bellowing, "Looks good!" Then he told us that the tumor had shrunk, the PET was clear, and Dixie was ready for surgery. It all seems like a blur now. I cried, of course. Like Uncle Ralph Gutierrez in this story, I'm a crier. I'm crying as I write this now. And then and now, I can still hear Dad. Whistling . . . and adding a subtle fist pump.

On April 3, 2017, exactly a month after Dad's death, Dixie underwent a thoracotomy that removed most of her right lung. Since then, she has been in remission, and I thank God every day for her good health.

For the past seven and a half years, I've had a ringside seat for the fight against cancer in America. Along the way, I've heard more than my fair share of conspiracy theories in waiting rooms across this country. These encounters, coupled with my own desperation, fear, and anxiety during Dad and Dixie's respective cancer journeys, formed the backbone for this story.

But while a conspiracy is at the center of this novel, the heart and soul of the story ask a more primal question: What would you do to save the ones you love the most?

Thank you for reading *The Boomerang*. The emotional terrain covered in this book is ground I know painfully well. I've walked every step, and I know that many of you have as well. But, as set out above, this story isn't about cancer. It's about the power of the human spirit. About family and love. About heroes emerging from the ashes, like Nester Sanchez's Apache attack helicopter.

Heroes do still exist. I know that for a fact. Mine has been dead now for more than seven years, but when the bullets start flying in my life, he is always right by my side.

Whistling . . .

ACKNOWLEDGMENTS

My wife, Dixie, inspired this novel in so many ways. Dixie is now seven years cancer-free, but her journey alongside my father's fight were the seeds of this story. Dixie's childhood and family in New Mexico were huge inspirations, as was her alma mater, Menaul School, and her many friends in New Mexico who lent me an ear and answered my questions.

Our children, Jimmy, Bobby, and Allie, are growing up, but the shared memories of prior trips to see their mother's New Mexico home contributed so much to this story.

My mom, Beth Bailey, is my number one fan. She is my rock of support, and I don't know what I'd do without her.

My agent, Liza Fleissig, loved this story from the moment I sent the synopsis to her. Liza's persistence and devotion to my career are unmatched. She is a dream agent and an even better friend.

My developmental editor, Ed Stackler, made incredible suggestions that helped this story fly. Thank you, Ed, for seeing my vision and making this novel better.

To Megha Parekh, Gracie Doyle, and my entire editing and marketing team at Thomas & Mercer, thank you for continuing to support my dream. This is our tenth book together! I still can't believe it.

Thank you once again to my friends Rick Onkey and Steve Shames for their early reads of this story.

My friends Mark Wittschen and Bill Fowler both gave fantastic input on military helicopters that informed this story.

My brother, Bo Bailey, continues to support my writing journey with calm and cool advice.

My friends Joe and Foncie Bullard from Point Clear, Alabama, are two of my favorite people in the world. Their support means everything to me.

My father-in-law, Dr. Jim Davis, is always so encouraging, and his positive outlook on life is like nectar for the soul.

My friend Dr. Jack Gleason, a radiation oncologist, was a great sounding board for questions, and I appreciate his help and expertise very much.

My niece, Bentley League, provided valuable insight on the political and social scene in Washington, DC.

My stepfather-in-law, Jerry Baca, who our kids call Pops, and my mother-in-law, Beverly Baca, a.k.a. Mammie, were tremendous influences on this story. Jerry's love of his family in New Mexico and the interesting stories that he and Bev shared of their time in Albuquerque provided a lot of the background for my research for *The Boomerang*. I dedicated this novel to Jerry's family.

Ralph Baca, Jerry's brother, is one of the greatest characters I've ever met in my life. Uncle Ralph, as we all call him, is quick with a joke and tells stories that will make you laugh out loud one second and cry the next. His tearful prayer for my wife's good health during our last visit touched my soul and inspired the character who bears his name in this story.

Ralph's son, Jeffrey Baca, was a one-man tour guide for Dixie and me during our last visit to New Mexico, and so much of Jeff's help plays out in this story, including our trek up the Sandia Peak, the jam-packed day we spent in Los Lunas, and our trip to Santa Fe. Seeing New Mexico through his eyes was so helpful. Thank you, Jeffie!

Ralph's daughter, Jeralyn Duran, and her fiancé, Sergeant Ryan Gray, were very helpful in showing us Los Lunas and hitting the landmark spots.

Leonard Baca, Jerry's youngest brother, was the first member of Jerry's family that I ever met, and our trek around San Diego watching Dixie run the Rock & Roll Marathon in the summer of 2001 is a memory I'll never forget. Leonard's infectious positive energy has been a blessing, as well as his sharing his wonderful family with us. Leonard's sons, Santiago "Santi" Baca and Amos Baca, have called me "cousin" since the day I met them, and my conversations with both helped me craft the dialogue and the family interactions in this story.

Elizabeth and James Chavez hosted two unforgettable Baca family get-togethers during our trips to New Mexico, and each party was so warm and festive. The food, the laughter, the arguments, and the family shenanigans that played out during these lunches were a great help to my writing and were also just a lot of fun.

Jerry's sisters, Lorraine Baca Clines and Ruthann "Auntie Ruth" Moss, along with Ruthann's husband, Johnny Moss, were so warm and gracious with their time. And while I never met Jerry's late sister, Carmen, I named a character in this story after her.

Dixie's wonderful friends Toni Morgan, Meredith Hutton, Caesar Gonzalez, Dominic Davis, and Megan Florez helped this story just by allowing me to be around them and listen to their stories of the Menaul School. Megan and her husband, David, hosted a wonderful party at their home where we ate pizza, roasted marshmallows, and had a merry time, and Toni gave us an incredibly informative tour of Menaul.

Dixie's late uncle, Jack Hettick, took Dixie and me up to a place called High Finance at the top of the Sandia Peak some twenty years ago to eat dinner. Jack was an interesting man, a character of the first order, and I've never forgotten that dinner or that nighttime trip up the Sandias.

My late uncle, Colonel Charles Stringfellow, invited our family to visit him and his wonderful wife, Jane, in Santa Fe, New Mexico, in the fall of 2015. Uncle Charlie and Jane met us at the Balloon Fiesta in Albuquerque at four in the morning, and the memories of that chilly morning, the incredible breakfast burritos, and the excitement of waiting for the grand ascension with Dixie and the kids informed one of the pivotal chapters in this story. Uncle Charlie was an incredible man who my family misses very much.

My father, Randy Bailey, died in March 2017, but there's not a day that goes by that I don't miss him, heed his wise counsel, and wish he were still here. Even though he's been gone for over seven years, I still write lines and imagine his reaction to reading them. I always will.

ABOUT THE AUTHOR

Photo © 2019 Erin Cobb

Robert Bailey is the *Wall Street Journal* bestselling author of the Jason Rich series, which includes *Rich Justice*, *Rich Waters*, and *Rich Blood*; the Bocephus Haynes series, which includes *The Wrong Side* and *Legacy of Lies*; and the award-winning McMurtrie and Drake legal thriller series, including *The Final Reckoning*, *The Last Trial*, *Between Black and White*, and *The Professor*. He also wrote the inspirational novel *The Golfer's Carol*. *The Boomerang* is Bailey's eleventh novel. The author lives in Huntsville, Alabama, with his wife, Dixie, and they are the proud parents of three children, two dogs, and two cats. For more information, please visit www.robertbaileybooks.com.